Leslie Ford is a pseudonym for an author whose fiction has been published to critical acclaim in Britain, America, Europe and Japan. Two of his novels are currently being adapted for the screen. He has three children aged from thirteen to twenty-three and lives in Cornwall, in a house overlooking the sea, with his American-born wife, who is also a writer, and their large, woolly dog.

DIMINISHED RESPONSIBILITY is Leslie Ford's first novel of psychological suspense and he is currently at work on a second.

Diminished Responsibility

Leslie Ford

First published in 1995
by HEADLINE BOOK PUBLISHING

First published in paperback in 1996
by HEADLINE BOOK PUBLISHING

A HEADLINE FEATURE paperback

10 9 8 7 6 5 4 3 2 1

ISBN 0 7472 5157 6

Typeset by CBS, Felixstowe, Suffolk

Printed and bound in Great Britain by
Mackays of Chatham PLC, Chatham, Kent

HEADLINE BOOK PUBLISHING
A division of Hodder Headline PLC
338 Euston Road
London NW1 3BH

Diminished
Responsibility

ONE

The nightmare started, as the very worst nightmares do, amidst the trappings of peace and normality.

It was six-thirty on a cloudless Sunday evening towards the end of May. Sally Jackson had been pleasantly occupied for the past half-hour in the kitchen of the family's airy thirties semi in Barnes, sautéing onions, rinsing beansprouts, shredding cloves of fresh garlic, and methodically chopping red and yellow peppers for the evening's stir-fry. Kit, her husband, was in the adjoining conservatory, dozing his way through the last of the colour supplements.

'That'll be our Emma home,' he called out lazily. 'I'll start setting the table.'

For a brief moment Sally was tempted to ask Kit to get the door. Because she knew it wouldn't be just Emma, her daughter, on the doorstep, but also Jonathan, her ex-husband. Then Sally reminded herself that she was a grown-up woman, and Jonathan was, after all, the man she had chosen first to marry, then to have a child by, and last but not least to divorce . . .

Sally slivered a carrot lengthwise with a viciously neat little stroke of the Sabatier, slipped off her apron and headed out into the cool, kelim-carpeted hall. The bell gave one more irritable little ring before she reached the door.

1

Somehow, out of a clear blue sky, it had started to drizzle. Sally's expectation was confirmed. Her ex-husband was waiting on the step with their thirteen-year-old daughter. As ever, he seemed impossibly tall. Emma looked paler than usual and, it seemed to Sally's critical eye, perhaps even a little thinner.

'Come in, quick, darling, before you get wet!' she said, though the rain was scarcely noticeable. Just an excuse to eagerly gather up Emma for a hug. 'Good weekend?'

'Of course,' Emma answered, turning slightly to smile at her father, who had made no attempt to move in out of the drizzle.

'Emma still has homework to do,' Jonathan said before Sally could ask any more questions. Father and daughter exchanged another swift glance, this time a guilty one.

'Horrible history assignment, Mum,' Emma said. 'But I've nearly finished. Honest.'

Sally frowned. 'Jonathan, you *promised* she'd get it done. I'm sure you're never this casual with your own students.'

'My students! We've got market-led education these days. They can do what they like! I am no longer *in loco parentis*, but merely a humble salesman of knowledge, dealing with honoured customers, purchasers of a service.'

'Well,' Sally retorted, 'Emma attends an old-fashioned institution where there's none of that Thatcherite nonsense. As you well know.'

Jonathan's mesmeric blue eyes met hers. 'As I well know.'

Sally looked away. She knew what he meant.

Implication, I only get to see my daughter every other weekend, you bitch, so get off my case.

Emma was shifting from foot to foot. Tense. She had inherited her father's height and skinniness along with his nerviness and his piercing blue eyes.

'Hey. Enough, you two,' she murmured.

Jonathan Quinn, Sally's first husband, was a gangling six-feet-four. His aquiline features, unruly hair, and salt-and-pepper beard gave him the look of a permanently angry prophet. Or, on the other hand, of a fairly successful politics lecturer, which he was. That old brown leather jacket and those scuffed sneakers gave the game away.

Sally sighed. She had plenty of energy, her own rather brilliant career, and had always been able to take care of herself. Yet when the pair of them – beanpole Jonathan, and Emma taller by the month – stood opposite her like this, she felt powerless, like a wind-up blonde doll with no key. Overwhelmed.

Sally decided as usual to retreat, to take refuge in practicalities.

'Look, forget it,' she said. 'Are you both still all right about keeping each other company at half-term while Kit and I are in Somerset?'

'Excellent,' Emma said. 'Do stop worrying, Mum.'

'Just checking.'

Emma made a face, then stood on tiptoe and gave her father a peck on the cheek. ''Bye, Dad. I'd better tackle that homework.' She turned to her mother. 'I'll just take a snack up to my room – no dinner for me, OK?'

Before Sally could protest, Emma slipped into the house, leaving Sally and Jonathan together, alone. Her ex-husband showed no inclination to leave.

'Em looks exhausted,' Sally said evenly. 'What do you think?'

'To tell the truth, I'm really concerned. She's been avoiding meals all weekend.'

Jonathan didn't spell out the problem. He didn't need to. For the past year or so their daughter had been in therapy for an anorexic condition.

'Well, don't let her miss next week's appointment with Dr Yardley,' Sally said. 'I know it's a bit of a nuisance, but do you mind driving her over there and waiting?'

''Course not. Only an hour. I'll find a caff and go and mark some papers.' There was a pause. 'Something else,' Jonathan said. 'The real reason Em didn't do her homework. Yesterday afternoon I settled her in her room with her books and nipped out to do the food shopping. I got back and Zak Paine was hanging around.'

'So?'

'Well, I know he's Liz's son, and she's your oldest friend, but—'

'Why shouldn't he drop over?'

'He was already on his third can of Special Brew, that's why!' Jonathan snapped. 'He's only sixteen. What's he doing getting tanked up like that? I mean, where's he get the money? Does Liz give him a drinks allowance?'

'What Liz does is her own business,' Sally countered defensively. 'Zak's a good kid at heart. Anyway, he and Emma have known each other all their lives!'

'Yeah, well, what I was getting round to is, I think his interest in Em is a bit more than brotherly these days.'

'Relax!' Sally said. 'They're both growing up. Relationships change. You're not jealous, are you?'

Jonathan ignored her jibe. 'I hear the boy's got the house to himself next week while you're all partying at Liz and Harry's snug little west-country retreat.'

'What do you expect them to do? Lock him out of his own home every time they take off on a few days' holiday?'

Jonathan's expression was fierce, unrelenting.

'Well, you can tell Liz from me, I'm not having Zak use my place as a pick-up joint,' he growled.

'OK, OK!' Sally paused. 'Listen, Jonathan, you're over-protective. You see problems where they just don't exist. For instance, you really don't have to deliver Emma right to the door. She's not nine any more. She has her own house-key.'

'Christ, you live a very sheltered life, Sal, between the BBC and beautiful Barnes. Don't you know, nowhere's safe these days?'

'But Emma will be fourteen in November!'

A shriek of adolescent laughter floated towards them from the conservatory. While Jonathan seemed to instil in Emma his own anxieties, his fatal self-pity, it was Kit who released her girlish exuberance. Stepfather he might be, but he had a way with her.

'You're sure it's all right?' Sally repeated, to cover the awkwardness of the moment. 'I mean, we could always take Emma with us to Liz and Harry's.'

'Why should there be a problem?' Jonathan said. 'Can you tell me when I ever missed a chance to spend more time with my little girl?'

'I was just asking because—'

'Because what? It's only Friday night to Wednesday, for God's sake. My own flesh and blood, parcelled out to me in days!'

Turning abruptly on his heel, Jonathan strode across the road to where his old Ford estate was parked. He got in and slammed the door behind him, like a man who has been wrongly accused of some terrible, unforgivable offence.

* * *

5

Emma had been persuaded by Kit to have a taste of Sally's stir-fry, then she had hurried off up to her room. Kit was now in the TV room, casting a desultory eye over the evening news.

'They're all crooks,' he said matter-of-factly. 'Look at that bloody cabinet minister. Lying through his teeth. Why do your telly people let 'em get away with it?'

Sally stroked his hair as she passed. He looked up, and his broad, open features creased in a smile. When Kit looked at her like that she knew she adored him, for his loving ways and his cool head, and that all the turmoil of the divorce from Jonathan had been worth while.

'Can we talk, darling?' she said.

'Sure.' Kit zapped the TV. The politician's smug face imploded and disappeared. Kit looked at her searchingly. 'Let's have it.'

Always straight to the point. Never ducked a problem. At forty Kit was managing director of an expanding software company, and the smart money was on him for the topmost job when the founder/chairman retired.

Sally perched on the arm of the sofa. 'Kit, I'm worried about Emma, or rather about her relationship with Jonathan.'

'Come on! He's her dad. She loves him. What could be more natural?'

'That's just what Dr Yardley always says. You men stick together, don't you?'

'It's obvious Emma doesn't find the weekends easy, but there's no question she wants to see Jonathan.' Kit shrugged. 'It's called a conflict, my love. Life is full of them, and many, like this one, are simply insoluble.'

'Oh, don't say that.'

'It'll sort itself out when she leaves home and goes to

college. Then she'll stop being a shuttlecock and start living her own life. Away from all of us. That time will come before we all know it.'

'Jonathan will be heartbroken.'

Kit laughed. 'Listen to you! One moment Jonathan's the clingy-monster, the next he's the poor deserted Dad! You can't have it both ways, my love.' He shrugged. 'All those emotions are pretty complicated at the best of times. When you divorce and there are kids involved, you get complications in spades.'

Sally thought about it, nodded resignedly.

'You sound like a newspaper article, but I know you're right. I'm sorry. Jonathan was on particularly trying form tonight. He makes me feel like the original scarlet woman.'

'He just knows how to push your button!'

'Because it was me who left, me who broke up his family . . .'

'Of course. But you weren't the only one who was suffocating in that marriage,' Kit said crisply. 'Jonathan was bloody miserable too, if he'd just admit it.'

'Maybe. But I have such a wonderful life now. You, this house, my job at the Beeb. And I get to be with Emma . . . I can't help feeling that all this happiness has been acquired . . . well, at Jonathan's expense.'

'In a way it has. Which is precisely why Jonathan's so angry and so sad. But the real question is, would you like to go back?'

'*God*, no. I just feel sorry for him.'

'Of course you do – you're meant to! Jonathan may be clever, but he's not emotionally strong. Emotional blackmail is the weapon of the weak, and he's using it for all he's worth.'

Sally bent down and kissed his forehead. 'But you're strong, Kit.'

'In some ways. In some.'

7

* * *

The sound was not so much a muffled scream as a long, dull moan.

Sally's instincts brought her awake before her brain could interpret the sound. Then she saw in the sparse moonlight that Kit was gone from his place in the double bed beside her. She knew he had to get up early to go to Leicester, but this was the middle of the night – the street-lights were still on outside . . .

The sound came again. Not quite so protracted this time, but with a plangent quality that chilled Sally's heart like nothing else. She knew it must be coming from Emma's room.

By the third, lowest moan, Sally was out of bed and moving across the dark bedroom towards the door. She stumbled over a pair of discarded shoes, then reached the moonlit clarity of the upstairs hall.

Emma . . .

Now Sally could see down the passage and in through the open door of her daughter's bedroom. Kit's broad, naked back faced her. A lacquered floorboard creaked under her foot, but Kit didn't react. He was bent over Emma's bed, apparently oblivious to Sally's approach.

Sally paused on the threshold and whispered: '*Kit* . . .'

He stiffened for a moment, then turned abruptly. He was dressed in nothing but a pair of boxer shorts. In the half-darkness his mouth was open like a guilty boy's.

'God, Sally. You frightened the life . . .' Kit's murmured reproach died away. 'I heard Em sing out, so I dashed along to see what the problem was. It sounded like she was being attacked, you know . . .' He glanced down at his own near-nudity, smiled awkwardly. 'Sort of didn't think to throw on a dressing-gown.'

Sally realised she must be staring like a Gorgon.

'How long have you been here?' she said. As she spoke, Emma stirred in her sleep, whimpered.

'Half a minute. I don't know. I just wanted to make sure she was all right. She's been talking as well . . .'

Sally moved to the bedside. Kit made way for her, edged back towards the doorway. She reached out and gently brushed back a stray strand of hair from Emma's forehead. The girl's face was frowning in a kind of uneasy concentration.

Then Emma muttered in a frightened and tiny but quite clear voice, 'No, Daddy. *No* . . .'

Sally looked round for Kit and he was gone.

When she came out of the room some minutes later, Kit was on the landing, looking broodingly out of the window at the darkened street.

'That is not a happy girl,' he murmured.

'What exactly did she say?' Sally asked softly. 'When you first went in there?'

Kit continued to gaze out of the window. 'She said, "You're not my Good Daddy. No. No . . ."'

'*Good* Daddy?'

'Yes.'

'I told you something was wrong.'

Kit finally looked at Sally.

'As I said last night, she's got a lot of conflict in her life. Kids say all sorts of stuff in their dreams.' He shrugged his powerful shoulders. 'You'd better get up for her next time, though. If there is one.'

'But I wasn't—'

Kit laughed softly. 'No, of course you weren't. I know that. But you may be able to make sense of the thing where I can't.'

9

He turned decisively towards their bedroom. 'Come on, my love. I've got to be up and at it in a couple of hours. Breakfast in Leicester with the Midlands sales force. Life in the fast lane, eh?'

Kit woke Sally with a cup of tea before leaving for his dash up the motorway. He had already got his own breakfast. Unmarried until he met her, he had never depended on Sally to look after him in that way. Not like Jonathan.

She watched Kit leave in the early morning light, backing from the garage, skilfully manoeuvring his sleek Mercedes in the silent cul-de-sac. One of the first jets of the morning rumbled overhead, lights still blinking, dropping steadily for its final descent into Heathrow. Then Sally lay in bed for a while, sipping tea. At seven she padded down to the kitchen and clicked on the *Today* programme, to stop herself thinking too much.

At a quarter to eight, it was time to call up to Emma. Her daughter appeared downstairs surprisingly promptly, spruce in her mauve Putney High uniform.

'You're up pretty bright. Even early too,' Sally said.

'Needed a good night's sleep.'

'So you got one? A good night's sleep, I mean?'

'Yeah.'

'Did . . . did you have any dreams?'

Emma looked puzzled. 'You all right, Mum?'

'Yes. Of course I am.'

'Where's Kit?'

'He's got a meeting in Leicester, remember? Had to leave at half-past six.'

'Oh, right.'

10

'I should be able to get home early this afternoon. We could take a walk on the Common after tea.'

'Could,' Emma conceded vaguely.

'I'll pick you up from school, perhaps . . . Or perhaps you should go to Jenny's, as usual, in case I'm a bit late.'

Jenny Anderson was a neighbour, a divorcée with a girl of Emma's age and an eight-year-old son. For two years now, since the Jacksons' last au pair had gone home, Jenny and Sally had enjoyed a very convenient arrangement: Emma stayed in the safety of the Anderson house round the corner until her mother or stepfather got home, and in return Sally paid half the wages of the nice Australian nanny that Jenny couldn't have afforded on her own. Perhaps next year Sally would be able to think of Emma coming home here to an empty house, but not yet.

'Have some toast,' Sally said with a helpless sigh, changing the subject.

'OK.'

Emma ate an entire two slices, slowly but surely. Sally watched, trying not let her daughter see she was monitoring each mouthful. Before they knew, it was time for them both to hop into Sally's little Volkswagen and start their respective days.

As promised, Sally came home from work slightly early, picking up Emma from Jenny's on the way.

She dumped her bagful of scripts on the sofa, put some coffee on, checked through the day's mail.

The sun had come out that afternoon. While Sally busied herself in the kitchen, Emma spread her books out in the conservatory. When Sally glanced through the connecting arch, her daughter was sitting peacefully at the table with the door open to the sunshine and the birdsong. An idyllic scene, except that Emma still looked worryingly pale.

'How're you doing?' Sally called through to her daughter.

'OK. Gym again this afternoon. I ache like anything.'

'You're supposed to be young and supple.' Sally frowned at her from the arched connecting doorway.

Emma shrugged, closed her book.

'Got much homework?' Sally said.

'Not for handing in tomorrow, no. Already done my maths and English. Then I've got to get into the big French project. "The Channel Tunnel: Is It A Good Thing?" In French.' Emma grimaced. 'At least five pages. By the week after half-term.'

'I'll be in Manchester then, so if you want any help, you'd better not do it at the last moment. We could tackle it now . . .'

Emma shot Sally a wintry smile.

'Not sure I can face it. *De trop*, y'know.'

'Or we could go for a wander on the Common,' Sally suggested, seizing her chance. 'After I've finished my coffee. I'd like that. Please?'

'Honestly, Mum, if you're so keen on exercise I don't know why you don't get yourself a dog.' Emma's look was affectionate but deadpan cheek.

'Brat. The answer to that is, because he – or she – would get lonely all day while we were at work, and because I couldn't talk to him, or at least not without being considered batty. Come on, girl. Walkies!'

Emma dashed upstairs and got changed into jeans and jacket. They cut through to Barnes Green, round the pond, then down to the Common. The fine weather had brought out the strollers, and Sally had to admit she was glad of them. The trees were thick and overhung the paths. When deserted the Common could be a little creepy.

They talked for a while about Emma's day, about half-term, then about the school trip to Paris she wanted to go on in the summer. It took Sally time before she came up with the big question.

'So you had a good time with your father?' she said.

Emma smiled. 'Excellent.'

'Is it OK, going up there every other weekend?'

Emma looked at Sally quizzically, as if her mother had just asked something eccentric, even slightly mad.

'I love staying with Dad,' she said firmly. 'I miss him – even if you don't.'

This girl can give as good as she gets, Sally thought ruefully.

'It's just that you seem a bit edgy lately,' she said. 'And – I hope you don't mind my bringing this up, darling – you're getting a bit picky with your food again.'

Emma sighed, nodded. 'I know. I've talked about it with Yardley. He says it's manageable. We decided it might have to do with my self-image now that boys are getting interested in me.' The therapy-speak tripped easily off her young tongue.

'Especially Zak?'

Emma looked straight ahead down at the path.

'Maybe.'

'What does that mean?' asked Sally, trying to sound light-hearted.

'We like spending time together, that's all. We always have.'

'Of course. But—'

'For God's sake, Mum, what is this all of a sudden? I've known Zak all my life!'

'Emma, I'm your mother!' Sally protested. 'Sometimes it's hard, adjusting to your suddenly being a teenager, and Zak being old enough . . . to be interested . . .' She touched Emma's arm in a half-controlling, half-pleading gesture. 'At the moment I just need to do a little reality-check, OK?'

Emma let her mother's hand rest on her arm for a moment, then gently pulled away.

'Fine. Why not?' she said, and clearly meant the opposite.

They walked on a little further in silence. Home-going commuter traffic was building up on Rocks Lane.

'You sort of woke us up last night, you know,' Sally said then.

Emma stopped in her tracks. 'What? How?'

'You were having nightmares. Kit went to your room first, then me. You were muttering in your sleep. Crying out. That's why I'm a bit worried, I suppose, darling. Am I being silly or what?'

'You *both* came into my room last night, Mum?'

'Yes.'

'I don't remember anything.'

'Really?'

Emma walked on for a while, pondering her mother's words.

'I . . . I do sometimes have weird dreams,' she admitted. 'Sort of bad things.'

'Bad things.'

'I think it's those video nasties Amanda's brother always puts on when we're around, just to scare us. Gory stuff. Creepy houses. You know. Amanda gets nightmares sometimes too. She told me.'

14

'So there's nothing else, Em?'

'No. *No.*'

'Really, honestly?'

Her daughter turned away angrily. Unnecessarily angrily, it seemed to Sally.

'You make me feel like a child,' Emma said heavily.

'Darling, of course you're not exactly that.' Sally hesitated, wondering how to put it. 'But on the other hand, in the scheme of things, thirteen is still quite young.'

She knew immediately she had got it wrong, that it had come out pompous, condescending. Emma's swift reaction confirmed her clumsiness.

'For God's sake, mother, will you get off my case? I'm absolutely fine! Just fine!'

TWO

For Sally, the week before the Whitsun holiday was hellish. The play she was producing ran into legal problems and needed a substantial last-minute rewrite. To add to the chaos, two of the actors came down with flu on the day they were due to record, so she spent Wednesday recasting, Thursday re-rehearsing, and all day Friday in the studio.

She managed to stagger home to Barnes by just after seven that evening. Jonathan had already come at six to collect Emma for her extended stay with him. Sally had no time to pack; she grabbed some jeans and T-shirts from the pile of clean but unironed clothes and literally threw them into a bag. Three hours later than planned, Kit's Mercedes finally joined the stream of traffic on the M4 as they headed for Harry and Liz's cottage on the edge of Exmoor. Sally was already fast asleep in the passenger seat.

The journey took over four hours, slowed by bank-holiday jams around Bristol. By the time they parked in the dark, silent lane outside the cottage it was almost midnight.

There was just time for greetings, a snack, and then bed. Despite, or perhaps because of the tensions of the trip, Sally and Kit ended up making glorious, urgent love in the spare room with its view of the distant Brendon Hills, while the stars gazed benignly down from a clear, unpolluted night sky. Then, childless for a week, released to play and rest as the fancy took them, Sally and Kit slept in long and late.

Around eleven the next morning, the men went off into nearby Williton to do the shopping for dinner. It was understood they would stop off for a quick pint on the way back. Sally and Liz hadn't seen each other since before Easter, and they were looking forward to a talk.

Liz made cappuccinos on the smart, matt-black little machine in the kitchen. The two old friends settled down at the scrubbed-maple table.

'All right?' Liz asked.

'Wiped out . . . But how about you?' Sally returned.

Liz laughed, pushed back her long dark hair. Where Sally was elfin-faced and blonde, Liz, her very oldest friend, was tall and dramatic, with full lips and ironic question-marks for eyebrows.

The two women had shared a room in college more than fifteen years before. In those days the 'All right?' exchange had become established as their private joke, particularly after a lively Friday night. It was all in how you said it. The years had passed; Sally had made a career at the BBC and Liz in Social Services, but the code was still as clear and as sharp as ever.

'Oh, I'm all *right*.' Liz looked at her friend shrewdly. 'Not so sure about you, though. Come on, out with it!' she pressed Sally.

'All . . . right . . .'

Sally's hesitant admission now came reinforced with a doubtful little hand-gesture.

'God! It's Kit! He's having an affair! I always knew he was too good to be true!'

Sally blushed. 'Kit? Oh no. He adores me. Really.'

'So it's you . . .'

'Whoa!' Sally snorted. 'Slow down, Liz! Actually, it's the other eternal triangle – or is it a see-saw? – me, Jonathan, and Emma in the middle.'

'Hmm. Is your ex still being wimpish about the divorce?'

Sally nodded uneasily. She never could get entirely used to Liz's brisk, not to say ruthless, attitude towards relationships. Until Liz met Harry five years previously, she had shown every sign of viewing men as attractive but disposable artifacts, things you might acquire for a season and then decide to chuck away, like fashion frocks or items of costume jewellery. Even Harry, Sally suspected, was probably still on trial.

'The old guilt-trip, of course,' Sally confirmed. 'And Emma's old enough to start taking sides. But I'm not sure that's really it.'

'No?'

'Hard to pin down. I do know that Emma's having eating problems again, though.'

'I thought she was doing well with that therapist you sent her to.'

'She was. And it isn't really a crisis. It's still classified as a sub-clinical eating disorder. But she's thinner than ever, and she seems troubled.'

'OK. Definitely cause for concern. What's this got to do with Jonathan?'

'I think staying every other weekend with her father in that cramped flat, month in month out, is getting to Emma.'

'I'm sure she can cope.'

'I wonder if she'd rather be home more but feels she doesn't want to hurt Jonathan's feelings.'

'You mean, since you've already hurt him, she doesn't want to compound it?'

Sally nodded. 'You think that's crazy?'

'Not at her age, no. Maybe she's more torn than she lets on. Kids often are.' Liz smiled wryly. 'Makes me glad Zak and I haven't seen his father since 1981.'

'Not all Emma's friends go to the same school, so weekends are the only times she can see them.' Sally shot Liz a questing little glance. 'For instance . . . your Zak's been following her to Jonathan's.'

'I take the hint.' Liz reached for a cigarette. 'The plot thickens. Has Emma been given contraceptive advice?'

'That wasn't what I was getting at. She's not even fourteen!'

'But she's very pretty.'

'She's only just started her periods.'

'Good enough.'

'For God's sake, it's *illegal*.'

'So's smoking marijuana. So's driving at seventy-five miles an hour on the motorway. People still do it, Sal.'

Liz, who often compared the joys of argument with a rally in tennis, was satisfied that her final, deadly lob had been a winner. She lit her cigarette, took a ruminative drag.

'Well, I can't control every minute of Zak's day,' she continued, 'but you can ensure Emma knows what's what. *If* they're sleeping together – which, actually, my dear, I think extremely unlikely.'

Despite herself, Sally was relieved by Liz's opinion.

'Emma's very definite about not being old enough for sex. "This isn't the sixties, you know," she said to me. Little minx.'

'She's a sensible kid. Takes after her mum. So,' Liz persisted, eyeing her keenly, 'the eating disorder's not that bad, and it seems as though Emma isn't having sex after all. Then there's got to be something else getting to you, my dear.'

Sally hesitated. 'Well, I'm not conscious of it as a problem, but I might as well mention it: Kit and I are trying for a baby of our own,' she said.

'But that's great!'

'I know. But all I can think of is how Emma will react! And I wonder if somehow Emma knows and it's somehow affecting her . . . Plus, of course, I don't need to tell you how obnoxious old jealous Jonathan will be about the whole thing . . .'

Liz made a face. 'Well, you know how I feel about Jonathan, Sally. I always distrust anyone who flaunts his integrity like the wounds of Christ!'

'He's an emotional vampire,' Sally agreed. 'It was one good reason I couldn't stay married to him. Well, now he's transferred his demands from me to Emma. Sometimes I get this feeling he's sucking the young life out of her.'

'You're going to have to discuss the problem with him. Clear the air. If you do have another child, it's going to change his relationship to Emma. Maybe for the better, who knows? But it might be a good idea to start preparing the ground now.'

'It's difficult. We just about manage the practicalities – who delivers Emma where and when, that sort of thing. But otherwise, to be frank, I'm talking total communications breakdown.'

'Well that's got to change!' Liz said firmly. 'Never mind what you two mixed-up adults think of each other. What about Emma in the middle?'

Liz was right. Sally had to get into some kind of real dialogue with Jonathan. She would have to do all the emotional work, but what was new about that?

'Yes,' she agreed. 'But what to do?'

'Cajole Jonathan into lunch somewhere,' Liz suggested. 'On him, of course.'

'We've got a lot more money than Jonathan. Do you know how low lecturers' salaries are?'

'Never mind that. If he's paying, he'll feel powerful and in charge.'

'Even if it's pie and chips at the local,' Sally countered ruefully.

'Knowing Jonathan's taste in food, *especially* then.'

They both laughed. The mood changed. Liz looked at her watch.

'Twelve-thirty. The men will be in the pub. I've got a bottle of Sainsbury's Sancerre in the fridge, and you're not pregnant yet, my dear, so why don't we see if we can empty it by the time they get back?'

'Why not?' Sally said. 'It's been a sober, hardworking few months since Christmas. This sounds like the decadent interlude I've been looking forward to, and it suits me just fine.'

Jonathan put aside the assignment he was marking, stretched, looked at his watch. Time for eats. He got up from his paper-strewn work-table, shambled towards the kitchen.

'Em!' he called out. 'Fancy strolling out for a burger?'

No answer. Jonathan wandered to the door of her tiny room.

It was a cramped flat: just a lounge, a kitchen/dinette, and two modest bedrooms in a grey little street the estate agents called 'Chiswick Borders' but everyone else knew as Shepherd's Bush. Even so, it was a stretch on his lecturer's salary. But at least he could have his daughter to stay, and give Emma her own space. At least they could be together properly, lovingly. Kit and Sally couldn't take that away from him, though Jonathan suspected that she, especially, would like to try.

Emma's room was empty. Then Jonathan recalled that a couple of hours back she had told him she was going to the shops. Something about getting Kit a present.

Come to think of it, though, Kit's birthday isn't until July.

Five minutes later found Jonathan steering his Ford estate into the busy shopping section of Chiswick High Road and looking for a place to park. No luck. He drove past the supermarket, past the pub, past the mimsy little decorator's shop that had opened just before Christmas, and finally past the burger bar where he had been planning to take Emma for lunch . . .

Through the picture window of the fast-food place he saw a striking young woman who looked vaguely familiar. For a split second Jonathan strove to match face with name, then quickly chided himself. This was no woman but a child. His child.

Emma. And she was with a young man. Zak Paine.

Jonathan spotted a vacant parking space thirty yards or so beyond. He swerved into it, going in forwards so that the corner of his tailgate ended up sticking a foot out into the traffic. He didn't give a damn about neat parking. All the same, he knew he had to keep control of himself, avoid embarrassing Em in front of all those people, so he lit one of the cigarettes he was trying to ration, and he sat in the front seat of his car and waited for the rage to die down.

I fume as I fume, Jonathan thought grimly.

Sally was probably right, he considered as his temper subsided. Jealousy lay at the root of it. But then what would that bitch know about a simple, basic emotion like that? For Christ's sake, she'd never had reason to be jealous of him while they were married. Probably, in fact, have been better if she had.

Feeling a little steadier, and – this was just as important –
with his story ready, Jonathan got out of the car and headed for
the eating-house.

Zak started visibly when he saw Jonathan walk into the
burger bar. At sixteen the boy was big for his age, looked older,
could even manage a little fuzz on his chin to go with the lank
hair and the ripped jeans. Zak half-got to his feet, Emma sat still
where she was and looked at her father . . . strangely . . .

'Hi,' Jonathan said. 'Didn't expect to see you, Zak.'

'No,' the boy mumbled. 'I . . . er . . . yeah, Emma and me
made a date to go shopping for Kit's present. You know, 'cos
I'm a guy I'd sort of know more . . .'

'Right.' Jonathan sat at the table, trying to act normal. He
was just going to have to tolerate this thing with Zak for the
moment. He couldn't bitch to Sally again without seeming
weird, obsessive. 'So what did you get? For Kit, I mean.'

Zak looked out of the window, embarrassed.

'We decided on a Gorecki CD, but they'd sold out of the one
we wanted,' Emma answered none too convincingly.

'Right. Have you eaten yet?' Jonathan said, looking at the
menu over the serving-counter, even though he knew it by heart.

'We were just having a quick coffee,' Emma explained
hastily. 'I would have said about meeting Zak, Dad, but . . .' She
made a vague gesture of ambivalence. 'You were busy marking,
and . . .'

'It just so happened that I'd bawled Zak out last week,
right?'

Emma smiled. Her father always forgave her everything
when she smiled. 'I 'spose so.'

Jonathan forced himself to smile back. 'Well, I'd planned to
get some burgers to take home,' he lied, 'but since we're all

here, why don't I buy us lunch? How does that grab you, guys?'

'Great,' said Emma. 'But I'll just have the side-salad, all right?'

There was a muffled crash from the cottage's tiny kitchen, where Harry and Kit were supposed to be washing up the things from dinner. Liz rolled her eyes.

'It's the country air,' she said. 'Plus the booze, of course. The locals down here are all total dipsos, you know. Harry insists it's part of the rustic charm . . .'

'Some drink to remember/Some drink to for-g-e-e-t-t!' crooned Harry as he entered, shaking his wire-grey shock of hair. He carried a tray bearing a cafetière and four coffee cups. 'Remember the Eagles? "Hotel California"? Wait a minute. Was it *drink*? Or *dance*? Ohmigod. My memory's going.'

'You're an embarrassment, you hideous old sixties relic,' Liz said. She turned to Sally, winked. 'I need a toy-boy, Sal, that's what I need!'

Harry grinned. 'I hear the vicar's son's available.'

'He's a seething mass of pimples!'

'You can't have everything.'

Harry set down the tray just a little too noisily on the kitchen table. Kit followed him, carrying a bottle of brandy and four tumblers. He towered over Harry by a good six inches – Sally always seemed to choose tall men, Liz the slighter sort. They looked like Mutt and Jeff. Kit delivered his load safely.

'I think we deserve another drink just for getting out of that kitchen alive, don't you?' he announced. 'A death-trap built for Elizabethan dwarves.'

Harry laughed. 'I sense contempt for decent vernacular building from you, Mr Jackson. Actually,' he said in a mock-whisper, 'this cottage isn't really Tudor at all. It was constructed in 1987 from a Swedish kit. The proportions are this way because the commissioning clients were Japanese.'

'Harry's started with the architectural jokes,' Liz muttered. 'There'll be no stopping him now.'

Her partner looked hurt. 'You're talking about a man who personally designed the first post-modern public convenience north of the Wash. More respect, per-leaze!'

'Respect?'

'Well, it was either accept the job or the practice went bust.'

Harry handed Liz a stiff brandy, sat down on the carpet next to her armchair.

'Coffee can wait, I say.'

'I haven't had so much to drink since the day I divorced Jonathan,' Sally said with a giggle as her husband joined her on the sofa. 'Do you remember?'

'I remember the bill for the champagne,' Kit retorted. He smiled blearily. 'Worth every penny, though.'

Sally lifted her glass. 'To divorce!' she toasted. 'And to marriage!'

'To having your cake and eating it!' chipped in Harry. They each took a sip. 'I've never understood that saying, actually,' he added thoughtfully. 'I mean, what's the point of having the bloody stuff if you *don't* eat it?' He gestured dramatically with his tumbler, almost swirling his remaining brandy over the rim.

'Careful,' Liz counselled, but Harry was in full flow.

'Cakes, toy-boys, all the pleasures of life,' he continued regardless. 'I was in Amsterdam on business last month, you know, and the thing was, it was all cake and all eating, that place. I mean, drugs and sex and everything all out in the open and being consumed shamelessly . . .'

'It's no different in the Borough of Barnes and Richmond,' Kit drawled. He turned to Sally. 'Is it, my love?'

She giggled. 'You really *are* drunk, Kit Jackson, if that's what you think.'

Harry nodded. 'She's right. The age of consent in Holland is twelve, for a start. Beat that!'

'Join it, mate, more like!' Kit guffawed.

The silence that followed was so sudden, and so profound, that it felt as if someone had pressed a mute switch.

Liz finally took a deep breath. 'Taste,' she hissed. 'We have a taste problem here.'

Sally glared at Kit. He shrugged, a big, embarrassed child.

'Joke,' he mumbled. 'Bad joke. Schoolboy joke . . .'

'Not funny, though,' said Liz in her soft but deadly voice. 'Because, for a start, you're not at school any more.'

'I don't see why there can be jokes about toy-boys but none about toy-girls,' Harry said, coming to Kit's aid.

'Because . . .' Liz's gaze on her partner was merciless. 'Because abusing young girls is about male power, and male irresponsibility, and male cruelty. That's why.'

'I'm sorry,' muttered Kit. 'Forget I said it.'

Liz glimpsed Sally's distress. With a visible effort, she reined herself in.

'What makes you think we're going to remember any of this in the morning, anyway?' Liz held out her empty brandy glass to Kit and made an imperious gesture. 'I'll have some more of this, actually. And for extra punishment, I'll make you stumble back into the dwarves' kitchen and get some ice.'

At about one in the morning, Sally emerged from the downstairs loo. The door to the garden was slightly ajar. She could hear Harry's and Kit's voices in the living room. A glance through the little window to the left of the door revealed Liz standing by the azaleas in the moonlight, smoking one of her occasional cigarettes. Harry couldn't bear them in the room with him, and Liz couldn't totally give them up. It got hard in the winter.

Sally emerged, whispered a greeting. Liz started like a frightened animal. Her look as she turned was almost wild.

'Oh gawd,' Liz said quickly, 'it's you! I still haven't got used to the quiet here. I'm easily spooked.' She indicated the pinpoint tapestry of stars above them. 'Don't get this in London, though, eh?'

'Listen, Liz, be honest, would you rather be alone?'

Liz shook her head with the deliberation of the still-slightly-drunk.

'Happy to be interrupted,' she said, 'but only since it's you.'

'I want to apologise again for Kit's stupid little crack about under-age girls. It was unforgivable. But it's just not like him. Really, not at all . . .'

Liz waved the hand with the cigarette in dismissal.

'Oh, Harry's every bit as bad when he's had a few. It's just that . . . well, sometimes I suspect I really don't like men much.' She shrugged. 'Even the nice kind of men that women like us marry.'

THREE

The Saturday night incident had raised tension. It could have made for a difficult few days, but in fact all turned out well. The pressure between the four of them dropped just as the weather-barometer rose.

Fine, sunny days took them out on to the hills every day. Meals were eaten in tea-rooms and pubs. Alcohol consumption retreated within decent bounds until the very last evening. Even then, no problems. No outbursts. No embarrassments.

The two couples parted on Wednesday morning with a sense of friendship renewed. Despite mild hangovers, there was a lot of laughter on Kit and Sally's drive back to London.

Jonathan appeared on time, and even he seemed at peace with his world. Emma, like a little wife, had persuaded him to buy a well-cut pair of khakis and some smart docksiders. He had even got himself a decent haircut.

If only Emma had seemed as at ease as the adults. Sally fancied she picked up again that tense, slightly feverish anxiety in her daughter when Emma and her father kissed each other goodbye.

'I'll miss you, ducks,' said Jonathan as they parted. 'I've got used to your company this week.'

'Yeah, Dad. We'll do it again.' Emma smiled. 'Next time

we'll get you some Timberlands. You'll look really cool.'

When Jonathan had gone, Emma made to go straight to her room. Sally managed to intercept her.

'So,' she said, 'did your dad find the time to drive you to Dr Yardley, and have you got all your half-term work done?'

'Yes, Mother. We were both very responsible.' A shy smile. 'You think Dad would let me get away with a thing like that twice?'

'No visits from Zak to distract you this time.'

'Only once.' Again, the shy smile.

'Ah.'

'Dad bought us all lunch, actually. Me and him and Zak.'

'He's getting more tolerant of the competition.'

'A bit.'

The shy smile turned coquettish. Emma tossed her head and continued up the stairs. One moment a vulnerable little girl, the next a young woman beginning to understand her power.

As for Sally, she didn't know if that look of her daughter's amused her or broke her heart. Soon there would be no child left in the house, it seemed. Only three adults, living together.

And perhaps – perhaps – a baby?

The next morning, after she had dropped Emma at school, Sally switched on the radio for the news. The announcer reminded her that it was the last day of May. Only then did it occur to Sally that she had missed her period. She should have menstruated around the time they went down to Somerset, if not a few days earlier. All the business with the play and the worrying about Emma had made her forgetful. That intense conversation with Liz Saturday lunchtime, about Jonathan and Emma and trying for a new baby, and even then she had been overdue!

Suddenly it was all Sally could think about. After nearly fourteen years, another child, another new life.

And this time the child would be fully hers and Kit's.

But what about the changes this would bring for Emma? And – though she hated to take him into account – Jonathan? How to manage the breaking of the news?

'Well, I peed into the little phial,' Sally said, 'and a ring appeared, just like it said. How reliable are these things?'

'These days, pretty much so,' came Liz's confirmation down the line. 'Gone are the days of prayer and mumbo-jumbo and take away the first number you thought of. You're a couple of weeks late?'

'Maybe a bit more.'

'I rest my case.' Liz paused. 'How does it feel?'

'Strangely frightening. When I think how it was when I got pregnant with Emma – you know – the little basement flat in Islington and me slaving away as dogsbody to that terrible woman at the World Service, while Jonathan was finishing his postgrad work . . . but somehow I'm more nervous, really nervous I mean, now . . .'

'That's because you know more. And because your life is, bless us all, a bit more complicated. I must confess, I wouldn't fancy going through it all again. On the rare occasions Harry starts making broody noises, I tell him motherhood'll turn me into an exhausted harridan with stretch marks who's lost interest in sex and talks about nothing but what the baba did today. Soon shuts him up.'

'Your description fills me with confidence, I must say.'

'Just kidding, honest!' Liz paused meaningfully. 'So when are you going to tell Kit he's going to be a dad?'

'I think I'll break this to everyone gently. God knows, Kit's waited long enough for this. He can wait another few days for full confirmation.'

'As I said, it's not like it used to be. The new self-test kits are pretty much spot-on.'

'Oh, I know. But it's not just that. You see, if I tell Kit now, I know he'll be absolutely over the moon. It'll be impossible for him to keep the secret, I know it. He'll rush off to tell Emma straightaway. I'd rather leave it till the weekend while she's at Jonathan's, so I can sit Kit down with a Scotch and give him the good news, we can celebrate just the two of us, and then we can decide how to tell her . . .'

'Come on. Emma will be thrilled, I'd imagine.'

'I certainly hope so.'

'Little Miss Caution. You haven't changed since college! Still, maybe you're right. Nothing wrong with a bit of mystery and suspense. And what's a day or two between friends?' Then Liz turned away from the phone. A voice was calling from her office door. 'And now, darling, I have to go,' Liz explained quickly. 'Got a meeting on children at risk. I mean, we think *we've* got problems. 'Bye, Sal.'

When she got home that evening, it was even harder than Sally had anticipated to keep her suspected pregnancy to herself, but she did it. She knew Kit longed for a child of his own, and it would be too cruel to raise his hopes and then disappoint him. Or so she told herself. Actually, it had occurred to Sally more than once during this roller-coaster of a day that perhaps she was more anxious about another child, and what it meant for the entire extended family, than she let herself admit. She needed time to think before it became public, irreversible.

In any case, there were still the same everyday worries. Primarily, of course, to do with the child she already had: Emma. To Sally, her daughter seemed even more withdrawn. She stayed upstairs until it was time for supper, then came down and ate – it seemed to Sally – quickly and mechanically before disappearing once more to her room to watch television.

The more she thought about Emma, the more the result of the pregnancy test receded into the background. Sally watched Kit as he poured himself an after-dinner Scotch.

'Something's very wrong with Emma,' she said. 'I'm her Mum. I can tell.'

Kit had started unscrewing the cap of the Malvern water. He paused, frowned. 'Right. But what?'

'I don't know.'

'I've ... well, reluctant as I am to admit it, I've been thinking Jonathan may have a point,' Kit said. 'About Emma and that boy Zak, I mean.'

'She denies it, darling. I have to believe her.'

'OK. But if that little bastard's been fooling around with Em, I'll have his guts for garters.'

'You're sounding just like Jonathan! Macho claptrap!'

'Em's a kid, Sal!' Kit said harshly. 'Just a kid!'

'That may be true, but you don't own her! Neither does Jonathan! She's her own person, Kit!'

Kit looked at Sally for a long moment, then nodded slowly. He added Malvern water to his whisky, fifty-fifty as usual, scooped up some ice from the covered bowl. It jangled into the tumbler like tense sound-track music.

'Oh, by the way,' Kit said then in a more normal voice, 'I've negotiated a new deal for our group health insurance. Gives us better coverage.'

'That's good,' Sally answered vaguely.

'Means we have to go in for a medical check-up, though. First thing on Monday.' Kit tapped her shoulder. 'You're not listening.'

'I am. I am. Right . . . a medical?'

''Fraid so. To get the new rate we have to prove there's nothing organically wrong with any of us.'

'Emma included?'

'Don't worry. Jock Macintyre has said he'll do the examination personally. We won't have to go through the sausage-machine like the rest of the staff.'

'Aha. Special treatment. Courtesy of the golf-club mafia.'

'I've been dealing with Jock for years. He's a nice guy. But he has to say he's done the exam or the insurers won't OK the new plan. All right?'

'Sure, but Monday's no good. I've organised a meeting for that morning,' Sally said. 'Preparing for the Manchester brainstorm. There's no rush, is there?'

'Jock says he can't do it any other time. Sorry.'

'You could have given us more notice, darling.'

'It's important. And Jock *is* doing me a favour.' Kit put his arm around her. 'Not getting your period, are you? You're pretty touchy.'

It was rare for Kit to put his priorities first in quite such a decisive way. Anyway, it was sort of a family thing, wasn't it?

'Oh, all right,' she relented, shaking him off gently. 'I'll switch the meeting to the afternoon. It won't make me popular.'

'You're a darling. It's good to get these things out of the way.'

Should she tell Kit now, before the check-up? Sally couldn't keep her mind off the tiny germ of life she imagined – no, felt –

34

inside her. She resisted an urge to throw her arms around Kit, say: *You're going to be a father! Doesn't that feel good?* But all at its right and proper time. She would talk to Dr Macintyre and make sure he kept her pregnancy quiet until Kit had been duly informed.

'Yes,' Sally said out loud with a secretive smile. 'Yes, it sure is.'

Emma spent Sunday with her friend Amanda – the one with the video-obsessed brother – and Kit played golf.

Sally was grateful for the opportunity to make some notes for the drama brainstorm she was due to attend in Manchester next week. She would be away from Tuesday to Friday, helping hammer out the ways they would take popular radio drama into the twenty-first century.

Prepare yourself for a storm of management jargon, Sally thought. *And give as good as you get.*

She already had her plan for the week: confirmation of the pregnancy should come on Monday, she travelled up to Manchester on Tuesday, then returned on Friday just in time to see Emma off for the weekend with Jonathan. This would leave her and Kit alone together on Saturday and Sunday, during which she could break the news of her pregnancy to him. They could celebrate together, then discuss how to tell Emma.

Neat. Right. Perfect. These things were all about management, and as a producer, management was what Sally excelled at.

Of course, it didn't all go quite to plan. Early Monday morning, just when she didn't need it, the morning sickness started. Sally threw up surreptitiously in the downstairs loo amid loud flushing so that no one would hear her. Who needed confirmation?

By the time they all left for the check-up at Jock Macintyre's practice, Sally looked and felt like hell. Luckily Kit seemed distracted by the morning's proceedings, which were extremely thorough and didn't see them out of the place until noon. As a consequence, Kit and Sally parted hastily. It was a contest as to who of the three of them was in the more irritable temper. Kit seemed on edge, which was not like him. Emma had to be packed off to school in a cab, which arrived late. Sally missed the first ten minutes of her meeting and would have had no chance to grab lunch, even had she been hungry . . .

It was five o'clock before she could ring the family planning clinic. The consultant there simply confirmed what the home-pregnancy test and the morning sickness had already told her: she was expecting a child in January of the next year. What joy. And what a huge change in all their lives . . .

Immediately afterwards, she called Liz, who got all practical and recommended vitamins for any tiredness, and ginger tea for the morning sickness – straight root ginger by the spoonful if that wasn't immediately available. 'Infallible,' she said. Sally dropped by the health-food shop on the way home, dosed herself up with Liz's recommended substances right outside in the car, surreptitious as a chocolate fiend or a secret drinker.

It was hardest of all, that final evening before leaving for Manchester, to keep from blurting everything out to Kit, especially as he still seemed on edge, as if under special pressure. How marvellous it would be to cheer him up with the news! But Sally held herself back. Get the business trip over. Another four days, she told herself, and all could be revealed. Then we'll tell Emma, she thought. Kit and I together. On Sunday night. Everything planned out and made safe and sound.

Management.

* * *

Despite another stealthy attack of nausea – not so bad this time, maybe the ginger was working – the morning of Sally's departure seemed like another triumph of organisation. Kit's company Mercedes was in for repairs, and he would borrow her Volkswagen while she was away. Of course, he could have hired another executive model, but it was part of his style as MD to set an example of frugality. Sally had ordered a cab for ten-thirty to take her to Euston.

'Don't forget, Dr Yardley tomorrow afternoon,' Sally told Emma as they walked out to the car. 'Take the bus, all right?'

'No problem. Have a good week, Mum.'

They hugged each other.

'You take good care of each other,' Sally said, planting a kiss on Kit's cheek. He still seemed uncharacteristically anxious and preoccupied. 'It'll be the weekend before we know it.'

'Right,' Kit responded, looking at her a little strangely. Then he got into the VW alongside Emma. She said something and he laughed, perhaps a little harshly. The engine came to life. A quick wave and the little car and its two precious passengers were heading out of the cul-de-sac and into the world.

Sally went upstairs to finish packing.

It was almost ten-thirty when the phone rang. Sally picked it up quickly, supposing there must be a problem with the cab. No one who knew her and Kit would bother calling them at home on a weekday.

'Hello,' the caller said in a cultivated Scottish burr. 'Could you please put me through to Mr Kit Jackson?'

The voice seemed tantalisingly familiar to Sally.

'This is his wife,' she said. 'Kit's at work.'

There was a short silence. Then the voice said, 'Oh gosh, I

believe I've got a wrong number.'

'Wait a minute,' Sally said, suddenly recalling where she'd heard it before, 'isn't this Dr Macintyre?' Silence. Sally persisted. 'You examined us all yesterday, remember? I'm pregnant but we agreed you wouldn't tell Kit. Surely you remember *that*?'

'Of course. And I have no intention of breaking that confidence.' Macintyre coughed coyly. 'You see, I'd intended to ring Kit on his direct line at the office, but . . . you know, the ones I have written down here are both 0181 numbers and I suppose . . .'

'You dialled the wrong one. Can I help, anyway?'

Macintyre's embarrassment was palpable, even over the phone.

'Well . . . er . . . it's sort of a personal matter, Mrs Jackson,' he struggled.

'Does it concern our check-ups yesterday?' Sally's voice become hard, insistent. 'I have a right to know.'

'Quite. Quite! But as I said, Mrs Jackson, it's . . . personal . . . Well, I'll see if I can catch Kit at the office, shall I?' Macintyre continued quickly. 'Awfully sorry to bother you. 'Bye.'

He hung up before she could reply.

Sally was left with a silence and a nagging sense of incompleteness.

Bloody men. She felt certain Jock Macintyre was holding something back. Perhaps the tests had revealed a serious health problem. Perhaps Kit was ill. *Oh God, what if her husband was keeping something terrible from her, like cancer?*

Or what if the foetus is damaged? Macintyre might well tell Kit but not her.

No. Don't be silly, Sal, she told herself. One easily

embarrassed Scots physician doth not a drama make.

Save it all up until the weekend. Everything would be fine.

Manchester.

Management.

FOUR

Most of it felt like a dream, but she could always remember those words he said to her, even when he hurt her and made her sore:

'I love you, and I'm your Good Daddy, so don't listen to what anyone else says about what's right or wrong. It's just we have to be careful, sweetheart, because the world doesn't understand . . .'

Emma came out of her stepfather's study, closed the door quietly behind her and stood for some moments on the landing, feeling the silence, where more words seemed to be coming from.

'We're like fugitives from the bad people, sweeping away our tracks, that others call memories, with brushwood as we go, so no one will follow or find us, Emma and her Good Daddy. The pity is, we lose so much. But we must do this because the grown-up world just doesn't understand . . .'

Emma moved forward, feeling as if she was floating. The dream continued. She reached the threshold of the room where her stepfather was sleeping. She heard his rasping breathing. She stepped in. In the warmth of the summer night, he had half-kicked away the covers. Her eyes accustomed themselves to the darkness. He lay on his back, the skin of his broad chest albumen-grey, shining slightly with sweat.

'You see, we can't let anyone find us. They don't understand. This precious thing we have. They don't understand. You're mine and I'll do anything, anything, to keep you . . .'

Emma reached the bedside, looked down on her sleeping stepfather. All she knew was what Good Daddy had told her. All she felt was cold hatred, channelled, programmed anger.

'Anything, anything . . .'

Emma held the carving knife in both hands, pointing the blade downwards at her stepfather's naked chest as it rose and fell gently, almost imperceptibly.

She took a deep breath, raised the knife, still gripping it in both hands. Then she exhaled and brought it down with all her strength, fine point first.

'There's only one answer, and your Good Daddy knows it . . .'

Emma's stepfather's eyes half-opened just before the point of the knife pierced his chest. His mouth formed a new shape. She didn't know if he was about to say something, or if he understood; either way, she didn't care.

'Good Daddy knows it.'

Not Good but Bad, said a voice inside Emma's head. *Not Good but Bad, Bad, Bad . . .*

FIVE

In the small hours of Sally Jackson's last scheduled night in Manchester, the keening chirrup of a bedside phone tore her out of a deep sleep.

She fumbled, found the light-switch, stared nervously at the phone for a moment, then snatched it up as if dealing with a small but dangerous animal.

'Yes.'

'Mrs Jackson?'

'Speaking.' Despite a late-night session with her discussion group in the hotel bar, she was instantly alert, as if in some mysterious way her body had prepared itself for this.

'Right.' Pause. 'This is the night manager. I'm very sorry to bother you at this time, but there's a lady and a gentleman downstairs in reception who need to talk to you on an urgent basis.'

Sally glanced at her alarm clock. It was five to two in the morning. She swallowed hard.

'Could I ask what it's about?'

'A police matter, Mrs Jackson. Can I bring them up?'

'Yes . . . All right.'

Sally eased herself out of bed, picked up her robe from the chair beside the wardrobe, sat back on the bed and waited. She felt weightless, insubstantial with anxiety. It felt like hours later when the knock came. Sally padded to the door. After checking the chain was secure, she opened up.

There were three figures outside in the softly-illuminated corridor. One man in a civilian suit, and a man and a woman in police uniform. The dimness of the lighting gave the whole tableau a bizarre, stagy quality, as if everyone was waiting for a curtain to go up.

The civilian was short and bald, sporting one of the hotel's staff identity badges on his lapel. The night manager. The first police officer was tall and broad-shouldered, with greying hair and a puddingy, comedian's face. His female colleague was youngish, short-haired, and looked very nervous.

'Mrs Jackson?' the policewoman asked.

Something in her voice forced Sally's heart into her mouth. She swallowed hard.

'Yes . . .'

The policewoman held out her identification. Sally stared at it stupidly.

'This is Mr Underwood, the night manager,' the policewoman said, indicating the short man, in case Sally hadn't seen his badge. She pointed to the uniformed man. A careful preparation of her ground. 'And this is my colleague, Constable Young. May we come in?'

Sally didn't want them to come in. She either wanted to be sleeping, dreaming, or – if this was the dream – waking up from it. But somehow she slipped the chain, moved back and said something which might have been 'OK' or 'of course'.

Then they were all in the room with her, grouped around her, and Sally asked: 'Please. what is it?'

'Mrs Jackson,' the policeman said solemnly, taking over the

speaking part as if by pre-arrangement, 'there has been an incident at your home in London.'

'Oh, my God . . .'

The policewoman, meanwhile, had moved to Sally's elbow and was holding her gently.

'A knife was involved. I'm afraid that your husband is critically injured,' the man's voice continued relentlessly in his soft Lancashire growl.

'What about Emma? Emma! My daughter . . .'

'She's . . .' He hesitated, groping for a form of words. 'She is unhurt.'

'Thank God! Where's Kit now?' The disjointed, jumbled questions tumbled from Sally's lips. 'Did they catch the person who . . . ?'

'It appears that your daughter may somehow have been involved in the stabbing, Mrs Jackson,' the policeman said heavily.

He stepped back, as if anticipating some kind of retribution.

Sally stared at him intently. For an instant she had the mad sense that sheer effort of will would make him a liar. But his face, for all its gentle concern, was unyielding. Then she felt the room slip and spin around her.

The WPC half-led, half-carried her towards the bed.

Sally had suddenly left her body and was afloat, watching everything from a distance, connected to this reality only by a fragile, tingling thread.

She heard the policeman say to the night manager, almost cheerfully, as if he had just got something very difficult off his chest, 'Right-ho, chum, why don't you make yourself useful and get the lady here a nice, strong cup of tea . . .'

Six

After the chill silence of the car down from Manchester, to enter the police station was to move finally and irrevocably from dream to reality: lights, people, ringing telephones and swirling emotions.

Sally walked into the reception area and there was Jonathan, his lanky body crouched on a plastic chair, shaggy head in hands. He looked up and straight at her, impaling her with the agonised intensity of his stare.

'Where's Emma?' Sally said.

He just continued to look at her, pale and gaunt. Then he started to rise, wringing his hands as he did so, as if casting something out.

'I said, where's Emma?' Sally repeated. Her own voice felt so small. It was like one of those dreams where you screamed and yelled and screamed but no one answered and you finally realised that no sound was coming out, and never would no matter how hard you tried.

Then Jonathan lunged towards her. Sally should have been forewarned by that strange piece of business with the hands.

He took her by the shoulders and he shook her. She caught words grinding out from between his teeth in rhythm with the shakes: 'Kit', 'monster', 'bitch bitch bitch' . . .

It was hurting. Sally pulled back, stumbling slightly. Jonathan threw up his hands, clutching at air as if wanting to strangle it.

'We were happy once!' he howled. 'We were *safe*. We were a *family!*'

'Jonathan. I'm sorry. Listen . . .'

Sally's words died away. Listen to what? What could she say?

'See what you've done now, you bitch! Satisfied?'

Oh God, Oh God . . . And there was only a half-hearted man's voice saying, 'Come on, Mr er . . . er . . .'

'She married that monster!' Jonathan stopped snatching and flung out an accusing finger. 'Want to know who gave him the chance to get at my daughter. She did!'

'Mr er . . . er . . .'

And then someone appeared between Sally and Jonathan in a flash of silver and red and white. Shining dark hair and scarlet lips, and a strong, London-accented woman's voice.

'OK, Jim, settle Mr Quinn down, will you? I need to have a word with Mrs Jackson.'

And there was Jonathan standing like a child, his mouth opening and closing, and a young policeman saying something quietly to him. And Sally herself felt a hand on her arm, and was being guided towards a pair of swing doors, and that same very definite woman's voice was saying:

'I'm Sergeant Lipari. Let's get out of here, Mrs Jackson. This is no good for anybody, is it?'

Then the doors swallowed them and Jonathan was gone. It was an enormous relief to Sally, but no actual comfort at all.

'My name's Cheryl Lipari. Tea, Mrs Jackson?'

Sergeant Lipari knew as she offered it how inadequate a

response it was to the anguish of the woman facing her across the table. But then what *would* really help Emma Quinn's mother? At least tea would warm her up. It must have been a long, wearing drive down from Manchester.

Sally nodded gratefully, listened as this exotically attractive policewoman issued an order to the WPC in the corner. She observed Lipari: thirtyish, big silver earrings, crisp white blouse with a chain at the throat, red cotton jacket – like the name Cheryl, the effect was definitely too much, Sally registered. Yet somehow, somehow she carried it off. Sally decided that too, *as if it mattered* . . . Despite her exhaustion, Sally now felt fiercely, preternaturally alert. Her lifesaver was to keep tracking the details, however apparently irrelevant. Every time the terror and the pain threatened to overwhelm her, she pushed them back fiercely, like an embattled crewman repelling boarders. *Keep noticing*, she repeated to herself obsessively. *You must notice everything*.

'Anything else you need?' Sergeant Lipari was asking with a new softness in her voice. 'Anything to help you through this, I mean. We have a doctor on call . . .'

'They already asked me that. I've never taken pills of any kind, and this is no time to start. I need my wits about me. For Emma – and for Kit.' Sally took a deep breath. 'How is she . . . how are they both?'

'Emma is in the building, Mrs Jackson. She's being looked after. I'm afraid she seems to be in shock: she's not reacting to us much at the moment. We haven't asked her any questions yet. When we do, a parent or family representative will be permitted to be present.'

Sally nodded automatically. 'Where's my husband?'

'He's still in the operating theatre at Charing Cross Hospital.

It sounds as if he won't be out of there until this afternoon.'

'Can't I see Emma? Please?' From tigress to supplicant in a matter of moments.

'I should think so. Soon.'

'How soon?'

'I'm sorry,' Sergeant Lipari said. 'This must be a terrible experience for you, but I – we – have a job to do. A serious offence has been committed.' She paused, weighing her words. 'The most urgent decision we have to take is whether a sample – what is called an "intimate sample" – should be taken from your daughter. You do understand why that would help us – and Emma – don't you? We need to know if there's evidence of . . . recent physical intimacy.'

Sally stared numbly at Sergeant Lipari for a long moment, then nodded.

'Good. You're being very brave, Mrs Jackson. Now, usually such an examination is performed by a police surgeon, but in fact it may be any doctor nominated by us. I personally feel it would be appropriate for a female paediatrician – Dr Walsh – to take the sample.' Sergeant Lipari paused. 'We'll need your permission. And, in this case, that of your daughter. Or at least – since she is not speaking – we may not take a sample against her objection.'

There was a silence.

'And if I say no?' Sally murmured at last.

'Mrs Jackson, do you wish to clarify this matter, or not?'

Sally didn't want the examination – she didn't want any of this to have happened – and a part of her, the weak, terrified part that couldn't keep the faith with Kit, feared what the examination would reveal. But of course, what Sergeant Lipari said should take place, must take place.

'Very well,' she said, barely audibly. 'And what then, Sergeant?'

'Well, as I said, your daughter is not talking at the moment. We shall be keeping her here at the station unless otherwise advised. The technical description of the current situation is that Emma is "not fit to be interviewed but fit to be detained".'

'So how . . . ?'

'At some point, perhaps during the next few hours or perhaps tomorrow, we shall try to ask her some questions. A social worker will be present. Plus a solicitor. One parent or other family-nominated person may also be in the room.'

'Not Jonathan – my ex-husband – and I together?'

'I'm afraid not. I'm sorry. These are the rules.' Sergeant Lipari sighed. 'This is awful for you, I know, but you and Emma's father will have to discuss the matter and agree.'

'I want to be there.'

'Fine. But you must agree with Emma's father to that effect.'

'Has Emma been charged?'

'No, Mrs Jackson. Not yet.'

'So is it . . . is there any possibility that she didn't stab Kit?'

Sergeant Lipari looked at Sally coolly but not unkindly.

'There was no one else in the house, Mrs Jackson,' she said. 'No sign of forced entry. Your neighbour found Emma in the living room clutching a bloodstained knife, one of a set of Sabatier implements from your kitchen . . .'

As Sergeant Lipari spoke those three sentences, Sally felt as if she aged ten years. Only now did she feel the full, crippling weight of the tragedy.

Jonathan's accusing words throbbed in her head like a drum: 'We were happy once! We were *safe*! We were a *family*!'

'. . . All the same,' Sergeant Lipari continued, 'your daughter is not strong, and your husband is quite a big man.' She looked at Sally carefully. 'Do you mind if I ask you a few preliminary questions?'

'No . . . of course not. Anything to help.'

'Thank you, Mrs Jackson. Now, did anyone else have a key to the house?'

Sally shook her head.

'Just the three of us – me, Kit and Emma.'

'And is there anyone Emma might have allowed access?'

'After midnight? Only my ex-husband, Jonathan . . . And Emma had school friends, though I can't imagine them coming round after midnight . . . Except perhaps for Zak.'

'Who is Zak?'

'My friend Liz Paine's son. He and Emma have known each other all their lives. He's sixteen, a bit wild, but—'

'In what way, wild?'

Sally felt put on the spot, forced into an obscure betrayal.

'I know he's started drinking a bit,' she said lamely.

'Drugs?'

Sally made a helpless little gesture.

'OK,' said Sergeant Lipari, making a note. 'And has he been in the habit of coming round very late?'

'He's always been able to treat the house as his own.'

'How did he get on with Mr Jackson?'

'Fine. Really, fine. If anything, Zak's problems are with Jonathan, Emma's natural father.' Sally looked away, avoiding the policewoman's searching professional gaze. Her voice dropped to a mumble. 'So . . . there's nothing for you there, Sergeant.'

'I have to ask you these questions, Mrs Jackson.'

Sally shook her head. 'Why? *Why?*' she murmured. 'Kit and

Emma adored each other. He was more like her best friend than
... you know ...' She bit her lip like a child who knows she has
said the wrong thing.

There was a heavy silence. Sergeant Lipari let it grow for a
while before she broke it.

'So they were close, were they?' she asked gently but
pointedly.

'Not like ... I mean not ...'

'Mrs Jackson, if Emma did stab her stepfather – or if she's
covering up for someone who did – then she must have had a
reason.'

'Not Kit. No.' Sally looked down at the scuffed and scratched
surface of the interview table. '*No*.'

'You never noticed anything out of the ordinary or, shall we
say, odd, in his relationship with Emma?'

Sally looked up defiantly, her eyes bright with defiance.

'Just a lot of laughter. And a lot of affection.'

WPC White returned with a mug of tea for Sally, black
coffee from the machine for her superior. Sergeant Lipari gave
Sally a few moments to take some nourishment, then pressed
on.

'Mrs Jackson, painful as this may be, I'm sure you understand
that we have to know as much as possible about the
circumstances,' she said. 'How long have you and Mr Jackson
been married?'

'Six years in April.'

'So Emma was seven at the time.'

'Well, yes.'

'Was Mr Jackson married before?'

'No.'

'Any children?'

'No.'

'Did he . . . did Mr Jackson have any long-term relationships with other women before he met you?'

'I think he lived with someone for a couple of years in his twenties. He had casual girlfriends, though. Plenty of them. When he wasn't working.' Sally leaned forward. Defiant. 'I'm perfectly well aware what you're getting at, Sergeant. There's nothing sexually odd about Kit, I assure you.'

'How did you meet?'

'I work as a radio producer. I was making a programme about the computer revolution. He was an adviser. It went on from there.'

'I see.' Sergeant Lipari made a note of that. 'Now, am I to understand that you are away from home a lot?'

'Each of us has to go away from time to time, yes. On business. Me much less often than Kit, actually.'

'OK . . . but nevertheless that would mean there were other times when Emma and your husband were alone in the house together?'

'Sergeant, for God's sake, I can't believe what you're implying!'

Sally's eyes seemed to be searching the perimeter of the room for some means of escape. Then she looked back at Sergeant Lipari. Now she was frowning with anger.

'These things don't happen to people like us!' she said in a low, hoarse voice. 'They just don't!'

Sergeant Lipari held Sally's furious glare, knowing it concealed fear and despair. Then she said, she hoped not too cruelly:

'I've been in the police for twelve years, Mrs Jackson. And if there's one thing I can safely say I've learned, it's that anything can happen; anything, and to anybody.'

'Oh God!' Sally slammed her tea down on the table. 'I don't know where to *be*! I don't know what to *feel*!'

'I really am sorry, Mrs Jackson. We are trying to be as gentle as possible with Emma. But we have to follow the correct procedures. Your daughter is still under fourteen, and therefore may not be considered wholly responsible for her actions, but I'm afraid you must understand that she's prime suspect in a section twenty case – that's attempted murder. Such an offence is a serious, grown-up business. We are holding her in custody because it is necessary to obtain evidence by questioning.' Sergeant Lipari seemed to soften fractionally. 'Please believe me, but none of us has ever been involved in such a case before, never. Not quite like this.'

Instinct told Sergeant Lipari to reach out and take Sally's hand, and to hold it firmly.

'You'll see Emma soon. I promise,' she said gently.

And finally Sally broke. She sobbed with pain and terror and exhaustion, clutching herself with her free hand but hanging on desperately to Sergeant Lipari with her other, rocking in her chair. Then, suddenly, she freed her hand from Sergeant Lipari's and stood up.

'Excuse me,' Sally mumbled. 'I think I'm going to be sick. I'm all right. This has been happening for some days now. I have something to take, but I forgot . . .'

Sergeant Lipari hurried Sally out of the room, escorted her along to the loo at the end of the corridor. Sergeant Lipari and WPC White stood outside the cubicle, listening to Sally's desperate retching.

Sergeant Lipari and the WPC exchanged looks.

'Are you thinking what I'm thinking?' Sergeant Lipari said.

'I'd say so, Sergeant. Not just the pressure, right?'

'No. And if she is expecting, and her husband did abuse her daughter . . .'

WPC White sighed. 'She can keep the posh house and the glamorous job. I'm glad I'm not Mrs Jackson, Sergeant. I really, really am.'

DC Derek Vaughan winked at the ward sister, patted the packet of Marlboro in the breast-pocket of his shirt.

'I think I'll just nip outside and do something for my health,' he said.

'Something bad, I guess,' said Sister Majukwu. Her finely-chiselled Ibo features creased momentarily into a smile.

'So ten, is it, Sister?' Vaughan asked. 'Can I tell them at the station that him in the side ward's due in the operating theatre at ten?'

'Yes. Mr Jackson will get the best surgeon in the hospital trust.'

'Wages of sin,' said Vaughan. 'See you in a bit. I'll ask Constable Gittings to stay outside the ward in case Jackson comes round.'

'About as likely,' said the sister, 'as a pig taking wing.'

Vaughan walked out into the hospital corridor, where Gittings was waiting. Gittings was short – just over the Met's minimum – and crop-headed. Vaughan stood over six feet tall, with thick wavy hair and even features that would have been handsome but for the broken nose he had acquired as a young copper, breaking up a disco brawl.

'I'll just nip back to the car. Said I'd contact the Lip back at the nick,' Vaughan said. 'You stick around here in case Jackson does a Lazarus.'

But Vaughan didn't go back to the car, which was parked in the staff parking area. A couple of minutes later, he emerged from the main doors of the Charing Cross Hospital. The commuter traffic was starting to build on the Fulham Palace Road. The sky was clearing from the south, but there was still the chill, petrol-scented damp of a London morning. Later there'd be dog mess added to the cocktail.

He lit his cigarette and headed for a public phone-booth.

Vaughan counted the rings at the other end of the line, tapping out a little tattoo as he waited.

'*Nine* . . . idle bastard . . . *Ten* . . . probably on the nest . . . *Eleven* . . .'

'Hello. Mulligan speaking.'

'Paul. Derek Vaughan.' He smiled. 'Yeah. Course I know it's early. I got something for you, haven't I? But you'd better be bloody quick off the mark.'

'Better be good. I'm listening.' The voice was polite, precise.

'Got a stabbing. Domestic . . . but with a twist. Worth a drink?'

'Depends on the twist.'

'I'm calling from the Charing Cross Hospital,' Vaughan explained. 'Got this guy in a side ward here, waiting for surgery. I've been with him since he was fetched in, about one in the morning. Thing is, looks like his stepdaughter got a kitchen knife and stabbed him half a dozen times. Or if she didn't, she stood by while someone else did.'

'Abuse case, right?'

'I think we can safely say.'

'So where was the girl's mother at the time?'

'Away on a business trip, apparently.'

'Not bad. Unhappy families. Career mother neglects the kid

57

. . . Don't know about getting me out of bed for it, though.'

'Except – get this – the stepdaughter's thirteen years old and looks like Kate Moss's younger sister.'

There was a sharp intake of breath on the other end of the line.

'Derek,' the voice said, 'you're an angel. I'm out of bed. I'm into my Calvins . . .'

In the police station's reception area, Jonathan sat with his chin in his hands, staring at a road safety poster.

Sally thought her ex-husband's eyes flickered slightly in her direction when she entered the room, but he didn't turn or move. The ten or so steps to where he sat seemed long, agonising, full of choices that were not choices. Where else could she sit but next to him? But what could she say?

The silence did not lift when she sat down.

It deepened.

Sally felt the heat of the tears welling up in her eyes.

'I've given permission for them to examine her,' she said. 'It might . . . it might help us to know what happened. After that, they need to ask Emma some questions. One of us is allowed to be present. I want it to be me, Jonathan.'

Now she could see the way her ex-husband's jaw was locked in rage, the eyes blind with pain.

'Jonathan,' Sally whispered. No response. 'Oh God. Whatever happened, it's my fault. If only I'd been home last night, I might have . . . *Whatever* happened, I could have . . .' Her voice faded almost to nothing. Her resolve not to fall apart, to trust the man she loved, had reached its lowest ebb, and she knew it. 'All of you . . .' Sally said, knowing she was talking not just to Jonathan, but to Emma and to Kit – and ultimately to her own embattled self. 'I'm sorry . . . but I won't let the grief take over. I'll make it up to you . . . I'll make sense of this terrible thing . . .'

Detective Superintendent Charles Garfield adjusted the knot of his polka-dot Charles Tyrell tie in one of those little automatic acts of vanity that had passed into station legend.

'So are we talking the obvious here?' he asked bluntly.

Garfield had one of those sharp-featured, clever London faces. He still wore his hair in a careful, centre-parted Mod style straight from the sixties of his youth.

Across the desk from him, Sergeant Lipari nodded cautiously.

'Of course, we can't know for sure,' she said. 'I've asked Joanna Walsh to come in and take an intimate sample. Then maybe we'll know if the girl was being sexual abused immediately before the incident.'

'Maybe? Can't you do better than that?'

'No, sir. Bar the presence of semen traces, or actual pregnancy, there's no such thing as certain proof of intercourse. Or, for that matter, loss of virginity. Contrary to popular belief.'

'And meanwhile the girl isn't talking. I know this is a politically incorrect thing to ask, but I wonder about her part in this affair. I mean, if it was a mutual sexual involvement—'

'With respect, we're talking about a relationship between a thirteen-year-old girl and a forty-year-old man – who happens to be married to her mother. I don't call that a sexual involvement in the proper sense, sir,' Sergeant Lipari retorted. 'The law classifies it as statutory rape. I prefer the word abuse.'

'Yes?' Garfield eased back in his chair. 'What about Sicily? Don't they get started young over there?'

'Well, sir, my parents actually come from near Pisa, and I was born in Ealing, so I wouldn't really know.' Sergeant Lipari was smiling now, but her brown eyes had taken on a glint that was unmistakably unamused. 'However, I'm inclined to believe that even in the *mezzogiorno* men don't routinely rape their pubescent stepdaughters.'

'Sex is a powerful force,' Garfield insisted gravely. 'It defies age and convention.'

'Listen, sir. That kid's in a state of shock, totally traumatised! We're not talking crime of passion here. For my money, it's got to be abuse. Pure and simple. In as much as abuse is either of those things.'

'Maybe you're right,' Garfield murmured, finding some interest in one of his pearl cufflinks. 'Just a suggestion.'

'Another thing,' Sergeant Lipari said. 'Jackson was a bachelor until he was thirty-five. Only one long-term relationship before his wife. Who, of course, already had a little girl when he met her . . .'

'You think he was attracted by the daughter even at that stage?'

'I don't know. But it's a possibility we have to bear in mind.' Sergeant Lipari hesitated. 'And it seems to me that there's another question we have to ask,' she said. 'Which is, did Emma Quinn actually physically stab Jackson, or was someone else involved? Her natural father, Jonathan Quinn? Or maybe the teenage kid the mother mentioned? Zak Paine.'

Garfield got to his feet and walked over to the window, which overlooked the neighbouring roof. He thought for a while.

'It's all circumstantial at the moment, isn't it?' he said heavily. 'Supposition. Based on the assumption that Jackson was abusing his stepdaughter. Which we may or may not be able to prove.'

'Absolutely. I mean, we could come up with completely different scenarios involving those other suspects. Let's even suppose for a moment that Jackson *wasn't* abusing her,' Sergeant Lipari said, warming to her theme. 'Let's assume the *boy*'s the one who's been having sex with Emma. Zak is round at Emma's house while the mother's away, Jackson gets suspicious, confronts him about it. They row, Zak loses his rag, stabs Jackson, then flees in panic . . .'

'And what about Emma? She was found holding the knife.'

'I was getting to that, sir,' Sergeant Lipari said. 'After Zak's gone, she manages to pull the knife out of her stepfather's chest, which is why she ends up holding the weapon. But meanwhile she can't handle the horror and the divided loyalty, so she retreats into deep, deep shock, which is where the officers at the scene – and now we – find her.'

Garfield laughed harshly, grudging respect rather than amusement.

'Nice scriptwriting, Cheryl. But what do you really think?'

'Of course, I'd be very surprised if it wasn't Jackson,' Sergeant Lipari answered. 'Meanwhile, let's get over the intimate sample hurdle. And, most important of all, let's see if we can help Emma to talk.'

With his shy smile and thick, gold-rimmed glasses, Paul Mulligan looked like a law student or an accountant. A discreet herringbone sports jacket and slacks covered his rangy frame, with a white shirt – always white – and a tasteful striped tie to complete the picture of social respectability that Mulligan's middle-class Barbadian parents had always preached to him as the highest social value. Because of this, and because he was black, people were always surprised – and often disarmed by him – even when they found out that he worked for a downmarket paper like the *Orb*. He owed a promising tabloid career to his superficial harmlessness.

Mulligan's gaze swept up and down the Thames towpath. Then he checked his Rolex, shivered slightly in the bright morning chill. The traffic was heavy on Hammersmith Bridge, but Derek Vaughan had promised not to keep him waiting. Mind you, even that mad bastard was hardly going to shoot down the bus lane with the blue light flashing on his way to a rendezvous with P. Mulligan . . .

A jogger passed him. Then a second came into view . . . no, it was DC Vaughan. The tall, athletic CID man, dressed in a bomber-jacket and jeans, approached at an easy lope. When he stopped he wasn't even a little bit out of breath.

They shook hands. Vaughan was about the same height as Mulligan, roughly six feet, but weighed at least a stone and a half more, all of it muscle.

Vaughan glanced quickly around to ensure they were alone.

'First, drinkie-poohs,' he said.

Mulligan reached inside his jacket, took out an envelope and handed it over.

Vaughan pocketed it without bothering to count the notes inside. In return, he slipped Mulligan a sheet of paper.

'It's all there,' Vaughan said. 'Names, addresses, et cetera. The stepfather in the hospital is one Christopher – known as Kit – Jackson, forty-odd, something comfy in computers. The mother is called Sally, divorced from the kid's natural father, works for the good old BBC, would you believe? The girl's called Emma Quinn, surname taken from her natural father,

Jonathan Quinn. A college lecturer, he is.'

An appreciative smile spread over Mulligan's smooth features.

'Brilliant, Derek. The chattering classes to the life! The girl banged up at your nick?'

'Yeah.'

'The mother there, too, I presume.'

'Quite tasty, actually, for her age.' Vaughan laughed. 'Could say the same about the kid.'

'You're sure this Jackson guy was abusing her?'

'For Christ's sake. I've outlined the circumstances. What do you think?'

'I think it's a great story whatever. And where exactly does Jackson work?'

'Computer software company. Business park just off the M25. It's all written down for you. Never say I don't earn my gravy.'

'Listen, if you or someone else from the scene-of-crime mob could snaffle a family photo from the house, it'd be worth big money, and I mean that.'

'I know. Too chancy, though. Been a bit of aggravation about our relations with the press.' Vaughan cast a wary eye up and down the towpath. 'Got to go, mate.'

'Discretion is the better part . . .' Mulligan's smile showed healthy white teeth. 'Call me when there's developments. Meanwhile, take it easy.'

'Yeah. See you.'

Mulligan stood watching DC Vaughan until the cop reached the top of the steps and disappeared on to Castelnau Road. Then he slid a matt-black mobile phone from his jacket pocket and punched out a number.

'Hi, Gary,' he said. 'Paul Mulligan here from the *Orb*. Got some personal details here for you to chase up. I want financial status, any standing orders at the bank, that kind of thing. Plus criminal convictions. And names of surviving parents and siblings. PDQ, OK? Quick turnaround gets you the usual bonus.'

SEVEN

'You see, we can't let anyone find us. They don't understand. This precious thing we have. They don't understand. You're mine and I'll do anything, anything, to keep you . . .'

To an outsider, it was as if a light had been turned off behind the child-woman's violet-blue eyes.

Emma Quinn was pretty, like her mother, Sergeant Lipari thought. But when she was grown up she would be quite a lot taller. Skinny. The girl was in that brief, poignant in-between period, facially like a young woman, physically still only part-developed. Emma sat on the bunk in one of the station's detention rooms, her arms wrapped protectively around herself, her legs crossed and her mouth slightly open. When they had brought her here in the small hours, she had been in a nightie and a coat. Since then someone from Social Services had found her a sweater and a pair of jeans. They were much too big for her; adult clothes for a vulnerable child.

Sergeant Lipari glanced inquiringly at the woman from Social Services, who nodded her assent.

'Emma,' Sergeant Lipari said softly, 'no one's blaming you for what happened. But we need to know why. Do you understand?'

The girl looked at her but did not speak.

'Do you understand?' Sergeant Lipari repeated.

There was no answer. She had expected none. That empty, directionless gaze was getting to her.

'Well, first Dr Walsh here is going to examine you. If you have any objection, please make it clear to us now.'

The paediatrician was a plump, moon-faced woman with, Sergeant Lipari knew, a couple of kids of her own.

'Hello, Emma,' Dr Walsh said gently. She opened her bag, took out a pair of rubber gloves. 'This won't take too long, I promise you. And it won't hurt. All right?'

Once the gloves were on, she turned to Emma and nodded.

'If you could just slip off your jeans.'

Emma didn't move.

'Or perhaps the lady here could help you . . .'

The woman from Social Services stepped forward and began to undo the top button of Emma's jeans.

Emma Quinn closed her eyes and screamed.

And screamed.

The woman from Social Services recoiled as if bitten, glanced anxiously at Sergeant Lipari.

'Emma, it won't hurt,' repeated Dr Walsh. Then to the woman from Social Services: 'Just be gentle. Let's see.'

Another approach was made.

Emma screamed again. She started to shake. Now it was Dr Walsh's turn to check with Sergeant Lipari.

'This is problematic,' she murmured. 'There can't be any suspicion of her being forced.'

Sergeant Lipari shook her head. She heard footsteps in the corridor outside.

A male voice said, 'All right, Sergeant?'

It was Turnbull, the station's custody officer, checking on

the peace of his kingdom. In the cells, Sergeant Turnbull was God. Only the duty super could overrule him, and that Garfield would do reluctantly.

'Yes. Fine.'

But of course it wasn't. This was the last thing they needed. This was dangerous territory. The woman from Social Services had already taken out her notebook and biro and was starting to make notes.

Dr Walsh said, 'If she won't let me examine her, then I don't know what we do.'

'No.'

It was then that Emma made her move. She reached out a still-shaking hand and grabbed the notebook from the woman from Social Services.

The woman looked around wildly.

Emma then took her pen too. Her face screwed up in concentration, she wrote unsteadily on the top sheet of the pad. She held it out to Sergeant Lipari.

Gently Sergeant Lipari stepped forward and took the sheet. Emma stretched herself out on the bunk, with her back turned to the three adults. The message of her body-language could not have been clearer.

And neither could the message on the council-issue pad, despite the shaky handwriting.

It was comprised of two words, and it said: WANT YARDLEY.

As Sergeant Lipari rounded the corner towards her own office, she saw DC Vaughan by the coffee machine.

'Morning, Derek,' she said.

'Morning, Sergeant.' Vaughan smiled his urchin smile.

'You look like hell, if I may say so.'

'You're no Robert Redford today either, *Constable*,' she said, and kept on going.

He fell in step beside her.

'We've both had a long night,' said Vaughan. 'That's why.'

'It's not over yet. Any news from the hospital?'

'So far as I know, Jackson's still in the theatre. Could be under the scalpel well into the afternoon. His chest looks like a Swiss cheese. He's only alive because none of the incisions went directly into the heart. Hundred-to-one chance, said the surgeon I spoke to.'

'We'd better keep someone there in case Jackson comes round and has something to say for himself.'

'Like "I done it, officer."'

'Words to that effect would make our job easier, wouldn't they? Emma Quinn's still not talking. Plus she's resisting providing intimate samples, so we don't know whether she was raped.'

Sergeant Lipari walked quickly into her office. Vaughan followed her. She was waiting for him just inside.

'Well,' she said, 'were you born in a field, Constable?'

Vaughan closed the door behind him. They both listened for a moment to the squeaking zip of a printer going in the next-door office. Then Sergeant Lipari stepped forward.

'Hello you,' she murmured, and reached out to stroke his cheek.

Vaughan pulled her towards him and kissed her full on the lips. She responded hungrily. Her fingers probed beneath his jacket, traced the muscles of his back. She could feel him hardening. Her own body started to melt. With an effort, she pulled away.

Vaughan laughed softly. 'Now there's a pick-you-up. Or is that a sexist term?'

'Yes, I think it probably is.' Sergeant Lipari took a deep breath. 'What do you tell your wife, Derek?'

'I lie. I say: a policeman's lot is not a happy one.'

Mulligan eased himself back in his seat. Beside him Trevor Yallop, a staff photographer from the *Orb*, was snatching some final pictures of the Jackson house fifty or so yards away. They would have got closer, but the scene-of-crime team had taped off the end of the cul-de-sac. A couple of them had just come out and made faces at the press boys. How they'd all laughed. Now Mulligan was talking into his trusty mobile and oozing shy charm.

'The thing is, Matron, I've been living up north for the past few years but I'm going to be in the area this afternoon on business,' he said. 'Mrs Jackson took me under her wing when I was just a young kid, straight off the boat. I know she's not really recognising anyone at the moment, but it's the principle of the thing, isn't it? I mean, I know how much it's costing her son Kit to do the right thing, and I don't want him to think he's the only one who cares. OK? Great, Matron, great . . .'

He killed the phone, snapped it back in its cradle.

Yallop, a gaunt cockney with close-cropped hair who affected the flak-jacketed Don McCullin look, snorted in amused derision.

'*Straight off the boat,*' he mimicked. 'You are an absolute disgrace to your race, Paulie old chap. That's what you are. Not politically correct.'

'So report me to the thought police,' said Mulligan. 'Listen, Trev, time you buggered off and got those piccies developed.

The rest of the pack'll be here soon. We've got to stay ahead, and I know how . . .'

EIGHT

'Mrs Jackson,' Sergeant Lipari said, 'after Emma had refused to be examined by Dr Walsh, she did something remarkable. She wrote something on a piece of paper. Does the name Yardley mean anything to you?'

Sally did a puzzled little double-take.

'Yes, of course. Dr Noel Yardley. He's the therapist Emma's been going to for her eating problems.'

'Eating problems?'

'Anorexia. In a relatively mild form, but worrying all the same.'

'Right. What kind of a timescale are we talking about, Mrs Jackson? With the eating problems and the therapy, I mean.'

'About a year. Perhaps a bit more.'

'And has the therapy been successful?'

'Pretty much. Certainly until recently.'

'Does Emma get on well with this Dr Yardley?'

'Oh yes. He's gentle, sympathetic, and very competent. As I said, until recently, Emma had been improving steadily. Her eating habits are still a bit eccentric, but no more than a lot of other teenagers.'

'And he's a doctor? Yardley, I mean.'

'Yes. He's a doctor of medicine and of psychology. Quite high-powered.'

Sergeant Lipari asked for Yardley's phone number, recognised it as somewhere in the classy end of Chiswick.

'Emma's message seemed to express a wish to see him,' Sergeant Lipari explained. 'Any objection?'

'No. Not at all,' Sally said. 'If that's what she wants. I'm thrilled she's started to communicate.'

'Yes.' Sergeant Lipari leaned back in her chair. 'Mrs Jackson, did Emma know that you're pregnant?'

'No . . . *no*.' The second time more definite.

'Your husband might have told her.'

'I told you earlier. He didn't know either.' Sally's fine hands were entwined so tightly that the knuckles had turned white. 'I could . . . I should . . . have told Kit straight after the self-test. There was no reason to leave it until the weekend, not really . . .'

'I can't believe you need to punish yourself about that, Mrs Jackson. You made a perfectly rational family decision. You couldn't have known.'

Sally made to say something, then bit her lip and looked away.

'Well,' Sergeant Lipari said, 'as you say, it's good that Emma is communicating just a little bit. We have to build on this, Mrs Jackson. Perhaps with her therapist's help.'

'Noel Yardley's a lovely man. You'll see.'

Superintendent Garfield's first question when Sergeant Lipari entered his office was whether she was ready to charge Emma Quinn.

Sergeant Lipari didn't answer that one directly. She told him about what Emma had written on the piece of paper after refusing to be examined. She told him who this 'Yardley' seemed to be.

'So?'

'Her mother says the girl and this man get along very well. Emma trusts him.'

'According to her mother.'

Sergeant Lipari nodded. 'She's resisting Dr Walsh. We could nominate this Dr Yardley to examine her. It's unusual, but it's not actually against the rules.'

'He's a man.'

'He's a fully-qualified doctor, sir. And if I'm right, Emma Quinn won't object to his examining her.'

'And if you're wrong? If the girl refuses him too?'

'Then we'll have to rely on other forensic or verbal evidence. At least we'll have given it a shot.'

Garfield's reluctant grunt of assent conceded Sergeant Lipari's point.

'Sir,' she continued, 'I've read that anorexia – like bulimia – is one of those things that can be connected with abuse. Sort of a rejection of growing up. The girl can't accept her adult sexuality because it's tainted by association with abuse.'

Garfield nodded again but looked faintly uncomfortable. This was not his kind of territory. Feelings, fears, deep stuff. Women's business.

'Yeah,' he said finally. 'Another brick in the wall, if we want it.'

'I've already rung Yardley. He's willing to come in first thing. OK?'

'Whatever. We have to make something happen.' Garfield sighed. 'And don't forget: evidence of abuse is one thing – it's motive, and it's potential mitigation, but the chief matter at hand is whether the girl stabbed her stepfather or not. At this rate we'll have to charge her without her having said a bloody word. And once we do, we'll be *sub judice*, and by law we won't be able to ask her any more questions. We need her to talk now. We need her to tell us what happened last night.'

'I'll ring Dr Yardley and ask him to come in later, sir,' Sergeant Lipari said. 'Meanwhile I'll have a word with the teenage boy. His mother and her partner have just brought him in, apparently. Then I'll have a go at the father. If someone else was involved in the stabbing of Jackson, those two have got to be our prime suspects.'

Sergeant Lipari's first sight of Zak Paine seemed to confirm her suspicions. He was big for his age, with longish fair hair. He wore a grimy sweater and torn jeans. Right down to the wispy blond fuzz on his chin, the boy was a ringer for that rock star who killed himself . . . Kurt Cobain. Sergeant Lipari's niece had been a big fan, posters all over her bedroom. But what really caught Sergeant Lipari's attention was the sizeable fresh bruise on the left-hand side of his face, running from the corner of the eye down to the bottom of his cheek.

'Sit down, Zak,' Sergeant Lipari said, trying not to stare.

Zak glared at her with a reasonable representation of alienated cool, but he also swallowed noticeably hard as he sat down.

'I've just been with Emma,' Sergeant Lipari continued. 'She's had a terrible night.' She looked pointedly at his bruise. 'Looks like you did too.'

Zak shrugged and said nothing.

'Where were you last night, Zak?'

'Out.'

The boy's accent was pretty accurate South London. Might

have been more convincing if Sergeant Lipari hadn't already known that his Mum was an assistant director of Social Services and her partner an architect. She decided to play it polite for now.

'Where, if I may ask?'

Zak glared at her a bit more, then reached into his shirt pocket and took out a packet of Marlboros and a box of matches. He slapped them down on the table between himself and Sergeant Lipari; waited for a reaction.

'You're over sixteen,' Sergeant Lipari said simply. 'And smoking's allowed. Now, where were you last night, Zak?'

He lit up, croaked through a cloud of smoke: 'At a club. Then we got in a mate's car and drove around.'

'Until when?'

'Late.' Zak smiled wolfishly. 'Or early, depending how you look at it.'

Sergeant Lipari met his teen braggadocio act with an impassive nod.

'OK. So let's get back to the previous evening. Did you go round to Emma Quinn's house first, before you went clubbing?'

'Nah.'

'But you could have.'

'Yeah. But I didn't.'

Sergeant Lipari looked up from her notes. 'Have you ever had sex with Emma Quinn, Zak?'

He returned her gaze, slit-eyed through the fog, then shook his shaggy head slowly and very definitely.

'Is that a no, Zak?'

'Yeah.'

'You're sure?' Sergeant Lipari's voice was hard-edged, insistent. 'Think carefully, Zak. You might get probation for

75

under-aged sex, especially since you're only just over the limit yourself. Attempted murder's a different thing altogether.'

'I *didn't*,' the boy insisted fiercely. 'She's still a kid.'

Sergeant Lipari had to admit his denial was convincing. No childish breakdown, but on the other hand no over-the-top macho stuff. Sex or no sex, though, it didn't mean he hadn't been present when Kit Jackson was stabbed. There were still the livid, fresh bruises to be explained.

'OK. You've had a few knocks on your face. Where did you get those, Zak?'

Zak screwed up his face, half a grin, half a grimace.

'Had a bit of bother on the street.'

'Which street?'

'Christ, somewhere in Stockwell. It was dark at the time, and I was a bit out of it.'

He must have sensed Sergeant Lipari's scepticism, because he drew hard on his cigarette and shook his head vigorously. He loved to feel his mane shimmy, obviously, even in genuine anger and distress.

'Listen, I wasn't round at Emma's place!' Zak repeated. 'And I never screwed her.' He looked at her shrewdly. 'But someone else did, right?'

Sergeant Lipari avoided his question.

'Did Emma have any other boy she spent time with?'

'Not as far as I know. Anyway, weekends she always seemed to be at Jonathan's place across the river,' Zak said with a humourless laugh. 'No chance of any guy sniffing round while Jonathan was on his little girl's case, I'll tell you that.'

'So Emma and her natural father are pretty close?'

Zak nodded.

'*Very* close, Zak?'

'You could say that. Jonathan's a bit of a sad bastard, to tell you the truth.'

'And what about Emma's stepfather, Mr Jackson?'

'I dunno. He was much easier than Jonathan, actually. I mean, with me and with Emma too. I'm amazed what happened last night, OK? The whole atmosphere at their place always seemed pretty laid-back.'

'Emma seems to have stabbed Mr Jackson. That's not a very laid-back thing to do.'

'I said it *seemed*, right? I didn't know that bastard Kit was abusing her. Jesus, can't you ask Emma about it herself? Why are you giving me this hassle?'

'Because Emma's very distressed, Zak. She won't talk. She won't react at all. In fact, she's in deep shock.'

Zak just looked at Sergeant Lipari for a long, tense moment. He didn't shrug or shake his head or anything. His essential prop, the cigarette, burned unheeded in his fine-fingered right hand.

'There must be a reason why she's like that, Zak,' Sergeant Lipari coaxed him. 'Do you have any idea what that reason could be?'

He stubbed his half-smoked cigarette out in the ashtray.

'Try talking to that arsehole Kit,' Zak growled. His cocksure mask slipped momentarily. 'Emma wouldn't have done what she did for no reason,' he muttered, avoiding Sergeant Lipari's penetrating gaze. 'No way. No fucking way.'

They had set up a little camp in one corner of the reception area, on four bright blue plastic chairs grouped around a standard ashtray. It was like a cruel, shabby parody of a dinner party. Cigarette butts and discarded tea and coffee cups littered the ground. The atmosphere between them was civilised, of course, but always on the edge of something else, more honest and more frightening.

'She just won't talk, the sergeant said,' Sally repeated. 'If only she would talk, we'd know.'

Liz drew on her tenth cigarette of the morning.

'Listen,' she said hoarsely, 'I grilled Zak all the way here in the car. He said quite definitely that he and Emma kissed and cuddled. But they *never* had sex. She wasn't old enough. I believe him.'

Jonathan snorted in disbelief.

'He was round my place at half-term. Tanked up on Special Brew. Who's to say he wasn't at Sally's last night in the same condition?'

'Oh, Jonathan . . .' Sally chided him wearily, and drew her coat around her, though it was warm in the room.

Harry reached out, took Liz's hand, half-comforting and half-restraining. But Liz stayed surprisingly calm. She gave Jonathan a long, cool look.

'I still believe him,' Liz persisted. 'And not just because he's my boy. See, Zak's all sod-you on the surface, but he's wised-up enough to realise that in situations like this a lie does you a lot more harm than the truth, however sordid.'

Jonathan shrugged angrily. It was like a surrogate act of violence.

'Well, if it wasn't him, then it must have been Kit!'

No one said anything to that. Sally flushed, looked away. She was determined to think nothing but good things. It was the only way.

'Well, somebody was abusing my little girl,' Jonathan pressed on with a grim insistence that dug in like gravel on open wounds, his as well as everyone else's. 'And no one said a bloody word to me until it was too late.'

Jonathan Quinn was good-looking in a gaunt kind of a way, but sizing him up across the interview table Sergeant Lipari had to fight an instinctive feeling of dislike. He was a whiner, not her type at all. On the other hand, he was Emma's father, and what he was going through at the moment was just about as rough as it gets. That gave him some rights in the sympathy department.

'OK,' Jonathan said, shifting uncomfortably in his chair. 'I don't know how to put this . . . because all those nice Guardian-reader's euphemisms disappear when it's your own daughter you're talking about . . . but . . . was Emma interfered with?'

Sergeant Lipari decided that if disclosure was risky, withholding might be worse. This was an emotionally damaged man she was dealing with, but certainly not a stupid one.

'We're not sure yet, Mr Quinn. She wouldn't let our doctor take an intimate sample. We're hoping she might allow herself to be examined by Dr Yardley, her therapist, who is, of course, also a qualified medical practitioner. Would that be all right with you?'

Jonathan gave her a long, cold stare with those deep blue eyes of his. They were disconcertingly like Emma's.

'So long as it's properly supervised,' he said in a flat, almost automaton-like voice.

'I'll be present, Mr Quinn. As will an experienced female social worker.'

There was an uneasy pause. Then Sergeant Lipari said:

'I'm told by people who know about these things that it's possible your daughter could have inflicted those stab-wounds on her stepfather – though only just.'

79

This was an exaggeration, but it gave Sergeant Lipari a chance to study Jonathan's reaction. Head thrust forward, he was stroking his beard, or rather rubbing it.

'Of course, it's amazing what strength rage can give someone, isn't it?' she continued. 'Even a slender girl of Emma's age. From my own personal experience, though, the only time I've seen such injuries they have been inflicted by one adult male on another.'

Jonathan looked at her steadily, nodded. Otherwise he betrayed no new emotion. Sergeant Lipari had been hoping for an over-reaction, something to give her a foothold in this man's secret emotional world, perhaps even his secret world of violence. His surface calm was disconcerting. Slightly unnerved, and beginning to wonder what the hell was going on here – perhaps he was still in shock, perhaps he was close to cracking – Sergeant Lipari decided to change tack.

'I've been talking to Zak Paine, Mr Quinn. You know him?' she asked. Jonathan nodded. 'He's only sixteen, but he's a big enough lad. He denies having attacked Emma's stepfather, though.'

For all his anger and pain, Jonathan Quinn couldn't suppress a sour but almost proud smile. 'So that leaves me as prime suspect, right?'

'It's my duty to check certain facts. Such as where you were last night.'

Jonathan clasped his own chest, swung his legs over each other. Again like Emma. The movement seemed to bring some life back into his gestures and facial expression.

'Well,' he said, 'I was at home. Alone. Marking students' essays.'

'The entire evening, Mr Quinn? Until you went to bed?'

'Yes. I'd spent the entire half-term holiday with Emma and I hadn't got as much done as I should. I still had marking and preparatory work to catch up on.'

'Can anyone corroborate this?'

''Fraid not. I was playing Mozart on the stereo, which my neighbour could probably hear, much to his disgust, but the sound of music doesn't prove I was actually there, does it?'

'Do you have a key to the Jackson house, Mr Quinn?'

'Nope.'

'OK. I'd like to ask you a personal question. Did you – do you – dislike Mr Jackson?'

'I loathed – loathe – him,' said Jonathan, placing careful emphasis on his words. Now there was passion rumbling dangerously inside him, like an earthquake warning. 'He broke up my marriage, Sergeant. I think that under his good-guy façade he's a ruthless egotist. It wouldn't surprise me to know he abused my daughter. If he did, I wish him dead.'

Sergeant Lipari looked up from her notebook. Jonathan Quinn seemed in a world of his own. He drew a deep breath through clenched teeth. His jaw was white with tension.

'But I wasn't at his and Sally's house last night,' he spat the words out. 'And I didn't stab him. I wish to God I had, before he drove my little girl to it.'

'Doesn't actually prove much,' Garfield said, poker-faced.

'No, unfortunately,' Sergeant Lipari conceded. 'It means that he could – I mean, just could – have got into the house and stabbed Kit Jackson, though.'

'The kid Zak was around at half-term too. He could equally well have nicked the girl's key. Or she could have given it to him . . .'

81

'Yes,' Sergeant Lipari said. 'I have to admit, if Jonathan Quinn is protecting himself at his daughter's expense, he's a bloody good actor.'

'Yes. Well, there's plenty of those around in this business, aren't there?' Garfield suppressed a yawn. 'You said you talked to the boy they thought had a thing for her. What's he like?'

'Zak, you mean? He's your typical young middle-class tearaway,' Sergeant Lipari said. 'As long as he doesn't kill himself with drugs during the next few years he'll straighten out and end up pretty much like his parents.'

'So what about him and Emma?'

Garfield was easier with this line of thinking. Whodunit.

'You want my gut feeling, sir?' Sergeant Lipari offered. 'I think Zak would have had sex with Emma if she'd let him, but she wouldn't. As for whether he was at the Jackson house when the stepfather was stabbed, your guess is as good as mine.'

'I don't like to guess, Cheryl. I never feel comfortable with too much speculation.'

'All right. My instinct is that Zak wasn't there, but we're checking on where he went that night. The boy was hanging out with a bad crowd. They may all be reluctant to state their exact movements.'

'Let's see about that, shall we?'

'I'll put Derek Vaughan on it.'

'One tearaway to catch another.'

'Sir?'

'Never mind. When's Dr Whatnot coming in?'

'Any time now.'

'Good. That should give us a bit more to go on.'

The rambling Edwardian house was called Chamberlain Grove.

It had been built for the owner of a chain of 'Home and Colonial' stores when God was still an Englishman and rural Surrey still felt closer to heaven than to the M25.

Of course, 1990s Britain had no Home and Colonial stores any more. But what it did have was lots of old people, and – providing they or their loved ones had the money to pay – the Chamberlain Grove Nursing Home was happy to look after them, either in the main house or in the three discreet extensions built in the mid-eighties when the private geriatric-care boom really got going.

Paul Mulligan eased his BMW down the drive towards the half-timbered house itself. The flowerbeds were ablaze: scarlet geraniums, purple gladioli, and sea-green hydrangeas just coming into bloom. He hoped he would be able to send his mum to a place like this when she got past it. Just like Kit Jackson had.

Mulligan parked and strode purposefully into the entrance hall, straightening his tie as he entered. Every inch the businessman.

The auxiliary who came out of the office looked Chinese, maybe Vietnamese. She squinted at Mulligan suspiciously. He grinned back.

Yes, Mulligan felt like saying. *Yes, I'm black, and yes, I'm about to tell you a lie. But not about that car outside. It's mine. Or the five hundred quids' worth of Armani jacket I've got on my back. I bought all of 'em. No, this is a little lie in the line of my well-paid work, honey . . .*

'Morning, Nurse,' was what he actually said. 'I spoke to the Matron on the mobile earlier. Here to see Mrs Jackson. Old friend of the family, in the area on business . . .'

The woman looked at him indifferently for a moment, then shrugged.

'Go recreation room,' she said. 'Mebbe Mrs Jackson watch TV. Otherwise room twenty-nine.'

The woman gave another eloquently contemptuous little shrug and retreated into the office, leaving Mulligan alone in the entrance hall. One of these days she'd need an operation on those shoulders, Mulligan decided. Repetitive insult injury.

The lounge was easy to find. Just follow the blare of the telly. From the doorway Mulligan could see heavily patterned velvet curtains drawn over elegantly tall windows. In the half-darkness, ranks of inmates sat as if planted in wheelchairs and on dralon sofas, staring at an Australian soap. Another care assistant, this time an angry-looking pop-eyed white girl with a shaved head and rings through her nose and eyelids, was sitting at the back, looking bored out of her skull.

'Yeah?' she said without getting up. 'Looking fer somethin'?'

The accent was Irish, the voice remarkably sweet if you ignored the message behind the glassy green eyes.

'Someone,' Mulligan corrected her. He smiled his professional smile. 'Mrs Jackson. I've known her since I was a kid. Just dropped by to visit her, say hi, you know.'

'Sure. Nearest wheelchair to the door. She won't have much to say to you, though. Alzheimer's.'

'I know,' Mulligan said. 'She wouldn't mind a walk round the grounds, though, eh?'

'Mind? She wouldn't know the bloody difference.'

Mulligan nodded sympathetically, advanced on to the woman identified to him as Mrs Jackson. He greeted her cheerfully in what he hoped was a familiar manner.

'Hi, Mrs J. How are you today?'

Stella Jackson looked at him blankly. It was really weird, Mulligan thought. She couldn't have been much over sixty-five, and she was well-preserved. If you'd seen her out in the street, you'd have taken her for mid-, even early-fifties. An elegant blouse, nice hair. But then there was that vacant stare . . .

'Fancy a stroll?' For a moment, Mulligan thought he discerned a tiny smile. 'Turn around the grounds?'

He released the brake on the wheelchair and trundled towards the door.

The rear gardens totalled a couple of acres, mainly put down to lawn. Concrete paths criss-crossed the greensward, swerving round regimented flowerbeds. A couple of inmates were sitting directly outside the building, catching the sun. One of them said hello as Mrs Jackson and her companion emerged.

Mulligan pushed the old lady around the perimeter path a couple of times, taking his bearings. By then he was ready. Making sure no one was looking, he steered towards an open fire door at the far end of the building.

'Thought we'd check out your room, Mrs J.,' Mulligan said as they entered an empty corridor. 'Number twenty-nine, right?'

It wasn't hard to find. With her being in a wheelchair, he had reckoned her room would probably be on the ground floor, and he was right. A pleasant enough little cubicle overlooking a corner that was shaded by a tall cypress.

Apart from a faint odour of incontinence, it wasn't too depressing a room. Pink frilly bed stuff, flowers on the windowsill – left over from her son's last visit? – and . . . yes . . . on the little corner table a collection of framed photographs, some in black-and-white but most in colour.

Mulligan parked Mrs Jackson by the window. He smiled.

'Nice room.'

And all the while he was giving the pictures the once-over. One black-and-white, probably 1950s, little Kit with Mum and

Dad, yes, as a boy you could see his resemblance to his father
. . . and . . . ah . . . in a plastic frame an eight-by-six colour job
of Kit, the wife . . . and the stepdaughter.

Kit is wearing a pullover, and he's got one arm around the
pretty wife and the other round the even more pretty stepdaughter.
Must have been taken within the last year, Mulligan thought . . .
perfect.

'Nice family,' Mulligan said.

He picked up a couple of the other photographs, then put
them down again, checking each time to see if Kit Jackson's
mother was watching. She seemed to be looking out of the
window. That was when he picked up the recent photograph,
turned his back on her and popped it in his jacket pocket. Then
he spun like a dancer and threw out his hands.

'So. Another quick turn and then back to *Home and Away*?'

Suddenly Mrs Jackson's eyes seemed to focus a little more
keenly.

'Kenneth!' she said in a well-modulated, penetrating, Home
Counties voice. 'There's a black man in the bedroom.'

Mulligan swallowed hard. All he needed was for her to have
a fit. He took a step forward towards her.

'It's OK, Mrs J. Just fine.'

Then Mrs Jackson smiled.

'Don't worry, dear,' she murmured. 'He must be one of the
staff.'

'Yeah,' Mulligan said quickly. 'Here to take you for a walk.
A nice walk in the garden. Then the end of your Aussie soap.'

In fact, there were cartoons on by the time Mulligan got Mrs
Jackson back to the lounge. Road Runner and the Coyote,
eternally chasing around their surreal cartoon version of the
Rockies. The inmates were still as quiet as before, but now the

Irish girl was sitting up in her seat, grinning and following the high-speed proceedings on the screen with excited glee. The rings on her nose and eyelids were jigging up and down all together.

'Cheers,' said Mulligan, parking Mrs Jackson back in her place near the door. 'That was nice.'

The Irish girl didn't even bother to look at him.

On the way out, Mulligan stopped by the Alzheimer's Disease collection box in the lobby. He took a five-pound note from his wallet. Then he smiled ruefully to himself, added another, and stuffed them both into the slot.

As Mulligan swung out through the doors and into the sunshine, there was sweat on his forehead but an unmistakable spring in his step.

Neither Sally nor Jonathan knew it yet, but their private horror had already made page two of the *Evening Standard*, City Prices edition, just under a report about delays on the Northern Line due to staff shortages.

The headline read: WEST LONDON STABBING MYSTERY: GIRL HELD.

'The man's teenage stepdaughter,' the piece concluded, 'is helping police with their inquiries. She cannot be named for legal reasons.'

And at the house in Barnes, two officers from the scene-of-crime team were looking over Kit Jackson's study.

One of them, checking the desk, opened an unlocked drawer and let out a long, low hiss of surprise.

'Oh boy,' he said, half to himself, half to his colleague. 'Oh boy. This guy was confident. A fool, even.'

The other officer closed a book he had been examining, replaced it in its position on the wall shelf.

'Which means?'

The man by the desk beckoned to him. He was holding up a piece of shiny computer paper. It bore a less than pin-sharp but perfectly recognisable image, like a newspaper half-tone. The officer glimpsed bare flesh, slender limbs.

'There's plenty more of this filth in the drawer. Look at these. Just bloody look at these and ask yourself why that girl stabbed him.'

NINE

Sergeant Lipari had gathered from Sally Jackson's comments that Dr Yardley had his attractions, and he was no disappointment. Emma's therapist was in his mid-thirties, good-looking in a boyish, serious kind of way. He wore a green cord jacket, designer jeans, and a pair of expensive-looking glasses. He had brought with him his black medical bag, ready to carry out the intimate examination if Emma allowed it.

Almost worth going to therapy myself, Sergeant Lipari thought. *Perhaps I could think of a problem. Not too serious, just enough to keep him interested.*

'Dr Yardley?' she said. He nodded. 'Cheryl Lipari.'

They shook hands formally. Yardley's grip was firm.

'How is Emma?' he asked immediately.

'Not great.'

Yardley frowned. 'I'm sorry. I thought I'd seen everything, but this one is hard to believe. Anything I can do to help . . .'

Sergeant Lipari led the way through the doors marked NO ADMITTANCE.

'Mind if I refuel first?' she asked.

'Pardon?'

But by now she was already at the coffee machine.

While they waited for her plastic cup to fill up, she asked

Yardley, 'Do you know Mr Quinn? Emma's father, I mean?'

'I met him once. Right at the beginning of her therapy. We had an initial session with the entire extended family.'

'What did you think of him?'

Yardley shrugged and smiled his professional smile.

'Right. Well, of course I haven't met Mr Jackson,' Sergeant Lipari continued, 'but I'll be frank. If you'd asked me before last night who was a potential child-abuser in that particular family set-up, I think I'd have picked Mr Quinn over Mr Jackson every time.'

Yardley nodded, but still in a way that didn't commit him to any particular view.

'Of course, such a superficial impression doesn't prove much,' he said. 'That's precisely why abuse cases can remain undetected for so long – because the men involved are often so damned plausible.'

Sergeant Lipari asked him if he wanted something from the machine. Yardley said he had already drunk enough tea today to sink an ocean-liner. They set off for Garfield's office, Sergeant Lipari taking hits of coffee as she walked.

'Off the record,' she asked between sips, 'assuming her husband was abusing Emma – and, of course, despite the strong circumstantial evidence, we don't know that for certain yet – do you think Mrs Jackson knew what was going on?'

'All human beings have a certain innate capacity for self-deception,' Yardley said. 'It's amazing how much we can choose to ignore if we really want to.'

'You must see a lot of that, I suppose.'

'Oh yes, Miss Lipari.'

'Sergeant,' she corrected him crisply. '*Sergeant* Lipari.'

When they got to Garfield's office, the superintendent wasted no time. He asked Yardley if he had ever suspected anything might be amiss in Emma's home circumstances.

Yardley smiled sadly.

'People think that because you're a therapist you're privy to every nook and cranny of your clients' lives. If only. Even children – because that's what Emma was and is – have pretty sophisticated defence mechanisms. They shut part of themselves off—'

'Not for ever, they don't,' Sergeant Lipari cut in.

'No.' Yardley nodded agreement. 'Repressed terror and anger can suddenly erupt, with tragic results. As may have happened in this case.'

There was a short silence, then Garfield said, 'Emma Quinn was being treated by you for anorexia, right? Isn't that one of those things caused by sexual abuse?'

Yardley hesitated. 'It's . . . well, it's fashionable in some circles to blame everything on abuse. And, of course, in this case we now have to suspect a connection.'

'You mean – she was clinging to her childish, undeveloped body because she didn't want to grow up?'

Yardley was probably used to people quoting tabloid-paper psychology at him. He smiled at Garfield with surprising warmth.

'Well, perhaps,' he said. 'In cases of divorce and remarriage, we do find regression on the part of the children involved. It could be, for instance, that Emma didn't want to feel she was competing sexually with her attractive, youthful mother – Mrs Jackson – and her mother's new, active lover.'

'You mean Mr Jackson, her stepfather?'

'Yes.'

'Speaking of which,' Sergeant Lipari said, 'one thing we're

not clear about is whether Emma knew that her mother was pregnant. By Mr Jackson. Did she mention anything of that kind?'

Yardley looked at her in surprise.

'No.' He seemed quite disturbed. 'This is the first I've heard of it.'

'When did you last see Emma?'

'Yesterday. At four in the afternoon.'

'So if Emma had known about the pregnancy, she might have told you?'

'Probably. We did our usual focus session on stuff that had come up for her during the previous week. I think she would have trusted me sufficiently to share something as important as that.'

'The pregnancy was confirmed just before Emma's mother left for Manchester, sir,' Sergeant Lipari explained to Garfield. 'According to Mrs Jackson, she was planning to tell her husband this weekend, while Emma was staying with her father on one of her regular access visits. Emma would have been informed on her return, she said.'

'So at the time of the stabbing, neither Jackson nor Emma knew that Mrs Jackson was pregnant?'

'Supposedly not,' Sergeant Lipari confirmed. 'But that doesn't mean Jackson might not have guessed. I was just wondering . . . If he had worked it out, then, given a sexual, exploitative relationship between himself and Emma, he might have told her about her mother's pregnancy for reasons of his own.'

Garfield looked disapproving. The presence of another man seemed to have made him less tolerant.

'More scriptwriting, Cheryl,' he said. 'Sure we haven't had enough for today?'

'Wait a minute, though, sir . . . Is it possible that Emma, having got entangled in this abusive relationship, found out about her mother's pregnancy, and this caused her to lose control and stab her stepfather? Out of anger, jealousy, a whole confused lot of emotions?'

'That's an awful lot of supposition, Sergeant,' Yardley said.

'But let's say I do suppose it.'

Yardley paused for thought. While he considered Sergeant Lipari's hypothesis, he took off his glasses and rubbed his eyes.

'Well, of course, small children can be quite insanely jealous of a sibling, step- or other,' he said eventually, replacing his spectacles. 'But it's very unusual for a teenager to react in that way. In fact, in my experience they're often quite pleased. It gives them a new role in the family. They have hope that things will return to what they see as "normal", that mother and stepfather will stop being red-hot lovers and become blissfully dull, dependable parents again. Which often happens, to the adults' mild regret.' He allowed himself a smile, then shrugged. 'I don't know. Everything you suggest is possible, I suppose.'

'Of course, the alternative is that Mr Jackson was abusing Emma over an unspecified period,' Garfield said with a look at Sergeant Lipari that clearly implied, *enough*.

'It's another possibility,' Yardley agreed.

'You don't sound entirely convinced,' Sergeant Lipari said.

'This is an unusual case and I'm trying to keep an open mind. I find it rarely benefits me or anyone else to jump to conclusions, to "accept the obvious".'

'Fair enough. Who was paying for her sessions with you, by the way?'

'Mr Jackson. Or rather, his healthcare plan.'

Sergeant Lipari frowned. 'That was quite a risk for him to

take, come to think of it. Surely she might have revealed his abuse to you at any moment, mightn't she?'

'Well, yes.'

'Then why didn't she?'

'I don't know, Sergeant. I'm a therapist, not a detective,' Yardley countered quietly but firmly. He glanced at his watch.

'OK,' Sergeant Lipari said. 'Let's move on. Emma's solicitor will be here soon. Now, would you say Emma was well-informed on sexual matters?'

'She seemed to me fairly streetwise for her age. These days even kids in nice suburbs have to learn the big-city ropes, don't they?'

'I'm afraid so.'

'Yes, well,' Garfield growled. 'I think you should get going with Emma Quinn now. Unless Jackson survives – and confesses – she's our only hope.'

'I hope she trusts me enough to open up,' Yardley said. 'But I'll tell you right now, I have no intention of rushing her. First we'll see if Emma's OK with a physical examination. Then we'll consider what to do. Your priorities are police priorities,' he added with a smile that was both disarming and subtly challenging, 'which means they are not necessarily mine.'

Emma Quinn had been resting. Sergeant Lipari entered her cell first, followed by the female social worker who had been present a few hours previously for Dr Walsh's failed examination. The female social worker, who did not especially approve of a male doctor's involvement in this process, stood to one side with her notebook at the ready.

'Hello, Emma,' Sergeant Lipari said quietly. 'Are you all right?'

The girl did not move from her bed. She looked at Sergeant Lipari out of a bloodless face. The violet eyes were just as intense, and just as blank, as before.

The policewoman knelt down and touched Emma's arm.

'We've got someone you know coming in to see you in a moment. You wrote down his name.'

The girl's eyes flickered.

'Yes, it's Dr Yardley,' Sergeant Lipari said. 'Shall I ask him to come in?'

Emma stared at her for some moments. It was not a yes or a no. But above all, it was not a scream.

Sergeant Lipari stood up slowly. Only then did she dare to exhale with relief. She still wasn't entirely sure they weren't making a mistake. But this was one first, tiny step.

She looked at the social worker, who seemed impassive. Then she went to the door. Yardley was waiting outside in the corridor with the custody officer. Sergeant Lipari nodded, moved back into the room.

Yardley came through the door, gently put down his bag.

'Hello, Emma,' he said, and smiled.

Moments passed. They had agreed that the slightest hostility, the slightest resistance, and they would call it off. The tension in the room seemed to suck out the air. Then, very slowly, Emma Quinn smiled back, and the atmosphere became breathable once more.

'I've been asked to give you a sort of a check-up,' Yardley said. 'Won't take a moment. Would that be all right?'

Slowly, almost imperceptibly, Emma nodded her head.

Garfield let out a long, low sigh of frustration.

'God isn't on our side, is he?' he said. 'All it would have

taken was a little trace, a little something . . .'

'Believe me, sir, no one's more disappointed than I am,' Sergeant Lipari said.

'What about the shrink?'

'Dr Yardley doesn't really have opinions, sir, as you'll have gathered from our talk earlier on.'

'But it was his idea to follow up with a talk session tomorrow, right?' Garfield demanded gruffly.

'I'd already been thinking along those lines,' Sergeant Lipari said with a slightly defensive frown. 'Yardley must have picked up on my thoughts. He's amazing like that. A mind-reader. Goes with his job, I suppose.'

'Maybe. Anyway, what do you think now?'

'I think we don't have much choice. No traces of semen, as I said, which would have been our only conclusive proof. Emma's not *virgo intacta*, but as we know there are all sorts of reasons why a young girl's hymen can be broken. So . . . we have to get her to talk.'

'You think Yardley can pull that off?'

Sergeant Lipari ran her fingers through her thick, dark hair in an unconscious gesture of tension.

'From what I witnessed in her cell a few minutes ago, sir, Emma Quinn probably feels safer with Yardley than with anyone else in the world,' she said. 'If he can't get her to speak, I don't know who can.'

'And how do her family feel?'

'Emma's solicitor has no objection. She foresees no difficulties persuading the parents.'

Garfield shrugged, looked out of the window. There was a pigeon fluttering around on the roof opposite. It was fully grown, but seemed to be taking flying lessons from another one.

'Yardley says he can come in around eleven tomorrow morning,' Sergeant Lipari persisted. 'He'll treat the whole thing like it's a regular therapy session. I suggest we get set up to record anything Emma says.'

Garfield grunted.

'Listen, I promised to phone him. I've got Emma Quinn's solicitor waiting to hear what our plans are. Can I take that as a positive answer?' Sergeant Lipari said.

'Sure.' Garfield let out a humourless little laugh. 'Wheel him in. Everybody loves a shrink. Judges, juries, the papers . . . Personally they give me the creeps.'

Emma's solicitor had arrived shortly after Yardley had begun his examination. Diane Worcester was a small, tough-looking woman in her mid-thirties. She always wore black, in this case a smart knitted suit.

Sally and she had become friendly while making a legal documentary some years ago, and they had occasionally socialised since. Sally admired the solicitor for her feminism, for her humanity, and for her stubborn determination. Three good reasons why she had rung her when the question of Emma's legal representation was raised.

Diane Worcester had been closeted with the police for the past twenty minutes. Now, as she emerged from the heart of the police station, square-shouldered and fierce-gazed, there was something about her terrier-like presence that Sally found both intimidating and immensely heartening.

Jonathan rose slowly from his seat. Even before he reached his full height, he towered above the tiny lawyer.

'How's Em?'

Diane Worcester didn't answer immediately. She put her

briefcase on the table and sat down.

'She's still very much in shock,' she said, addressing herself to Sally.

Jonathan eased himself back into his chair. 'I think we knew that,' he said testily.

'The doctor – Yardley, the man who was Emma's therapist, has given her something to help her sleep. She's physically OK, it seems. Anyway . . .'

'What about the examination?' Jonathan asked harshly. 'The intimate one?'

Diane Worcester examined their haggard, exhausted faces. Her own features softened.

'Dr Yardley was able to carry out the intimate examination in full. It was inconclusive. Emma is not a virgin in the traditional sense, but there can be all sorts of reasons for that.' Diane Worcester's frustration was clear. 'More to the point, no traces of semen or any other matter were found. In other words, there appears to be no medical evidence that Emma was sexually abused.'

Jonathan swallowed hard, looked away.

'So . . . Dr Yardley has agreed to return here tomorrow morning,' Diane Worcester said. 'To try and help Emma find her voice.'

'Emma . . . still hasn't spoken?' Sally asked.

'No. That's the problem. The police would like to firm up their position by taking a statement from your daughter before laying charges.'

Jonathan frowned angrily. 'Are you out of your mind giving them permission to do that?'

'I have done nothing of the kind,' Diane Worcester said crisply. 'Not yet. I'm here to ask your opinion.'

'Wait a minute, if she admits she did it, they'll be able to charge Emma,' Jonathan said.

'Mr Quinn, they are going to do it sooner or later anyway.'

'My little girl will end up in jail.'

'That depends what sort of statement she makes – if any,' the solicitor said. 'On the positive side, once charged, she could even, technically, be granted bail, though in this case, given her disturbed condition and her "at risk" status, I'd have thought that unlikely. The other advantage is that once a suspect is on remand, he or she can't be questioned by the police any more. Then we can start to construct her defence.'

'Sounds like she wouldn't have any.'

'Not so. The sooner we can establish abuse, the better.'

Sally started. 'But you said . . . I mean, the examination showed—'

Diane Worcester looked at her sharply. 'Because there was no evidence of intercourse immediately before the stabbing, that doesn't mean abuse had not occurred on previous occasions. We have to countenance the possibility that Emma acted in self-defence, before abuse could once again occur.'

Sally looked at the floor. *Think only good things about Kit. No matter what . . .*

'The encounter – not a formal interview – is due to occur at eleven tomorrow morning,' Diane Worcester continued briskly. 'One parent may be present as well as myself.'

'I'll be there,' said Sally, looking up. 'I think we have to give Emma a chance to speak.'

Jonathan opened his mouth to say something, then thought better of it. After a short silence, he asked Diane Worcester, 'How long can they hold Emma?'

'Another forty-eight hours or so.'

'But if we held out—'

'Mr Quinn, I think the police already have more than sufficient evidence to support a charge,' Diane Worcester reminded him. 'The question is not whether Emma will be charged, but whether we allow Yardley to encourage her to speak.' She paused. 'What do you think?'

'Yes,' said Sally. 'We have to know what happened. And I trust Dr Yardley. One thing, though. As well as being present at the interview, I'd like a few minutes with my daughter beforehand. To reassure her.'

'I'll see what I can do, Sally.'

Jonathan stared into space for a while, then gave a shrug and a little nod, scarcely more than a twitch of the head.

'All right,' Diane Worcester said. 'Of course, I'll be there as well, to ensure there's no funny business. And I intend to defend your daughter's welfare quite aggressively. However, what Emma needs now is a night's sleep.' She turned to Sally. 'If I were you, I'd go home and do the same.'

'Home?' Sally echoed her faintly. 'I . . .'

'You need all the strength you can summon for the days ahead.' Diane Worcester looked at her watch. 'I'll let the police know that we agree to Dr Yardley's presence at tomorrow's interview. Then I'm afraid I have an important meeting back at the office. It was all I could do to get over here for an hour. I'm sorry.'

Then the lawyer was on her feet, briefcase once more firmly in hand. Sally rose too, slowly and shakily, like an invalid.

'Please,' she said, 'could I have a private word . . . ?'

Again Diane Worcester looked at her watch. Jonathan said, 'I need a smoke. I'll go outside, get some air.'

He walked quickly away, leaving the two women together.

'How can I help you, Sally?' Diane Worcester asked.

'It's Kit. I can't help myself. I want to see him,' Sally said, and just to say his name was like lifting a stone from her heart. 'But you all seem sure . . . that he abused Emma.' She looked pleadingly at the other woman. 'How can you be so certain? I mean, there's still no direct evidence . . .'

Diane Worcester said nothing for a long moment. Then she shook her head.

'I can only guess how hard it must be for you to accept what's happened,' she murmured. ' I know you're still in shock, but I have to be frank: I believe your husband is culpable. He's obviously a sick man, Sally.'

'But what should I *do*?' Sally blurted out, tears welling.

Diane Worcester looked at her levelly. 'Try to forget about Kit. Don't judge him. You can't. In fact, there's nothing you can do for him at the moment – it's the surgeons and doctors who'll decide if he lives or dies. Just think of Emma. She needs you to be on her side. And she needs you to be *strong*.' She reached out and patted Sally on the arm. 'Get a good night's sleep, for your sake and for everyone's. Even Kit's, if you like.'

Sally nodded slowly. 'Of course.'

'I'll see you in the morning. This could be a landmark case.'

'Yes?'

'Abuse as provocation. It might even open our way to a plea of diminished responsibility.'

'My daughter is not a landmark. She is a human being,' Sally said.

Diana Worcester did not waver. 'It will be tough for you, I know, Sally, but there'll be no shortage of support. This is one we're going to win.'

'Win?' Sally echoed faintly. 'Win *for whom*?'

Jonathan had reappeared and was waiting with barely suppressed impatience for the conversation to end. Diane Worcester patted Sally on the shoulder. Then, with a swift nod to Jonathan, she swept out of the police station. After she had gone, Sally stood for some moments, staring vaguely into the middle distance. Then she glanced bleakly at her ex-husband.

'I don't know where to go,' she said, her voice thick with despair. 'I can't go home, not yet, perhaps not ever ... and I can't face Zak and Liz and Harry.'

Jonathan looked at her almost shyly.

'I've got a spare bedroom, Sal. Where Emma sleeps. You can stay as long as you need to.'

'I don't know.'

'We may have been apart for six years, but we're in this together,' Jonathan persisted. 'I've got the car here ...'

Sally still did not move. She looked around the reception area, at the door Diane Worcester had come through. Somewhere on the other side of it was Emma, mute and traumatised. As for Kit ... from a practical point of view Diane Worcester might have a point, but ...

Oh God. Think only good things.

'Sal,' her ex-husband repeated, taking her arm. 'You've got to make a decision.'

Sally came out of her half-trance and focused on him. At this moment he was gentle, strangely relaxed. The father of her child. The one fixed point in a world gone mad. Through the fog of exhaustion and shock, she made a decision to leave everything until tomorrow, to take what refuge was available. Diane Worcester was right about one thing at least. Sally had to remain strong. For everyone.

'OK. Thanks,' she said. 'The police have your phone number?'

Jonathan nodded. 'We can be here in fifteen minutes if anything happens. Both of us.'

He took hold of her arm and guided Sally towards the door.

TEN

Sergeant Lipari took a final gulp of coffee, swore not to go back out to the machine again today. Or at least not before she finished her report.

Vaughan breezed in without knocking. He had been grey with tiredness when she last saw him an hour ago. Now he was hyper.

'Want to know the latest find at the Jackson place?' he asked.

'Go ahead.'

Vaughan faced her across the desk, resting his weight on his hands. He wore a peculiar look of triumph mixed with embarrassment, like a teenager who has managed to smuggle a copy of *Penthouse* into the house and hide it under his bed.

'Listen to this: in a drawer in the stepfather's study – not even locked, for Christ's sake – they've found an envelope with sophisticated computer-generated images of young girls. Stark naked, showing all they've got.'

'Jesus.'

Vaughan started to pace around the room, then cracked his knuckles and turned.

'And you know what, one of the pics is of the daughter!'

Sergeant Lipari read Vaughan's fascinated disgust, and

found herself wondering if he had seen the image, and what it made him feel.

'See, Jackson was in computers,' Vaughan continued. 'All fits, doesn't it?'

'Like a glove...' Sergeant Lipari took a deep breath. 'Forget the lack of medical evidence. No jury in the country would convict that girl for murder now.'

'You got it, doll. But meanwhile, as usual with these bastard nonces, everyone who knows Mr Christopher bleeding Jackson keeps telling us what a nice guy he is.'

'I hear present tense. What's the word from the hospital?'

'Came out of theatre an hour ago, but still unconscious,' Vaughan answered almost distractedly, as if this was a minor detail, as if Kit Jackson's life or death didn't matter any more. But he was slowly calming down.

'So Jackson still can't talk. On the other hand, we're not into murder yet either.'

'Exactly.' Vaughan turned away and started pacing the room again. 'Getting a whiff of press interest, though,' he said. 'Neighbours must have been talking. Sooner or later there'll have to be a press conference.' He grinned. 'If so, I daresay Mr Garfield will suddenly acquire a high profile, though they'll trot you out for the caring sharing bits.'

To her surprise, all Sergeant Lipari felt was dazed and inexplicably sickened. Why couldn't she share Derek Vaughan's euphoria? Perhaps because she was a woman? Because she saw the necessity of the hunt but couldn't enjoy the details of the kill?

'Child abuse. Broken families. Computer porn,' she said. 'Dream stuff for the tabloid reptiles. Be nice if we could keep them at bay for twenty-four hours. Preferably until we can get a statement from Emma Quinn.' She looked back at her almost-completed report. 'Probably too much to hope for, though.'

Vaughan returned to Sergeant Lipari's desk, leaned over and gave her a furtive peck on the cheek. His fingers brushed her face.

'It's eight o'clock,' he said. 'Aren't we entitled to knock off for the day? We're talking about an open-and-shut case. All over bar the media feeding-frenzy.'

'All bar the bit Mr Garfield and I are going to have to handle, you mean.'

'I suppose so. But nothing more's going to happen until tomorrow. Come on, Cheryl. Your flat's only five minutes away.'

Sergeant Lipari smiled despite herself.

'Are you trying to get me the sack, Derek Vaughan?'

Vaughan smiled back. Half-wolf, half-pleading child. He was never simply one thing at a time. Perhaps that was why she had fallen for him. That, and the way he undressed her and touched her.

'Get you the sack?' he mimicked. 'No way. You know me.' He lowered his voice. 'I just want you *in* it.'

'Jesus. You're not subtle, are you?'

'Some things in life are straightforward.'

Sergeant Lipari hesitated, then made a wry little face.

'I've got to finish this report.'

'Ten minutes?'

'Twenty.'

'Call it fifteen, Cheryl my darling.'

'Done. Just stop distracting me. Go and wait in the canteen.'

'Distracting you with what?'

'Making me want you, you bastard. Making me want you.'

* * *

Every time Sally tried to fall asleep, something in the room seemed to bring her jarring back into full consciousness. And then she was even wider awake for a while, like a driver who has almost fallen asleep on a long journey, for whom the flash of danger, the panicky, correcting wrench on the wheel, brings an enlivening surge of adrenalin.

Then Sally would lie with her eyes open, gazing around this room, a parallel child's world she had never seen before tonight. Emma's room in Jonathan's flat. Posters of the same pop groups and actors as at home in Barnes, but with one or two small changes, such as one of *Jurassic Park*, which Emma had been to see with Jonathan. Plus a huge teddy on the beanbag (very Jonathan) in the corner. Of course, to Kit and Sally Emma always insisted she hated teddies. Children were so adaptable. And in their way they liked difference. It helped to keep things clear. Or seemed to . . .

Christ, I desperately want a cigarette, Sally thought. I feel so sad and so empty, I don't care what happens to me. Except I have to stay alive and well for Emma. And . . . perhaps Kit was dead. But they would ring her if he was, surely? And, as she had told herself a hundred times during this longest day and night of her life, tomorrow Emma would talk, and Kit would regain consciousness. Tomorrow, instead of mystery there would be reasons. Tomorrow, instead of confusion, certainty.

There was the sound of a police siren, very near. Another surge of adrenalin. The sound passed. Then, it could have been one minute or ten later, another sound, a footfall in the doorway. Sally started, rolled over and looked across the darkened room. A tall, male figure. A fraction-of-a-second's fantasy that she was at home, not at Jonathan's, and this was Kit, her beloved Kit, come to tell her all was well.

'Who is it?'

Of course, a stupid question.

'Me. It's my flat, remember?'

Sally sighed and clicked on the bedside light. There was her ex-husband, wearing just his dressing-gown and looking childishly uncertain.

'What do you want, Jonathan?' she asked.

He shrugged, smiled painfully. A lock of hair fell over his eyes. He made no attempt to brush it away.

'I couldn't sleep, Sal.'

'Neither can I. Sleep feels like a betrayal.'

'Of Emma?'

'Of . . . everything.'

Jonathan took a step forward. Sally, in a small act of faith and a determination to stay strong, had taken some more of the ginger tea from her travel-bag before turning in; she remembered now that Jonathan had already put away a couple of large whiskies by then. Perhaps he had made further inroads on the bottle since.

'I couldn't stay away,' he continued. 'I know I promised, but . . .'

'Jonathan, go back to bed.'

But he came a little closer and then paused. When they had first met, as students fifteen years before, he had also come into her room and stood hesitantly. Then there had been attraction, erotic tension, the promise of something powerfully sexual once shyness was overcome. This was something much more complicated. All Sally sensed was his loneliness and his desperation. Then came a strange realisation: as she looked at Jonathan, pity suffused her like an erotic charge.

Sally shivered, though it was not cold here.

'Go back to bed,' she murmured, not even convincing herself.

'You see, Sal, it's been so long since . . .' And he was at the bed, pushing aside the duvet. 'I just want to hold you,' Jonathan said, and eased himself on to the narrow mattress beside her.

Surprising herself again, Sally did not resist. She even found herself moving slightly to allow him.

He put his arms around her and lay there for some time. Their breathing regulated to a single tempo. Then Sally felt Jonathan's fingers move under the T-shirt she had worn to bed, despite the warmth of the summer night.

'Jonathan . . .'

'Please.'

And she said nothing more. His hardness was comforting and even after all these years familiar. Above all, it signified life, not death. Fleetingly, Sally knew she would loathe herself in the morning for this, but somehow it didn't stop what was happening. She opened her palm on the cool skin of her ex-husband's back and began to caress him, as he caressed her.

'*Shit!*'

She was on top of him, riding to climax, when the phone rang.

'Leave it!' Vaughan hissed urgently. 'Leave it . . .' He pulled her down on him.

And Sergeant Lipari came, in short spasms with the phone still ringing, and finally collapsed across him, panting and incongruously giggling. She lay there like that, full of him, for a few more moments, staring balefully at the phone. Then one naked arm snaked out and picked it up.

'Yes. Lipari,' she said. She shivered. Vaughan was still in

her, still pulling her close. She glared at him.

'Cheryl? Garfield here. Did I wake you up?'

'No, sir.'

She saw Vaughan's grin as he realised who was on the line. The fleshly sound was loud and unmistakable as they pulled their bodies apart and she rolled back on to the pillows. Surely, she thought, Garfield had heard and knew what she had been doing.

Perhaps.

'Pity,' the superintendent growled. 'Right, I've got a copy of the *Orb* in front of me. Early edition. It's got a sodding great colour photo of Christopher Jackson and his stepdaughter plastered across the front page and a headline: "IS THIS THE BEAST OF BARNES?"'' Pause. Ominous pause. 'Are you listening to me, Cheryl? Can you work out what this means?'

'It means someone at the *Orb*'s managed to get hold of a picture, sir. Happens all the time.'

'Happens too bloody often! This is an inside job, Cheryl!' Garfield hissed. 'Someone on our investigating team flogged the *Orb* that photo, and by Christ I'm going to find out who's responsible and nail their fucking goolies to the garden gate!'

'I think we'd better discuss this in the morning, sir.'

'Too bloody right. And I want action. Got that?'

'I'll do what I can.'

'I want you in my office first thing.'

'Of course, sir. We've got the therapist coming in for Emma Quinn at eleven, don't forget.'

'Right. But I want to see you before that: eight o'clock sharp, in my office. Maybe I'll get your shrink to service my head while he's at it. I think the big end's gone. Goodnight.'

'Goodnight, sir,' Sergeant Lipari said sweetly, and replaced

the phone. She yawned and stretched, then turned to Vaughan.
He was oddly watchful. 'The *Orb* got hold of a photograph of
Jackson and Emma,' she said. 'Mr Garfield is sure they got it
from one of us. Presumably for money. He's out for a scalp.'

'I know. I could hear him from here.'

'Well, any suggestions?'

'Nah.'

'Helpful as ever, Derek dear.'

Vaughan had lit a cigarette. He offered it to Sergeant Lipari.
Usually her refusal, like his offer, was routine, but this time she
took a puff. Sergeant Lipari looked at the clock. It was just
before midnight.

'You never go home, do you?' she said.

'Why, do you want me to?'

Sergeant Lipari said nothing. Suddenly, just minutes after
wanting this man more than anything or anyone in the world,
she needed to be alone. Vaughan didn't fit in here: perhaps in
bed, but not elsewhere in the neat, elegant flat she had treated
herself to after divorcing her husband. *Jack the Lad. Why do I
always go for Jack the Lad? Maybe I could use a shrink as
well*, she thought.

The benefits with her ex-husband, adulterous rat though he
was, had been his money and his charm, both of which came
from ten years at the top of the rag trade. How else but from a fat
divorce settlement could Sergeant Lipari have afforded this
spacious flat in one of the nicest blocks in Richmond? Derek
Vaughan, for all his straight-up-and-down attractions, was
neither rich nor especially charming. Last but by no means
least, Vaughan was also married, and not to her. However, at
this moment, this seemed a distinct advantage, Sergeant Lipari
realised with a sudden flash of insight which she had never

really had before. Because all at once she wanted him to leave her world and go back to his own.

'Well? You want me out of here?' Vaughan pressed her.

'I do think you should go home,' Sergeant Lipari told him finally. 'I've got a sod of a morning ahead tomorrow. Another session with Emma Quinn, this time with her shrink on hand, and now the business with this bloody photograph. I need my sleep.'

'Why can't I kip here?' He snuggled closer.

Suddenly Sergeant Lipari felt intensely, unfairly irritated by Vaughan's persistence, his assumption that anything he did or said was going to be all right with her. Again she recognised a tiny but significant turning-point in their relationship.

You either start to pull out, or you go further in, she thought. *There's never any standing still, is there?*

'Come on, doll,' Vaughan coaxed softly. 'Why not?'

'Because I don't want your marriage falling apart on account of me,' Sergeant Lipari said a little lamely. Then she found herself switching on to the offensive: 'We're having an affair, OK. I like what we do in bed. But I don't want to live with you.'

'You've been at the assertiveness training again.'

'I'm studying for my Ph.D., Derek, didn't you know?'

Vaughan smiled, stubbed out his cigarette in the ashtray.

'All right. I'll go home. But first . . . I mean, you got yours, didn't you? Even with Mr Garfield hanging on the line.' He reached for her hand, directed it downward. 'Come on. One for the road . . .'

It took Sergeant Lipari another irritating but not entirely unpleasurable half-hour to get rid of him.

ELEVEN

Sally's first conscious thought was of Emma; pale, silent Emma, whose life had become a nightmare.

Her second was of Kit, silent also in a sleep that might have no end. Perhaps today she would sneak off and see him – *damn* the clever lawyer – she had to see him while he was still alive. Touch him. Comfort him, if that was somehow possible. Sally was absolutely sure, in that first clear moment of waking, that Kit was innocent. She had no explanations for anything. *She just knew.*

At least Jonathan had gone back to his own bed. It was not even that their sex together had been bad: it had simply been wrong – wrong because all they had both really needed was to hold each other, hold each other and no more. In marriage it had been the same, Sally recalled. Sex so often confused with comfort, desire with affection. But Kit had known the difference. That had been a revelation. It was why she had left Jonathan and gone to live with him.

Perhaps Sally had needed to remind herself, all over again, of why she had broken up her first marriage. Certainly this was the only explanation of last night that made any sense, or left her with any shred of self-respect.

The digits of the bedside clock read seven-fifteen. She felt a vague background nausea, but nothing she couldn't handle. For the next few weeks, she promised herself, that ginger would always be by her side.

Sally eased herself out of bed. First stop was the bathroom, to wash thoroughly between her legs. Then, sick at heart still but also calm and determined, padded through to the living room. She picked up the phone, dialled Liz's number.

'Hello, Liz Paine.' Sally's friend's voice was thick with sleep but its tone indicated a mind on full alert. 'Is that Sally?'

'Yes. I know it's early—'

'Christ! At last, darling! I've been worried sick! Where have you been?'

'I meant to give you a call last night, but . . . you know . . . after everything . . .'

'Thank God you've rung now. After we left the police station, we took Zak out for an Indian,' Liz explained hastily. 'I'd expected a message on the answering-machine when we got back, but instead there was just the press round-up at the end of *Newsnight*. I saw the tabloid headlines. Darling—'

'What tabloid headlines?'

'About Kit.'

'What are you saying?'

'He's in the papers. But we can discuss that later.' Liz was brusque, all business. In her element. 'Now Sally, where are you, for God's sake?'

'At Jonathan's.'

'Boy, you must have been desperate.'

'I suppose I was. After the argument about Zak, I thought things might be difficult with you lot.'

'Don't be silly,' Liz countered firmly. 'We talked it through last night over the lamb pasanda, and we really want you to stay with us.'

'But Zak—'

'Oh, Zak may be a stroppy little bastard at the moment, but he understands why you had to tell the cops about him, and why they had to haul him in. I just wish he'd tell us exactly where he was the night before last . . .' Liz sighed. 'I'll phone in sick. Just give me half an hour. We'll come and get you. Don't worry. You'll be safe here.'

'I have to be at the police station at eleven. Noel Yardley's coming in to see if he can persuade Emma to talk about what happened. I want to be there. By law I can be. At least I'll see her, Liz.'

'No problem. It's only just gone seven now. We can get you settled in here and then I'll drive you into the police station.'

'Are you sure? About my staying, I mean.'

'Completely.'

Sally heard the entryphone buzzer by the front door, looked around irritably. Had Jonathan gone out to fetch something and forgotten his key? Then there were voices in the street.

'Just a minute,' she told Liz.

Sally put down the phone, walked over to the window. She parted the curtain and looked out into the street. At first it looked bizarrely like a protest demonstration, or a film being made on location. People wandering aimlessly around, mostly men but one or two women, spilling from the pavement into the street, calling to each other. Men festooned with cameras, looking bored. One of the crowd stepped back from the door and looked up. She caught his eye. He smiled up at her, and Sally realised that this was neither a demo nor a film. They were reporters, here for her and Jonathan.

She picked up the phone once more.

'Oh Christ,' she said softly, as if afraid the crowd outside could hear. 'The press. They've found us.'

'I'm coming, Sal. Hang on.'

After Sally had replaced the phone, she turned to go back to Emma's bedroom. Her ex-husband was standing in the kitchen doorway, holding two steaming mugs of coffee. She knew it was cheap instant, because she recognised its ersatz-acorny smell. He wore his dressing-gown and a shy smile.

'Hi,' he said. 'They're still outside, but at least I've dissuaded them from trying to get in.'

Sally nodded. 'Liz is coming to get me,' she said. 'I'd better start packing.'

'I thought, I mean, last night—'

'I was confused, Jonathan. My fault. We both needed comfort.'

Jonathan put the coffees down on the little side-table.

'But there's plenty of room here. It doesn't have to be like that. Really.'

Sally started to move towards the bedroom.

'I'm married to another man, Jonathan, and he's fighting for his life. Despite what's happened, I still feel love for him. And I feel responsible.' Sally paused, but Jonathan said nothing. She turned towards the spare room. 'I'll get my things.'

Sergeant Lipari was five minutes early. Garfield didn't keep her waiting. He wasn't malicious that way. On the other hand, he made no effort to gild the lily.

Already at his desk, her boss merely grunted a good morning and gestured for Sergeant Lipari to sit down. Then he tossed a copy of the *Orb* on to the surface between them, composed his fingers into a steeple, and studied Sergeant Lipari's reaction.

Sergeant Lipari examined the cropped happy-snap of Kit Jackson and his stepdaughter, Emma. Lipari had never seen a picture of Jackson before. She was mildly surprised to note that he was nice looking, with a slightly plump, sensible face and humorous eyes. Emma looked very pretty – fully alive and happy, the colour version of her current, pale-grey self.

'The photograph must have come from the house,' Garfield said quietly. 'Which means one of our scene-of-the-crime team must have passed it to a reporter on the *Orb*. For a consideration, goes without saying.'

Sergeant Lipari finally tore her eyes from the picture.

'You're sure this came from the scene of the crime, sir?'

'Where else?'

'Family—'

'Both Mrs Jackson's parents are dead. She's got one sister. In Australia. Mr Jackson's an only child. His mother's in a home somewhere, apparently.'

'Neighbours—'

'Cheryl, the paper had the picture well before the rest of the press pack even got a whiff,' Garfield said in that mock-patient way of his that so often preceded an explosion. 'I had the deputy commissioner on the phone to me last night.'

'Sir—'

'He was climbing the fucking wall, Cheryl.'

'Fair enough, sir,' Sergeant Lipari said mildly. 'But what exactly do you expect me to do about it?'

'This has happened before at this nick. Now it's happened once too often. It's got to stop. If you've got any suspicions, share them with me now.'

'I'm afraid I don't have any suspicions, sir.'

119

Garfield leaned forward. 'Well, you'd better acquire some. And when you've got them, talk to me. The deputy commissioner's already whacked in a protest to the paper. Of course, they deny the picture was procured for them by one of our officers, but they would, wouldn't they?'

'With respect, they might be telling the truth.'

Garfield shrugged heavily. 'I want this case sorted quick, Cheryl. I want to know who supplied the happy-snap to the *Orb*, and I want whoever stabbed Mr Jackson charged – so everything's nicely *sub judice*, the tabloids leave us alone, and we can get on dealing with the rest of the local mayhem. Got that?'

'Sir, I can't make promises about the photo,' Sergeant Lipari said. 'As for the case itself, we all want a result there. But we can't cut too many corners or we'll be making a different kind of trouble for ourselves.'

'Then just make sure you don't.'

Sergeant Lipari felt something tighten in her gut. Oh, she liked that sudden 'you' Garfield had popped in there. And then there was the simple-minded male belief that anything, even the heart of a damaged child, could be repaired by hard work and determination. Life as a football match. 'Work-rate' and 'guts'. The old steamroller.

Vaughan was waiting for her by the coffee-machine. He looked exhausted and a touch chastened. Sergeant Lipari guessed his wife might not have been entirely satisfied with his explanations about the previous night.

She told him about Garfield's little lecture, the threat to the investigation team.

'The Governor's being a bit naïve, if you ask me,' Vaughan said. 'The press have got a million ways of getting what they want. We don't know the half of it.'

'Well, we'll have to learn, won't we?' Sergeant Lipari said simply. 'And fast.'

Sitting on the narrow single bed in the daughter's room, Sally listened to the sound of voices outside Jonathan's flat. Mutterings, arguments, occasional laughter. Now and again someone would call up from the street: 'Mrs Jackson? Are you in there, Mrs Jackson?' Then there would be a pause, followed by: 'Mr Quinn?'

Sally had her bags packed and ready. They still contained the clothes she had taken with her to Manchester, five days and what felt like an entire life ago. Jonathan, who had disappeared into the bathroom twenty minutes since, seemed to have taken up permanent residence there.

Of course, Sally felt guilty. It didn't change the fact that she had to get out of here. There were certain practical things she and Jonathan might have to do together in the coming days and weeks, but that was as far as it went. Along with the guilt she felt a kind of satisfaction with her own toughness, a feeling that somehow she could use it for the sake of Emma and Kit. Somehow.

The toot of a horn outside. Sally leant over to the window and twitched the curtain. Yes, it was Liz Paine's little Renault, forcing its way through the ratpack of journalists. Liz, who was driving, looked furious. Beside her Harry had a look of wry concentration. While Sally watched, her heart lightening just a little, Liz manoeuvred as close to the building as she could. She and Harry clambered out. They firmly locked both doors and headed for the front entrance to the flats.

Sally got to the entryphone before it buzzed.

'Liz?'

'Yes.'

'Don't let any of those creeps in, will you?'

'Are you kidding?'

Sally pushed the door-release button, took a breath and waited. When the doorbell rang, she checked through the spyhole. Through its fish-eye she saw Liz and Harry, alone in the strip-lit hallway.

The two women fell into each other's arms. They stayed that way even while Harry pushed them in, as if they were some tableau on wheels, and closed the door behind them. Sally cried a little, sadness and relief.

'Don't say a thing,' Liz said gently, dabbing Sally's eyes and cheeks with a tissue she had produced from somewhere in her usual miraculous practical fashion. 'Let's just get you out of here. Plenty of time to talk later.'

Sally spoke anyway.

'I've already rung the police,' she said, gabbling her words slightly but not ashamed, not with Liz. 'Emma's woken up.'

'She'll be fine,' Liz said.

'Will she?'

'As fine as can be expected,' Liz qualified her assurance slightly.

Sally nodded distractedly. 'Please . . . please can we get out of here?'

'Where's Jonathan?'

'In the bathroom.'

Harry had meanwhile found his way through to the spare room and retrieved Sally's bag. He was standing meaningfully by the door.

'Ready? Let's go, Sal,' Liz said. 'By the way, I've taken the liberty of ringing your boss – Gareth, wasn't it? – anyway, the one who once asked me to run away to the Seychelles with him – and he said they're all thinking of you, and you've got leave of absence until everything's sorted out. So don't worry about that.'

'Liz, you're a miracle,' Sally said, planting a kiss on her friend's cheek before they separated and turned towards the door. 'I just don't know what—'

Then the bathroom door opened and there stood Jonathan.

'Hi, Liz. Hi, Harry,' he said. Absurdly, he seemed desperate to appear normal. His voice was slightly hoarse. Had he been crying as well?

Harry put down the bag. He shrugged awkwardly.

'Sally rang us . . .'

Jonathan nodded. 'Come to take her away?'

'It's what she wants,' Harry said softly but with a hint of steel.

'And Sally always gets what she wants, right?'

'She's in a very difficult position, Jonathan,' Liz said. 'And this is no time for reviving old grudges. Sally's got to keep strong. For Emma.'

'And for Kit?'

Sally glanced at Liz, who looked at Harry. He opened the door.

'We'll talk some other time, Jonathan,' Sally said. 'We've both got to stay strong for Emma. I'm sorry I can't stay, but it's not possible. I'll be at the police station later this morning. See you there?'

Jonathan just stared at her. All the way out through the door, along the hall, and down the stairs. Sally looked up as they prepared to open the door on to the street. He had followed to the top of the stairwell, was simply staring down, coldly and intently, through flight after flight.

Perhaps Jonathan could *kill someone*, Sally had time to think in the instant before Harry opened the outside entrance. *Dear God, what had poor Emma seen two nights ago that did this to her?*

Then Liz slipped a scarf around Sally's head and bundled her out into the street.

Voices immediately started shouting, 'Mrs Jackson! Mrs Jackson!'

There was the light, wheezy click of camera-shutters, the cicada-whirr of motor-drives, a confusion of faces and hands and arms, a copper-blue morning sky wheeling overhead as Sally ducked and dived, evading eager grasps. Liz was right behind her, pushing. Harry was battering his way through with her travel-bag. Within seconds they were at the car. The back door opened and Sally was propelled inside. Someone tried to get in with her, but Liz wrenched him out and joined Sally on the back seat. The lock snapped shut. Some business in the front, then the front door slammed as well. Muffled curses outside; loud, growled oaths from Harry in the driver's seat. Faces were still pressed to the window, gibbering like damned souls, as he started the engine.

The Renault pulled away in first gear, its engine rising quickly to an angry snarl. Harry didn't change up until they were doing twenty-five and heading for the main road.

Sally sat hunched and ashen in the back seat like a sick old woman. Liz patted her on the shoulder.

'You made it,' she said. 'You survived the hell of the tabloids. Now it's poor old Jonathan's turn.'

'Yes,' Sally said. 'Poor old Jonathan.'

In his parked BMW, Paul Mulligan finished noting the number of the Renault. Yallop was heading back from the mêlée outside the flats, like a hunter home from the kill. Mulligan picked up his mobile and dialled. Derek Vaughan had started whining about getting into trouble with his DS. Well, one more favour and he might let him off the hook. Might.

Vaughan walked into Sergeant Lipari's office while she was on the phone. She gestured for him to sit down, mouthed, 'Just a sec', and finished the conversation.

'OK,' she said, after she had replaced the receiver. 'That was the hospital. Guess what? There's a real chance Jackson might pull through. His wife will have to be informed, though I'm not quite sure what she'll do with the information.'

'So he's conscious.'

'We should be so lucky. Could be a day, could be a month, even a year. Failing a confession from Emma Quinn, we'll have to make our own case.' Sergeant Lipari looked at her watch. 'Which reminds me, the girl's therapist is due here in about ten minutes. Any confirmations of Zak Paine's movements on the night of the stabbing?'

'He was at a club in Stockwell until around midnight, pretty much as he claimed. Loads of witnesses to that.' Vaughan checked her reaction. 'Disappointed?'

'The attack on Emma's stepfather occurred around twelve-thirty. Say he did leave Stockwell at midnight. That still leaves Zak just about enough time to cab it over to Barnes for the main event.'

'You serious?'

'I'm just saying we have to be absolutely sure he couldn't have been there.'

125

Vaughan shrugged in a half-amused, half-resigned way that reminded her of her own Italian father. She guessed Vaughan would shrug more and more like that as he got older. Just like her father.

'He left with a couple of kids who are known as casual drug-dealers,' Vaughan said. 'Mainly cannabis, nothing really heavy. Middle-class teenagers, like him.'

'The three of them were under the influence of drugs?'

Vaughan nodded. 'I have a feeling this is the real reason why Zak's pretty vague about the rest of the night.'

'God. Sixteen,' Sergeant Lipari said. 'Mind you, my cousin Marco was raised with a rod of iron. Soon as he left home, he got straight in with a druggy crowd in Soho, ended up on probation for possession, lucky not to get bird. What can you do?'

'What I suspect Master Paine's nice progressive parents are going to be doing from now on, which is keeping a bloody sight closer eye on him.'

Sergeant Lipari nodded thoughtfully. 'Maybe he didn't go to the Jackson house, and maybe he wasn't involved in the stabbing. All the same, we'd better know exactly who he was with and where he went. For the record.'

'We'll talk to the other kids. I guess if they're prepared to back him up, it puts Zak out of the picture.'

'Yes. Which, unless Emma had a very secret companion we don't know about, leaves us with her sad, angry father, Jonathan Quinn.'

'Him again.'

'He was listening to Mozart, he says. On his own. Saw no one, spoke to no one until we came and knocked on his door at two o'clock.'

'He could certainly have made it over to Barnes and back, couldn't he?'

'He could indeed, Derek. He could.'

Zak was still up in his room when Sally arrived at Liz and Harry's place, a large, untidy Victorian house set just back from Wandsworth Common. You could get lost in it, Liz always used to joke. Especially if you really wanted to, and Sally assumed that was exactly what her daughter's childhood playmate would want to do.

So, Sally was surprised when Zak appeared downstairs within minutes of her arrival. Liz had gone into the kitchen to make coffee. Barefoot, dressed in a Metallica T-shirt and an old pair of sweatpants, the boy managed to look sheepish and faintly truculent at the same time in a peculiarly moving adolescent-male way.

'How's it going, Sal?' Zak asked. 'You all right?'

'Surviving,' Sally said, 'I'm grateful to your mum and Harry for rescuing me.'

'From Jonathan?'

Sally felt herself blushing. She had sort of half-meant that, but the earnest expression on Zak's face made her feel ashamed.

'The press had surrounded the place,' she explained. 'It was like an armed siege, except they were shooting cameras.'

'Right.' He shuffled from one bare foot to another. 'And Emma?'

'She was still asleep when I rang earlier. I'm going to call again in a bit. I'm going to be able to see her later this morning.'

'Give her . . . yeah, give her my love when you see her, will you?' Zak said. He took a cautious step forward. 'Listen, I'm sorry . . . this is really terrible . . .'

To Sally's amazement, he came right up to her, took her round the waist and kissed her on the forehead. Then he stepped back just as quickly, surprised at his own action.

'Thanks,' Sally said softly. 'Thank you for that.'

'Cool,' Zak muttered. 'I'll see you later, OK?'

And he fled back upstairs.

Sally wandered through to the kitchen. Liz was filling the kettle.

'I think Zak and I just mended the little hole in our fence,' she said.

Liz shrugged. 'This has given him a shock. It's given us all a shock. Do you want to go through to the living room and settle down near the phone? I'll bring you something to drink . . .'

'There's some of that ginger tea in my bag.'

Liz smiled wryly. 'I'll make you a cup. Anything to eat?'

Sally shook her head and went back through into the familiar surroundings of the living room, where she had sat so often, during dinner parties, teas, or just chatting with Liz. God, she remembered bringing Emma to Zak's tenth birthday here. Balloons, cakes and jellies, an entertainer, well-regulated childish screams of enjoyment . . .

Liz glided in with the ginger tea, set it down.

'I've got to ring the office,' she said. 'I'll do it on Harry's work line. You see how Emma is, Sal, and decide when you want to go into the station. I'm happy to be your chauffeur for the day – for the week, if it helps.'

'For today would be great. I think I'll be all right after that. But thanks anyway.'

Sally rang the police station and spoke to Sergeant Lipari. Emma was awake. She had taken a few sips of tea but refused food. Lipari confirmed that Sally could have a few minutes with her daughter before the session with Yardley. Also – Lipari's manner became cautious, even oddly apologetic – it seemed that Kit's condition had stabilised. He was still unconscious and on the critical list, but he was getting no worse.

'I assumed you'd want to know, Mrs Jackson,' the sergeant said.

'Yes . . . of course. Thank you.'

Sally put down the phone, took a sip of the soothing tea. Then, quite suddenly, as if moved by some outside force, she found herself ringing the Charing Cross Hospital. Moments later, she was talking to the sister on the ward where Kit was in intensive care. The sister confirmed Lipari's account. Mr Jackson was unconscious but stable. That was important. Stable. When would Mrs Jackson be in to see him?

Don't they know? Sally thought. *Don't they know what the police are saying my husband did?*

You can visit any time, day or night, in intensive care, the sister explained. Then she asked Sally if she was all right.

'It's . . . it's hard to say, really,' Sally said.

She put the phone back in its cradle. Liz found her some minutes later, crumpled over the arm of the sofa and weeping like a child.

'Sally, darling. What is it?'

'I rang the hospital about Kit! I couldn't help myself!' Sally sobbed. 'I just couldn't help it – I wanted to see him, you know . . .'

Liz sat down beside her. 'And is he . . . ?' she began solemnly.

'No! He's stable, they said.' Sally's voice rose to a desperate, incantatory wail. 'Sta-ble, sta-ble, sta-ble!'

TWELVE

Diane Worccster folded her arms across her small, chunky body in a classic defensive attitude. Her grey-green eyes searched the small group in Garfield's office with an intensity that brooked no contradiction.

'It has to be understood right from the start that Emma Quinn is not a criminal but a *profoundly* traumatised child,' she said. 'I'm here to ensure that she's treated with the care, respect and consideration due to her.'

Garfield looked pained.

'Miss Worcester, that goes without saying. This is a difficult and delicate case.'

'I'm glad to hear you acknowledge that so clearly, Superintendent! We'll make a new man of you yet!'

Garfield suddenly discovered a speck of something on the lapel of his usually immaculate cashmere-mix jacket.

'The thing is, though,' Sergeant Lipari rescued him, 'we *are* dealing with a case of attempted murder. Now, there's still the possibility that Emma didn't actually stab her stepfather. And what I'm saying is, the man – or woman – who did could still be running around free.' She paused. 'In the light of this, you do understand our urgent need to talk to Emma, don't you?'

Diane Worcester rummaged through her bag, fished out a

stick of sugar-free chewing gum and popped it into her mouth.

'It's in all our interests that the events of the night before last are clarified,' she said. 'That's why the family and I have not opposed a visit from Dr Yardley. However, my client must come first,' she continued. 'There's no way I'll let you play games with Emma's sanity.'

'Miss Worcester, we're bending over backwards,' Sergeant Lipari said carefully. 'Mrs Jackson will be allowed to see her daughter before the interview, which is not strictly necessary. Emma is not being treated as anything other than a distressed young girl.'

It was Yardley's turn to intervene now.

'I'm not concerned with prejudging this case but with putting Emma back in touch with the human race, Miss Worcester,' he said. The sharpness in his normally easy-going tone came as a surprise to Sergeant Lipari. 'I hope Emma will emerge from shock and be able to help us and, most importantly, herself. If not, she will need expert treatment. As her therapist, I shall be the first to support and indeed facilitate such treatment. In the meantime, I think I am experienced enough, and I know this child sufficiently well, to be given a chance to talk to her this morning, don't you?'

He had coloured slightly, but his eyes were calm as he met those of Diane Worcester. She chewed mechanically, holding his gaze, her arms still severely folded.

I wouldn't like to be a witness who gets on the wrong side of her, thought Sergeant Lipari. *Or a client, for that matter.* She inwardly let out a silent cheer when the solicitor was first to look away.

'What I'm saying is, Emma's not going to prison,' Diane

Worcester muttered. 'No matter what she may have done to . . . this person . . .'

'I'm with you there. Whatever she did. Whatever her reasons,' Yardley said. His voice was kind and reasonable again.

There was a knock on the door. A WPC put her head in and said Mrs Jackson had arrived.

'Still OK for her to spend a few minutes with Emma in her cell?' the WPC asked.

'Sure. It's what we agreed,' Sergeant Lipari said. 'We'll go to the interview room and wait. No special rush, OK?'

They got to their feet. Yardley granted Diane Worcester a dignified smile.

'Testing time,' he said. 'Shall we see if Emma's ready to open up a little?'

A policewoman from something called the Family Support Unit led Sally into Emma's cell. The place was small and sparsely furnished but not as dungeon-like as Sally had feared. The policewoman had explained that there were different kinds of cells: ones for violent street criminals and ones for other categories, and this was the second sort.

And in any case Sally had eyes only for her daughter.

Emma was sitting on the bed when the cell door opened and Sally got her first glimpse of her daughter since the morning she had left for Manchester. Emma half rose to her feet, expressionless. But by then her mother had flown across the room and taken her in her arms. She felt Emma respond, not quite as she would have before, but there was life and love there, and Sally could hope at that moment that all things were possible.

'Darling, darling, darling . . .'

Sally felt her own tears dampening her daughter's neck. She pulled back, sniffing, looked into Emma's eyes.

'Darling . . .'

The girl smiled slightly, then just burrowed into her mother's shoulder like a baby.

Sally had no idea how long they stood there like that. Until the policewoman said very softly, 'We should be getting along to the interview room, if that's all right.'

She nodded. 'Emma,' she whispered, 'Dr Yardley's going to have a chat with you. I'll be there.'

Emma looked up at her, dry-eyed. A tiny motion of the head.

Oh please, Sally thought, *smile properly, don't just stare at me like a lobotomised thing, please . . .*

But what Sally said, in her best, most cheerful, Mum-will-make-it-better voice, was, 'You'll be just fine, I promise.' Another tiny motion of Emma's head showed she had heard her mother. 'Now come on, darling. Let's go and see Dr Yardley, shall we? You asked for him, and he's come to talk to you.'

Emma Quinn was seated at the interview table with a social worker to her right. Diane Worcester positioned herself to the girl's left. Sally Jackson was tucked unobtrusively into the corner. Yardley entered and sat at the table, directly opposite Emma.

'Emma,' Sergeant Lipari said softly. 'Dr Yardley's come back to see you. All right?'

The girl showed no reaction. She was almost translucently pale. Her lips were slightly parted. She was breathing shallowly through her mouth.

Sergeant Lipari looked up to check the video-camera light was on, then said softly:

'Dr Yardley would like to talk to you. He'd like to help.'

Yardley didn't immediately answer his cue. He sat for some time just looking at Emma and smiling. The plan was to behave as if this were the beginning of a normal therapy session at his consulting rooms.

'Hello, Emma,' he began eventually. His voice was conversational but with a subtle touch of gravity. 'I didn't ask you about it yesterday, but you've had a bad time since we last talked. A terrible thing happened, isn't that right?' He paused. 'Would you like to tell me about it now? Do you feel able to?'

They waited. Then Emma's eyelids flickered. She swallowed. Something had got through. What, and how this infinitesimal bridgehead could be exploited, no one could tell – except maybe Yardley, Sergeant Lipari prayed; except this remarkable man.

'Fine,' Yardley continued evenly, 'take your time. We have lots of time. Everyone here wants to help you. Everyone here wants to know the reason for what happened the night before last, but only so we can help you.' Pause. 'All right, Emma?' Pause. His voice became a coaxing whisper. 'All right? No need to talk if you don't want to. Just nod if you understand what I'm saying.'

Another hiatus. All around him was heavy with tension, but Yardley appeared to sit easily, for all the world as if he were companionably alone in the room with Emma and they had an eternity to decide whether, if ever, they were going to talk.

Emma responded with a tiny, barely perceptible movement of the head. Up, down.

Sergeant Lipari found herself exhaling like a spent swimmer coming to the surface. She glanced quickly at Sally Jackson just to ensure that the girl's mother wasn't about to break down and shatter the moment, but Sally was silent, absolutely concentrated, as if willing her daughter into communication. Even Diane Worcester had stopped chewing her gum. She was as transfixed as the rest of them.

Yardley stayed just the way he was. He let moments pass.

'Why?' he asked then. 'Emma, *why*?'

A tear emerged from the corner of Emma's left eye. Otherwise she seemed perfectly, eerily impassive.

Yardley didn't seem to react. Then Sergeant Lipari noticed that beneath the table, out of Emma's sight, the fingers of his left hand were drumming soundlessly on his thigh. As if to give that hand something to do, Yardley directed it into his pocket and produced a monogrammed handkerchief. Slowly, obviously to avoid alarming Emma, he took off his gold-rimmed glasses and slowly gave them a wipe with the handkerchief. Then he replaced them, put away the handkerchief, quietly cleared his throat.

'Why, Emma?' he repeated with a hint of urgency.

If a pin drops now, I'll be for a cardiac arrest, Sergeant Lipari thought, her eyes fixed on Emma. *Dear God, I can't bear this*.

The movement was small at first. Just a twitch of Emma's mouth. Like the first tiny tremor of an earthquake. A moment later, another. And another... until the girl's face was trembling, her mouth opening and closing silently, straining for expression. The first sound that came out was a high-pitched croak that broke in its middle. Then a howl. Then Emma Quinn raised her slender fists and crashed them down on the table.

Finally out came a word: 'BAD!' And another: 'BAD DADDY!'

The look on Diane Worcester's face was a mixture of fascination and panic. She laid a hand on Emma's arm, but the girl ignored her. She began rhythmically to thump the table-top, and a litany came pouring out, shrilly rhythmic and insistent:

'HE SAID HE WAS A GOOD DADDY, BUT HE WAS BAD, BAD, BAD!'

THIRTEEN

Sally walked unsteadily out through the door marked 'Private', glanced unseeingly around the reception area. She looked ashen. Liz was at her side before Sally could even register her presence.

'News?' Liz murmured.

'They've charged Emma,' Sally said simply.

'Ohmigod. Dear Sal.' Liz put her arms around her unresisting friend. 'So, Emma told them what happened?'

'Yes . . . yes . . . Or sort of. I mean, it's obvious somebody's been abusing her. She calls him her "Bad Daddy" . . .'

Liz nodded. 'Was it? You know . . .'

Sally shrugged abruptly, more like a spasm of pain wracking her upper body.

'Emma's named no names,' Sally said quickly, a little too quickly. 'She may have started communicating again, but she's still very blocked . . . but of course it's what everyone thinks. Personally, I—'

Suddenly Sally could speak no more. She sat down abruptly in one of the blue plastic chairs with her head in her hands, her normally immaculate blonde hair hanging in tangled strands across her face, and she sobbed.

'That's the bad news, I suppose,' she said after a while in a very small but quite rational voice. 'The good news is, now she's on remand we'll be able to visit her every day. She'll be in something called secure accommodation. It's a local authority thing. A sort of kids' home with locks.'

'I know.' Liz dropped a wry little grimace. 'I'm in Social Services, remember? They're good places. Trained staff. In fact, I picked some of them myself.' She paused. 'Shall we get out of here? Just for a bit?'

Sally shook her head. The colour was starting to return to her face, the focus to her eyes.

'Not yet,' she said. 'Jonathan and I are being allowed a visit before she's taken away. Just a few minutes. They said any time now.'

'OK. Well, afterwards we should get Emma some clothes and stuff from your place,' Liz suggested. She looked levelly at Sally. 'Listen, I can do it, if you can't quite manage going back to the house yet.'

'No,' Sally countered with a new firmness. 'I want to get those things for Emma, and I also want to pick up my car. I'll need it.'

Liz looked at her doubtfully. She knew Kit had been using the VW while Sally had been away, right up to the night he was stabbed.

'You're sure?'

Sally nodded. WPC White appeared at the door and gestured for her to come back to see Emma.

'You'll come to the house with me?' Sally asked plaintively. 'You'll hold my hand?'

'Of course. How could I not?'

Liz took Sally's hand in hers and squeezed.

'Thanks.' Sally held on to Liz fiercely. 'I must go there, you see. I must feel the place. It will help me decide what to do next.

I know I'll still have a daughter when all this is over. It could help me know if I'll still have a husband as well.'

Sally released Liz's hand, shook herself like a small, sleek creature emerging from sleep, and followed WPC White back into the interior of the police station. This strange official labyrinth, which had been so intimidating at first, so frightening, was now becoming as familiar as the corridors of the BBC or even the rooms of her home.

The amazing adaptability of the human animal.

The infinite strength of the female protecting those she loves.

As she walked back into her office, Sergeant Lipari's heart was pounding, whether with shock or triumph it was hard to tell.

She called Vaughan in.

'Well, Emma spilled the beans,' she told him. 'He'd been abusing her for about a year. At least, someone called her "Bad Daddy" had.'

'She didn't mention Jackson's name.'

'She sort of can't. Blocked. I've talked about it with Dr Yardley. It's going to be a while before the poor kid can think straight again. If ever. He hopes they'll let him continue with their course of therapy.'

'Got to be Jackson, though, hasn't it? The only question left is, did she actually stab the bastard, or was someone else involved?'

'Yes.'

'Any clues?'

Sergeant Lipari shook her head. 'Emma's still got no memory of the actual stabbing,' she said. 'You should have seen her when she got in touch with her feelings, though. She had enough anger in there to turn fifteen stepfathers into salami!'

'But do you think she could be protecting someone? Her natural father? Zak? Whoever?'

'Whoever.' Sergeant Lipari paused. 'The evidence Emma just provided is probably enough to convict Jackson of abuse.'

'And also to convince a jury that she stabbed him?'

'Yes. Oh, I think so.'

'You're presuming Jackson survives.'

'It's something we have to accept as a possibility.' Sergeant Lipari sighed. 'Can you imagine, Derek? We've had to charge a thirteen-year-old girl. She'll be up before the magistrate in the morning. The law says we have to treat her like a *criminal*!'

Vaughan shrugged. 'Life is tough. I bet she doesn't do time, though.'

'Not if her brief has anything to do with it!'

Vaughan smiled. His confident smile. 'Right. Anyway, from our point of view what this means is we have a solid-gold result!' He looked at his watch. 'Just got to nip out and talk to someone. Then how about I buy you a spot of lunch to celebrate?'

'Terrific,' Sergeant Lipari said with a wry smile. 'Harvey's? The River Café?'

Vaughan was already on his feet. He laughed.

'See you in the Golden Lantern. Half-one. If you get there first, order plenty of prawn crackers.'

'We'll be able to visit you as often as we want to, they've told us,' Sally said.

She glanced at Jonathan. He was trying to smile. The pain on his face was unmistakable, unbearable.

Emma nodded slowly. She looked pale, exhausted, as if she had just gone through the crisis of a severe illness – which, perhaps, she had.

'All right, precious?' Jonathan said, moving a little closer.

Again Emma nodded mutely. Somehow it was almost more disconcerting than no reaction at all.

'And I'm going to get some clothes for you from home. Plus a few of your other things,' Sally added. 'I'll bring them tomorrow. All right?'

'All . . . right,' said Emma, so quietly it would have been easy to miss it.

Jonathan and Sally caught each other's eye. Then the three of them came together in a hug, and all of them were crying.

Twenty, thirty seconds later, the door opened. They separated. Emma sat down again quite abruptly. Sally turned and saw Cheryl Lipari standing just inside the room.

'I'm sorry, but I think our time has to be up,' said Sergeant Lipari. 'The doctor says Emma needs rest.'

'Don't worry, precious,' Jonathan said quickly. 'Mum and I will come and see you every day.' He paused. 'And I'll make sure you never see . . . *him* . . . again . . .'

His hate-filled reference to Kit stung Sally like a physical blow. She forced herself not to react.

'Be brave, Emma my darling,' she said with a smile.

Sergeant Lipari nodded to the WPC who had been supervising the visit. The younger woman led Emma out. Emma turned once, and Sally thought she smiled.

'So you've charged her with attempted murder, Sergeant?' Jonathan said harshly when his daughter had gone. 'I can't believe it!'

'As matters stand, I'm afraid we have no alternative.'

'For Christ's sake, she's a child. And the provocation—'

'I understand your feelings, Mr Quinn, but that will be for the court to decide.' Sergeant Lipari cut him off firmly. She turned to Sally Jackson. 'Can I get you anything from the machine? Tea? Coffee?'

Sergeant Lipari sensed the extremity of Sally Jackson's anguish, and recognised its quality as quite different to that of Jonathan's outrage. She knew instinctively that Sally's suffering had a great deal to do with Jonathan's reference to Emma's stepfather. This woman was being torn apart by incompatible feelings: anxiety for her daughter, yes, but also a lingering loyalty to the man she had loved and lived with for six years and whose child she was carrying. What would Sally Jackson do about *that*? Lipari wondered. After all, Emma was alive, and with therapy and love would, surely, somehow rebuild her life. Kit Jackson, on the other hand, was fighting for his own existence: even if he survived he would face a shaming trial; one that at the moment could have only one outcome.

Sally refused the offer of a hot drink. Pale with exhaustion after the agonies of the visit, she made her excuses. She had to go now. Her friend was waiting for her in reception. No, Sally told Jonathan, she would be fine. Just fine.

For her part, Sergeant Lipari left the room with an irrational but nagging sense of things being not quite right. She desperately needed to talk to someone she could trust, and Derek Vaughan would have to do.

They met on the third floor of the multi-storey car park. Vaughan, who had come on foot, appeared at the top of the pedestrian stairs and saw Mulligan leaning against the bonnet of his gleaming-red BMW at the far end of the level. When he saw Vaughan, the reporter waved but didn't move. The thirty yards or so the DC had to walk indicated a subtle shift in the power-relation between the two men. Vaughan realised this only too well, and was not indifferent to the thought.

Vaughan drew level with Mulligan's car. The reporter raised first his backside from the bonnet, then an eyebrow in inquiry.

'There you go,' said Vaughan, handing over the slip of paper.

'Thank you.' Mulligan passed him the promised envelope.

'This is the last time I access that computer for you,' Vaughan said.

Mulligan must have caught the tightness in his voice.

'You're pissed off, aren't you, Del?' he said, and smiled. 'You don't think I'm treating you with sufficient respect. Interesting feeling, right?'

'The commissioner's on the warpath over that bleeding photograph of Jackson and his daughter,' Vaughan said, ignoring Mulligan's needling. 'How did you get it?'

'Trade secret.'

'They think somebody from our nick supplied it. The commissioner's breathing down your editor's neck.'

'Well, don't you worry your pretty little head. My editor's neck is pure, breath-proof brass,' Mulligan assured Vaughan cheerfully. He looked at his watch. 'I'd buy you a drink, but I guess you'd rather not be seen with me around the traps at this delicate juncture. Right?'

'Right.'

'Pip-pip then, old boy,' Mulligan said in a passable Bertie Wooster accent. Then he switched to an American ghetto growl. '*Re-spect!*'

Vaughan turned and walked back to the pedestrian exit. Even after he had started down the stairs, he could still hear Mulligan's deep, rumbling laugh echoing through the concrete echo-chamber of the car park.

FOURTEEN

When they drove into the cul-de-sac where she, Kit and Emma had lived for so many years, Sally expected her heart to tighten, and it did, like a muscle that has been asked to do too much. But the overall feeling was a kind of fearful watchfulness. As they drew up outside the house and Liz hauled on the handbrake in that decisive way of hers and killed the engine, Sally felt like one of those people in besieged Sarajevo you saw on the news, trying to look normal as they walked the streets in permanent expectation of a sniper's bullet.

Of course, there were no snipers. There were not even any cameramen to shoot. A curtain twitched, though, across the street, at the house of Carolyn Bayliss, the shipping agent's wife with the screechy voice, who had always drunk too much and laughed too loudly at the Jackson family barbecues.

'Is this all too much?' Liz asked. 'I mean, coming straight from seeing Emma . . .'

'No. It's fine.' Sally took a deep breath.

Liz too had noticed the hints of prying life in the silent street. She patted her friend's shoulder.

'Courage, my dear.'

My daughter is still alive. My husband is still alive, Sally thought. *What have I to fear? Only the neighbours and the press. And they cannot really hurt me.*

They got out of the car, walked up the short path to the door. It was five days since Sally had left for Manchester. Already there were weeds in the front garden that hadn't been there before. The roses needed spraying for blackfly, she couldn't help thinking as she selected the front-door key from her bunch. She unlocked first the deadlock, then the Yale. Such efforts to stop the dangers from outside – when they were all within.

Then they were out of the morning sun and into the cool, wood-floored downstairs hall. The familiar pattern of the kelim running its length. Home. Facing Sally was the framed Matisse poster she and Kit had brought back from Paris two years ago. She caught sight of her own grey, puffy face in the mirror. The door to the living room stood half open. The deadlock clicked shut behind them. A satisfyingly heavy, secure sound.

It all looked so tidy, so normal. Sally half expected to look through to the conservatory and glimpse Emma finishing her homework. Or to hear Kit call down from his study, welcoming her home from this nightmare trip into another, grotesque reality.

For a while Sally stood rooted to the spot, unwilling to break the spell.

'The place is full of ghosts,' she murmured eventually, half to herself. 'Except everyone's still alive.'

'Take your time,' Liz said. 'Take this one very easy.'

'Yes.'

Sally took a step forward, then another.

'You want to go straight up to Emma's room, love?'

Sally nodded. *Want* was hardly the right word for her feelings, but it would do.

She slowly led the way up the stairs and along the landing.

Past Kit's study, made out of a tiny spare bedroom, to their right, and on to Emma's room right at the end.

Sally paused at the threshold.

There was all the familiar clutter, down to the unmade bed. One door of Emma's wardrobe was half open, revealing a couple of skirts hanging, a pair of jeans. There was a paperback book on the floor by the bed, upturned to keep Emma's place. On the shelves Kit had built, Emma's CD player and her little twelve-inch television. Plus her Walkman, with an untidy profusion of tapes piled around it.

'Some clothes. And the Walkman. I know her favourite tapes. They might help . . .'

It got comfortingly mechanical for a while after that. The two women busied around, packing clothes into a little grip-bag, sorting out what tapes to take. Sally picked up the paperback. A Judy Blume novel. She packed that too, first slipping a bookmark into the page Emma had reached before . . . well, *before*.

Ten minutes later, they were ready.

'OK?' said Liz. 'Shall we go?'

Sally hesitated. 'Can you wait a minute?' she said then. 'I . . . I want to have a little look around. On my own.'

'Right. I'll be downstairs, having a ciggy. Shout if it gets too much for you.' Liz gave Sally a little hug. 'It'll help you get strong, I think,' she murmured.

Sally watched Liz disappear down the stairs with the bag of supplies for Emma, then took a deep breath and walked right down the other end to her and Kit's room.

Someone had covered the bed with a blanket. Sally didn't know whether to be grateful for that or not. She had braced herself for the sight of blood on the mattress, for that was where

Kit had first been attacked. In the event, she couldn't bring herself to remove it. Otherwise there was no sense of horror. Only sadness, emptiness. A sense of a phase of life over. Was that a bad sign? Was that worse?

Sally was tempted to make for the stairs, for the safety of Liz's smile and a quick retreat to the outside world. Instead, she forced herself to retrace her steps and make her way to Kit's study. This was important work she needed to do now, she sensed. Grief work. She needed to get strong, Liz was right, and this was part of the process.

Kit's desk was tidy. Not surprising: he never left it a mess, either at home or at work. There was the photograph of himself, Sally and Emma, taken on holiday in St Lucia the previous year. Otherwise there was just his yellow legal-pad for notes, his electronic organiser, his desk-diary . . .

Sally shivered. She thought of the pornographic material the police had found in one of the desk's drawers. She went into what the frisson meant, tried to get a sense of wrongness, of evil, but instead of getting stronger the feeling faded. Again just sadness, hollowness. She took a step up to the desk, flipped open the desk-diary, looked up the pages covering the previous week.

There were only four entries. Three referred to things Sally already knew about.

The first, for Monday, read: '*Medical: a.m.*' The next, for Tuesday, read: '*Sal to Manchester: 10:30.*'

Then, under Friday: '*Sal returns from Manchester, p.m.!*'

The poignancy of the jolly little exclamation mark, the affectionate longing of those words, were almost too much for her.

The only other entry looked like a business thing. It was

under Wednesday and consisted of a hastily-scribbled note: *'N.Y. 1:00.'*

Maybe Kit had had to phone New York from home, late. He often took or made transatlantic or transpacific calls from home, to fit in with the time-zones. Kit the workhorse. At the company's disposal right round the clock.

Sally closed the diary. Then there was a bit of a blank, as if she went into a dream. The next thing, she was standing in the kitchen with Liz's arms around her.

Liz was saying over and over, 'Are you all right? Are you all right?'

Finally Sally managed a nod and started to come to.

'I . . . I still can't believe . . . that Kit . . .'

'Don't think about that now, Sal. This place got to you. It's inevitable. Quite understandable. It's going to take a while before you can handle this. Maybe a long while.'

'I don't feel . . . bad . . . The place, you see . . .' Sally groped for words, then gave up and just said in a small voice, 'Do you mind if I stay at your place for a while longer? I couldn't manage it full time here. Not yet.'

'No one would expect you to,' Liz said. 'There's a bed for you with us for as long as you please. A week, a month, a year . . .'

'Thanks.' Sally ran a hand through her hair, took a deep breath. 'Come on, let's get these things out of here. I'll take them over to Emma in the morning.'

The waiter had just brought the third plate of prawn crackers when Vaughan arrived at the restaurant. He ordered a drink on his way in.

'Thank God you're here to help me with these,' said Sergeant

Lipari when he arrived at the table. 'I have a feeling they're *very* fattening.' She pushed the plate in Vaughan's direction. 'Get stuck in!'

Vaughan seemed preoccupied. He didn't even touch the prawn crackers.

'What's up?' said Sergeant Lipari. 'Are you ill?'

'Nah.'

'Had an upset?'

'Honestly, I'm fine.'

Vaughan finally took a prawn cracker and chewed on it half-heartedly. A glass of lager was brought. He downed half of it in one gulp.

'OK,' Sergeant Lipari said, determined not to be deterred from what she needed to say. 'Derek, I hope you're sitting comfortably, because I want to suggest something pretty strange. And I want you to consider it very carefully.'

Vaughan drank some more lager and grinned lasciviously.

'If the suggestion involves us both taking off our clothes, doll, I'll tell you now, I'm in favour.'

Sergeant Lipari smiled. It was a pretty unconvincing stab at Vaughan's usual form, but a step in the right direction, a sign of normal life. Must be the lager.

'Be serious,' she continued, wagging a finger. 'Now, imagine I'm a very messed-up young girl. My parents are divorced, but I'm still close to my natural father and spend every other weekend with him.'

Vaughan groaned. 'Sweetheart, this is supposed to be a celebration. The case is *finito*! We have a result!'

'Yeah, well it's my party, Derek, so indulge me.'

Vaughan toyed with his second cracker, then popped it into his mouth like a protest.

152

'OK,' he said in a voice that expressed martyred patience. 'So you're Emma Quinn, in other words.'

Sergeant Lipari nodded.

'My natural father – Jonathan Quinn – cleverly poisons my mind against my mother's new husband.'

'Mr Christopher Jackson.'

'Right. So, gradually I get to think that everything Kit Jackson does is evil, and everything Jonathan does is good. Even – ' Sergeant Lipari's dark eyebrows were furrowed in deep concentration – 'even if it's Jonathan who is actually abusing me . . .'

'Which is why you go bananas in the middle of the night and stab your innocent stepfather? Give me a break, Cheryl.'

There was a pause while the waiter brought the food. Vaughan turned to the waiter, held up his now empty lager glass.

'And another Dortmunder, OK?'

'If you're feeling under pressure, that's not the way to handle it,' Sergeant Lipari said irritably.

'Feel like reporting me? Think I need *counselling*?'

'For God's sake, Del.'

The waiter went away. Sergeant Lipari took a mouthful of food, then picked up the thread of the case again.

'Weirder things have happened than what you suggested just now,' she said. 'Kids are put in extreme positions by these situations, their loyalties are tested. It might be impossible for Emma Quinn to admit to herself what her real father is doing, so she—'

'The stepfather had kiddyporn in his study! Including a picture of Emma!'

'Someone else could have planted it there. We've already

established that Jonathan Quinn could have stolen Emma's house-keys.'

Vaughan eyed Sergeant Lipari's chow mein with feigned concern.

'I'd ease up on the monosodium glutamate, Cheryl, I really would.'

'Listen, I'm just playing devil's advocate. Given the circumstances, I've still got to have Jackson ringed as the abuser, but I'm not prepared to discount the possibility that it was Emma's natural father, Quinn, who actually stabbed him.'

'Which is why she cracked up.'

'Yes. Just imagine you're thirteen, an abused kid, and then you witness that particular little scene! Wouldn't you just try to blot it out?'

'Yeah. Absolutely. But I repeat: we have a solid case here.'

Vaughan's second lager was set down beside his plate. He picked up the glass, took another big swallow. A flush was spreading beneath his skin, starting from the cheeks. Sergeant Lipari decided she couldn't be bothered to nag him. He didn't usually drink to excess at lunch. Maybe his wife was giving him a hard time. At this precise moment, she realised, she didn't actually care all that much.

'All the same,' Sergeant Lipari said, 'we've got to be careful with these loose ends. If Jackson survives, it'll be months before he's fit to stand trial. People change, and so do their stories. Memories get hazy. A clever defence lawyer will find the gaps in our case and exploit them. And he'll also do his best to tie Emma in knots – presuming she's capable of giving evidence. God knows, kids of her age can be pretty suggestible.'

For a moment Vaughan seemed far away. Then his rugged features creased in a smile.

'Forget it, Cheryl,' he said. 'As my old Irish granny used to say, Jackson's guilty as all hell and purgatory put together. He'll get bird. And I'd take bets he'll have a fatal accident within a twelvemonth. One thing about decent honest criminals, they really hate a nonce, and after his trial he'll be the most famous nonce in the country.'

The two cars approached the house in Wandsworth slowly and in convoy: first Liz's Renault, then the little VW Sally had brought back from Barnes. There was only one parking space directly outside the house. Liz parked thirty yards or so away, leaving the best spot for Sally.

Sally opened up the hatchback of her car to get out Emma's things. She turned, and saw a tall, smartly dressed black man standing on the pavement between her and the front gate of Liz's house, smiling at her. Liz was still occupied locking the Renault.

Sally did her best to look normal. 'Yes?' she said. 'Can I help you?'

'I hope you don't mind,' the man said in a pleasant, educated voice. 'My name's Paul Mulligan, Mrs Jackson. I know about what happened with Emma. I'm here to help you. Can we talk?'

What to say? He was polite, disarmingly well-spoken, and now she had recovered sufficiently to notice, behind those glasses he seemed to have kind eyes . . .

'Talk?' Sally stammered. 'I . . . I mean . . . what do you want to know?'

Mulligan moved closer.

'I want to hear *your* story,' he coaxed. 'And Emma's. I want to help you put the record straight. For a start, your husband—'

But now Liz was rushing towards them, her face set in a

mask of grim determination, an avenging angel in designer jeans and sweatshirt. She stomped up to Mulligan, pushing herself between him and Sally.

'How the hell did you find us?' she snapped. 'Which paper are you from?'

'Madam, I am an investigative reporter,' Mulligan said gravely, in a way that managed to combine dignity with obvious evasion. 'I'm writing a story about child-abuse. Just trying to get at the truth, that's all.'

Liz took the bag of Emma's belongings from Sally's unresisting grasp and started to push her friend towards the front gate.

'Bugger off!' she hissed at Mulligan.

'Listen, Mrs Jackson,' he persisted, hopping beside them. 'I'll protect you. You talk to me and we'll keep the rest of the press away. That's a promise. We'll make sure it's *your* story the public hears.'

'I said bugger off!'

Liz swung at Mulligan with the bag full of Emma's things. When he stepped back, she ducked through and closed the gate behind herself and Sally.

'We are now on private property,' Liz said firmly. 'And this woman is not talking to anyone.'

It was then that she saw Mulligan's photographer shooting from the other side of the street. Sally was standing against the front door, eyes wide, biting her lip, like a rabbit caught in headlights.

'And you thought you had enough problems,' Liz murmured. She set down the bag and slipped her front-door key in the lock. 'How wrong can a girl be?'

* * *

'Spot of this?' Liz asked, holding the unstoppered whisky decanter above Sally's ginger tea. 'Single malt and ginger. And it's afternoon. Nice and wicked.'

Sally shook her head. 'Tempting. But I need a clear head. Also . . .' She patted her stomach.

Liz poured herself a slug into her own mug of black coffee, took a sip and rolled her eyes.

'Wonderful.'

Sally looked at her levelly.

'Something happened between last night and this morning,' she said. 'Apart from realising I couldn't stay in the same room with Jonathan for more than half an hour at a time, I got in touch with a stubborn refusal to deny the man I've been in love with for the past six years. And whose baby I'm carrying.'

'For God's sake, Sal. He—'

'—abused Emma,' Sally finished for Liz. 'Supposedly. But did he?'

'Yes. I have to say I think so.'

'Everyone else thinks so too. But nothing I saw or felt at the house led me to that conclusion.'

'Darling, you can't be serious.'

Sally realised that all this was getting to Liz too. Her friend, the indestructible, was vulnerable after all. All the same, she took a deep breath and pressed on.

'Listen, even if I can't love Kit any more. Even if – do you understand this, Liz? – it turns out that I have to hate him for the rest of my life, I need to be clear about who Kit is and . . .'

'Yes?'

'. . . Well, to be sure whether he abused Emma – or not.'

Liz downed a large swig of fortified coffee.

157

'Just try to concentrate on Emma,' she said. 'She's the one who needs you.'

'Of course. I'll visit her every day. But . . . I must find out about Kit. If he had sad and terrible secrets I have to find out about them. For my sake and for Emma's.'

Liz shrugged impatiently, almost peevishly.

'So far as Kit's concerned, there's only one serious question you have to answer,' she said. She fixed Sally with a searching gaze. 'Be honest. Are you sure you want Kit's baby?'

There was a silence.

'I don't know,' Sally said then. 'Of course, the baby isn't responsible for any of what's happened . . .'

'Think of Emma. Could she live with Kit's child?'

Sally looked at her bleakly.

'I know I have to make a decision, but first I have to try to make sense of things. Don't you see?' For all her exhaustion, her bewilderment, her near-despair, Sally felt sure she was right, that at this moment she was stronger than Liz, more able to cope with this chaos. 'The world – our world – has gone mad. But I have to understand,' she said. 'I have to, or I'll go mad too.'

Liz shook her head.

'I'm sorry, Sal. I'll always be here for you, but I can only go so far with you along that road.'

'You've already come far enough. There's some things I have to do, some places I have to go, on my own.'

Constable Harris saw someone looking in through the ward doors. Hard to tell if it was a man or a woman. The corridor lights had been lowered after the night-shift came on.

When the doors swung open and the slight blonde edged in,

Harris instinctively got to his feet and straightened his tie. She was in her late thirties, fifteen years or so older than him, attractive, wearing a summer frock and carrying a shoulder-bag. He could see she was tense and he could tell she was lonely.

'Hello,' she said. 'I've come to see Mr Jackson.'

'I'm sorry,' Harris said, 'only authorised persons.'

'I'm Kit Jackson's wife. I'm entitled to see him, aren't I?'

Harris hesitated. Along with the tension and the loneliness he could also sense a high-strung determination in this woman.

'Do you . . . I mean, I have to ask you this . . .' he said, 'but do you have any proof of identity, madam?'

Sally reached into her bag, still keeping her gaze fixed on the young policeman, and fished out her wallet. She took her eyes off him only to find her driver's licence.

He examined it, nodded. 'OK.' But he didn't move aside.

Sally could see him wondering if he should look through the rest of her bag's contents. Solemnly she offered it to him. He took it, blushing slightly, and quickly checked the contents, presumably searching for weapons. Only then did he let her through the door into the side ward where Kit lay.

There were machines and tubes everywhere. The only one whose function Sally recognised was the plasma drip attached to his right hand. Kit was propped up on the bed, oddly still and peaceful, as if he had been trapped here by this web of equipment and at some point had simply given up, dropped into the sleep-state the occasion demanded. His chest and arms were all bandages. His face was pale. All the same, it seemed as if he might open his eyes any moment, smile and say something.

Sally took a step forward.

'Hello, Kit,' she said. 'Hello, darling.' She felt a prickling in the back of her neck, turned instinctively and saw the young policeman looking in at her. He had been joined by a nice-looking young nurse. Their gaze was both curious and conspiratorial, like children looking at adults through a keyhole. The faces disappeared when they realised Sally had noticed them.

When she looked back at Kit, her vision of him had changed. Now he seemed like a sleeping baby, infinitely innocent and vulnerable. She wanted to hold him. Instead she leaned forward, stroked his forehead. It was damp but cool. She kissed the spot she had touched.

Then, on impulse, Sally stepped very close to Kit and took his hand, the one where they had inserted the big, bruising plasma drip. Careful not to dislodge the needle from its place in the fat vein of his forehand, she held the tips of his unresisting fingers against her stomach.

'Kit, I never got a chance to tell you that I was pregnant,' she said softly. 'I thought a few days here or there didn't matter, do you understand that? But would it have made things different somehow if I'd told you? They say the beating of a butterfly's wings in Borneo can unleash a storm in America. Does that work in reverse? Can changing a detail mysteriously prevent disaster too?'

Sally stood there by the bed for some time, apparently talking to herself, sharing her feelings with Kit and the baby. Finally, when she had said everything she could dare or bear to say, she sat down on the ugly red plastic chair by the bed.

She looked at her unconscious, wounded husband, the man everyone had picked for a monster. And she thought, and she prayed, and she waited.

FIFTEEN

Despite everything, Sally and Jonathan had agreed that for Emma's sake they would present a united front. They met outside the secure accommodation building, which was just off Roehampton Lane. The atmosphere between them was guarded and cool, but somehow made intimate by their duty to Emma.

Apart from the high walls outside and the locked doors and windows, the place looked like a modern, slightly spartan boarding-house. They saw very little of the secure accommodation itself. After a brief interview with the house father, they were shown into a comfortable, though recognisably institutional lounge room, where Emma and a care assistant were waiting for them.

There were the same big hugs as there had been the day she was charged. Emma seemed a little healthier in colour. Apparently she had managed to eat something. When the clothes, the Walkman, and the tapes Sally had brought from Barnes were handed over to the care assistant for checking, Emma smiled.

Then they sat together on a seventies-style multi-unit sofa.

Emma spoke haltingly but with more assurance than she had shown before, although there was still a disconcertingly regressed aspect to her presence. She told them the place wasn't bad. The staff were kind. She hadn't seen much of the other kids. She wished . . . she wished she could come home . . .

'Darling,' Sally said quickly, 'we believe in you, Dad and I. Really. You'll be out of here once this is sorted out, I know it.'

She regretted her words immediately. They might be true, and they might not. Which made them empty. Before she could qualify the statement, Emma suddenly fixed her with a grave, intense gaze.

'Where are you going to live now, Mum?' she said suddenly. 'Will you go back to living with Dad now?'

Sally was dumbstruck. As she struggled, Jonathan cut in on her behalf.

'Your Mum's staying with Liz and Harry,' he explained. 'Remember Liz and Harry?'

'And your friend Zak?' Sally added quickly, watching closely for Emma's reaction.

Emma looked first at Jonathan and then at Sally. She nodded. 'You'll be safe there,' she said.

Sally let out a forced little laugh that she hated herself for.

'Of course I will.' She took Emma's hand in hers. 'I promise you won't ever have to go back to the old house, darling. The one in Barnes, I mean.'

Emma said nothing for a while. Then she frowned.

'It's funny,' she whispered. 'I don't remember the room where it kept happening. Just the voice and the way he touched me . . .' She looked away. 'But I know it was him.'

Jonathan moved in, took her other hand. 'It's all right, darling.'

Emma looked at him and gave a pained little smile. 'You're a good Daddy, aren't you?'

There were tears in Jonathan's eyes as he smiled back at her.

'Yes,' he said softly. 'Of course I am, my precious. Of course.'

After the heavy outer doors of the building closed behind them, Jonathan and Sally stood together in the car park for some moments, unable to speak. Then Sally turned hesitantly to Jonathan, who was lighting a cigarette.

'Isn't it strange?' she said. 'When Emma thinks of the abuse, she doesn't actually see Kit.'

Jonathan tossed away the spent match, blew a dismissive puff of smoke.

'That's not exactly what she said, Sal,' he countered. He shrugged his slightly stooping shoulders. 'Anyway, she's still suppressing a hell of a lot. Unsurprisingly. She'll need years of therapeutic help to get over this. Maybe they'll let Yardley see her on a regular basis. She trusts him.'

Sally nodded. 'But . . . you'd think . . . I mean . . . Look, I'm sure there's more to this than the police will admit,' she said in a rush. 'I'm not really happy with the way they're handling the case. I'm going to Kit's office this afternoon and—'

Jonathan turned on her. He loomed like a tall, angry crow.

'Sure!' he snapped. 'And everyone there will tell you what a great guy he is!' He tossed away his half-smoked cigarette and stamped on it. 'For God's sake, woman, will you stop protecting him? Admit it: you married an animal. If you start pretending that bastard didn't abuse my Emma, I'll swing for you!'

'Jonathan. Please . . .'

'I mean it! And if he gets off, I'll bloody well swing for him!'

Jonathan grabbed Sally's shoulders and squeezed, his strong, long fingers just inches from her neck. There was murder in his eyes. Sally had seen him angry before, many times, but this was a new level. At a moment like this, her ex-husband could kill.

And what else could he do? What else that he might regret later, try to cover up at all costs?

'That hurts!' Sally panted. 'And it won't stop me. Listen, Jonathan, I'm beginning to think you protest too much!'

How she found the strength to say that, she would never know. The eyes continued to bore into hers for a few moments more, the fingers to press.

'You . . . you can't be suggesting . . . Jesus, you bitch!' Jonathan murmured.

'Why not? You're always so bloody over the top! You're always too much!'

Jonathan dropped his arms to his sides. He stood staring at Sally with frightening intensity, his mouth working as if struggling to find words.

'You're mad,' he said, spitting the words out like bad food. 'I . . . I never want to speak to you again. If you have something to communicate to me about Emma, ring my solicitor.'

Jonathan turned on his heel and strode off towards his car without another backward glance.

Sally watched Jonathan drive away. As his battered Ford disappeared around the bend in the road, an elderly lady came up to her and asked her if she was all right. She realised now that she was trembling.

'I'm OK, thanks,' she mumbled. 'I had a little accident, but I'm fine.'

And in a funny way, this was true. Sally knew she was alone now, Kit's only ally, and it was oddly liberating as well as frightening. At that moment, with the old lady still eyeing her with kindly concern, it became clear to her what she had to do.

Sally drove back to Liz's house slowly, gathering strength, regaining her nerve. For the first time, she saw her ex-husband not just as an embarrassment, an irritation, but as one of the enemy, perhaps even – the thought had seared her mind like lightning during the row with Jonathan – *the* enemy.

It was three o'clock that same afternoon when a very different-looking Sally parked her VW Golf in the visitors' section outside the offices of Quantum Software. She stood for a moment, listening to the roar of the M4 half a mile away. Then she smoothed down the impeccably tailored jacket of her Nicole Farhi suit, picked up her leather Fendi shoulder-bag, and headed for the main door of the building.

The reception area was all marble and exotic greenery, with a specially commissioned glass sculpture of a microchip poised on a plinth in the middle of the room. That had been Kit's idea, two years ago. Jill, the receptionist, stopped talking on the phone as Sally approached. She quickly got to her feet, failing to hide her astonishment beneath a faint smile of concern.

'Mrs Jackson,' Jill said. 'Hello. Well . . . I mean . . . how are you?'

'Holding up,' Sally said. 'I have an appointment with Fred in five minutes.'

'Right . . . how's . . . ?' Jill blushed.

'Kit?' Sally filled in for her. 'He's unconscious but stands a good chance of survival. My daughter is recovering from shock.' Sally nodded in the direction of the leather sofa in the corner of reception. 'I'll wait. Don't worry about me.'

Just at that moment, one of the phones on her desk rang. With evident relief, Jill plunged back into her work.

Among the computer magazines on the circular glass table Sally found a copy of *Country Living*. She flicked through the photographs of charming cottages and happy, creative couples, unable to read, almost unable to focus, concentrating solely on looking normal, 'handling it'. She had no idea how much time had passed before she heard a familiar, subtly foreign-accented voice.

'Sally?'

She looked up. Fred Hanek was standing over her, hands behind his back, rocking on his heels in that deceptively coy way of his. The founder and chairman of Quantum Software – Kit's immediate boss – was balding and tubby. He compensated for the first by having his hair cropped very short, and for the latter by always wearing tailor-made Savile Row suits, cunningly cut to disguise his pear-shaped figure. Neither the haircut nor the suits were, however, what Sally or anyone else first noted about Fred Hanek. What grabbed everyone at first sight were his sable-brown eyes, full of cleverness. His expression revealed a rigorous intelligence that had made him top of his year at the Charles University, Prague, in computer science, set for a brilliant career in his native Czechoslovakia. But the year in question had been 1968. He had fled that autumn after the Russian invasion, and his brilliance had since made him a rich man in England, his adored and adopted country.

Sally rose and put out her hand. Hanek shook his head, smiled and drew her into his arms for a hug.

'How is Kit?' he said finally.

'Alive,' Sally answered simply.

'And Emma?'

'Recovering.'

Hanek looked around, saw Jill watching them from her perch at reception. A junior managerial type Sally vaguely recognised had come into the lobby and was also casting curious glances in their direction. He looked away when Hanek met his eye, pretended to study a file he was carrying.

'Come on, Sally,' Hanek said softly. 'Let's go to my office. We can talk there privately, as friends, all right?'

To get to Hanek's office they had to pass through the open-plan work-space where Quantum's seventy or so employees sat at their desks and screens. Everyone tried not to stare. One or two even succeeded.

The last time Sally had been here was at Christmas, for the company party. Then the whole floor had been festooned with tinsel and bunting. Ever-changing computer-generated images had been projected on to the ceiling for the disco. Now that she was a teenager, Emma had also been invited for the first time. Sally's fondest memory of the party was of her stick-thin daughter on the disco floor with plump, ungainly Hanek. His idea of dancing remained the one current in Prague student dives, circa 1967 – a cross between the Watutsi and pioneer-camp callisthenics that threatened the life and safety of any other dancer within five feet.

Hanek led the way. His office, with Kit's slightly smaller one next door, was glass-walled, giving a view of each other and of the work floor. Sally knew the room was actually soundproofed – the glass was thicker than it looked – but all the same she felt terribly exposed, even when the door closed behind them. Hanek, in his usual understanding way, sat her down on a sofa in the far corner, as far from the outside world as possible, and took a seat opposite her.

'Coffee, Sally?' he said.

She shook her head.

'Perhaps it is not such a good idea that we came here. Our wonderful, modern, open-plan office . . .' Hanek shrugged.

'It's OK, really,' Sally insisted.

Leslie Ford

Just then the intercom buzzer sounded. Hanek frowned, pushed the button.

'I told you I was not to be disturbed,' he growled.

Then Sally saw a look of embarrassment and indecision cross Hanek's face. He picked up the phone and put his hand over the mouthpiece.

'Please?' he murmured to Sally. 'It is a big American client. Kit had been dealing with him. You understand, the deal must be clinched . . .'

'Yes. Of course. Kit would expect you to press on.'

'Thank you. Two minutes, maybe three only. I promise.'

While Hanek spoke to the American client, Sally stood up and wandered around. She tried not to stare next door, but it couldn't be helped. Her eyes kept being drawn back to Kit's office on the other side of the glass. She knew the office was exactly as he had left it the previous week, before the stabbing, with its desk, phones, computer work-station. Even the family photograph . . .

Suddenly, looking at the computer screen in Kit's office, Sally remembered the computer-generated pornography the police had found in Kit's study. She had never seen the images, but she could imagine only too well. At that moment, the single, unblinking eye of that screen became obscene, voyeuristic, evil.

Hanek had finished his phone call.

'Sally?'

She did not turn round. 'Yes . . .'

Hanek padded across to her.

'You are OK?'

Sally realised she was all but pressed up against the glass screen separating the two offices. Hanek gently took her by the

168

arm and steered her back to the sofa. They sat down again.

'I think the deal is solid, by the way,' Hanek said. 'I have said Kit is in hospital. I was not specific about other matters.'

Sally nodded. 'Life goes on. You have a living to make.'

'Bad publicity is not the only thing on my mind,' Hanek said. 'However, I would be dishonest if I did not admit that it is, shall I say, *one* of the things.'

He shrugged in his dignified Central European way.

Hanek's words were genuinely caring and considerate, but it was not in his nature to hide anything from Sally. She really couldn't blame him. She hadn't come here to be cosseted from reality.

'Kit would have done the same.'

'Yes. And now I assure you there will be no more interruptions.'

'Thanks,' she said, then took a deep breath. 'You must be wondering why on earth I would want to come here.'

'My dear Sally, when you requested a meeting I did not feel it my place to ask your motives. However, I presume your coming here has to do with Kit.'

'Yes,' Sally said. 'You see, everyone's assuming that my husband did something terrible and that he deserved what happened to him. Everyone, that is, but me.'

Hanek looked at her steadily, like an intelligent, cynical Buddha.

'I have seen many bad things in my life,' he said eventually. 'Living in the communist bloc during the fifties and sixties, I am no innocent when it comes to knowing what my fellow human beings are capable of. However, of Kit I would never have thought such a thing as is being suggested. Never in one million years. I would have trusted him with my life, and those of my own children. You cannot reproach yourself that you did the same.'

'You're being very sweet, Fred,' Sally said, 'but I didn't come here fishing for a character testimonial. I'm just trying to understand what happened. And to do that I need to ask you a few questions.'

'Please. Fire away.'

'Right. Now . . . as you know, I was away on business when it happened, but did Kit seem at all strange to you in the way he behaved in the last day or two before the stabbing? Did he seem worried, for instance?'

Hanek frowned. 'Last day or two? Well, that I cannot say. He was, of course, absent from work.'

'Absent?'

Hanek registered Sally's look of shocked disbelief and shrugged.

'You did not know this? Kit called in sick two days before. Said he had flu.'

'This . . . this was on the Tuesday?'

'Correct.'

Sally briefly experienced a kind of vertiginous terror. *She didn't want to know any more secrets about Kit.* A moment later, her mind began to swirl with possibilities.

'I left for Manchester that same morning,' she said, the words tumbling out. Hanek's calm gaze encouraged her to confess. 'Kit drove off to work as usual, planning to drop Emma at school on the way. He was driving my car because his company one was in for repair; a bit later a cab came to take me to Euston . . . What time did he actually call in sick?'

'Quite early, I think. I was enjoying my first cup of coffee of the morning, I saw he was not in his office, and Jill downstairs told me he was not coming in that day. Must have been about ten.'

'He *could* have returned home later the same morning, then. But why?'

'Perhaps he felt ill while on his way to work?' Hanek suggested.

'We spoke on the phone that evening, after I had arrived in Manchester. He didn't mention it.' Sally looked pleadingly at Hanek. 'You had no idea anything might be amiss?'

Hanek hesitated, uncertain how far to go in expressing an opinion.

'Maybe . . . yes, maybe Kit seemed a little preoccupied the last week or two,' he conceded reluctantly.

'Yes,' Sally said. 'You see, I suspected something had come up as a result of that insurance check-up. You know, for the new company health plan.'

Now it was Hanek's turn to look perturbed. 'I'm sorry?'

'You must remember,' Sally pressed him. 'Ten days or so ago. We all went to Dr Macintyre's in Richmond for a thorough check-up. It was to do with Quantum upgrading all its employees' health cover.'

Hanek threw up his plump, expressive hands in exasperation.

'It is my turn to learn something,' he said. 'I am completely ignorant of any such upgrading. And I would certainly have known, because this is my company. I own it.'

'Kit said—'

'Perhaps, Sally. But this is the first I hear about it. Maybe Kit wanted increased cover personally. Maybe you misunderstood what he told you.'

'No,' Sally replied fiercely, surprising herself with how definite she felt and how firm she sounded. 'I'm a producer. My life is detail, getting things right. I know I didn't make a mistake.'

Hanek said nothing, just waited politely for her to continue. Now Sally was sure there were only two alternatives: either she was falling apart, or Kit really had lied to her about the check-up.

But why? Sally's heart began to pound. This was one of the keys to the mystery, she thought. The first and perhaps the most important.

SIXTEEN

'The thing is, Doctor,' Sergeant Lipari said, 'Emma wouldn't tell us what *actually* happened. She keeps repeating the *fact* of the abuse – she's absolutely clear about that – but when it comes down to concrete details . . .'

At the other end of the telephone line, Noel Yardley's voice was calm and patient but with a hint of professional command.

'It may take time before she opens up fully,' he explained. 'In an ideal world, we shouldn't be pushing her for that sort of information at this stage.'

'Yes, I understand that. The puzzling thing is, from what her mother said, Emma seemed genuinely fond of Jackson. Even now, she's been heard to ask if he's going to get better.'

'Clearly her feelings are ambivalent,' Yardley said. 'Hence, perhaps, her distinction between the "good" and "bad" daddy. They may be the same person. This kind of thing is quite common in domestic abuse cases. And, given the power of parental archetypes – 'scuse my jargon – perfectly understandable.'

There was a knock on the door. Vaughan stuck his head in. Sergeant Lipari mimed shooing him away. He mimed looking crestfallen and disappeared again.

'Perhaps we'll get to hear Jackson's side of things,' she continued. 'If he survives.'

'Yes, what's the situation there?'

'Still unconscious but his chances of pulling through are getting stronger by the day.'

'That would be helpful. You could come at the problem from another direction.'

Sergeant Lipari enjoyed the sound of Yardley's cultured, imperturbable voice. It reminded her of the nice priest she had confessed to as a little girl. Except the priest had been old and fat, not thirty-something and good-looking. Unprofessional thoughts.

'Tell me, Doctor,' she said, 'when did you last see Mr Jackson?'

'A couple of months ago. He and his wife came to see me to discuss Emma's progress.'

'And?'

'At that time Emma seemed to be doing well.'

'I mean, how were *they*? In terms of their relationship.'

'They seemed, to an outside observer – even a trained eye, you might say – like a happy, well-adjusted couple.'

'That seems to have been the general impression. Different story now,' Sergeant Lipari added wryly. 'Though Mrs Jackson is holding up fairly well. She's stronger than she looks, I think.'

'Perhaps. She could also be in a state of profound denial,' Yardley said. 'To be honest, I've sort of been hoping she'll feel able to talk to me at some point. I believe I could help her deal with this stuff, or at least face the facts.'

'Can't you contact Mrs Jackson and suggest it?'

'Not really. Etiquette. Anyway, nothing worse than an interfering shrink.'

'I suppose you're right.' Sergeant Lipari suddenly had an inspiration. 'Tell you what,' she said, 'maybe I'll suggest it to her when the opportunity arises.'

'That might well be the solution, yes.'

It occurred to Sergeant Lipari that Yardley had been hoping all along that she would suggest what she had just suggested. She had experienced the same feeling about her decision to let him handle the interview with Emma. He was one hell of an operator when it came to people, that was for sure.

'Meanwhile, is it OK if I ring you at odd times for professional advice?' she said. 'All the psychology at this police station is strictly amateur, I'm afraid.'

'Of course, Sergeant,' Yardley said with a laugh. Was there a hint of flirtation there? 'Any time. To you, twenty-four-hour service.'

In the visitors' car park at Quantum Software, Sally punched out a number on her car phone.

'Hello. The Macintyre Practice,' said a well-spoken voice a few moments later.

'I'm a patient of Dr Macintyre,' Sally said. 'I need to speak to him, please. It's extremely urgent,' she added in her most polite-but-insistent manner.

'I'll see if Dr Macintyre is available. Who shall I say is waiting?'

'Sally Jackson. Kit Jackson's wife.'

The phone played back some Vivaldi while Sally held on, sweating in the heat of the car. The weather had turned warm and muggy. The music went on a little too long. When the receptionist finally got back to Sally, her voice was subtly guarded.

'Dr Macintyre is busy with a patient at the moment. Perhaps he can ring you back?'

'I absolutely must speak to him,' Sally said. '*Now.*'

'Mrs Jackson, I can only suggest that he rings you back. He is in the middle of a procedure.'

'Is that so?' Sally was surprised at the icy determination that suddenly crept into her own manner. 'Well, listen, I'm not getting off this phone until Jock Macintyre has agreed to see me. This afternoon. Would you tell him that? It's about my husband, Kit, and it is literally a matter of life and death.'

There was a silence. Then the receptionist asked her to hold again. More Vivaldi, flowing on and on, matchlessly beautiful and, in Sally's mood, madness-inducing.

'Hello? Mrs Jackson?'

'Speaking. Don't worry. I'm not going anywhere yet.'

The receptionist swallowed audibly and took a deep breath.

'I'm awfully sorry,' she said, 'but Dr Macintyre has a very important meeting immediately after surgery. He'll ring you at home as soon as he's free—'

Sally slammed the phone back in its cradle, turned the ignition key. The Golf's engine roared into life. She shot out of the car park, heading for the motorway.

Dr Macintyre's private-patients-only surgery was in an elegant, leafy little sidestreet just back from Richmond Park. It was about half-past five when Sally parked her car across the road from the Grade Two listed building. She strode purposefully up to the blue Georgian door, pushed the little bell next to the discreet sign that said, PATIENTS PLEASE RING. The buzzer sounded immediately, and the door gave.

First hurdle crossed.

Sally walked into the pastel-schemed waiting room. She ignored the two well-dressed patients there and locked gazes with the receptionist. The woman, forewarned by Sally's body-language, half rose, looking alarmed.

'I'm Mrs Jackson,' Sally said. 'We spoke earlier. I demand to see Dr Macintyre.'

The woman drew herself up to her full height. She was fortyish, tall, slightly horsy-looking, with a Sloaney accent. *The merchant-banker's-discarded-first-wife type*, Sally classified her with a ruthlessness born of desperate determination. *No sweat.*

'I'm sorry,' the receptionist said, slightly shrilly. 'He is with a patient. These are his consulting hours, and unless you have an appointment . . .'

Second hurdle . . . to be leapt.

Sally turned and marched towards the door to the right of the receptionist's desk marked 'Dr J.M. Macintyre'.

She heard a voice wail, 'But Mrs Jackson!' Then she opened the door and walked in.

Jock Macintyre, a stocky, square-faced man who brushed his thick hair back in silver wings, was talking to an elegant middle-aged woman patient. For a moment neither of them acknowledged Sally's presence. Then, quite suddenly, they both turned. The woman's face expressed irritation, Macintyre's surprise – rapidly superseded by horror. Under other circumstances the scene might have been comic.

'Sorry to burst in on you, Dr Macintyre,' Sally said, 'but I need a word.'

Macintyre nervously straightened the burgundy and lemon Hermes silk tie that so perfectly offset the seriousness of his chalk-stripe suit.

'Mrs Jackson. Really . . . I was going to ring you . . .'

He was looking past Sally. She realised that the tall receptionist must be hovering in the doorway behind her. Well, if that woman tried anything, Sally could manage a vicious backwards kick . . .

'Ah, Henrietta. Would you please get Mrs Jackson a cup of tea?' Macintyre said almost plaintively. 'I'll see you immediately after Mrs Galway-Jones. If you'd just—'

'I don't want any tea,' Sally cut in. 'And I'm not moving from here. Perhaps this lady would like to wait instead?'

Macintyre came to a decision. With a helpless little I-must-humour-this-lunatic gesture he turned to the woman and said, 'Mrs Galway-Jones? This is unusual, but . . . I think my other patient here has a pressing problem . . .'

The woman rose slowly, in cold silence, staring at Sally, then swept out.

'It's all right, Henrietta,' Macintyre said, still looking behind Sally. 'Mrs Jackson and I won't be long. Perhaps you could offer Mrs Galway-Jones some coffee?'

The door closed behind Sally and she relaxed fractionally.

Macintyre managed a vague wave of the hand.

'Sit down. Please.'

'I'm OK the way I am,' Sally said. 'I've got two questions for you. The supposed health-plan check-up. What was that really about? And what did you have to say to Kit the other morning that was for his ears only?'

Macintyre got up and walked to the window, stared out as if hoping for inspiration – or perhaps for a helicopter to airlift him out of the room. Then his shoulders slumped and he turned.

'I was helping Kit out, that's all,' he said in a quiet, defeated voice. 'He said he wanted you all checked out quietly. And he was especially concerned about Emma. Wasn't sure the therapist she was seeing had got to the root of her problems. Thought it might be something physical . . .'

'There was no upgrading of the healthcare scheme!'

'No.'

'So what was it about?'

'Oh, the examinations were perfectly genuine.' Macintyre coughed in embarrassment. 'It's just that Kit didn't want either you or Emma to suspect the real reason behind it.'

'Which was what?'

Macintyre coloured visibly. 'Kit . . . I mean, you must understand, I knew him as a man of absolute integrity, one who completely adored both you and Emma, Mrs Jackson . . . Kit . . .'

'Yes?'

'He asked me to check for any signs that Emma was . . . shall we say, sexually active.'

The Kit Sally was hearing described to her seemed like another person altogether from the husband she loved and trusted. Or was it always like this? She remembered the argument on the night Kit had announced the medical examination; her own taunt about 'macho' attitudes. Men were different. *Even*, as Liz had said once, *the ones women like us marry*.

'I can't believe this,' she said. 'A virginity check?'

'Oh no. Nothing so old-fashioned. But he said he was worried she'd been fooling around with boys at a dangerously young age, and you wouldn't talk about it, so . . . Well, I asked her if she had started menstruating – as you probably know, she is. I . . . er, also did a bit of discreet cross-questioning. You know, one can usually tell with young girls . . .'

'Did you do a physical examination?'

'Enough to establish that she was not using contraceptives.'

'And that she's not technically a virgin.'

'Insofar as this is possible or relevant, yes. The breaking of the hymen can occur as a result of many kinds of non-sexual activity.'

'Absolutely! What you did to Emma counts as assault!' Sally snapped. She knew everyone out in the waiting room would be listening, and she just didn't care. 'And it was pointless, anyway! Jesus! What a filthy, stupid little male conspiracy!'

'Mrs Jackson, really—'

'You lied to me the morning I left for Manchester, you bastard,' Sally said coldly. 'If you had told me the truth then, things might have turned out differently. Christ Almighty, I could have you drummed out of the medical profession! Now, tell me a good reason why I bloody well shouldn't!'

'Please. It was a favour, Sally. Kit was really upset, really concerned about Emma. I felt sorry for the guy.'

Macintyre's Glaswegian accent was coming through more strongly as he lost his private-doctor cool.

'Plus you got a fat fee,' Sally said. 'Well, what I really want to know is, did you tell Kit what you just told me? That Emma was no longer a virgin, I mean.'

Macintyre nodded slowly.

'I also told him that this didn't necessarily prove anything. We spoke later that same day. After I had phoned and got you. He had sworn me to secrecy, Sally, don't you understand? He didn't want to worry you. That was typical of him. He said he thought somebody . . . of course, he wouldn't say who . . .'

As Sally walked out through the smart Georgian door, she was flushed with a kind of sour triumph, but her anger against

Macintyre and Kit was already fading. In its place was a kind of puzzled wonder.

If Kit had been abusing Emma, why would he go to such elaborate, even bizarre, lengths to arrange an examination?

For God's sake, why pay to provide proof of the very thing he should have been trying to hide?

Even shortly after midnight, the atmosphere in the hospital ward was still oppressively warm and muggy.

On the corridor the lights had been dimmed, and someone had propped open the double-doors leading out into the courtyard. A cooling breeze wafted into the building, eddied past the sister's office and the sluice room, infiltrated even into the side ward where Kit Jackson lay unconscious.

After four hours on duty, Staff Nurse Yvonne Grainger was dying for that paradoxical pleasure: a cigarette in the fresh air. But first there were some routine tasks to perform. She emerged from the office, covered the short distance to the side ward. No sign of the friendly young policeman who was supposed to be on watch there. She went into the room. Everything seemed fine. Mr Jackson looked so peaceful. He looked so nice. It was impossible when you looked at him like this to believe the things the papers said about him.

Staff Nurse Grainger checked the patient's drip, his pulse, his temperature. She would get one of the auxiliaries to help turn him later, to prevent bed sores.

But first . . .

After one final, gentle primp of the pillows, Staff Nurse Grainger left the side ward and looked out through the open doors into the courtyard.

As she had suspected, Constable Harris was out there,

having a quiet smoke in the shadows. He could see her framed in the softly lit doorway. Aware of this, she patted her hair and smiled. He moved a little into the light and waved. He wore a cheeky, sod-the-regulations grin. Irresistible. Especially since Harris was young and really quite good-looking. He had slightly protruding, pixie-like ears, but the rise of Tony Blair had made even those sort of fashionable.

Staff Nurse Grainger looked around, saw no one, and decided to take a chance. Ciggies could be quickly discarded, in any case, if they spotted anyone approaching.

Harris produced a cigarette and a light for her without a word being said. She giggled. He giggled. A conspiracy was re-established in the sultry darkness.

Within moments Harris was asking Staff Nurse Grainger if she fancied a drink on her night off. She found herself saying yes, that would be very nice, and by the way her name was Jackie. *Mine's Kevin*, he said with a grin. *As in Costner.* They looked up at the sky, trying vainly to spot stars, and they looked at each other.

Behind their backs, the corridor lights glowed softly. The building was defenceless. They paid it no attention.

SEVENTEEN

Sergeant Lipari was tired and slightly hungover after a colleague's hen-party the night before. Lots of booze, male strippers, shamelessly enjoyable all-girl hilarity. Home at two in the morning, up at seven.

And then, within moments of getting to work, the news that someone may have tried to kill Kit Jackson.

'The hospital trust is setting up the usual internal inquiry,' she told Garfield later that morning. 'On the face of it, no one can tell whether the drip was removed by accident or malice.'

'One of your boys was supposed to be there,' Garfield said, giving Sergeant Lipari one of his weaselly looks. 'Right in front of the door. Have you spoken to him?'

'Kevin Harris.' Sergeant Lipari shrugged. 'He claims he heard something outside and went to investigate. Left the side ward door unguarded for about five minutes.'

'You think Harris is telling the truth?'

'I'm unpersuaded. I suspect he was out there for ten, having a crafty smoke with the nurse on duty.'

'If someone did get in there and have a go at Jackson, Harris is in serious trouble.'

'Apparently, the nurse had been in Jackson's side ward just a few minutes before,' Sergeant Lipari said. 'Checking up on him. She said she looked in every hour or so. Anyway, she also noticed that Harris wasn't at his post outside, so she went into the courtyard and found him there.'

'Where they exchanged Silk Cuts and passed the time.'

'As I suspect, yes.'

'So there was an opportunity for someone to have interfered with Jackson's drip, Cheryl, right?'

Sergeant Lipari nodded slowly.

'And if the nurse hadn't remembered leaving her bleeper in the side ward, and if she hadn't gone back for it and noticed the plasma drip had become disconnected, Kit Jackson would be a dead man.'

'My heart bleeds.'

There was a silence. Then Sergeant Lipari cleared her throat.

'I wish someone had seen fit to ring me at home about this, sir. Last night, I mean.'

'Come on, Cheryl. You were strutting your stuff at Julia Verney's hen-night. What would have been the point?'

'They could have left a message on my machine, sir.'

'Sure. Cheryl, the fact is that the amount of alcohol you consumed last night is written all over your gaunt, drawn face. Like every other female from this station who went out on the razzle last night, you are this morning one of the walking dead. God knows what state you were in when you got home.'

Sergeant Lipari bit back the rejoinder that rose to her lips. Something along the lines of: No matter how pissed you were, sir, or what time of night it was, you'd always expect to be kept up to date on a development like this – the prime suspect on your case being on the receiving end of a possible murder attempt is, after all, no trivial little detail that can wait for tomorrow.

'Well, if someone did try to finish off Jackson, I want to find out who,' Sergeant Lipari said.

Garfield looked none too enthusiastic.

'Let's see what the hospital inquiry establishes, shall we? I'll give Harris a personal bollocking, anyway. To encourage the others, as they say.'

'Sir, if someone did try, they might try again. I don't know if we can wait for the inquiry.'

Garfield was staring out the window. 'Yes, well,' he said. 'I was going to talk to you about that. I mean, now that Emma Quinn's been charged, I think it's time to move on, don't you?'

'Move on?'

'You know we're seriously overloaded, Cheryl. We're also coming in for some stick over the heath rape case. I need a fresh face on that and, hangover notwithstanding, I'd suggest that not-so-fresh face could be yours. Once you've got the Emma Quinn case off your desk.'

'We had a possible attempted murder last night, sir.'

'Perhaps. That remains to be seen.' Garfield was staring at Sergeant Lipari in a watchful way that brooked no contradiction. 'Meanwhile, the world keeps on turning, and I can't afford to have my most presentable FSU officer tied up on just one case. One case where we already have a result . . .'

Garfield paused meaningfully. Sergeant Lipari realised she was going to get nowhere by a frontal assault.

'OK,' she said. 'I've still got a heap of paperwork before I can hand the case over to the CPS. Say, Wednesday?'

Garfield thought about that, did his own calculations, nodded assent.

'Can I tell them you'll give a press conference on the heath rape case, say, Wednesday afternoon?'

'Yes. Yes, that'll be fine. I'll arrange everything.'

Garfield smiled. 'Good girl.'

Sergeant Lipari waited until she was out in the corridor before she indulged herself in a long, silent scream. Then she collected a strong black coffee from the machine and headed back to her office.

There, on top of the pile of paperwork, Sergeant Lipari found a note on her desk to ring Sally Jackson as soon as possible.

Sally Jackson looked at her watch. Almost ten. Harry was at work, Zak was at school, and Liz had gone shopping.

She paced around the living room, eyeing the phone on the low Indian table, willing it to ring. She desperately needed to use this interval of privacy to talk to Sergeant Lipari. They had assured Sally she was in the building. Surely she would ring back soon?

Sally sat down, closed her eyes, concentrated on her breathing. She needed to be calm for this conversation. There must be no question in the sergeant's mind that she, Sally Jackson, was any less than collected and rational; the perfect witness.

The phone rang. Sally, wrenched out of her trance, lunged forward and grabbed it as if her life was at stake.

'Yes?'

Sally realised the hand that held the phone was shaking.

'This is Sergeant Lipari from Richmond Police Station.' The voice was friendly but professional, warm despite the nasal London vowels. 'You left a message for me to ring, Mrs Jackson.'

'Oh. I did. Right. Thank you so much for calling back.'

'That's OK.'

There was a pause. Sally detected a slight wariness in the

woman's voice, or maybe a hesitancy, as if she was wondering whether to tell Sally something. If so, she obviously decided against it.

'So, what can I do for you, Mrs Jackson?' Sergeant Lipari said then.

'Oh . . . I sort of wanted to talk,' Sally said. 'You see . . . you remember I mentioned the medical check-up we all had just before . . . you know . . . ?'

'Yes. What about it?'

'Well, I told you it was something insisted on by Kit's company. That's what he told me. But yesterday I saw Fred Hanek, Kit's boss, and he said he knew absolutely nothing about it.'

'Would Mr Hanek normally? Know about it, I mean?'

'Yes. It's his company. Fred's the chairman but very much a hands-on one. Kit was always complaining how Fred insisted on keeping track of everything down to the last paper-clip. With something as important, as potentially expensive, as a change of health-plan, he would definitely have known.'

'I see. Go on.'

Sergeant Lipari's voice was interested but neutral.

Sally took a deep breath.

'So, then I spoke to the doctor who had actually examined us – Kit, Emma and me, that is. He's an acquaintance of Kit's, you see, and he admitted to me that Kit had set the whole thing up, to see if Emma was being abused. The point is, this proves—'

'Do you realise what you're saying, Mrs Jackson?' Sergeant Lipari cut in. 'This is extraordinary behaviour on your husband's part. And the doctor's too.'

'Well, yes, but the point is—'

'Why would he have done this if he was abusing Emma?'

'Yes. Exactly.'

'It's a good question. But what you just told me could, of course, *equally* indicate that Mr Jackson knew he was in trouble – that the whole history of abuse was about to be revealed – and so he was taking extreme measures in an attempt to pre-empt the crisis. And extreme measures they clearly were. They might, however, have helped him if it came to his word against Emma's.'

Sergeant Lipari's voice was relentless, pitiless. 'After all, who would suspect a man who actually seemed to be arranging proof of his own guilt? Right? The trouble is, of course, that in the first place the action itself shows desperation – exploiting a personal friendship with the doctor in what can only be construed as a conspiracy. Secondly, Emma's loss of her hymen is really neither here nor there. Surely Mr Jackson would have known that.'

Suddenly Sally could no longer continue to feign calm.

'For God's sake,' she snapped. 'He's a man! I don't think he did know! Can't you see that Kit might be innocent, that what he did might have been naïve and strange and even wrong, but he was doing it for the right reasons? Can't you conceive of it at all?'

She knew she must sound hysterical, but she couldn't help herself. And in that moment she didn't care. Where did reasoning get her? Could evidence and reason break down the official walls of certainty that had been built around this case, around the sufferings of her husband and daughter?

'Of course I can conceive of what you suggest, Mrs Jackson,' Sergeant Lipari said finally. Her voice was gentle but firm. 'But . . . well, you'll understand this because you're a career woman yourself. Some people say women don't handle authority well.

188

They say we get sidetracked by detail, they say we get emotionally involved.'

'But what about the medical examination! Kit *arranged* it!'

'And asked the doctor – his friend and co-conspirator – to keep it secret.'

'Can't you at least talk to Dr Macintyre?'

'I'm sorry, Mrs Jackson,' Sergeant Lipari said. 'I can't go back to my superior and reopen the inquiry on the basis of a single anomaly, especially one that's ambiguous in its implications. I'd risk being accused of letting my heart rule my head. Of course, if you wish to make a statement at some point, you're welcome. Though I don't think it would help your husband. Or Dr Macintyre, for that matter.'

'Well, I don't care how you look to your superiors, Sergeant,' Sally said. 'This isn't a feminist issue for me. It's a matter of my husband's innocence, his life . . .'

'I'm sorry I can't be more helpful, Mrs Jackson. I really am.'

There was a long pause. With grim insight, Sally realised that the burden of proof was totally on her. Unless she could provide incontrovertible evidence that someone else had abused Emma, that someone else had somehow arranged the terrible events of the past Thursday night, the police – even the nice, clever, sympathetic ones like Sergeant Lipari – would never listen to her.

'Could I ask you a personal question?' Sergeant Lipari said, breaking the impasse.

'I suppose so.'

'I just want to know if you've spoken to your ex-husband, Mr Quinn, lately.'

'Oh, yes.' Sally let out a harsh, humourless little laugh. 'I most certainly have. We visited Emma yesterday and ended up having a furious row. A sort of a terminal one, you might say.'

'And might I ask what about?'

'About my husband. Jonathan accused me of caring more about Kit than Emma, trying to defend the indefensible. He said he'd swing for him if there was any chance Kit might "get off", as he put it.'

'So you would say he was extremely angry? I mean, violently so?'

'Potentially, perhaps. Jonathan's violence has always been verbal rather than physical, though. At least until now.' Sally paused. 'I have to tell you one more thing. I . . . well, half accused Jonathan of having unnatural feelings about Emma.'

'Mrs Jackson—'

'That was why I called it a terminal row. Is it really so impossible? Don't natural fathers abuse their kids too?'

Sally knew she must sound vindictive, crazy, but she had to say it.

Instinct told Sergeant Lipari not to mention the previous night's incident. Sally might ring him, and she wanted to catch Jonathan Quinn unawares. And, for God's sake, this was the same scenario that she had suggested to Derek Vaughan, only half-speculatively, over lunch yesterday. If only this supposedly open-and-shut case would get itself closed and stay that way. All the same, there was no way she was going to encourage Sally Jackson in this line of thinking.

'I need to talk to him about a couple of things,' Sergeant Lipari said calmly, making no comment.

'Well, he's at home on compassionate leave, same as me.'

Sally could hear paper rustling at the other end. As if something was being written down. Then Sergeant Lipari spoke again. Her voice was livelier, more directly interested.

'Thank you, Mrs Jackson.'

'When it comes to believing Kit might be innocent, I really am in a minority of one, aren't I?' Sally said.

'It's not that, Mrs Jackson—'

'I don't blame you, Sergeant. You didn't live with the man for six years. But I did. He was a wonderful husband and stepfather.'

Silence again. Again, there was no answer to that.

Instead, Sergeant Lipari said carefully, 'I'd like to make a suggestion, Mrs Jackson. Is that OK?'

'Yes, Of course.'

'It sounds to me like you need someone to talk to,' Sergeant Lipari said. 'Someone you can develop your thoughts with. I'm a policewoman, and I'm very busy. But . . . I was talking to Dr Yardley the other day. He's been a very real help to me, sort of as an expert consultant. Anyway, I know he'd be glad to help you too, in a personal capacity, except he really doesn't want to appear intrusive.'

'You think . . .'

'Whatever happens, I think it's important you regain your emotional strength, don't you?' Sergeant Lipari persisted. 'For your own sake, and for Emma's.'

This woman's sure I've lost my mind, Sally thought. *They all are.*

'Thanks anyway, Sergeant,' was what she actually said in reply.

'I wish I could do more.'

'You've done enough. 'Bye.'

Sally replaced the phone and sat for some time with her head in her hands. Her eyes were damp with tears, but somehow she was too exhausted to cry properly.

She checked the time. Liz would be back soon. And Liz . . . well, Liz was practical and kind, and Sally's oldest friend, but she believed Kit was an abuser too. Like Sergeant Lipari, Liz would probably interpret the check-up story in ways unfavourable to him. She hadn't reminded Sally about Kit's silly little joke about under-age girls in Holland, but then she didn't need to . . . Sally could talk to Liz about anything, except about the husband she had loved and still loved.

Sally reached for a Kleenex from the dispenser on the table, dabbed her eyes. Then she found a number in her Filofax, picked up the phone and dialled.

Sod Sergeant Lipari. Sod the police, said the voice inside Sally's head. *Sod the bloody lot of them. There's only one person who'll definitely listen to me. He'll listen to anyone. It's his job and he's brilliant at it.*

'Hello?' she said when the number answered. 'Could I speak to Dr Yardley, please? It's Emma's mother. Yes, Sally Jackson.'

Sergeant Lipari stared balefully at the paperwork piled on her desk. She felt tired, emotionally drained, and guilty for having given poor, confused Sally Jackson the brush-off, even though she knew she had no choice. All this, and it was still only ten-thirty in the morning.

What wouldn't let her go was Sally Jackson's description of her row yesterday with her ex-husband. *I'll swing for him*, Jonathan Quinn had told her. Too much of a beautiful coincidence? Of course, the hospital authorities weren't even sure someone had tried to kill Kit Jackson. All the same . . .

Before she knew it, Sergeant Lipari had the phone in her hand and was dialling Quinn's number.

The phone at the other end rang for some time. She had

almost decided to hang up when a male voice answered, thick with sleep.

'Hello? Mr Quinn?' Sergeant Lipari said, trying to sound cheerful but sympathetic at the same time, as if all was plain sailing, mere formality.

'Sure. Who's this?'

Quinn was grim, guarded. Maybe he wasn't easily fooled.

'Sergeant Lipari from Richmond CID. I'd like a chat,' she continued brightly. 'Oh, just to fill in a few details . . . Actually, I'm happy to keep things informal . . . Cottage pie and a beer? Sounds fine. See you at twelve-thirty. 'Bye.'

Sergeant Lipari checked the name of the pub Quinn had suggested as a rendezvous. Somewhere off the arse-end of the Goldhawk Road. But then, college lecturers were even more badly paid than policemen.

She was still wading through her paperwork when Vaughan walked in half an hour later.

'Problem solved,' he announced.

'What particular problem would that be, Derek?'

Vaughan's relationship with his wife? The mystery of the missing plasma drip? Sergeant Lipari could think of at least fifteen just sitting here.

Vaughan didn't pick up on her sarcasm. Or perhaps he chose not to. He sat on the desk and leaned forward confidentially.

'The problem of the pic in the *Orb*,' he explained. 'The one of Jackson with his stepdaughter. Turns out the original was nicked by a reporter from Jackson's mother, who's in a nursing home somewhere in Surrey. Totally gaga, poor old dear.'

'Nice. What Christian gentlemen they all are.'

'Yeah. The journo pretends to be an old family friend, doesn't he? He organises things so's he's left alone with her in her room – which is full of family mementos and photos; he slips the offending snap in his pocket, and there you go.'

'Right.' Sergeant Lipari raised an eyebrow. 'So who turned over that particular stone and discovered the reptile beneath?'

'Little me. I worked out it was the only other possibility apart from the house. Quick phone call, confirmed someone had been round there to see the old lady. Fitted the description of the *Orb* reporter, who is, I have to tell you, black, which considerably aided the process of identification.'

'Congratulations. Mr Garfield will be very chuffed indeed.'

'Yup. End of story.'

What he had just said was a bit strange when Sergeant Lipari came to think about it. *End of story*? File under 'enigmatic'.

'You think so?' she said.

'Sure. We're off the hook.'

'You've got no political sense, Derek, did you know that?'

'What do you mean?'

'I mean that far from being over, this one's set to run and run. The reporter concerned has put his paper seriously in the wrong. The commissioner's going to grab his chance and go for the jugular – unjustified accusations against our officers by the gutter press, et cetera. He'll complain to the paper's proprietor, and the owner'll kick the editor's ass. The editor will then turn on our poxy little journo – who'll find himself in very deep doo-doo,' Sergeant Lipari concluded with a weary smile. 'Now there's a cheering thought for you, eh?'

'Abso-bloody-lootly,' agreed Vaughan vaguely, as if he already considered the subject seriously passé. He looked at the papers on her desk. 'You don't look too keen on those. What d'you say, doll? Golden Lantern again?'

'Not today. I have a lunch date with Jonathan Quinn, Emma's father.'

Vaughan was alert once more. 'Oh really?'

'Yes. Really.'

'And what would that be in aid of?'

'Something he said to his ex-wife yesterday – before the bother at the hospital – makes me think I should have one last word with our Mr Quinn before I let the governor move me on to any other business.'

'This case is supposed to be all over bar the paperwork, doll. Mr Garfield ain't gonna to like it.'

'He ain't going to know about it, Derek. Not from me. And not from you, either,' Sergeant Lipari added waspishly. 'You should look at it this way: he'll like it even less if we screw things up in full-frontal view of the tabloid press, won't he?'

EIGHTEEN

It was just after one when Sally arrived at Noel Yardley's consulting rooms in Chiswick. There were two bells: one for the practice, the other – marked simply 'Private' – which Sally knew was connected through to the therapist's personal flat on the first floor.

Yardley opened the door himself. His receptionist had obviously gone to lunch.

'Hello, Sally,' he said in that dignified but almost teenagerishly friendly way of his, ushering her through into the tiled hallway. 'Great you decided to give me a call. Let's hope I can help.'

'You already have. You brought Emma back from outer space.'

'Oh, I'm afraid she still has a way to go. I can't lie to you on that score. But I think there's a good chance she'll come through this. It may take time, that's all.'

Yardley led the way through the empty waiting room, through a pair of open double doors, and into the light, airy space where he held his therapy sessions. It was about twenty-five feet by twenty, with his desk at one end, lots of book-lined shelves to its right and left, and a couple of wing armchairs by the fireplace.

'When was the last time you were here?' he asked.

'A couple of months ago, maybe three,' Sally said. 'With Kit.'

Yardley nodded. 'Sit down.' He indicated one of the armchairs. 'Since we don't have much time, I think we should keep our first talk pretty casual, don't you?'

Sally flopped down into the armchair, just as ordered. God, she was so tired; tired of taking everything on her own shoulders, of fighting and being confused and alone . . .

Sitting down opposite her, Yardley folded his hands and looked at her with a mixture of friendly curiosity and concern.

'Is there anything you really – I mean *really* – need to discuss?' he asked softly, and opened out his hands like a priest prepared to give blessing. 'Of course, we could start with Emma . . .'

'Actually, I want . . . need . . . to talk about Kit,' Sally answered. 'Does that sound really weird?'

'Not at all. He's still your husband. You loved him, and that doesn't change from one day to the next.'

Yardley held Sally's gaze, his soft brown eyes glowing warmly with sympathy and understanding.

'I can't get him out of my mind. I know I should be concentrating all my energies on Emma, but that's just not the way it's been.'

Sally knew she was on the edge of tears. The stabbing. Kit and Emma. The pregnancy. Jonathan. She felt as if she were teetering above a vast, seething volcanic crater of existential and emotional instability. Yardley was her only hope. He was not here to judge, only to help. He would be her lifeline.

'Well,' Yardley said matter-of-factly, 'whatever the outcome of the legal investigation, you *must* continue to think about Kit, for the sake of your own emotional health.'

'God, I'm so relieved you said that,' Sally murmured. 'Everyone else seems to have written Kit off as an abuser who got what was coming to him.' Her fists were tightly clenched on the arms of the chair. 'They think I should just blank him out, forget him . . .'

'And you don't feel you can go along with that.'

'No, I can't.'

'You're a very honest and courageous woman, Sally,' Yardley said. 'I can support you totally in all this.'

'Thank you.' Sally paused. 'You see, I've been to the hospital to visit Kit, and the fact is that my feelings – my instincts – for him are still strong, despite what he's supposed to have done to Emma.'

Yardley paused, glanced up the ceiling, then back at her with a kind of gratitude, as if he had found something up there to bring to the discussion.

'Just so long,' he added, choosing his words carefully, 'as you don't deny the real possibility that your husband might have behaved very badly, even criminally, with Emma, out of some very extreme impulse of his own. Can we consider that, or is it too far out for you at the moment?'

'I don't think he did abuse her.'

'Feelings are, of course, important, Sally, but—'

'Wait a minute. Please. Secondly, you see, there are one or two facts in the abuse scenario that don't seem to add up.'

'We're on solid, practical ground here, are we?' Yardley asked.

'Yes. Absolutely.'

Now the tears finally brimmed over. Sally let out half a dozen big, howling sobs, then pummelled the sides of the chair in her frustration. The sobs turned into snorts of anger and pain.

199

Yardley offered the box of Kleenex and waited patiently until he thought Sally was ready to continue.

'Can you go on?' he said.

She nodded. 'See, the week before . . . the stabbing, we all . . . me, Emma, Kit . . . went for a medical at a local doctor's.' The words poured out like a flood that had been pent up too long. 'Kit told us it was a health insurance check-up,' Sally continued, 'to do with upgrading our cover. But it wasn't really. The insurance story was just a smoke-screen. Kit had secretly arranged the whole thing with the doctor, who is a friend of his. You see, he was trying to establish if Emma had been . . . interfered with . . . sexually.'

Yardley looked shocked. 'Somewhat unethical.'

'But perhaps well-meant.'

'And, on the face of it, a very strange thing to do if he actually *was* abusing her. Is that what you're saying?'

'Exactly!'

Despite the pain of recall, Sally smiled through her tears in sheer relief. At last a fellow human being was listening to her but not judging.

'Have you talked to anyone about these things?' Yardley asked gently.

'Sergeant Lipari said it was probably just a sort of very clever defensive move because Kit knew there was going to be trouble.'

'Well, of course, that's plausible,' Yardley conceded. 'But that's not really the point. She wouldn't admit any other possibility, right?'

'No. She wouldn't. I won't say she was completely unsympathetic, but . . . she doesn't seem to want to even consider that I might have something to contribute. I think she's frightened all the men she works with will accuse her of being all emotional and girlie, not tough enough to be put in charge of an investigation like this.'

'And what about your family and friends?'

'I haven't told anyone else. Liz would just be too shocked to look at it rationally, I think. As for Jonathan – Emma's natural father, you met him once – if I try to defend Kit in any way at all, he just gets angry and . . . sort of violently defensive . . .'

'Well, for him this is just old stuff in a new form.'

'Yes. He always hated Kit.'

'Sally, this must have been the last straw for you. First you're hit with all the horrors of the past few days. Then no one will listen to your thoughts about them. It must make you feel crazy.'

'Oh, yes,' she said gratefully. 'You're the only one who seems to understand. What . . . what do you think I should do now?'

'Wearing my shrink's hat,' Yardley said thoughtfully, leaning back in his chair. 'Well, wearing my shrink's hat, I would say that at the moment you just have to talk to whoever you need to, say whatever you like; feel the feelings – logical and illogical, reasonable and unreasonable, so-called appropriate or so-called inappropriate.'

'And . . . if you could forget you're a professional therapist? If you were just a friend reacting to what I just told you?'

'I shouldn't really do that, Sally,' Yardley said. He was unable to hide a sly, puckish smile. 'But I suppose it *is* my lunch-hour. Which makes me sort of a quasi-civilian. In which case I'd have say that those bastards have given you a hard time. They should have listened to what you said – and acted upon it. For the general peace of mind. Not just yours, but everybody's.'

'Well, if they won't hear the things I say about Kit, I'll have to make them listen, won't I?'

'Careful, Sally. Apart from anything else, you are still in a very vulnerable emotional state.'

'Never mind that,' Sally said fiercely. 'I want to know if you'll help me. Not just emotionally but in a practical way.'

Yardley looked at her for a long moment, then nodded. 'I'll try. As long as it's not illegal or physically dangerous.' He glanced at his watch, in the quick, apparently casual way of the caring professional whose every moment is spoken for. 'And as long as I can spare the time.'

The pub was a 1970s pseudo-Victorian conversion of the kind Sergeant Lipari harboured a special loathing for. Jonathan Quinn had insisted on meeting in the public bar, which, because she was on time and he wasn't, meant her sitting alone at a corner table, nursing a warm tomato juice and being ogled by a platoon of overweight jobbing builders. When they weren't guzzling pints of draught lager they were overdosing on pork scratchings. The place made the Chinese restaurant she and Vaughan frequented look like the Savoy Grill.

Sergeant Lipari's own ex-husband had taken a perverse pleasure in inflicting horrible pubs on her. In his case they had been in the East End, near his warehouses. Same difference. Mental cruelty with an alcoholic tinge.

When Jonathan appeared, he seemed unaware he was late. Maybe he had really lost track of such mundane considerations. He certainly didn't look too together. Pale, tense, distracted. He quickly ordered himself a pint of bitter and got another tomato juice for Sergeant Lipari. He asked her if she wanted to eat. She took a glance at the leaden Scotch eggs and the curling contents of the 'salad' bar and told Jonathan she was on a strict diet. Sadly, it involved skipping lunch.

'I like this place. It's authentic,' he said, decanting his six-feet-four of nervous energy into the confines of a leatherette-covered chair. 'Authentically fake, that is.'

He wasn't smiling. Sergeant Lipari decided to take it easy, let the conversation ramble a bit, then hit him with her news and check his reaction.

'Thanks,' she said, indicating the tomato juice. 'So, this has been a nightmare. My heart goes out to all of you. But at least Emma has started to communicate, and we seem to have a picture of what happened. A bit fuzzy on detail, but there you go.'

'Yes. There we go.'

Jonathan had taken a couple of big swallows of beer and his glass was already half empty. Sergeant Lipari remembered Vaughan yesterday in the restaurant. *Men under pressure. Predictable or what?*

'How do you feel, Mr Quinn?' she asked quietly.

Jonathan thought for a moment, then shrugged his bony shoulders. 'Angry, Sergeant.'

'That's natural. I mean, if this happened to my daughter—'

'But it hasn't!' Jonathan interrupted harshly. 'Do you actually have any children, Sergeant?'

'No . . .'

'Anyway, I don't think you understand me right. Yes, I'm furious about what that bastard Jackson did to Emma, but my real anger's reserved for Sally, my ex-wife.' Jonathan shook his head in embittered disbelief. 'She's started to stick up for him! Would you bloody believe it?'

'Stick up for him? You mean she's defending Mr Jackson?' Sergeant Lipari asked. 'In what way precisely?'

'You know . . . she can't believe he'd do such a thing. She

claims Emma's being vague about the details, et cetera . . .'

'Well, your daughter is still a bit hazy about some aspects of the incident. It's hard for Mrs Jackson being pulled both ways.'

'*What do you mean, both ways?*' Jonathan barked. 'There's only one direction she should be moving!'

He struck the table with his balled fist, rocking the glasses. Heads turned. There was a muffled curse from over by the dartboard as someone missed a double top. Jonathan leaned in closer.

'Listen,' he hissed, 'I want Jackson tried, and I want him punished! I used to be a card-carrying liberal, but life changes you, doesn't it? I hope they lock the bugger up and throw away the key! Jesus, I wish there was a death penalty for what he did!'

Sergeant Lipari, meanwhile, had been monitoring the outburst carefully.

Could be a performance, she thought, but if so a very good one. If this man is aware that Kit Jackson almost died last night, he's putting on a bloody good show of ignorance. On the other hand, people can be desperately convincing when they really need to be . . .

She decided on shock tactics.

'We suspect someone may have tried to inflict their own death penalty on Mr Jackson last night,' Sergeant Lipari said. 'There was an incident at the hospital that remains unexplained. Whatever happened, Mr Jackson was very lucky to survive.'

For a moment Jonathan seemed dumbstruck. Then his expression changed to one of grim delight.

'Well, well,' he said at last. 'If someone had a go at the bastard, whoever it was, good luck to them!'

He raised his empty glass in a toast, then jumped to his feet. For a moment Sergeant Lipari had a crazy notion that Jonathan was going to make a run for it. What he actually did was to sweep off back to the bar for a refill.

Sergeant Lipari waited for his return, aware that the snacking builders were still eyeing her. It was like being left alone in the lions' cage while the trainer nipped out for a moment. She was tempted to flash her warrant-card, just to see their faces.

'OK, well, we need to eliminate potential suspects, Mr Quinn,' she said, poker-faced, as Jonathan took a sip of his second pint. 'Can you tell me where you were at eleven o'clock last night?'

'I was in my car,' he said, more level now. 'Heading back towards London, actually.'

'Where had you been?'

'I'd driven out to Ash Ridge Common – one of my favourite places. I was born near Tring in Hertfordshire, so I've known that part of the Chilterns since I was a kid.'

'Did you have any particular reason for being there, Mr Quinn? Did you visit or meet anyone?'

Jonathan shook his head.

'I wanted to get my thoughts together,' he said. 'I wandered around the woods for a bit until it started to get dark. Then I had supper at a pub. Headed back to the M40 and arrived home about half-past eleven.'

'Can anyone corroborate this account of your movements, Mr Quinn?'

'I was alone, if that's what you mean. I don't have a lodger – I'd like to, but the spare room's reserved for Emma's visits – and I don't have a girlfriend.'

'I see.'

Jonathan sensed her scepticism. The catharsis of his curse on Kit Jackson seemed to have calmed him, brought him back from some private place, somewhere angry and voluble but all the same almost as remote as that his daughter had retreated to after the stabbing.

'Are you married or in a relationship, Sergeant?' he asked.

'No . . . not at this precise moment.'

'Right. Then, unless you're working, can you easily prove where you were most nights?'

Sergeant Lipari felt herself flush, and wondered if he had noticed it too.

'Point taken,' she conceded, trying to sound as if it didn't matter.

'Listen, I'd been sort of walking off my anger . . .' Jonathan said. 'As you can see, I have plenty of it. Sally and I had a terrible argument after we saw Emma yesterday afternoon.' He looked at Sergeant Lipari closely. 'That's it, isn't it?' he said, his eyes suddenly blazing with fury once more. 'Sally told you all about our row! The bitch!'

'Mr Quinn, the subject came up. What I want to know is, did you really tell her you wanted to kill Jackson?'

More of the beer went down. Jonathan slowly lowered his glass. It hit the table with a soggy little clunk.

'Yup,' he said, 'I said that. But as I told you before, I didn't stab him the other night. Emma is the most important thing in my life. I love her more than I can say. And because I do, if I was going to commit an act like that, there's no way I'd do it in front of her. By the same token, it wasn't me who had a go at finishing him off. Oh, I've got a big mouth. I know that. But I've been to university. Appearances to the contrary, I'm a nice middle-class man.' Jonathan laughed sourly. 'Deep down I'm just too civilised for primitive blood-vendettas. Or, if you were going to be brutal, you might say I just don't have the guts . . .'

* * *

'Goodness,' Yardley said. 'I'm sorry, but I have a client arriving in five minutes. This will have to do for today.'

Sally heard the front door open, the click of heels on the hall-way tiles. Fiona, Yardley's receptionist, was back from lunch.

'Would you like to come back tomorrow?' Yardley asked.

'Can I?' Sally answered almost plaintively. 'It's just so good to talk and not be treated like a neurotic idiot.'

'I can fit you in tomorrow afternoon for a proper one-hour session.' Yardley looked at her appraisingly. 'I'll confess, it's Emma's regular weekly slot. But you don't think she'd mind, would she?'

'No. No, I'm sure she wouldn't.'

'Well, Sally, I'd recommend some serious relaxation work, some focusing on your feelings. Sound all right?'

'You're very kind. You really don't know how kind.'

'Nonsense, Sally. Emma was my client. Something went terribly wrong for her, and for your family dynamics. What happened may turn out to have been one single person's fault – if one can use the term in this context – but its consequences are everybody's responsibility. I know I can help Emma, and I hope I can help you. I mean that. Absolutely.'

'I wish I could talk to Kit. I wish I could talk to Emma, ask her the truth . . .'

'You need to, and one day you will. Perhaps in the not too distant future.'

They got to their feet, but Yardley made no attempt to rush Sally away. She was grateful for that.

'It's . . . it's funny,' she said, 'but I was always such a worrier where Emma was concerned. Accident, illness, strangers in the park. The usual things. But I never anticipated this particular nightmare.' She paused. 'You know I'm pregnant, don't you?'

Yardley nodded. 'Sergeant Lipari mentioned it. I thought I'd let you bring the subject up. If you wanted to.'

'Well, after what's happened I don't know if I should be bringing another child into the world.'

'Perhaps it's one of the things we should talk about over the next few days,' Yardley said softly.

'Yes. Do you have any . . . I mean, I know you're not married . . .'

'I have been, though,' Yardley said hesitantly. He gave Sally a sad little smile. 'No children, I'm afraid. We never got round to starting a family before . . . before my wife died. I'm a widower, you see.'

The shock of what Yardley had said struck Sally like a physical blow.

'Oh my God. All this time we've been sending Emma to you, yet we had no idea – I'm so *very* sorry.'

'It was some years ago.'

Yardley's gentle dignity made Sally feel aware, even ashamed, of the demands she was making. Tragedy is universal, she thought. Her own present pain was simply more complex, more public, and above all more new.

'So . . . you know how it is,' Sally said. 'And you know all about healing, and the time it takes.' Shyly she offered him her hand. 'Goodbye, Doctor Yardley.'

'The name's Noel,' Yardley said.

He squeezed her hand. The smile came back, this time boyish and friendly. Finally he began to lead Sally towards the door.

'Please, please do call me Noel. It's important to me that you do that.'

NINETEEN

When Sergeant Lipari got back from seeing Jonathan Quinn, she was told to report to Superintendent Garfield. A matter of urgency.

Good news travels fast, she thought, and her suspicions were borne out.

Garfield was beaming chummily, rubbing his hands with pleasure. He told Sergeant Lipari to take a seat, but himself continued to pace around the room.

'Guess what?' he said triumphantly. 'The *Orb* reporter who nicked the photo of Jackson's mother – guy called Mulligan. Well, his editor's been made to sack him! Orders from the proprietor. The commissioner's like the original cat who got the cream.'

Perhaps Sergeant Lipari was still thinking of Jonathan Quinn, and Emma, and Sally Jackson, none of whom had anything to celebrate, but she failed to match her superior's glee.

'I bet,' she said, struggling to keep the irony out of her voice.

Garfield didn't seem to register her reservations.

'Meanwhile, this Mulligan character's threatening to call in his union and take the whole thing to a tribunal.' He laughed out loud. 'Plus – I mean, get this, it's like a TV drama, isn't it? – it turns out this bloke with the Irish name is *black*! So we could

209

end up with the Race Relations Board in on the act as well. Can you believe it, Cheryl?'

Sergeant Lipari still failed to match Garfield's delight.

'First, sir, I thought you wanted a low profile on this case from now on. Not conducive to the quiet life, though, any of what you just told me.' She sighed. 'Second, to tell you the truth, if I really think about it, I have to sympathise with the reptile. He's done nothing a hundred other reporters wouldn't do under the circumstances. He was just unlucky. His proprietor decided to sacrifice him for political reasons.'

Garfield's grin faded a bit.

'I see you're not in an optimistic frame of mind today, Cheryl.'

'I'm relieved our boys and girls are in the clear.'

'Oh, yeah. Mulligan's still making noises about bribery, but he won't name names. I reckon he'd been fiddling his expenses, claiming for non-existent informants. You ask me, this is all about him getting the paper to settle out of court.'

'I hope you're right.'

''Course I am.' Garfield clapped his hands. 'So, the Jackson case goes upstairs to the CPS and the commissioner chalks up a win in his war against the press. Everybody's happy. I hope you've got the paperwork ready.'

'Paperwork?' Sergeant Lipari echoed absently.

'For the CPS. To get the Jackson case wrapped up.'

Sergeant Lipari hesitated.

'Actually, sir, I'm not entirely sure the case *is* quite wrapped up,' she said. 'In my opinion there're a few important details that still need clarification. I spoke to Jonathan Quinn today—'

'For Christ's sake! What the hell do you think you're doing?'

'Sir, please bear with me for a minute. Listen. Quinn denies trying to kill Jackson. On the other hand, it's clearly something he talked about. His wife will vouch for that. Plus he's got no alibi for the time it happened.'

'He's some sort of academic,' Garfield observed, as if that explained everything. 'Bit of a wimp, isn't he?'

'A very *angry* wimp.'

'Cheryl, I cannot believe I'm hearing all this.'

'I've tried the gentle approach. This time I'd like to pull Quinn in and have Derek and the others give him some heat. Then he might have a bit more to say.'

'The girl picked up a kitchen knife and stabbed her stepfather. Surely you can't doubt that?'

'I'm ninety-nine per cent sure, yes. But that still leaves a one per cent chance of another scenario. According to that, someone else did it and she's shielding him, and that man was her natural father, Jonathan Quinn. In fact there's even another, related possibility: what if Quinn was the abuser? What if Jackson found out about it, and Quinn stabbed him?'

'Now you say this? *Now*? And why should the girl then accuse Jackson?'

'Whatever he may have done, Quinn's her natural father. She'd have been confronted with an awesome conflict of loyalties. I talked to Dr Yardley, the shrink, and he says he wouldn't rule such a thing out.'

'Come on, Cheryl,' Garfield said. 'Emma Quinn stabbed Jackson because he'd been molesting her. Damned near killed him! You know how much determination that took, how much reason she'd have to have? Christ, the knife practically weighs as much as she does!'

'Sir, she can't remember a whole lot—'

'But what she does seem very sure about is that Jackson was abusing her!' Garfield sighed deeply. 'What *is* your problem, Sergeant?'

Garfield's voice had turned ominously calm and reasonable. Sergeant Lipari knew this was when he was at his most dangerous, but she decided to press on anyway.

'If I could have a couple more days. Maybe I could get the therapist back. He could talk to Emma again . . .'

But even before she could finish her sentence, she could tell from the look in Garfield's eyes that the full-stop had been drawn, the book closed.

'Listen, there's a limit to how long we can waste resources on this one!' Garfield snapped. 'The girl's confessed. She'll probably get off, and there'll be feminists dancing in the streets. Next thing she'll have her own show on Channel Four. Youngest talk-show hostess in history. Jackson will either die of his injuries or spend the rest of his natural in jail. Fine!' He loomed over Sergeant Lipari and spoke slowly and precisely, as if to a recalcitrant child. 'We have a *result*. I think it's time we got back out there and started catching some proper villains, don't you, Cheryl?'

One last try, Sergeant Lipari thought. She kept hearing the desperation in Sally Jackson's voice. *For God's sake, can't you see that Kit might be innocent?*

'What happens if Emma gets her marbles together and suddenly retracts her accusations against Jackson?' she suggested. 'It's been known.'

'Cheryl, she was found in the classic locked room – all right, locked house – with a bloodstained knife in her hand. The same knife that was used to stab her stepfather.' Garfield raised his eyes to an unseen heaven. 'The forensic evidence alone should suffice. What more do you want?'

'I'd like to be absolutely sure no one else was involved, that's all.'

'For Christ's sake! Listen, do you have any evidence? You remember evidence, Cheryl? It's what judges and juries require in order to convict people.'

There was a long silence. The fact was that no, Sergeant Lipari didn't. All the same, this was not the way she had planned this interview. She knew Garfield was thinking *typical woman*, and in this case, she was forced to admit, he might have some right on his chauvinist side. Maybe Sally Jackson's wheedling had got to her after all. The evidence that wasn't really evidence, the wild accusations against her ex-husband, Jonathan Quinn . . .

'I want those papers with the CPS before you go home tonight, OK?' Garfield said, realising he had won this round.

'Very well, sir.'

'No evidence, no case. That's how it is.'

Sergeant Lipari understood the finality in his voice. She got to her feet.

'Well, we'll just have to hope that Jackson pulls through and can be interviewed,' she said, unable to resist having the last word.

Garfield looked at Sergeant Lipari steadily. His eyes were suddenly cold.

'I'll save my prayers,' he growled softly. 'I've got a teenage daughter of my own.'

'Our priority is simple, though perhaps not obvious,' Diane Worcester said, placing her elbows firmly on her crowded desk and fixing Sally and Liz with a gaze that did not encourage

213

disagreement. 'It is to ensure this case goes the right way.'

'Which means?' asked Sally sharply.

The solicitor shot her a look of mingled surprise and irritation. 'Mrs Jackson,' she said, 'we have to face the real possibility that your husband will survive and become fit to stand trial. It may seem at the moment that we have an unassailable case, but you'd be surprised how a good barrister can undermine such a case in court.'

By the time of Sally's return from her first session with Yardley, her post-therapy 'high' had given way to exhaustion. Liz had forced her to eat some lunch, put her to bed for an hour, and then driven her back over the river and on to Gale, Masimba & Worcester's offices in Holborn for a four-thirty appointment.

The partnership, operating from these cramped offices in a Victorian block behind Rosebery Avenue, had become well-known for handling tricky 'women's' cases – battered wives criminalised for striking back at violent husbands, incidents of sex and race discrimination, and a much-publicised case involving a custody claim brought by a man whose wife had left him for another woman. The partnership's success record was excellent, and at first it had seemed like a wonderful idea to hire Diane Worcester as Emma's solicitor. Now neither Sally nor Liz, for their different reasons, was quite so sure. In Diane Worcester's presence, matters seemed a little too clear-cut for comfort.

'I was under the impression it was your job to help my daughter defend herself against a charge of attempted murder,' Sally said. 'Not to "get" my husband.'

'Mrs Jackson. If abuse by your husband can be proved, there's a very good chance that Emma will be set free.' Diane Worcester looked at Sally over the top of her amber-framed spectacles. 'Are you seriously suggesting that he did not abuse your daughter? Because it's clear someone did.'

'What can I say?' Sally murmured. 'I know what happened, happened. But until it did – for whatever reason – Kit wasn't just a wonderful husband. He and Emma were really good friends. How often can that be said of a step-parent and a child? I thought I was so lucky in that respect.' She shook her head wearily. 'How can I tell the court anything else?'

Diane Worcester frowned darkly. She looked at Liz for support, but Liz was looking at the law books that lined the shelves either side of the desk.

'Mrs Jackson,' the solicitor said then, 'you can tell the court what you like. *We* want a conviction. And we're damned well going to get it.'

'*We!*' Sally burst out. 'You keep talking about somebody called *we*! Who exactly do you mean?'

Her voice must have carried right through the building. Zoe Masimba, Diane Worcester's Ugandan-born partner, popped up in her office next door and glanced through the glass partition to check no violence was being done.

'Everyone . . .' Diane Worcester cleared her throat, slightly flustered, but not for long. 'Everyone,' she continued more firmly, 'who's fighting to see justice done for an abused child, and for the thousands of others who are powerless to fight back as Emma did so magnificently! By we, I mean you, me, Liz, Sergeant Lipari . . . all of us women, as chance would have it. If chance is what it is.'

'And would this *we* include Jonathan, Sally's ex-husband?' Liz put in.

'Oh, he has his own agenda, I think, don't you?' Diane Worcester smiled knowingly at Sally and Liz in turn.

Finally Liz spoke. 'He's not the only one,' she said quietly. 'Here's my friend Sally, who's hoping against hope that her husband is innocent.' She then looked unblinkingly at Diane Worcester. 'And here's a woman who doesn't care if he's innocent or not, so long as she gets the right result for her cause.'

'Mrs Paine—'

Liz frowned and rejected Diane Worcester's protest with a wave of her hand. 'Excuse me, but I haven't finished!' Liz pointed to herself. 'And lastly here's a woman who just wants her son to be left alone to survive his adolescence, and her friend to regain her daughter, and if possible her happiness – and never mind who did what, though of course those who commit crimes must be punished.'

She paused to catch her breath. 'Now, I'm aware that none of this sounds particularly noble or good for the "cause",' she continued, 'but it's all honest and human. So shouldn't we all let things take their natural course and, dare I suggest, agree to disagree?'

Diane Worcester opened her mouth to speak, then decided against it. Sally put her head in her hands.

'It's time I took Sally home,' Liz said. 'All this can wait for another day. And as far as I'm concerned, that's exactly what it will do.'

Harry went to pour Sally some wine. She put her hand over her glass, shook her head. A half-cleared plate of spaghetti al pesto lay in front of her on the dining-room table.

'Not for me.'

'Fair enough.'

Harry topped up his own glass, offered the bottle to Liz,

who had none of Sally's inhibitions.

'I need to keep a clear head, no hangovers,' Sally elaborated.

Harry laughed. 'It's OK. No explanations required. Sometimes a body needs alcohol, sometimes it doesn't. Up to the owner of said body which it's to be.'

Sally nodded. 'You've been marvellous, both of you. I . . . I hope I'm not causing any problems between you and Zak.'

'No way,' said Liz. 'It's good for him to have to deal with real life, and real, injured people. I have a chastened son, and in a way I'm glad of it.'

'It's just that he always rushes off upstairs straight after dinner.'

Liz laughed. 'You think that's because of you?'

'There's something not right, though,' Sally insisted. 'Do you think he still has a problem with me?'

'Could I suggest something?' chipped in Harry, 'It seems to me that the lives of several people Zak loves are not right, so neither is he.' He paused. 'Maybe you should talk to him a bit more. Maybe he feels *you* have a problem with *him*.'

Liz nodded agreement. 'Zak can't go out, so he goes upstairs and makes himself a little world up there. You remember I took him to the computer supplier last weekend. Well, we upgraded his system, including a nice new modem. Until he was fifteen or so, he used to spend his whole time playing games on the thing. Then came his "wild at heart" period, which he's just put on hold. As we speak, Zak's roaming the Internet, cruising the information super-highway. OK. The equipment is expensive. Costs us another fortune in phone bills, but at least we know where our boy is at nights.'

'Cyberspace, to be precise,' said Harry. 'Just as many crazies out there, of course, but no drugs or booze – and no violence, except the virtual kind.'

'The . . . er . . . patient wouldn't mind some coffee, actually,' announced a voice from the doorway.

The three adults turned guiltily. Zak was standing there, looking wry and only slightly irritated. How long he had been listening to their conversation, it was impossible to tell, and no one was about to ask.

'Darling,' Liz said, 'hello.'

'Do go on, Mother dear.'

'Nothing bad was being said.'

'Except that I'm the boy with the problem. I'm the one who can't be let out into the community.'

Liz didn't know what to say to that.

'Help yourself, Zak,' Harry said on her behalf, pointing to the thermos coffee-pot in the middle of the table. 'Sally was worried about her relationship with you. That's why the subject of you came up, not because you're some kind of nutter.'

'Well, there's no problem,' Zak murmured, staying firmly where he was. 'I've known Sally – and she me – since I was a baby. Why should I have a problem with her?'

'Zak, dear, it's just that a lot's happened in the last week,' Sally said. 'Maybe we should have talked about it more.'

Zak shrugged. 'Any time. I know you've had a lot on your mind.'

'Still want that coffee?'

'Oh, yeah . . .'

Sally got to her feet.

'Then why don't you and I have coffee together? I know what: why don't you show me your new computer equipment that Liz was telling me about? Just spend a bit of time together. Take my mind off things too. OK?'

'I'm a bit old for bedtime stories now.' Zak grinned. 'But I do remember when you used to come over and baby-sit me – when Mum was out with one of her men. That was her scarlet-woman phase . . .'

'Zak!' Liz looked appalled for a moment, then spluttered into laughter.

Five minutes later, Sally and Zak were established at the work-station in his room, eyes fixed on the screen of his VDU. The definition of the images was astonishingly sharp.

'I can't believe it,' Sally said. 'At work I've seen the big computers they use for special effects and titles and so on. I know they cost a whole lot of money. I just didn't realise home computers were this good these days.'

'Power. Yeah.'

'And you can send and receive images from just about anywhere in the world?'

'Yeah, well, I get my access to the Net through Compuserve,' Zak said. 'It's a sort of commercial thing and a bit naff, I mean you're supposed to have your own unique connection. Anyway, it's like joining a club – you know, they tend to give newcomers a hard time, till you've paid your dues. They can be a bit sniffy and try to blind you with jargon and that kind of thing.'

'It's just like NASA HQ in here,' Sally said.

'Right. One small step for man,' Zak answered with a laugh, and punched out a sequence of codes.

'What does it all do?'

'It's connected by a modem to a phone line – you know that . . .' He paused, turned to Sally, all fresh-faced enthusiasm, completely dropping his school façade. 'I mean, I've been at this since I was sort of ten or eleven, but now the modem's so incredibly much faster, and these days the Net . . . well, the Net changes everything. I used to belong to a fantasy-game bulletin-board, and that was pretty much it, but nowadays . . . you can do anything, go anywhere, talk to anyone.'

Sally nodded. 'Kit's . . . Kit's company's been developing software for these processes. He says it's amazing what they can do, and in a year or two it'll be out of sight.'

'Yeah. It all used to be pretty slow and crude. I suppose that's why I got bored with it for a while back there. But with the stuff I've got now, you can do *really* neat things. Watch this.'

Zak continued keying, then waited expectantly. A message flashed up: WHO GOES THERE?

Zak typed in: THE WANDSWORTH KID.

ENTER! the screen said.

'I've known this guy since I was twelve and he was a year older. His name's Kevin Spacek but he calls himself the Spartan.' Zak explained. 'Got a thing about ancient Greece. Anyway, we linked up through a fantasy-gaming mag. We used to play fantasy games – "Dungeons and Dragons" kind of things. Now we share more sophisticated stuff.'

'Where is he?' Sally asked.

'Los Angeles,' said Zak with a sly little grin. 'Van Nuys, to be exact. In the San Fernando Valley.'

'Phone bills. I just can't conceive of the phone bills.'

'My mother and Harry know about it, Sally.' Zak's look hardened slightly. 'It's part of the deal.'

'And have you ever met the Spartan?' Sally said, changing the subject.

'Not physically. But I know him better than most of my friends at school.'

Suddenly the screen exploded into colour and light. A samurai warrior came hurtling towards them. It was detailed, fast-moving, and of astonishing graphic quality.

'Uh-oh,' said Zak. 'The Spartan wants to play . . .' He turned apologetically to Sally. 'Just a couple of minutes, to keep him happy, OK? Question of Netiquette.'

'Oh yes. It's fascinating. I want to know all about it.'

So for a few minutes two digital samurais swiped and ducked and dived. Heads were lopped off, a village saved from bandits, a maiden – pneumatic and flimsily-dressed – defended. Zak won once, lost twice, then signed off.

'The quality of the images is astounding,' Sally said. 'I noticed the girl there, especially . . .'

'Yeah. Hem. Well, this is actually a pretty low-key game. You can use the Net for this kind of thing, or for searching out information, or just chatting, you know, sort of cyberspace penpalling or whatever.'

'Whatever?'

'Well . . . sometimes . . . sort of weird stuff . . .'

'Oh yes? What kind of weird?' Sally pressed him.

'Well, part of the fun sometimes is getting into places you shouldn't be, right?'

'Perhaps.'

'Come on, it's a feature of misspent youth, right? Like scrumping apples used to be.'

Sally looked at Zak shrewdly.

'I think that what you're referring to is called hacking,' she said, 'and it's very naughty indeed.'

Zak just smiled and moved on.

'Next thing I want is a CD-Rom drive,' he said. 'You can get encyclopedias, dictionaries – I mean, the big Oxford one that usually comes with a magnifying glass – plus it plays music, birdsong, whatever you ask it to look up. And again the images are really high-resolution. Amazing.'

'Is this CD-Rom business the information super-highway?'

'The I-way, they call it.' Zak shrugged. 'A CD-Rom is more like a service area, if you see what I mean. Sort of a Happy Eater. The I-Way itself moves all the time, it's fluid, like the Internet . . .'

Suddenly the realistic image of the half-naked girl in Zak's Samurai game recalled to Sally the vivid pornographic images they had found in Kit's study. She closed her eyes, swallowed hard. And all she could see was Emma's face superimposed on one of those vulnerable bodies. *It wouldn't go away.*

'You all right?' Zak asked, tapping her on the shoulder.

She opened her eyes and found herself staring at Zak, as if returning to reality.

'It's been a long day, and it's catching up on me a bit. Don't worry, though, I'm fine.' But, of course, Sally wasn't really 'all right'. What she had just been looking at gave her a serious case of the shivers.

'Amazing, right?' Zak said.

'It's all very wonderful,' Sally said, 'but it's got a dark side, hasn't it? I mean, no one can really control what comes over the phone line to your computer, or any of the other thousands and thousands of computers linked up like this.'

'No,' Zak looked genuinely puzzled. 'But why should you worry about that?'

Of course, he didn't know about the paedophile images found in Kit's desk, or at least Sally didn't think so.

'"Oh brave new world that has such people in't",' she said.

'Shakespeare,' said Zak. 'Huxley was just quoting, wasn't he?'

'Yes.'

'And who said this boy wasn't getting himself an education?'

Sally laughed despite herself. 'Well, Zak, I'm for bed. Thanks for the show.'

As she made her way along the hall to the spare room, Sally was thoughtful. This had been Kit's world, the one he had inhabited when they were apart and he was managing director of Quantum Software. She knew the company was developing several software packages for this fast-growing market. This was the world Kit and his peers were handing on to the kids. Everything available, good and evil, noble and sleazy, at the press of a switch, the twitch of a mouse. And no matter what governments or parents or anyone else tried to do, these kids would be able to access it all.

Nothing hidden. Everything possible.

The possibilities should have been thrilling. Twenty years ago, Sally would have viewed them just as Zak did.

Now? Now freedom seemed threatening. Infinite possibility inferred infinite evil rather than good. The inevitable corruption of age, the inevitable corruption of experience, the knowledge that even the most harmless, idyllic way of life can conceal poisonous secrets.

Original sin. The believers had something there. After nearly forty years on earth, Sally suddenly thought she saw what they meant. She still couldn't believe in their God, but she could see what they meant.

Sally wished she could un-know the world. She wished she could be innocent again, live in blissful ignorance with Emma and Kit. And she knew she never would. Never.

TWENTY

Mid-morning Sally drove over to the secure accommodation to see Emma, knowing Jonathan wasn't planning to visit until the afternoon. She wanted to spend time alone with her daughter.

Sally had lain awake half the night before, going over and over her conversation with Yardley, haunted by its implications. '*I wish I could talk to Emma, ask her the truth,*' Sally had admitted just before the end of their session.

Yardley seemed to understand. '*You need to, and one day you will. Perhaps in the not too distant future.*'

By dawn Sally had come to a feverish decision. The questions had to be asked of Emma now, by her mother, however difficult for both of them.

Emma seemed unchanged. Articulate but in a childlike kind of way. Affectionate, but as if she was separated from everyone by thin, impenetrable glass. She showed no curiosity about why Jonathan wasn't there too.

'So, how are you feeling?' Sally asked after they had hugged and sat down on the sofa together.

The duty social worker, a big, friendly man named Tony Hutchinson, was in the room, just as he had to be, but trying not to be too intrusive.

'Not excellent, Mum. Just OK.'

225

Do it. Do it now, Sally told herself.

'Darling,' she said, trying to keep her voice as normal as possible. 'I want to ask you something. All right?' Emma nodded. 'I want to ask you two questions.' She paused, then slightly lowered her voice so as not to alert the social worker's protective interest. 'The first is, did you stab Kit?'

Emma looked at her in a curiously blank but direct way. Sally might just have asked her, 'Is this the way to the underground?' or whether she had brushed her teeth this morning.

'Yes,' she said finally.

'No one else was there?'

Sally's daughter shook her head.

'Why? Emma, why?'

'Because he was bad.'

'What do you mean by bad, darling? What *exactly*?' Sally wondered if she'd pressed too hard.

Emma hesitated. Her violet-blue eyes clouded with pain.

Sally could see that Tony, the social worker, was casting concerned glances in her direction, but she knew she had to keep going.

'Darling. Why was Kit bad?' she said.

'He . . . he did bad things!' Emma answered, and started to sob.

Now Tony was on his feet.

'Mrs Jackson,' he said gruffly, 'we can't have Emma being upset. I think it might be better if you just confined yourself to family chat, don't you?'

'Yes.' Sally reached over and held Emma in her arms. 'It's all right, darling,' she murmured over and over. 'It's all right now.'

Then came the other part of her plan for the day. Sally drove over to the Charing Cross Hospital. Her intention was to sit by Kit's bedside until it was time to go for her second session at Yardley's consulting rooms, which were only a ten-minute drive from there. After what Emma had just said, this had turned into the hardest part of all.

At first after Sally arrived, everything seemed the same, just as it had with Emma. Stasis.

Kit lay there, propped up on the pillows and besieged by his tubes. He seemed in a light sleep, just like he looked sometimes when he nodded off over the Sunday papers. Sally sat watching him for twenty minutes or so, as she had on other days.

'*God, I wish you could make this man innocent despite everything,*' she kept murmuring to herself, repeating it like a prayer, a mantra. Sally had two mantras: the first was, 'Make Emma well' and the second was, 'Make Kit innocent'.

But there had been a change. In her heart, she was beginning to acknowledge that Kit might not be innocent; that he had done terrible, unforgivable things to her daughter. It was only an effort of mind, of the will, that kept Sally insisting on the possibility that this might not be so.

It was while she was saying, 'Make Kit innocent' particularly hard that he seemed to her to open his eyes slightly and turn towards her. Sally leaned forward, took his hand.

'Kit? Are you there?'

And she was sure he smiled . . .

Sally gently put down her husband's hand and ran to the door.

'Nurse!' she called out once she was in the corridor, ignoring the policeman on duty.

Sister Majukwu appeared from her office, concerned.

'Mrs Jackson. What is it? Is your husband all right?'

'Sister! Kit just opened his eyes! He smiled!'

Five minutes later a doctor was on the scene. He did a series of checks, then joined them in the sister's office. A tall young Indian named Patel, he managed to combine a patrician manner with a kind of twinkling warmth.

'Mr Jackson is definitely becoming more aware of the outside world,' Patel told Sally. 'We, have noticed this before, which has given us hope that he may recover.'

'Is there anything we can do?'

'Only what you do already. Come to his bedside, talk to him.'

'He may be able to talk again one day?'

'We hope so.'

It was only then that Sally glanced at the office clock. It was ten to two.

'Oh God. I'm late for an appointment.'

There was no time even to say goodbye to Kit. Sally ran out of the office, headed for the visitors' car park.

It was just after two when Sally arrived in the street outside Yardley's practice. And there wasn't a single meter free. Aching with frustration, she drove round the block once, twice.

By the third circuit, Sally was thinking of taking a chance on a resident's parking space, even though she knew they checked regularly for permit-stickers and, living south of the river, she didn't have one. Then, as if in answer to her prayers, a van started to manoeuvre out of a metered parking space up ahead. She waited, then zipped into it.

It was ten past two when Sally pressed the entry-buzzer and was admitted to Yardley's consulting rooms. Yardley was friendly as ever, and totally non-judgmental about her lateness.

As soon as the door closed behind her, Sally told Yardley about Kit.

'But that's great.' Yardley smiled. 'Did you speak to the doctor on duty?'

Sally nodded. 'It looks as if Kit's slowly coming out of the coma. Nothing's for certain, but apparently the chances are getting better with each day.'

Only then did Sally tell Yardley about her time with Emma, her questions and the girl's answers.

Yardley looked at her keenly.

'I wouldn't have questioned her quite so closely quite so soon, but perhaps it was for the best,' he said. 'Are you satisfied that she was telling the truth?'

Sally nodded reluctantly.

'The next few months will be a very telling time for all of you,' Yardley said. 'Especially if – or should I say when – your husband is able to speak and account for his actions. You will be presented with some decisions.'

'I know. I'm thrilled . . . but also apprehensive.'

'Good. That's the right mix of emotions, I think.'

Yardley indicated for her to take the chair opposite his.

'That's as maybe, Noel. But on the way here I felt so tense I could explode.'

'Well, we'll deal with everything as it comes, OK? Now, I hope yesterday's session was helpful. What we really need is for you to relax. So take it easy. Try to ease your grip on the arms of the chair. Let your muscles loosen . . .'

'But perhaps I need to talk. I have the decision about whether to keep Kit's baby or not. I'm so frightened. I know I shouldn't have it, for everyone's sake, but I just don't seem to be able . . .'

'Of course. Don't worry about that now, though.' Yardley's

kind, intense eyes were locked into Sally's. She sensed her whole body untightening. Her feet and hands were starting to feel heavy. 'That's it,' he murmured. 'Let go. You're completely safe with me, Sally. Relax and listen to my voice . . . listen to my voice . . . There . . . See how easy it is?'

'Yes.' Faint, dreamy.

'You trust me?'

'Oh yes.'

'Wonderful . . .'

He passed his hand over her eyes and they didn't flicker.

'We're going to share a secret,' Yardley murmured then. 'A secret word. When I say it, you're going to feel exactly as you feel now, trusting, loving, completely and unconditionally cooperative. Shall I tell you it?'

'Please.'

'*Daydream* is the word, Sally. What is it?'

'Daydream.'

'Good. Daydream is *our* word. When I say it to you, whatever else is happening, you'll become like you are now, completely trusting and cooperative, because whatever I say to do is for the best, OK?'

Sally nodded and smiled. 'The best.'

'Yes. You can trust me, you see, Sally,' Yardley said. 'You can trust me completely . . . trust me *absolutely* . . .'

When Sally stepped out on to the pavement just under an hour later, her mind was still filled with conflicting images, and the voices in her head were still arguing, but her body was much less tense.

Sally retraced her route towards the parking bay where she had left her Golf, thinking about the session with Yardley that had led to this new state of relaxation. He had told her she was mentally and physically exhausted. This must have been why she could remember so little about the fifty or so minutes she had spent with him in that room. In fact – although he was far too polite to tell her so – she must have been asleep during the greater part of the session.

Yardley was so *accepting*. That was the wonderful aspect of it all. And every time she spent with him left her stronger, more able to do what she knew she had to do . . .

Which was to have the abortion. Now was no time to have Kit's child – not for her, for Emma, or even for the child itself. As for Kit, he didn't even know she was pregnant. *She would make sure he never knew. And if – no, when, as Noel Yardley kept insisting – Kit regained consciousness, then matters would explain themselves.*

So there was one crucial decision reached. Yardley had even agreed to organise the whole thing, make an appointment with a gynaecologist friend, supply the necessary medical certificate. There would be life on the other side of this terrible crisis. And Noel Yardley had helped to make it possible.

Sally arrived at her car, unlocked the door and flicked off the alarm. Once in the driver's seat, she thought, *What I need now is some nice, uplifting music.*

There were usually a few tapes in the glove compartment. Sally clicked it open. There were three or four in there. But what caught her eye was a large, folded sheet of pink paper. She frowned, picked it up, opened the paper out.

It was a parking ticket. Borough of Chiswick and Hammersmith. From the previous week, while she had been in Manchester and Kit had been using this car, because his Mercedes was in for repairs.

The date was Wednesday, the day before Kit had been stabbed.

The time was 1:20 p.m.

The offence: parking in a resident's bay without a permit.

The place: in exactly this same street, right outside Noel Yardley's consulting rooms.

Of course. Kit hadn't found a meter. He'd been in a rush, taken a chance . . .

For some moments Sally sat staring at the parking ticket, unable to believe the evidence of her eyes. She realised that her hands were shaking.

Nevertheless, her mind was working with a kind of icy, almost cruel clarity. Memories of the past week came flooding back.

Now Sally remembered Kit's diary entry for that Wednesday: *1:00 – N.Y.*

Of course, she had thought that 'NY' stood for New York. Now she realised it stood not for a place but for a person.

'N.Y.' had stood for Noel Yardley.

Why had Kit come here? What had happened? Had this been why, the very last time he spoke to her, he had been so cagey?

Sally refolded the parking ticket and put it in her bag. She sat in the car, feeling as if she were tipping into madness. Too much in one day, too much . . . She couldn't go back and ask Yardley any of the questions that were coursing through her brain. He had gone straight on to another patient at three o'clock, when she had left. Sally knew he usually worked through until six or seven.

Perhaps Noel Yardley had been protecting her from something terrible? Perhaps the police were too?

Sally picked up her car phone, punched out the number for Richmond police station, her mind racing with the questions she wanted to ask Sergeant Lipari. But when someone at the station answered, she killed the phone and slid it back in its cradle. No, Sergeant Lipari would only give her a lecture about the heart ruling the head. As for Liz, she had gone back to work today. She wouldn't be home until quite late.

Oh God, perhaps this was all a dream . . . or a nightmare . . .

Sally's jaw tightened. The one thing she wasn't going to doubt was her sanity. She turned the key in the VW's ignition. What she needed, she told herself, was a good, mind-clearing walk on Putney Heath.

Then she would know what to do next.

There must be an explanation for this.

If there wasn't, where else could she turn?

Sally ran a hand through her hair, pressed her lips together, and rang the bell marked 'Dr N.B. Yardley'.

She waited twenty seconds and rang again.

After a full half-minute, Sally let out a little grunt of frustration, took a deep breath, and punched the other button, the one that said 'Private'.

'Yes?'

The familiar voice that rustled down the intercom was crisp but approachable.

'Dr Yardley? It's Sally Jackson.'

'A surprise, but a very pleasant one,' the voice said. Quite natural, unruffled. 'Do come in.'

A buzz. A click. Sally pushed her way in and found herself at the bottom of a sculpted hardwood staircase. The stair carpet looked oriental, the walls had been delicately ragged and dragged and everything else by someone who knew what they were doing.

Yardley was waiting on the top landing, in tan khakis and a navy sweatshirt.

'Welcome to my humble abode,' he said.

There was a shyness in his manner outside the consulting room which was almost touching.

'I hope you don't mind me dropping round,' Sally said, suddenly unsure of herself. 'Something . . . came up . . .'

'Of course. Fine. I said I'd make myself available when you needed me, and here I am. Come in.'

The living room was mostly Indian-import furniture – a day-bed serving as a coffee-table, ornate hardwood occasional tables to match the banisters on the stairs – with big, comfortable colonial-style Lloyd-Loom chairs to lounge in. There was no overhead lighting. The lamps were all mounted on Middle-Eastern oil jars. Very nice.

'Can I offer you a drink?' Yardley said. 'I've got a respectable white Burgundy chilling in the fridge.' He smiled. 'Never mind your condition. A few sips won't hurt you. Trust me, I'm a doctor.'

Keep it casual, Sally thought, and said, 'Why not?'

Above the fireplace hung a mirror in a big oriental frame. The wood was one of those unusual rainforest ones: maybe Paduk. Sally could see her and Yardley's reflections in the glass. Maybe it was the soft lighting, but she thought she looked less haggard than she had expected – or rather, feared. For what it was worth, in that moment in the mirror, she and Yardley made a handsome combination.

'Do sit down,' he said, and wandered off towards the kitchen, which lay at the end of a short hallway. He whistled an operatic aria as he went, that soaring one from Donizetti's *Lucia di Lammermoor*.

But Sally somehow didn't want to sit down. She took the opportunity to prowl around the living room, get the feel of the place. There was the pop of a cork from the kitchen, the clink of glasses being taken from a cupboard. Off to the right of the hall she saw Yardley's study through its open door: all steel and blond wood, with a big VDU staring out at her amid a mass of other computer-type equipment.

Sally saw Yardley emerge carrying the bottle – carefully, by the neck, so as not to warm it with his hands – and the glasses. She stepped back into the room.

As Yardley poured the white Burgundy, he chatted away quite naturally. He told her he got his supplies from the Wine Society. This was a new consignment, arrived just before the weekend, and he hoped it was as good as usual.

She accepted the drink, took a sip. 'Very nice.'

'Good,' said Yardley with a smile, inviting her to take a seat. 'The Society doesn't usually let one down.' He nestled back in his chair. 'So how can I help you, Sally? As you can see, I'm off duty, but so long as it doesn't involve anything more strenuous than a goblet of plonk and a friendly ear, I'm at your disposal.'

'Right.' Sally put down her glass on the table between them. 'Noel . . . do you mind if I ask you something?'

'Of course not. I assume that's what you're here for. Fire away.'

Sally screwed up her courage.

'I know Kit was here last week. Did you see him?'

Yardley had been in the process of raising his own glass to his lips. He paused, smiled ruefully.

'Yes,' he said.

'Why didn't you tell the police? Why didn't you tell *me*?'

Yardley sipped his wine thoughtfully for a few moments.

'Sally, I made a decision,' he said at last. 'Wearing my shrink's hat rather than my dutiful citizen's. You see, I suspected that you'd seek support from me, and I thought that if you did I'd be able to help you, but I sort of suspected that if you knew I'd been talking with Kit I'd be tainted and you wouldn't feel able to open up, which is essential if you're to heal . . .' He snatched a breath. 'Phew! Long sentence! Anyway, it seemed to me that I wouldn't be telling the police anything they didn't already know.'

'I see,' said Sally weakly.

Yardley looked at her sadly, though he didn't shy from eye-contact.

'You're upset, Sally. I can tell. Maybe I did the wrong thing.'

Sally avoided that one.

'What did you and Kit talk about?' she asked.

'Emma, first of all. Kit went on a lot about the medical examination, and his suspicions about some teenage boy.'

'Zak? He's the son of my oldest friend, Liz.'

'Sounds right. Kit even railed against Jonathan, your ex. Added to which, he talked about your anxieties, which he said were undermining your own emotional health . . .'

'The police would say all that talk was just a smoke-screen, to confuse the situation if the abuse came to light,' Sally said. 'Like the medical examination. Like his whole pose as the jolly, caring stepfather.'

'If that was your husband's game, Sally, he played it very skilfully. I was convinced at the time. Now, of course, I don't know.'

Sally closed her eyes. *Think only good . . .*

236

Yardley paused, as if wondering whether to go on.

'In fact,' he said then, 'Kit asked me outright what I'd think if I was asked to take you on as a client . . .'

Sally opened her eyes again. 'Asked by whom? Me? Him?'

'I don't know. I suppose the implication was, he might talk you into it.'

'And what did you tell him?'

'The truth. That I couldn't really be your therapist and Emma's at the same time.'

'Oh.'

'Except now, of course, I can help you, because Emma is getting help elsewhere . . .' Yardley sighed. 'Listen, Sally, if you don't think we can work together any more, we can call this off now.'

There was a silence.

'I don't know if I should tell the police,' Sally said at last.

'I can't stop you. The choice is yours.'

'Would it affect your career?'

'Who knows?' Yardley made a little maybe-yes-maybe-no gesture with his right hand. 'Not terminally, though, I'm sure. We shrinks are the modern priests, they say. Well, I can plead the sanctity of the confessional.'

Sally looked at Yardley, felt her chest tighten with pre-emptive anxiety. If she did this to him, she would never see him again, and then she would have no one.

'Thanks for being honest with me,' Sally said. All at once she felt inexpressibly weary and depressed. 'Anyway, the police feel they have the case wrapped up. I think they just don't care any more . . .'

'That's not true,' Yardley said. 'They care a great deal. Or at least Sergeant Lipari does. But in the final analysis it's up to her boss. He's a tough cookie, I can tell you. To him, the evidence is simply overwhelming. And, of course, we should remember that he has a lot of other equally serious cases to deal with.'

Sally got to her feet, leaving her wine unfinished.

'Yes. And now I'll let you get on with your work.'

Sally turned to leave. Then, on impulse, she stepped up to the door of his study and looked inside. There was a document on the screen; what looked like a series of very lifelike, detailed drawings of parts of the brain. The quality of the images was extraordinary.

Yardley joined her in the doorway.

'This is where it all gets done, of course,' he said pleasantly. 'My research and article-writing, that is.'

'You remember we were talking about Zak earlier?' Sally said. 'He showed me his computer system last night. It was pretty amazing to a novice like me, but not nearly as impressive as what you have here.'

'How much do you know about computers, Sally?'

'Kit used to talk about his work. He ran – runs – a software company. Oh, and I can word-process. Sort of.'

'So you can play the penny-whistle,' Yardley said. 'Well, this is the equivalent of a symphony orchestra. It's the most powerful system available to private users at the moment. It puts me in instant touch with other therapists and specialists all over the world, all the major data-bases, plus the Internet, which I'm sure you've heard of. Not as interesting as some claim, by the way. It's anarchy out there – unless you know exactly what you're after and precisely who has it!'

'Never mind. Anyway, the resolution-quality is quite fantastic.'

'The images you see are digitally processed, which is why they're so sharp.'

'That's the CD-Drive thing, is it?'

'I thought you were supposed to be ignorant.'

'Zak was raving on about all that last night.'

'Well, yes, it is a CD-Rom drive. And in a few months it'll probably need upgrading again . . . Soon we'll be able to order up films and documentaries at the flick of a switch over an ordinary phone line.'

There was still polite enthusiasm in Yardley's voice, but he was surreptitiously looking at his watch, as he had done that afternoon when they had started to over run.

'Better go,' Sally said, dutifully picking up his cue.

'Sorry. Got a paper to write, and the deadline's right on top of me,' Yardley said. 'So, can you conceive of coming to tomorrow's session?' He smiled boyishly. 'I promise you, I have no more secrets in store about Kit's activities.'

'It would be stupid to give up now, wouldn't it?' Sally said.

'See you tomorrow then?'

'OK. Good luck with your paper.'

It wasn't until she was back out in the street, away from Yardley and his voice and his kind eyes that something happened to Sally. Her world tipped again, as it had tipped so many times in the past weeks.

She got back in her car, started the engine.

It would be stupid to give up now.

Sally's own words came back to her, but with their meaning turned through a hundred and eighty degrees. She felt frightened, daring, triumphant, all at the same time.

Oh yes, very stupid. In every possible way.

TWENTY-ONE

Sally listened at the door of Zak Paine's room. There was music on the stereo. He was in. And Liz and Harry were still both out. Now was the time, or never.

Sally knocked, waited for a count of three, then opened the door.

Zak was sprawled on the bed in his usual uniform of torn jeans and T-shirt. He looked at Sally through a blur of cigarette smoke, smiled.

'Come in,' he said.

She closed the door behind her. Zak rolled lazily towards the edge of the bed, sat facing Sally.

'Hi. How's Emma?'

'Not too bad. She looks a little more human every day, but she's still not saying much.'

'Question of time.'

'Yes.'

The music was an angry thrash, but melodic. 'Nirvana,' Sally said.

'Ten out of ten.'

'Emma has one of their records.'

'*Records*? Oh no.'

'You know what I mean: CDs, tapes, whatever . . .'

Zak got to his feet, took a step over to the armchair in the corner, swept the pile of clothes from it, bowed politely.

'Take a seat. Please.'

'Thanks.'

'Can't supply you with a drink. You won't want a ciggy. Can't offer you much else except my own company.' The boy appraised Sally with a bleary shrewdness. 'Want something in particular? Or are you just feeling lonely?'

'Well, I could do with a little company,' Sally admitted. 'But . . . well, I have a request too.'

'Go ahead.'

'Not much. Just a bit of hacking.'

Zak raised an eyebrow, glanced at his computer in the corner.

'Hey, Sally,' he mumbled. 'I know we talked about—'

'This is not a joke. I'm absolutely serious,' Sally cut in. 'I know you do that stuff for fun. Now I want you to do it for me. Or, more precisely, for Emma.'

Zak wandered around the room, frowning. There was a slightly sweet smell in the air, mingled with tobacco smoke. Sally wondered if he had been doing some dope. The scent was certainly suspicious. She hadn't been at college in the seventies for nothing.

Zak stopped, turned and faced her. He was wearing a wicked grin.

'OK,' he said. 'I mean, how can I refuse?' He squinted at her keenly. 'This is strictly off the record, agreed?'

'Strictly. I'll never tell a soul without your permission.'

'Thanks.' He sat down at his desk, flicked the switch on the computer system, waited for it to warm up. 'Who – or what – do you want to hack into?'

'I can't tell you that.'

'Is the system protected?'

'I don't know. Perhaps.'

'Well, all I need is for you to give me the phone number.' Zak shook his head in wry disbelief. 'Who'd believe it? Sally, Mum's oldest, straightest friend, hires a hacker.'

Sally handed over the piece of paper on which she had written Noel Yardley's private phone number.

'There you are,' she said, her voice icy with determination. 'Get going.'

Zak was in.

The process had been terrifyingly easy. Now twenty minutes after first hacking into the computer on the other side of the river, he was still roaming its open files, checking through with a thoroughness that belied his casualness, like a burglar who knows the places where house-owners keep their valuables. Zak seemed completely at home in this world, more so than in the real one. He knew its possibilities, its rules and how to break them.

'Aha,' he said softly after keying in yet another request. 'We have a locked file.'

Sally looked at the screen of Zak's computer. It was blue, and blank except for the request: PASSWORD (LOCKED).

'Damn,' Sally said. 'Why did I think it would be simple? Is there anything we can do about it?'

'Depends whether he's – is it a "he" . . . ?' Sally nodded. 'Well, it depends whether he's interested in deterring casual strollers or seriously concerned to protect his secrets,' Zak said, sucking through his teeth. 'Looks like a middling-difficult password system to me.'

'Yes. But can you get round it?'

Zak looked at Sally out of the corner of his eye. 'You are keen, aren't you? What are you expecting to find in there?'

'I don't know.' She returned Zak's gaze until he looked away, then repeated: 'Can you get round that protection, Zak?'

'Maybe,' he said. 'He's set it up to protect against more than the casual intruder. Even fairly savvy Net-users probably couldn't crack it.' Zak smiled cockily, rubbed his hands in anticipation. 'However! It shouldn't be a problem to a seriously experienced hacker such as myself.'

Zak keyed in an instruction to his computer, sat back with arms folded, as it started to rack through an unseen list.

One minute passed, then two. And suddenly a word flashed up on the screen: 'KINDERGARTEN'. A second later, Zak was into the file and it was asking him what he wanted next.

'Easy-peasy,' he muttered.

'How did you do *that*?'

'Oh, you can get programmes,' Zak said. 'Commercially available. Crack just about any locking system given time, but you have to know a few extra tricks yourself.' He laughed. 'They even build in a time-delay to make it look harder than it actually is.'

'God, it's scary.'

'Yeah, well, not many people know that. And those that do don't sleep easy at night.'

Sally looked back at the screen. 'What is this stuff? It looks different.'

'This is part of an outside bulletin-board file that's been saved on to your man's hard disk.'

'What's a bulletin-board?' Sally asked.

'The origin's obvious. Like those cork boards people have in the kitchen. But what it actually is, is a sort of cyberspace meeting-room. I mean, it connects like-minded users with a central space where they can check in with each other and exchange information and other kinds of material.'

'It's got a phone number in the top corner there.'

Zak squinted at the screen.

'Oh, right.'

'Where is the bulletin-board, then?' Sally asked. 'I mean, actually, geographically, in the real world?'

'Dunno. I've got an international code book somewhere, though.' Zak smiled impishly. 'Has been known to come in handy . . .'

He found the code book under a pile of games cassettes, tossed it to Sally, who wrote the number on the screen down on a scrap of paper and leafed through the international lists.

'Wait a sec . . .' She looked up, frowning. 'It's Amsterdam,' she said.

'Right.'

'So, what's on the screen now?' Sally demanded. 'That's what they call a menu there, isn't it?'

'Yeah. Exactly. Want to see what's for dinner?'

Sally nodded. Her heart was pounding. She strove to keep up a calm façade, even though she knew she was close to something awesome and terrible.

In response to Zak's commands, the screen flashed up the request SELECT *NYMPHFILE* Y/N?

'Yes,' Sally said quickly.

Now she felt as if she were floating inside her own head, about to lift off, but her mind was cool and clear. Some tigress-like survival instinct had taken over. She would not stop until she knew, knew for certain. No matter what the knowledge brought.

Zak pressed 'Y' and a numbered list appeared: 1) LOLITA . .
. 2) FANNY . . . 3) TWINTIME . . .

Zak's fingers hovered above the keys. He hesitated, glanced
at Sally.

'This stuff you've got me into looks . . . ah, pretty sleazy,
actually,' he said quietly. 'You realise I won't be eighteen for
another year and two months, Sally.' Attempting to make a joke
of it.

'You're old enough to drink and do a few drugs,' Sally said
harshly. 'You're old enough for this.' She indicated the list,
shuddered. 'You choose, Zak. I can't.'

'OK. You're the boss.' Zak frowned, selected TWINTIME.

A high-definition image appeared that made Sally's gorge
rise. Two young girls, roughly Emma's age, naked on a bed,
displaying themselves for somebody's camera.

The request *PLAY?* flashed on and off persistently.

'Who . . . are . . . those children . . .' murmured Sally.

Zak's lips were pressed together in embarrassment. He
couldn't meet Sally's eye.

'Jesus,' he said, all his playful bravado gone.

And then the screen went blank.

There was a shocked silence.

'What the hell happened there?' Sally was the first to speak.
Zak shrugged his shoulders.

'Someone at the other end cut the connection. I mean,
probably they pulled the modem jack out. Brutal but effective.'

'Why?'

'I'd guess, because they found us poking around in their hard
disk and they didn't want us there.'

'So what do we do now?'

'Er . . . we've got the number of the bulletin-board in

Amsterdam. We could dial it direct. Except that usually you need to get accepted, sort of.'

'Like joining a club,' Sally said with conscious irony.

'Yeah. And with . . . well, the naughty lines, they make you pay and stuff before you can access it.'

'Credit card?'

'That'll do nicely.'

'You seem to know a lot about this business, Zak.'

'Sure. It's like browsing on the top shelf at the newsagent's. But I never got involved with really pervie stuff like we just saw.' Zak eyed Sally cautiously. 'Promise you won't tell Mum or Harry, OK?'

'I promise. Now let's try the bulletin-board direct.'

Zak put them through. The system was protected, of course, and by a far more sophisticated system than Yardley's. There was no indication of how you 'joined'.

'Probably you have to be personally introduced,' Zak suggested. 'And judging from the security they've got themselves, it has to be really hardcore stuff. Whoever your man there is – it's all right, I don't want to know – he must be really into that scene. One of the inner circle or whatever.'

'Could you hack into it?'

'I could give it a go. Probably be a lot harder than the private pervert's system, though, 'cos they're pros. We could be here most of the night trying.'

Sally nodded. 'I get the message. It doesn't matter, anyway.'

'So what now?'

'Why don't we see if the guy on the first number's reconnected himself? You never know your luck.'

Surprisingly, the computer was already back on line, but their excitement was short-lived. The protected files they had accessed half an hour earlier had been removed from the hard disk altogether. All trace of contact with the paedophile bulletin-board had been carefully eliminated.

'Well, we know it wasn't a power-cut that blanked the screen earlier,' Zak said. 'He wanted us out of there. Once he'd done that, he cleaned up his disk, and no hanging about.'

'Could he have traced us?'

'Not unless he had specialised equipment.' Zak let out a nervous laugh. 'Jesus, Sally, who is this dude?'

'I can't tell you. And you mustn't say anything to anyone about what we've done tonight. Not until I've done what I have to do.'

'Fair enough.'

Zak knew enough not to push her.

Sally stared at the screen. Yardley's harmless professional files twinkled innocently at her in their neat listings. They began to blur in front of her eyes. The poison had been taken out of them, and now they didn't interest her any more.

'Turn it off, for God's sake, Zak,' she said, suddenly weary and sick at heart.

Zak obliged, found his cigarettes and lit one.

Sally breathed out in a long sigh of frustration. She unballed her fists, a warrior who had faced her opponent only to have him vanish from the field of combat.

'What now?' Zak asked.

'Well, what I'd really like to do is go downstairs and pour myself a large vodka and tonic from your mother's drinks cupboard.' Sally smiled bitterly. 'Then I might go and stick my head down the toilet. Any more questions?'

248

TWENTY-TWO

The clock said eight forty-five when Liz and Zak finally hurried out of the house – the boy still clutching a slice of breakfast toast – and Sally could commandeer the phone in the living room.

The hardest thing had been saying nothing to Liz last night, especially after a large vodka and tonic, but she didn't want another argument about Kit. In any case the only person worth convincing was somebody who could do something about it – which meant Detective Sergeant Cheryl Lipari.

Sally brought her ginger tea into the living room, sat down and dialled Cheryl Lipari's number.

It rang for some time. Then a man's voice answered.

'Constable Vaughan speaking.'

'Detective Sergeant Lipari, please,' Sally said decisively.

'I'm afraid she's not at her desk today. In fact, she's out of London on police business. Can I help you?'

Sally bit her lip in disappointment. 'No . . . I need to speak to her personally. When will she be back?'

'Tomorrow. Are you sure I can't help you . . . I'm sorry, you didn't give your name . . .'

'It's Mrs Jackson. Emma Quinn's mother. Yes, we've met. Could you take a message?'

'Of course.'

Vaughan was cool, polite, but she sensed a faint after-bite of sarcasm. Sally hadn't liked Vaughan much when she had met him, and she liked him even less now.

'Well, please tell her that Zak Paine and I have been busy, and we've found out something very disturbing about Dr Yardley. Noel Yardley. Got that?'

'Yes.'

'Have you written it down?'

'Yes, Mrs Jackson. I've written it down.'

'I don't suppose there's any way the message could be got to her wherever she is. Doesn't she have a mobile?'

'I'm afraid not, Mrs Jackson.'

Sally knew Vaughan was humouring her; she could picture the face he was making into the phone, but what the hell.

'But if Sergeant Lipari does come back to the office today—' Sally began.

'She won't,' Vaughan said crisply. 'But she'll definitely be in first thing tomorrow.' Pause for emphasis. 'She is an *extremely* busy officer.'

'I know,' said Sally, undeterred. If necessary she would break down the door to get into Sergeant Lipari's office, but she'd see about that tomorrow. 'I'm not wasting her time, I promise. You will make sure she gets my message?'

'Of course, Mrs Jackson.'

'And you'll tell her what I said.'

'Oh yes.'

'Thank you, Constable.'

It was only after Sally had put down the phone that the panic hit her. The one thing she had not reckoned on was that Sergeant Lipari would be so totally unavailable. No point in going above her. Superintendent Garfield, Sally knew, was even less sympathetic than the constable she had just spoken to. Sally drank the rest of her soothing tea in worried gulps. She wrapped her arms around herself as if cold, though it was a warm June day outside, and she felt herself tremble with anxiety.

Suddenly Sally was aware of being terribly, terribly alone – more alone than at any time since the night when Kit had been stabbed and her life had changed so irrevocably.

But what to do next? She had an appointment with Yardley just after lunch . . .

Several times as she sat there, Sally was tempted to pick up the phone, ring Yardley and cancel the appointment. There was no reason why he should connect her with the invasion of his computer's hard disk, but if she suddenly failed to turn up, he might, just might, start to become suspicious.

No. Best to brazen it out, get through the day, and speak to Sergeant Lipari first thing tomorrow morning. In fact, there might be a chance this afternoon to probe a little, see if her new view of Noel Yardley enabled her to penetrate his armour.

And now to the routine. Something to eat. Then to Emma, and to Kit. Visiting them would give Sally strength, the ability to get through this crucial day.

There was light at the end of this tunnel of horror. She was sure of it.

'How was Emma today?' Yardley asked.

'Slowly coming back to us, I think, Noel.'

'Excellent. And Kit?'

'He opened his eyes a couple of times. They say he's aware of what's going on around him but can't yet communicate.'

'That's wonderful news. And how are *you*, Sally?'

'Oh, fine. Much better, thanks.'

Nothing about Yardley seemed changed. Sally was shocked by how calm she felt. Really calm. It was like a betrayal of her experience, how easy it was to be with this man, despite what she knew about him. Perhaps she should have been pleased with herself, but she wasn't fooled. Yardley was extraordinarily seductive, and all the more dangerous for that.

'Terrific,' Yardley said with every indication of satisfaction. 'Well, since you're in somewhat more robust shape today, let's really have a go at getting into those feelings, shall we?'

'All right.'

'So relax. *Daydream* . . .'

Yardley was looking straight at her, his brown eyes kind and tranquil. Bottomless. Despite her wariness, her determination not to be controlled by him, she felt her fears really dropping away, her whole body becoming pleasantly heavy.

A while later – perhaps a minute, perhaps an hour, Sally didn't know or care – she heard Yardley's voice, soft and compelling:

'Daydream,' he repeated.

And the tiny, helpless remnants of her anxieties were dispelled.

He sighed. 'I should have done this yesterday when you told me you knew about Kit's visit. I thought I could just talk to you and everything would be all right, but I was mistaken. Very silly of me. But never mind. We can undo the harm, can't we? Do you trust me, Sally?'

'Yes. Of course.'

'Good. So safe. You trust me completely. You can tell me anything, everything.' There was a pause. Then Yardley stroked her hand. 'Do you know who I am, Sally?'

'No . . .' Sally said, but she was smiling. She was a girl once more, and this was a game.

Yardley laughed softly.

'You do know who I am, but I'll tell you anyway, shall I? So you know you're safe.'

'Yes.'

'Well, darling, I'm your *Good Daddy*. You'll do anything for me, won't you?'

'Oh yes.'

'You'll tell me everything.'

'Yes.'

'So first I want you to tell me what you were doing last night. You were playing with a computer, weren't you?'

Sally nodded obediently. 'Yes. And I got frightened, so frightened . . .'

'Of course you did.' He paused, sighed. 'You don't understand, do you? You're just like all the rest of them. You don't understand the beauty of what Emma and I had together. This is why we had to hide it.' There was a hint of silky anger in his voice. 'It's so sad when a truly beautiful thing is spoiled.'

'I'm sorry. Really.'

'It's all right, it's all right. You can make it up to your Good Daddy. Just listen to what I have to say. Listen precisely to what I tell you to do . . .'

'The things I do for you,' said Vaughan, drawing lazily on his regular-as-clockwork after-sex cigarette.

'Oh, I hadn't noticed much beyond the basics, actually. At least not tonight.' Sergeant Lipari, propped up on one elbow, was only half-smiling as she spoke.

Vaughan glanced sideways at her. 'You accusing me of not knowing my job?'

Sergeant Lipari's smile broadened. She reached over and flicked his right nipple.

'You do it to your satisfaction, I'm sure.'

'I've had no complaints until now.'

'It was a joke, Derek.'

'Yeah, well, enough of such jolly banter. It's not what I meant. I was referring to fielding your funny phone calls while you're off in Birmingham chasing rapists.'

'What funny calls?'

'Ones from Mrs my-husband-is-innocent Jackson, that's what. She rang this afternoon.'

'You should have told me before.'

'Come on. She's off her trolley. Jesus, she only wanted me to page you in Brum, didn't she?'

'Well, why did she want to talk to me, Derek?' Sergeant Lipari asked urgently. 'I mean, did she tell you what she wanted?'

'Sort of.' Vaughan idly stroked Sergeant Lipari's naked shoulders with his free hand. 'Claimed she and Zak Paine had discovered something "very disturbing" – I quote – about Dr Yardley. The shrink who got Emma Quinn to talk, right?'

'What could she possibly mean? He's a very distinguished man.'

'Apparently. Anyway, sounds to me like, now her ex-husband's finally been eliminated from inquiries, Yardley's her suspect now. Anything but admit Kit Jackson interfered with his stepdaughter. Who's next on her list once Yardley's been cleared, you reckon? Lord Lucan? Martin Bormann?'

Sergeant Lipari didn't laugh. She shrugged off Vaughan's caresses, reached over and plucked the burning cigarette from between his fingers. After a couple of puffs, she handed it back to him and made a face.

'Disgusting habit, Derek.'

'Thanks.'

Sergeant Lipari lay back on the pillows, her gaze thoughtful.

'Well, that's what we have to consider,' she muttered. 'Sally Jackson's either completely batty or an extremely brave and persistent woman whom we've all seriously misunderstood.'

Vaughan put up his hand. 'Please, miss, I vote for batty,' he said in a childish, piping voice.

'I just wish I could make my mind up about that, I really do.' Sergeant Lipari glanced at the little clock beside her bed. It was almost half-past eleven. 'Christ, Derek, ain't you got a home to go to?'

'Just about. At least I did when I left for work this morning.'

'Well, go to it, will you? I've driven a total of two hundred and ninety-five miles today, I feel like I've interviewed the entire female population of the West Midlands, and I've got three of them coming down tomorrow morning to attend an ID parade.'

'Plus you've got to return Mrs Jackson's call. Poor baby.'

'Listen, Derek, give me a break from your chirpy sense of humour, will you? I'm absolutely wiped.'

'But I promised Mrs Jackson on your behalf, darling, and you can't let me down.'

'No way I'd ignore the poor woman, anyway. To tell the truth I still feel there's loose ends there. I'm very curious about Sally Jackson and her affairs, Derek. I still want to know what really happened. And I want to know what happens next.'

'Oh yeah. Sure. Life's just one big soap, isn't it? Script by Cheryl Lipari.'

'There's something in that, actually. I suppose that's why I keep doing this job,' Sergeant Lipari said. 'Even though it means dealing with lots of seriously warped and wicked men – sorry, it *is* usually men, Derek – on both sides of the law.' She could see Vaughan was avoiding her gaze. 'Because I'm curious,' she murmured. 'Because I need to know.'

TWENTY-THREE

Sergeant Lipari clicked away at her report on the Birmingham trip. The words were starting to run into each other. She needed a break from this bloody screen, she decided. Come to think of it, maybe she needed a break from this whole bloody job.

Taking a big sip of coffee, Sergeant Lipari picked up the desk-phone and dialled the number Sally Jackson had left with Vaughan the previous day. Emma's mother answered on the third ring.

'Mrs Jackson, this is Sergeant Lipari from Richmond Police Station,' she began. 'Good morning.'

'Oh, good morning. How are you, Sergeant?'

Sally's voice was, surprisingly, almost spookily calm.

'Fine,' Sergeant Lipari said. *I feel like hell, actually, but that's not the point. What I want to know is, what's your problem?* 'How are you?'

'Bearing up. I think I'm gradually coming to terms with some major decisions.'

'Good.' *This conversation is surreal.* 'But I believe you had a problem yesterday – you left a message. You needed to speak to me. As a matter of urgency.'

'Oh, that. Yes . . . I was concerned about something to do with Noel Yardley,' Sally said. 'But it's all right now.'

'Are you sure? According to the message I got, you'd made some very disturbing discovery about him.'

'I think the man who took the message must have got things a bit garbled.' Sally sounded genuinely puzzled.

'He's been trained not to do that, actually, Mrs Jackson,' Sergeant Lipari said, allowing a little ice into her manner. 'Constable Vaughan is a very experienced officer.' *And if he's made a fool of me, I'll bloody well kill him.*

'Well, I'm very sorry to have bothered you. As I said, everything's fine now. I misunderstood something Noel told me. Thanks for ringing anyway, Sergeant.' Sally paused, then continued in the same level voice. 'I've decided not to have my husband's baby,' she said. 'It's impossible. Noel's been so helpful in empowering me to make the decision. He's even made the appointment for me at the clinic next week.'

'I see. Will—'

'Perhaps Noel will be able to help Emma too. I'm sure that with therapy she would recover so much more quickly. Would the authorities allow that?'

'I don't know, Mrs Jackson. We shall have to see. If I were you, I'd speak to your – I mean, Emma's – solicitor.'

'Yes. Perhaps you're right. Diane seems very confident Emma won't be given a custodial sentence.'

'You realise I can't comment on that, Mrs Jackson.'

'Of course. Anyway, thanks again for your understanding, Sergeant.'

Sergeant Lipari left just enough of a pause to make her point. 'You're welcome,' she said then.

She put the phone down, frowned deeply, then paged WPC White.

When White put her head in the door, Sergeant Lipari

asked her if Vaughan was around.

'Somewhere.'

'Tell him I want to see him. Now. If not sooner.'

White shot Sergeant Lipari a doubting look. 'Right you are, Sergeant,' she said hesitantly. 'OK.'

Vaughan appeared five minutes later. Obviously briefed by White that something was amiss, he looked wary and cocky at the same time. Typical.

'Sit down, Derek.'

He sat down, folded his arms.

'That message from Mrs Jackson,' Sergeant Lipari said. 'She gives a different version. You weren't pulling my leg, were you?'

Vaughan frowned, sincerely perturbed.

'No,' he said firmly. 'I mean, I think Mrs Jackson's off the wall, but I wouldn't kid you about a thing like that. More than my job's worth. You know that.'

'I'll ask you again. Was your account of your conversation with her completely accurate? Tell the truth, I just want to know.'

'Listen,' Vaughan snapped. 'I think you misunderstand.' He lowered his voice. 'Cheryl, what goes on between you and me outside this station is one thing, but work is work. I conveyed the content of that conversation to you under irregular circumstances, as we both know, but I assure you my information was a hundred per cent accurate.'

Sergeant Lipari still said nothing. Vaughan eyeballed her with fierce challenge in his gaze.

'I made notes at the time, Sergeant,' he said in a normal voice. 'You may inspect them should you so wish,' he added formally.

An uneasy silence hung between the two officers. This was serious stuff, and they both knew it.

'OK, Del,' Sergeant Lipari murmured at last. 'I believe you. In which case, I have a feeling something very funny's going on. I just wish I knew what.'

'*No comprendo*,' said Vaughan with a nervous little laugh.

'She denied anything was wrong. Anything at all. "Just a misunderstanding", she said.' Sergeant Lipari paused. 'Two possibilities: either Sally Jackson's fallen in love with her shrink; or she's gone completely round the twist and doesn't know if she' s coming or going.'

'Or both.'

'She sounded really uptight to you, is that right?'

'Absolutely.' Vaughan plucked an imaginary taut string. 'Wired to the nth degree, thank you very much.'

'You're sure Sally Jackson mentioned the name Zak? She and he made this so-called discovery together?'

'Cheryl—'

'OK, OK!' Sergeant Lipari granted the exasperated Vaughan a sour-sweet smile. 'Now clear off. I've got a phone call or two to make and I don't want any distractions.'

Zak Paine was sitting in the school library, supposedly researching an assignment on colonialism. What he was actually doing was reading Philip K. Dick's *Do Androids Dream of Electric Sheep?*

When Mr Hammond, the deputy headmaster, hurried into the library and peered around, Zak didn't bother to hide the book. Hammond was a sixties survivor type who believed that self-motivation and self-esteem were the keys to the kingdom. All the same, Zak had never seen Hammond so agitated. He almost looked . . . well, sort of stern . . .

'Zak Paine, gotcha!'

Hammond approached in loping strides, his greasy grey-blond mane shaking. As he reached Zak, a cowlick of long hair dislodged itself, revealing a bald spot.

'Sir?'

'Someone to see you.'

'Yeah? Who?'

Hammond lowered his voice. 'A policewoman, actually.'

'Oh.' Zak swallowed hard. 'Right.'

They'd found out where he'd been the night Emma stabbed Kit. Oh, sh-e-e-e-t . . .

The dark, attractive detective sergeant was waiting for Zak in Mr Hammond's office. Hammond hustled him through the door and stuck around with his tongue practically hanging out. It was really gross. The deputy head stayed in there for quite a while, fussing over her, asking her if she wanted coffee, even after she had made it quite clear she wanted him to leave. Zak was tempted to ask Sergeant Lipari if she wanted him to turf Hammond out.

Eventually Hammond went, and so did a great deal of Zak's bravado. Sergeant Lipari might be sexy in an upfront, wears-a-bit-too-much-jewellery sort of way, but when you were on her own with her in a room she could give you a look that froze your blood.

'Take a seat, Zak,' she said.

She sat down in Hammond's battered leatherette swivel-chair. Zak subsided into the one opposite her. He was in what passed for uniform. Suddenly he looked less like a child-man, more like a man-child – and a very nervous one at that.

'I'll bet you were hoping you'd never see me again, Zak,' Sergeant Lipari said.

'You said it.'

'Don't bother with the bravado, Zak. I'm not here to catch you out.'

'Oh yeah?' He smiled crookedly. 'I guess you still want to know what I was doing between the hours of two and three a.m. on the night of Thursday the twenty-eighth of May, right?'

'Wrong.'

Sergeant Lipari locked on to Zak's gaze. He was the first to turn away, pretending to check his watch.

'Your friends had tried to sell some cannabis to someone in a club. You were just along for the ride, but that didn't stop you copping a warning clout from the professional drug-dealers who thought the three of you were trying to muscle in on their patch,' she continued matter-of-factly. 'You were lucky they decided you and your mates were just a bunch of middle-class innocents and not worth the trouble, or you'd probably still be in hospital. But I don't care about that.'

Zak Paine reddened, furtively glanced around as if the walls might have ears. 'It was a stupid thing to do,' he said.

'Yes. Wasn't it? I wouldn't chance your arm again, if I were you.'

'So what do you actually care about, Sergeant?' Zak muttered.

'I care about finding out who abused Emma Quinn. Plus, maybe, who stabbed Kit Jackson. And why. How about you?'

'Yeah.' Zak shrugged. 'I care about that too. Especially the thing with Emma.'

Sergeant Lipari let the silence deepen, then leaned forward on the desk and asked softly: 'I want you to describe to me what you and Mrs Jackson were doing the night before last.'

Zak's face betrayed a mixture of puzzlement and suspicion.

'Why can't Sally do that herself?'

'Oh, she has,' Sergeant Lipari lied blandly. 'I just need your side of things, because everyone remembers different details, and every detail counts. You had an adventure with a computer, didn't you?' she added, carefully vague. 'And you found something pretty disturbing.'

Zak thought about that, then shrugged.

'Yeah. Computer porn, wasn't it? I was amazed. Sally, of all people! She asked me to get through . . .'

'Yes?'

'Well, you know, hack into this number,' he corrected himself. 'We found some porn files in there. Hard stuff, I think. Young girls. Only then whoever's computer it was realised we were in there, and he cut us off . . .'

'Right. And this person was . . .'

'I dunno. Sally wouldn't say.' Zak looked at Sergeant Lipari with some of his old distrust. 'Didn't she tell you?'

'Where was this computer?' Sergeant Lipari demanded, realising her only chance was to push on regardless, steamroller the boy into spilling out all the events of his and Sally's wild night at the computer.

'It was a London number,' Zak said.

'Did you write it down?'

Zak shook his head. 'All I remember is, it was an 0171.'

'You're sure you can't remember more than that?'

'Nah.' He caught Sergeant Lipari's frown of frustration, smiled slowly. 'But it was tied into a bulletin-board in Amsterdam. That's where the hardcore porn had been downloaded from. I noted it down so Sally could look up the code. I should be able to find that number for you if you want it, Sergeant. No sweat.'

Sergeant Lipari made it back to the station with twenty minutes to spare before the rape witnesses from the Midlands were due. She hastily summoned Vaughan.

'Listen, Derek,' she said, 'I have a problem. I've got to show my face at this bloody ID parade. If I don't, Mr Garfield will want to know why.'

'Why should that be a problem, doll?'

'Ease up on the familiarity when we're on duty, will you?' Sergeant Lipari muttered. Then she relented. After all, they were alone. 'Sorry, Del. I'm edgy. Fact is, I just spoke to Zak Paine. The night before last, he and Sally Jackson hacked into a private computer. It carried hardcore paedophile porn in its memory. Young girls.'

'Sweet Christ-on-a-crutch! Whose computer was this?'

'Zak doesn't know. Mrs Jackson wouldn't tell him. But from the message she gave you the following morning, I'd guess it must have been connected with Noel Yardley.'

'Except now Mrs Jackson denies anything's wrong.'

'Exactly. That's what's puzzling. It was her idea to hack into the computer, apparently, and she was deeply shocked by what she found in its memory, Zak said.' Sergeant Lipari sighed. 'I just don't understand what the hell's going on. I can't work out her motivation. I know how determined she was to get to the bottom of this. Why should she suddenly roll over and go helpless?'

'Maybe she's cracking up.'

'Maybe. But why now? Why not any other time over the past ten days?'

'Pass.'

Sergeant Lipari looked irritably at her watch.

'Shit.' She got to her feet, started hunting for the file on the Putney rapist. 'Right,' she said as she searched, 'I want you to do something for me, I want you to run a check on Dr Noel Yardley. His professional and personal background, qualifications, financial status, all that kind of thing. I want the basic information when I come out of this bloody meeting at lunchtime.'

'Cheryl, listen to me. Let's consider what Mr Garfield would say if he caught me doing this.'

'He won't.'

'I wouldn't bet on that. He's got your number, I'd say.'

Sergeant Lipari found the file she wanted, slapped it down on her desk, turned and faced Vaughan, hands on hips.

'*Just do it, Constable*,' she said. 'And if you tell anyone what you're up to, especially Mr Garfield, I swear I'll make you wish you'd never been born.'

Vaughan took refuge in his cheeky-chappie charm. 'Oh, I love you when you're angry.'

Mistake. Sergeant Lipari wasn't having it, not today.

'You've never really seen me that way, Derek,' she told Vaughan. 'You may think you have, but you're wrong. I'll see you after the meeting. Make sure you've got something for me then, OK?'

'Yes. Sir. Wasn't there a well-known Italian dictator whose name ended in "i"? Mussolini . . . Lipari . . . Are you and he by any chance related?'

'Just *piss off*, Derek. And when you get out there, tell WPC White I want her in this office, plus Constables Davidson and Travis.'

Sergeant Lipari thought Vaughan gave a satirical click of the heels before he turned and left the room, but by then she was thinking ahead, and she just didn't care what he did so long as he got her what she needed.

Sergeant Lipari got back from the ID parade half an hour later than she had hoped.

The whole exhausting exercise had not been a great success, considering the time and expense it had cost. She looked up irritably when Vaughan swept into her office, brightened when she saw the file under his arm.

'How did it go?' he asked.

'One yes, one no, one maybe,' Sergeant Lipari said. 'I'm pretty sure we've got the right guy, but Christ knows how we'll prove it.' She paused. 'Don't stuff me about, Derek. You got something for me?'

Vaughan nodded. He produced the file with a flourish, tossed it on to her desk.

'It's all in there,' he said. 'Dr Noel Bartholomew Yardley, thirty-seven years of age. Medical degree from Oxford University, postgraduate psychiatric training in London. Married for six years, no kids. Wife, Jacqueline, died in 1988.'

'Of what?'

'Dunno.'

Sergeant Lipari grunted noncommittally.

'All right. How long's Yardley been practising as a psychotherapist?'

'It's in the file.'

'Read it to me, Derek. I'm tired. My brain hurts.'

Vaughan made a face, retrieved the file, glanced quickly through his notes.

266

'Ah . . . hang on a sec . . . Want all the details?'

'That *was* the idea, Derek.'

'Right. You asked for it.' Vaughan read in a precise monotone. 'Dr Yardley set up shop in 1982. He has published several articles. Also a book about anorexia – presumably that's why Mr and Mrs Jackson sent the girl to him. Anyway, Yardley's a member of the Association of Psychotherapists, plus also the British Society for the Advancement of Therapeutic Hypnotism and an adviser to several bulimia and anorexia research groups—'

'*What did you say?*' Sergeant Lipari cut in sharply.

'When?'

'Just now.'

'Adviser to several—'

'No. Immediately before that.'

'Er . . . Therapeutic Hypnotism. Society for the Advancement of. He's a member, apparently.'

'That's what I thought. Interesting. Very interesting.'

'I suppose so. See it on telly, don't you? Mate of mine went to one of them to give up smoking. Cost him a small fortune. Worked, though.' Vaughan grinned. 'Only trouble was, every time someone said, "Want a ciggy?" he took all his clothes off and gave a rendition of "Let Me Entertain You" . . .'

'I want to know what Yardley's wife died of, Derek. OK?'

'Could take a while.'

'Don't let it. I want to know about Yardley's wife. And I particularly want to know if he's ever been in any kind of trouble with the law, or with any professional body on account of misconduct.'

After Vaughan had gone, Sergeant Lipari spent some time staring at the English Country Cottages calendar on her office wall, telling herself yes, then no, then maybe.

You could well make a complete idiot of yourself here, my girl, Sergeant Lipari thought. *But if you do, then sod it. Better than letting somebody else do it for you.*

The ID parade and her irritation with Vaughan both forgotten, she found a number in her address book, then picked up her phone and dialled.

'Carl Thompson,' a voice answered.

'Hello, Mr Thompson,' she said. 'Detective Sergeant Lipari here, from Richmond . . . Yes, we met when you were an expert witness in the Cruttwell fraud case last year . . . I'm in pretty good shape, and you?'

'Not bad. Busy.'

Sergeant Lipari took a deep breath and dived in. 'I'm sure you are, but I've got a favour to ask, and it's urgent. I don't know how to put this really, but I do remember – you know, we were chatting during one of the breaks – I remember you said you have considerable experience with hypnotism.' Her laugh was edgy. 'You see, the thing is that I sort of need a crash-course in it. How soon can you come in to my office? No, I don't want to give up smoking, or impress my friends, or get on the telly . . .'

TWENTY-FOUR

Sally had completely forgotten Liz was working at home today. When the knock on the door of her room came at about eleven, she started.

'Yes?'

Sally could feel fear in her own voice. Was she finally cracking up? Couldn't possibly be. Noel had told her she was making really good progress.

Liz entered, carrying two cups of coffee. She handed one to Sally, sat down in the guest bedroom's single armchair.

'You all right?' she asked.

Sally shrugged. 'There are bound to be days like this, aren't there?' she said. 'Noel warned me there'd be downs as well as ups. I was on a climbing curve yesterday, I've taken a tumble today. The old roller-coaster, he said.'

'You've made a big decision,' Liz said. 'About the baby, I mean.'

Sally nodded. Should she tell Liz about the slightly weird phone conversation she had experienced with Sergeant Lipari this morning? Maybe not. Maybe . . .

'So what are you planning to do today?' Liz asked.

'Oh,' Sally said, 'I don't know. Not a lot. Just rest. I'm seeing Noel at three. I'll feel better after that.'

'You're sure there's nothing you want to discuss?'

'No . . .' Sally remembered now. Noel had been very clear that there were some things you didn't discuss, even with your closest friends. 'No, Liz. You're very sweet. But I'll be fine. I'm handling it.'

Carl Thompson was short and bald, so bald that his head looked shaven until you noticed the sparse, fair winglets of hair over his ears. Once he had possessed a head of hair so bleached-blond as to be almost white. Pushing sixty, despite his arid pate he seemed younger, perhaps because he had an energetic manner and smiled a lot. Thompson was a clinical psychologist with over thirty years' experience, specialising in frauds, control-freaks and cultists.

'Another weirdo?' he said when he was shown into Sergeant Lipari's office. 'More exotic than Cruttwell?'

Sergeant Lipari smiled wryly. 'No one could be more exotic than Cruttwell, but I think this one may be a lot more dangerous.'

Bill Cruttwell had been a systematic bigamist and fraudster who had seduced well-heeled, ageing ladies all over south-west London with a patter that was half brush-salesman and (and this was his unique selling point) half religious-cult leader. He even had a small clique of genuine true believers to back him up; he would take his ladies to meetings where he was fêted like a guru. Then he would organise private marriage and 'betrothal' ceremonies in which he usually 'acknowledged' them as 'spiritual brides'. Not too long after, he would separate them from various bank accounts and properties before suddenly moving on to another way-station on the spiritual path.

It had taken months of work by Sergeant Lipari to nail Cruttwell. Thompson had been a valuable aid in establishing the man's psychopathic credentials in court. 'A sort of non-violent Charles Manson,' was Thompson's description of him at the trial. For months after Cruttwell had been sent down for five years, the psychologist had received threatening letters from the man's former followers, promising him death, hell and worse for having 'crucified the messiah'.

Thompson sat down opposite Sergeant Lipari.

'Hypnosis, you say? A backstreet practitioner doubling as con-man?'

'Nope. Degrees from Oxford and London Universities. Respected professional.'

Thompson raised a pale, bushy eyebrow.

'And what's he been up to?'

'I can't say for sure.'

'Sergeant Lipari, I hope you didn't bring me here on a fool's errand.'

'Wouldn't dream of it.' Sergeant Lipari paused. 'All right. I have reason to believe that this man's been abusing a young female patient. The problem is that everyone else here thinks it was her stepfather. That's why I'm being cautious.'

'And you think he's been doing it while the girl was under hypnosis?'

Sergeant Lipari nodded. 'Nothing made sense until I found out that my suspect was a qualified hypnotherapist. The girl stabbed her stepfather, you see, then recalled nothing about it – except that the stepfather had supposedly abused her. The conclusion to jump to was obvious: she stabbed him out of rage, desperation, whatever. Meanwhile, though, there was confusing evidence accumulating . . .'

Sergeant Lipari gave Thompson an edited run-down of Sally Jackson's discoveries.

'OK,' Thompson said when she had finished. 'This sounds intriguing. But I don't think I can help you unless I can talk to either the girl or the suspect. Preferably both.'

'Obviously, it might be hard to arrange the latter. And the girl's still under medical supervision. What I want to know is – again I'll put this cautiously – can it be possible that he did what I think he might have done?'

Thompson hesitated. Both eyebrows furrowed. He had very expressive eyebrows, as if they were speaking for the rest of his long-gone hair. Then he nodded.

'It's possible. But as I said, I'd need to speak to both of them.'

Impasse. Then suddenly Sergeant Lipari remembered the interview where Yardley had made his 'breakthrough' with Emma.

'Carl,' she said. 'I've just recalled that we taped an interview between the therapist and the girl.'

'Where?'

'Here. In one of our interview rooms. He had been treating her for a year or so for anorexia. It seemed like a good idea to get him to come in. To help her to open up . . .'

'Is that so? Well, Sergeant, I'd very much like to see that tape.'

Sergeant Lipari got to her feet.

'Could you wait here, Carl?'

'Sure.' He looked at his watch. 'I've got an hour at the most, though.'

'I'll have that tape for you in ten minutes.'

'Fine.'

Sergeant Lipari left Thompson in her office and sought out Vaughan.

'Any luck on the questions I asked you about Yardley?'

'Doesn't seem like Yardley's ever been in trouble. Got the

coroner's office calling me back about the wife's cause of death.'

'Good. They can call you on your mobile,' Sergeant Lipari said. 'Meanwhile, I've got Jim and Maggie looking busy on the Heath rape case, which frees us for the afternoon.'

'Oh yeah? Looking hot for the shrink, is it?'

'Warmish. By the end of the day I want to be able to go to Mr Garfield with something on Noel Yardley. At the moment I've got a guy by the name of Carl Thompson in my office – he's a clinical psychologist and an expert on hypnosis, among other things.'

'I can just see Mr Garfield listening to him . . .'

'We'll cross that bridge when we come to it. For now, I want you to get hold of the videotape of Yardley's interview with Emma Quinn – the one where she seemed to confess—'

'Oh my goodness gracious, we've really made up our mind now, haven't we?' Vaughan cut in acidly.

'Maybe.' Sergeant Lipari felt herself redden slightly. All she needed was Vaughan reminding her what a fool she might be about to make of herself over this one. 'Anyway, you've got ten minutes to find us a spare interview room with a tape player and set it up for me. I want Thompson to watch – ' she smiled crookedly and chose her words carefully – 'the bit where Emma broke down and started talking about the abuse . . .'

Sergeant Lipari was wielding the remote. Carl Thompson sat close to the screen. Vaughan had been sent off back about his business. She wanted to be alone with Thompson. And especially she wanted to spare him Derek's hypnotist jokes.

Sergeant Lipari had run through the tape until they were reasonably well into the tense confrontation between the therapist and his client. As it happened, this was even the same interview

273

room where it had taken place. To look around and see the same furniture, paint scheme, windows and doors as on the video screen, was eerily dramatic.

The angle of the camera was such that it took in Yardley and Emma on opposite sides of the interview table. Sergeant Lipari could not be seen. Diane Worcester was just visible to Emma's right. God, the young girl had looked terrible. Dead. Living dead.

' . . . *Everyone here wants to help you*,' Yardley was saying, his voice soft and warm. '*Everyone wants to know the reason for what happened last night, but only so we can help you.*' Silence for a long moment. '*All right, Emma? All right? No need to talk if you don't want to. Just nod if you understand what I'm saying . . .*'

Back in the present, Sergeant Lipari glanced at Thompson. He was watching impassively, his surprisingly slim, sensitive hands placed on his knees. He was still, stiller than she had ever seen him. Totally concentrated.

When she looked back at the screen, it was after Emma had first given that tiny nod, showing she was in touch, however remotely, with the world. Yardley had just picked his moment to repeat the key question.

'*Why? Emma, why?*'

It was invisible from the point of view of the video camera, but Sergeant Lipari could still remember seeing Yardley's fingers drumming on his thigh, betraying the tension. Now out came the monogrammed handkerchief, off came the glasses. The therapist wiped the lenses absently while he waited. On the other side of the picture, Emma sat impassive, seemingly still enclosed deep within herself.

Time passed. It had seemed like hours then, but the tape

showed it was only a handful of seconds. Yardley put away the handkerchief, waited.

'*Why, Emma?*' he whispered then, throaty, insistent.

Though she knew it was coming, the breakdown that followed was so intense that Sergeant Lipari could hardly bear to watch. It took great restraint for her to resist hitting the 'Off' button.

'BAD . . . BAD DADDY . . . !' Emma pushed out the tear-soaked words.

Sergeant Lipari glanced at Thompson. Still the solemn, concentrated stance.

On the screen, Emma began to rock, ignoring Diane Worcester's protective hand on her arm, and now the tears were turning to anger, and the voice from a blurred croak to a furious scream of accusation:

'HE SAID HE WAS A GOOD DADDY! BUT HE WAS BAD, BAD, BAD . . . !'

Sergeant Lipari continued to play the tape through. Thirty seconds later, on the screen, Yardley had carefully moved aside and Sergeant Lipari had taken his place to ask the girl questions about this 'Bad Daddy'.

Then, quite suddenly, Thompson said: 'Could we hold it there for a moment?'

Sergeant Lipari started in surprise. Then she nodded, obediently freeze-framed the tape. There was silence. Thompson turned to her. His face was unreadable.

'Did the girl give a specific name later?' he asked calmly. 'For her abuser, I mean?'

'Only "Bad Daddy". Bad Daddy did things to her. That was what she kept repeating. No forename or surname. Draw your own conclusions. We certainly did.'

'Yes. Quite understandably.'

'What do you think?' Sergeant Lipari asked urgently.

Thompson seemed not to hear her. 'Now I'd like to go back to just before she first spoke. Before the fellow there gets the handkerchief out and cleans his glasses. Do you have a frame-by-frame progression mechanism on that machine?' Sergeant Lipari nodded. 'Then take us through on that, will you?'

The flickering slow-motion sequence followed. Again Thompson watched everything in tranquil, almost meditative silence. Emergence of handkerchief, doffing of spectacles, rhythmic cleaning, replacing of glasses and hankie. Then what seemed like a long wait . . . only seconds in real time, the gentle *whoosh-whoosh* sound of the frame-by-frame progression adding to the strangeness . . . and the girl's mouth starts its anguished, accusatory movement . . .

'OK. Stop,' Thompson ordered, his voice suddenly authoritative. 'And give me the remote control, please.'

Sergeant Lipari handed it over. The psychologist played it back yet again, took them through, froze it just as Yardley was replacing the glasses on his own nose.

'See?' Thompson said quietly. 'The business with the fancy little handkerchief. That's chummy's signal.'

'What signal?'

'It's called post-hypnotic suggestion, Sergeant,' Thompson explained. 'Through giving instructions to the girl while she's under hypnosis – brainwashing her, if you like – he can make her do things when she emerges back into conscious life. We all know that from stage and television hypnotists. They use it to play games, make their subjects look ridiculous, and call it entertainment. But a skilled hypnotist such as this man can do serious damage. He can manipulate his subject's subsequent feelings, the workings of her mind.' Thompson paused. 'Even her memories.'

'Oh God,' Sergeant Lipari murmured. A terrible thought had suddenly occurred to her. 'I told you the girl's mother's been seeing him since the stabbing. Could he also have done that to her?'

'Of course.'

'Without her realising it?'

'If he's clever, yes. From what I've seen, I'd say he is. Extremely.'

'Which is why she might have denied this morning just what she was burning to tell me yesterday.'

'Did she have a session with him between the two occasions?'

'Yes. She genuinely believes she didn't really find out anything disturbing about him. If what you say is true, between then and now he must have reprogrammed her, wiped certain memories and replaced them with others. In the same way, Emma was made to believe her stepfather abused her, whether he actually did or not. Oh God. Surely it's not as mechanical as that?'

'Well, it's partly down to the hypnotic techniques, but . . . Sergeant, do you know what psychiatrists are talking about when they refer to transference?'

Sergeant Lipari thought of the background reading she had done for the FSU course.

'Sort of . . . falling in love with your shrink?' she suggested.

Thompson smiled wryly. 'As succinct a definition as any.'

'You think—'

'I'd imagine so. In both the mother's and – we'd better face this – the daughter's case. It would certainly give him a head start, wouldn't it? I mean, they really want to believe him . . .'

Sergeant Lipari shivered. 'He had a year to work on Emma.'

'That could lead to a very strong degree of transference between therapist and patient, and also a thoroughgoing subconscious control. Particularly in the case of a suggestible adolescent.'

'Of which Emma would not be aware?'

'Not consciously, as I said.'

'And the mother?' Sergeant Lipari followed up quickly. 'What about her relationship with the therapist?'

Thompson pursed his lips. 'How many sessions has she had with this man?'

'Three, I think. I don't know for sure if he hypnotised her on all those occasions, but I strongly suspect it.'

'OK. Well, he may have given her specific hypnotic instructions, I suppose, which she's likely to carry out if they're triggered. But his overall control of the mother probably won't be nearly as strong as with the daughter.'

'Just specific instructions, you said? And Mrs Jackson would respond to any signals according to those instructions?'

'Yes. If they've been well planted by your chap there,' Thompson said. 'Think of it this way: in the case of her daughter he's had a whole year to lay complicated minefields to protect his power over her, whereas in the mother's case there'll be just a few booby-traps.'

'Let's hope I can spot them, because the next thing I have to do is to talk to her and make her aware of what's been happening.'

'Give me an hour with her and I might be able to map out a few of the booby-traps, Sergeant, and with any luck start to defuse them.'

'Would you be willing to work on Emma's minefield too?'

'Yes. Yes, I'll try. But don't think I'll have cleared it in an hour. Or even a month. Or—'

'Or ever?' Sergeant Lipari finished for him.

'Ever is a long time,' Thompson said. He sighed. 'On the other hand, the human mind is a very complicated place.'

On the way back to her office, Sergeant Lipari scooped up Vaughan.

'Get this, Del,' she said when her office door closed behind them. 'There's a real possibility that Jackson's innocent. A probability, actually.'

'Christ.'

'It's the hypnotism. Yardley can make people believe things happened that didn't – and the other way round.'

'How the hell do you work that one out, doll?'

Sergeant Lipari described how they had re-run the tape of the 'breakthrough', outlined Thompson's observations.

'What we were watching on that tape was a signal,' she explained. 'A signal for Emma to come out of an imposed state of shock and go through the little routine that implicated Kit Jackson as her supposed abuser.'

'Yardley programmed her to stab her stepfather and then blame him for abusing her?' Vaughan shook his head. 'That is wild, that really is wild.'

'Well, it doesn't really matter at this stage who actually wielded the knife,' Sergeant Lipari said. 'The important thing is, Yardley made it happen. He primed Emma to cover up for . . . for him . . . the one person in her life she should have been able to trust. And he was the abuser all along.'

'The real "Bad Daddy" . . .'

Sergeant Lipari nodded grimly. 'And it may not have been

the only command he planted in Emma – or any of his other patients. Who include, by the way, the girl's mother. Which explains why she suddenly lost her memory of the night before last.'

She picked up the phone. 'If I'm right, I need to get to Sally Jackson before he damages her the way he did Emma. Meanwhile, I want you to go through Yardley's life with a fine-tooth comb. Every little detail. Movements, finances, anything suspicious in his past.'

Vaughan smiled wryly. 'You don't want much.'

'I want to know what colour socks he wears, if it shows a hint of loopiness, got that? And make it fast, Del. I get the feeling we don't have all that much time.'

TWENTY-FIVE

It was lunchtime, bright but a little breezy. They sat outside at Delices de France in Barnes. Sergeant Lipari needed some fuel. She had a double espresso and a pain au chocolat, Sally just a cappuccino.

'Thanks for coming,' Sergeant Lipari began. 'It's a haul for me to get down to Wandsworth.'

'Takes me out from under Liz and company's feet,' Sally said with a shrug. 'Anyway, I love dear old Barnes. Pity I can't move back. Not yet.'

On the Common across the road, two Slavic nannies had met and were chatting volubly while their little English charges dozed in their baby-buggies. Their guttural conversation drifted across to where Sergeant Lipari and Sally had met.

'I'll say one thing for the troubles in Yugoslavia,' Sally observed drily, 'they may be horrific, but they've solved the servant problem in south-west London. Half the toddlers you meet these days speak better Serbo-Croat than they do English.' She scooped some chocolaty foam off the top of her coffee. 'So, what can I do for you, Sergeant?'

'I'll tell you in a moment. Meanwhile, how are you feeling?'

'Much better, I think. It's tough, but I'm coming to terms with everything. What Emma did, and why. And – ' Sally

281

sighed – 'with the way Kit has to die for me now, whatever happens to him in the hospital. Doctor Yardley's been such a big help. I can't tell you how grateful I am to you for your advice.'

'My advice?'

'You told me I should give him a ring, remember?'

'Ah . . . yes.' Sergeant Lipari nodded wryly. *Good old me*, she thought ruefully. *Actually, I was just trying to get rid of you. Little did I know.* 'I'm glad you brought the subject up. Tell me, what exactly do you do in your sessions with Dr Yardley? I'm fascinated.'

'Well, Noel – that's what he insists I call him – is helping me to come to terms with my feelings of loss and anger and sadness.'

Brain-washing is right, Sergeant Lipari thought.

'But what exactly *happens*?' she pressed Sally, trying to keep the impatience out of her voice.

'We talk.'

'About what? Please, this is very important.'

Sally looked a little puzzled, but seemed content to oblige.

'He . . . encourages me to let go, I suppose. This helps me to get into a deeply relaxed state. Time flies. And I come out of the session feeling much better.'

'That's it? You're conscious all the time, Mrs Jackson?'

'Oh, the first time I fell asleep,' Sally admitted with a shy little smile. 'Noel said it was because I was so profoundly exhausted and stressed. Not just by what happened the night Kit was stabbed, but also by the unconscious knowledge of Kit's true nature that I had been carrying around with me for months, even years before then.'

Sergeant Lipari made no comment on the details, just tucked

them into her mental file for future reference.

'Have you fallen asleep since then?'

'I'm not sure exactly what you mean,' Sally said. 'I've certainly experienced deep, deep relaxation. It gets you on to another, liberating sort of level of consciousness. Like a meditation.' She smiled faintly. 'You should try it, Sergeant. It might help you unwind. You look as though you need it.'

'Thanks. Some other time, perhaps. So you feel you've changed radically since you started seeing Dr Yardley?'

Sally nodded in very definite fashion.

'The other thing is, I'm not going to have the baby. I just can't. As I told you on the phone, Noel's made an appointment for me next week at a private clinic. He says he'll organise everything, and give a complete course of counselling afterwards. It's best for me and, of course, for Emma. How could she live with Kit's baby? Noel will see us both through this, he's promised . . .'

The evil bastard, thought Sergeant Lipari. *Oh God, the evil bastard. Yardley really wants this woman to end up with nothing.*

'Mrs Jackson,' she interrupted crisply, 'I'm going to have to come straight out with this.' She remembered what Carl Thompson had said about the booby-traps in Sally Jackson's mind, but steeled herself and pressed on. 'I no longer necessarily believe that your husband, Kit, abused Emma. It's possible that you were right all along. I was wrong – we were all wrong – and Kit is completely innocent. I owe you an apology.'

Sally froze in the act of lifting her cup to her lips again. Her mouth hung open like a small girl's. Her eyes were locked into Sergeant Lipari's. She said nothing for a long time. Something like fear was glinting faintly behind that patched-up façade of tranquillity and acceptance, and Sergeant Lipari meant to fan that spark, carefully but ruthlessly.

'I don't know what you mean,' Sally muttered eventually.

'I'm saying your husband could be innocent after all.'

'I can't listen to this.'

Frowning, Sally rose as if to leave.

The group at the next table were starting to eavesdrop. Sergeant Lipari ignored them. She reached over, gently took Sally's arm, all the time keeping eye-contact.

'Please, you must hear me out,' she said. *Not so much a booby-trap as a wall*, she thought. *If I can just get through this, we'll have what we want. The rest can wait for Carl, so long as I can get Sally there.* 'You must. Sit down. Sit.'

Slowly Sally obeyed, but she was uneasy now. Anxious. She reminded Sergeant Lipari of one of Cruttwell's wronged women, still denying he could have cheated her even when faced with overwhelming evidence of the fact. Sally's whole emotional equilibrium at this point was still reliant on her continued belief in the comforting lie rather than the devastating truth. It was vital Sergeant Lipari kept talking, she knew that, to get through the recently planted barrier in Sally Jackson's mind. What she said next went against more written and unwritten rules than she could count, but she didn't care. There wasn't time for that.

'I have reason to believe that Noel Yardley is a pervert with a taste for young girls like Emma,' Sergeant Lipari told Sally. 'He possesses enormous personal charisma. He is also a skilled hypnotist,' she explained. 'So skilled that he can hypnotise people without their even realising it.'

'I don't believe you. He helped Emma. He helped me,' Sally said with a plaintive little laugh. 'You really don't know how it was. I'd started to go mad before you sent me to Noel. Now I'm sane.'

There was still a blankness in Sally Jackson's gaze that Sergeant Lipari found unnerving.

She realised she was going to have to batter this one through and risk upsetting Sally's delicate emotional balance. And Thompson was spot-on about the 'transference'. There was absolutely no question about it.

Emma's mother was to all intents and purposes in the process of becoming Dr Yardley's slave. It was just that he hadn't had time yet to break her thoroughly.

'Mrs Jackson, the night before last you asked Zak Paine to hack into Noel Yardley's private computer,' Sergeant Lipari said. 'When he did, you found evidence of hardcore paedophile pornography featuring young girls of Emma's age. Then you were suddenly cut off by Yardley. He had realised someone was checking out the contents of his computer.'

'I remember nothing—'

'Listen. Please. The next morning you tried to ring me. Unfortunately I was in the Midlands. But you left a message which was enough to make me suspect Yardley. Then, when I rang you the next day, you denied everything.' Sergeant Lipari thought she saw a flicker of fearful recognition in the eyes of the woman opposite her. Perhaps it was an illusion, but this was the encouragement Lipari desperately needed; the sign that, as Carl had said, there were parts of Sally Jackson that Yardley didn't yet control. 'In the meantime, you see, Yardley had hypnotised you and got at your memories.' She held hard on to Sally Jackson's hand. 'You must believe me when I tell you this.'

Sally shook her head. A little less certainly?

'If you don't believe me,' Sergeant Lipari said, 'then talk to Zak. He'll confirm everything I've said. Everything.'

'No. I mean, I want desperately to think that Kit is innocent. But I've got over my fantasies about that. Noel is a prominent professional. He's helped Emma – for God's sake, he all but *cured* her . . .'

Sally's pleas died away. She looked down at the fake-marble table.

'Mrs Jackson . . . Sally . . . I can imagine how it must be for you to take this on board,' Sergeant Lipari said. 'You trusted Yardley with your daughter, and now you've trusted him with your sanity. But I want you to at least consider the possibility that he is the man who abused your daughter, and is also responsible – directly or indirectly – for your husband's terrible injuries. If my suspicions are justified, then Yardley is a sick, vicious pervert. A dangerous psychopath. You must listen to me,' she persisted in an urgent whisper. 'You must help me. I need you.'

Slowly Sally looked up and faced Sergeant Lipari.

'But . . . I honestly remember nothing about it. The computer, the supposed time I spent with Zak, the phone call the next day. *Nothing.*'

Somehow, despite the denial, Sergeant Lipari knew she had her. Her heart beat faster.

'I believe you completely,' she said. 'I don't even want to discuss that for the moment. I just want to know exactly what you did in your consultation with Yardley yesterday. Can you tell me?'

Sally frowned. 'I . . . remember being very anxious at first. I can't remember why. But then we talked things over in a very easy way. I became very dreamy, calm. I just . . . well, I felt better than at any time since before the tragedy . . . Lighter, sort of . . .'

'And you have no memory whatsoever of the images that you and Zak accessed on his computer.'

Sally shook her head. She looked drained of all energy, all confidence.

'Mrs Jackson, you found out that Yardley was a member of a computer pornography ring based in Amsterdam. But between your message to me and our conversation this morning he reprogrammed you to deny it.' Sergeant Lipari paused. 'Will you admit the possibility that you've been abused by Noel Yardley, just as Emma was?' she asked softly. 'Not physically – I'd guess he's not really interested in grown-up women – but mentally. Your memory has been raped by him.'

'Perhaps Zak is lying,' Sally suggested in one last, feeble act of defiance. 'Perhaps he came to you—'

'Zak didn't come to us,' Sergeant Lipari corrected her quickly. 'I found him. At first he was reluctant to talk about it. But he saw what was in those computer files. He just didn't know who they belonged to – because you didn't tell him.'

Sally put her head in her hands.

'But I can't help it!' she murmured desperately. 'I *trust* Noel! I need him!'

'Of course you do!' Sergeant Lipari's tone turned harsh, insistent. 'Because he *told* you to. Listen, please – Yardley is a compulsive, utterly ruthless abuser who'll do anything to avoid arrest. It's my – ' she looked steadily into Sally's eyes – 'I mean, *our* job to catch him and put him away, so that he can't exploit his position and his charisma to damage any more young girls.'

'But how?' Sally said desperately. 'Even if it's true, how?'

Sergeant Lipari had been waiting for something like this

question. She had her answer ready.

'Listen to me carefully,' Sergeant Lipari said. 'You've been brave, you've been persistent – even when people like me refused to believe you – and now I have to be those things on your behalf. Do you understand?'

Sergeant Lipari waited for Sally's nod of agreement before continuing.

'I've called in an expert and absolutely reliable hypnotherapist, Carl Thompson,' she said. 'He's prepared to re-hypnotise you and try to find out what Yardley has been telling you, what he has planted in your subconscious without your knowledge.'

There was a long silence. Sally stared out across the road and over the Common. Traffic passed in front of her eyes but she didn't seem to see it.

'Oh, dear God, Sergeant,' Sally said at last in a low, hopeless voice. 'You've left me no one to trust.'

Sergeant Lipari leaned across the table and took Sally's hand. She did not resist.

'Mrs Jackson . . . Sally . . . it's my turn to ask, as a police officer but also as one woman to another . . . Please, will you help me? Will you talk to Carl Thompson? He may find nothing – no subconscious demands, no mental booby-traps; but if he does, it will be an enormous help in establishing Yardley's guilt and – just as importantly – in helping Emma to get better.'

There was another long pause. Then Sally nodded. The movement was almost imperceptible, but Sergeant Lipari felt relief flooding through her body.

Thank God. Thank dear God . . .

'I should tell you I have an appointment with Noel Yardley this afternoon,' Sally said then.

'When?'

'Four o'clock.'

'OK. You've got just under two hours. Ring him and say you're not feeling well. Cancel. Don't let him persuade you otherwise,' Sergeant Lipari added. 'I suppose it might arouse his suspicions, but we just can't risk letting him back in your mind at this stage.'

'I understand that.'

'So, can I tell Carl you'll come for a session with him at around six?'

'Yes.' Sally shot Sergeant Lipari a tiny, anxious smile. 'And what . . . what if all this just goes to prove that Noel Yardley is innocent, Sergeant?'

Sergeant Lipari had no idea what to say to that. She got to her feet. 'Excuse me,' she said. 'I'll just go inside and pay the bill.'

TWENTY-SIX

Sergeant Lipari arrived back at her car to find a message on the pager from Vaughan. She called in to the station, got him on the line.

'At last,' he said, sounding pleased with himself. 'How's Mrs Jackson?'

'Spooky.'

'I'm not surprised. Anyway, I've got a few interesting facts for you.'

'Go on.'

'First, our Dr Yardley is a traveller. Seven trips to Amsterdam in the past year. Bought tickets direct from KLM on plastic. Also, he's been paying fairly whacking credit-card bills to this – whadjamacallit – bulletin-board where he gets the porn.'

'Good. OK. You said facts, plural. What else have you got?'

'The late Mrs Yardley. She committed suicide.'

Sergeant Lipari caught her breath. 'How?'

'Jesus, give me a break, Cheryl!'

'It could be important. I want the details by tonight, by the time Sally Jackson's finished her session with Carl Thompson.'

'We'll have to get hold of the original coroner's records.'

'*Just do it, Derek!* Talk to you later.'

Sergeant Lipari killed the mobile, slotted it back into its

cradle. Suburban life flowed gently round her as she sat in her car and measured the full horror of the picture that was emerging of Dr Noel Yardley, distinguished therapist.

The main thing was not to be afraid of thinking the unthinkable. That had always been Yardley's defence. *In the comfortable, well-meaning suburban world of the Jacksons and people like them, who would ever believe such bizarre and extreme things?*

Sergeant Lipari's mind was racing. Oh, I bet the late Mrs Yardley knew a thing or two about you, Noel, she thought. I bet at first she just couldn't believe it either. Then by the time she could, it was too late. *You programmed her to die.* Just like Sally Jackson. Except Sally left that message for me yesterday. And she got herself a witness, because she involved Emma's young friend, Zak.

Clever Sally Jackson.

Lucky Sally Jackson.

'Sweet Jesus Christ, Cheryl!' Superintendent Garfield erupted. 'You're planning to run a bleeding music-hall act in my nick! Am I hearing this correctly? Am I?'

'What I need to do has nothing to do with showbiz, sir,' Sergeant Lipari answered patiently, determined to stand her ground this time. 'I've seen the telly,' she said. 'I know these guys use post-hypnotic suggestion for cheap entertainment – to make people do silly things they'd never consider doing otherwise – but I assure you it can be very, very serious in the hands of someone who knows what he's doing, like Yardley.'

'You've been running around south-west London on the Jackson case when you're supposed to have been dealing with a high-profile rape. Now you've decided you want an obviously deranged – I mean, understandably damaged – woman put under hypnosis in one of my interview rooms.' Garfield had become ominously calm. 'You've flipped too.'

'Sir, there was at least one classic case in the States where a hypnotist influenced a client to commit murder—'

'Date? Names?'

'Carl Thompson told me.'

'I see. So it's bullshit.' Garfield sighed. 'Anyway, everyone knows you can't hypnotise someone to do something they really don't want to do.'

'Oh yes you can. If you do it the right way,' Sergeant Lipari retorted firmly. 'I mean, if you tell a girl to take off her clothes in front of an audience of leering guys, she'll probably snap out of her hypnotic state and refuse. But if you've carefully suggested to her that there's nobody there, that she's at home and it's her bedtime, and she's perfectly safe – in other words, if you've carefully created a system of illusion . . .'

'So, have I got this straight?' Garfield interrupted. 'Doctor Yardley has been putting Emma Quinn under the influence during these therapy sessions and then abusing her. She wakes up, she remembers nothing. Neat,' Garfield commented sardonically. 'OK so far?'

'Well, yes, but—'

'*But* Mr Jackson, Emma's stepfather, *somehow* gets wise to him. So, to save himself from being exposed, Yardley *somehow* plants the child porn in the stepfather's study to incriminate him.' He ticked off the points on his fingers. 'Then, again *somehow*, without even being there, Yardley gets this skinny thirteen-year-old to pick up the Eversharp from the kitchen, trot into Jackson's bedroom as he sleeps, and turn her stepfather's substantial torso into gruyère cheese. All on a kind of delayed-action hypnotic programme. Correct?'

'Actually, yes. Well done, Mr Garfield. Except I don't know if Yardley was there at the house when Jackson was stabbed. No one was seen coming or going, but I suppose the question is still open.'

The superintendent raised his eyes to heaven. 'Cheryl,' he murmured, 'this is Richmond-on-Thames, not *The Twilight Zone*!'

'That's exactly what I thought until today, sir. But I've changed my mind.'

'That's not the point. The point, Cheryl, is that we already have a clear-cut *result* in this case. Just give me one concrete piece of evidence that what you're claiming could be true.'

'One, sir? I'll give you quite a few.'

And Sergeant Lipari told him about Sally Jackson's bizarre behaviour, Zak Paine's account of how he and she had hacked into Yardley's paedophile porn store, Carl Thompson's view of Emma's taped confession, Yardley's frequent trips to Amsterdam, Yardley's wife's unexplained suicide . . .

When she had finished, Garfield said nothing for a while, nothing at all.

At first Sergeant Lipari feared this was the eerie calm before a new, more violent Garfieldian storm. But as the silence deepened, she realised that for the first time since Emma Quinn's apparent confession, the superintendent was giving this case some serious thought. He was a sceptical man, and sometimes a bully, but he was not stupid, and he was very anxious not to blot his command's copybook in a high-profile case like this.

'I still think you're bullshitting me, Cheryl,' Garfield growled eventually. 'It's all still strictly circumstantial.'

Yet something in his tone told Sergeant Lipari she had won; Garfield just didn't want to admit it. The thing now was to let him save face.

Men, she thought, *doncha just love 'em?*

'Perhaps, sir, and I can't guarantee anything,' Sergeant Lipari said. 'But what we discover later this afternoon from Sally Jackson might change all that. Things have started going seriously wrong for Yardley, so he's going to have to make a move.'

'Why now?'

'Think about it, sir. Zak Paine was involved, Yardley probably knows Mrs Jackson rang me, because he then programmed her to deny it when I called her back. But how long can he keep the lid on? He's just buying a bit of time at the moment. And a bit of time is what I need too. Please.'

Garfield got up and went to the window. He stood there, hands behind his back, staring out, for some moments. Then he turned back to face Sergeant Lipari.

'How long?'

Gotcha, Sergeant Lipari thought.

'Twenty-four hours,' she said quickly. 'That's all. If by any chance I'm wrong, then no harm done. If I'm right, we've been saved from making a terrible mistake. Sir, think what the tabloids would do to us if they knew we'd had this evidence handed to us, but done nothing with it!'

Garfield heard her out, then shrugged heavily.

'OK,' he said. 'Just be very, very careful. I don't want my nick a laughing-stock. I can't have that, understood?'

'Yes, of course, Noel,' Sally Jackson said.

'Good. No problem, then.' Even over the telephone, Yardley's voice was even-toned, smoothly compelling. 'You know exactly what we have to do?'

'Yes.'

'Fine, Sally. You know what to tell Sergeant Lipari?'

'Yes.'

'That's very good. Now, darling, who am I?'

'You're my Good Daddy.'

'Good girl.' Yardley's voice was so warm, so loving. 'Now, your Good Daddy will say goodbye, and so will you. Then he'll count to three, and you'll put the phone down, and when you've done that you'll remember absolutely nothing of this conversation. You'll recall a very simple little talk with my receptionist, just as we agreed. But you will know what to say to Sergeant Lipari, and you will know what to do when you next hear my voice say our special word. All right?'

'Yes.'

'Goodbye, Sally. I hope you feel better soon.'

'Goodbye, Noel.'

'*One . . . Two . . . Three . . .*'

Sally replaced the phone, breathed a sigh of relief. Thank God it was only Fiona she'd had to speak to.

She went through to the kitchen to make some coffee. As she spooned the powder into the cup, she felt an unexpected stab of anxiety. She realised that she needed to talk to Sergeant Lipari now, before the session with this hypnosis expert of hers. She had to talk to the sergeant about her feelings. And on her own terms.

After she had made the coffee, Sally took it through into the living room. It was three-thirty now. There was still time. She set her mug down on the table, picked up the phone.

Sergeant Lipari sounded harassed, but Sally felt really clear.

It was her right to do this. Naturally Sally wanted to help the police, but she was a human being, she had to talk on her terms.

'How are you, Mrs Jackson?' Sergeant Lipari said. 'Did you talk to Yardley?'

'No, thank goodness. I got his receptionist, Fiona. I just told her I wasn't feeling well and said I'd ring tomorrow.'

Sergeant Lipari turned away from the phone for a moment to say something to a man in the room.

'Good,' she said then. 'Listen, do you want us to send you a car? For your appointment at six, I mean.'

'No . . .' Sally hesitated. Perhaps it was irrational, but somehow she had to assert herself. 'I've got my own car, as you know.' She paused. 'Actually, I've been sort of wondering . . . I mean, I haven't been having second thoughts as such, but . . . Well, before this session, could we drive somewhere, take a walk, talk? You know, woman to woman?'

There was a momentary silence at the other end.

'I've got a lot on,' Sergeant Lipari said. 'You must realise that.'

'Oh, I do. I just . . . I don't know, I feel it's important for me and for everyone else involved in this awful tragedy that we're absolutely clear about what we're doing. Bear with me. Please.'

'Well . . .'

'See you in twenty minutes, Sergeant?'

A deep sigh from the other end of the line. 'OK, Mrs Jackson. If you really think it will help.'

'Thank you.'

Sally put down the phone. She knew she had done the right thing. The warm glow she felt just went to prove it.

TWENTY-SEVEN

Constable Orchard was half-way through the *Telegraph* crossword and going like an express-train when he heard footsteps approaching. He looked up to see a pleasant-looking man approaching. The man wore a white coat and was carrying a stethoscope. A doctor. One Orchard hadn't seen before, but then he had only done two shifts here since they had taken Harris off the job.

Orchard got to his feet. The doctor nodded a cheerful greeting, made to go past him and into the side ward where Kit Jackson still lay unconscious.

'Excuse me, Doctor,' Orchard said.

The doctor turned, surprised.

'Yes, Constable?'

'Could you identify yourself, sir?'

'Of course. My name's Dr Venn. I'll be keeping an eye on Mr Jackson for the next few days while Dr Patel's away on leave. Do come into Mr Jackson's room with me if you feel you should . . .'

Orchard hesitated, thought of his crossword.

The doctor winked.

'I won't tell if you won't, Officer.'

Orchard smiled sheepishly. 'Fair enough.'

'Good-oh!'

The doctor pushed open the door and went inside. Orchard looked in through the window, saw him already purposefully busy, checking the drip. As he watched, the doctor moved on to feel the patient's pulse. He seemed completely at ease, a skilled physician going about his routine. Seeing Orchard looking in, the doctor flashed him that easy smile.

Great bedside manner, you had to hand it to the guy, Orchard thought with mild envy. *All the birds fancy doctors, right? That's why.*

Orchard went back to his seat outside the door, sat down.

Twenty-four across. *Mail exploits disorganised emir to aid fraudster.* Too hard for the moment. Better to try twenty-two down. That should supply a couple of letters for twenty-four.

A couple of minutes later, the white coat swept back out of the door.

'Thank you, Officer. 'Bye for now,' said a cheery, confident voice.

Orchard grunted acknowledgement. He didn't even look up.

Oh yes, Orchard was thinking. Twenty-four across. I-M-P-0-S-T-E-R. Great.

Sergeant Lipari emerged from the police station to find Sally Jackson waiting in her car with the hazard lights blinking. She bent down to address Sally through the open window of the Volkswagen.

'Hi. How are you?'

'Fine,' Sally said. 'Except, you know, maybe I'm suffering from claustrophobia, all those rooms and cars I've been sitting in lately. I've got this wild urge to be out in the sunshine.'

'We could leave your car here and walk down to Richmond

Park,' Sergeant Lipari suggested. 'It's close by. And it's certainly got plenty of open space.'

Sally shook her head, smiled shyly.

'I want to drive to Putney Heath. It's . . . well . . . my neighbourhood. Please hop in, Sergeant.'

Sally started the engine. Sergeant Lipari calculated the odds that Sally might refuse to see Carl Thompson if she tried to insist on Richmond Park. She decided they were too short, opened the door, and clambered into the passenger seat.

Sally pulled out skilfully, exited from Red Lion Street and tucked herself into the stream of vehicles heading eastward on Sheen Road. It had just turned half-past four, and the rush-hour traffic was starting to build. Nothing wrong with her driving. That seemed like a good sign.

Sergeant Lipari unwound a little. Sally didn't seem keen to talk in the car. She let her be for while.

'So, Sally, you're having a problem with the idea of seeing Carl Thompson, are you?' she asked her as they crossed the river.

Sally frowned, prepared to turn left.

'We'll go down Rock's Lane, I think,' she said. Then she answered Sergeant Lipari's question. Sort of. 'It's not really that. The fact is, I'm still having a problem with your theory that Noel Yardley has been doing these awful things.'

'The facts seem to support it, Mrs Jackson. What can I say?'

Sally nodded calmly.

'My world's been turned upside down more times than I can count in the past week or two. Today you did it again. Perhaps I just need to talk about the problem, OK?'

'Of course.' Sergeant Lipari waited a beat. Then said, 'But

you will let Carl Thompson hypnotise you?'

Sally made no answer for a few moments.

'One thing,' she said eventually. 'I suppose it's true that if Noel Yardley is guilty, then . . . well, Kit's innocent.'

'Yes,' Sergeant Lipari answered. 'That's exactly right, Mrs Jackson.' She paused. 'You'll have your family back.'

They turned across into Rock's Lane, where the stream of commuter traffic coming from north of the river was thick. In half an hour it would start to jam, but for now it was still moving steadily.

As Sally accelerated away from the junction, her car-phone began to bleep in its cradle.

Sally picked it up.

'Yes? Sally Jackson's mobile.' She waited, listened. 'Of course. Fine, yes,' she said. 'Absolutely fine.'

Then Sally replaced the phone.

They drove along for a while in companionable silence. Sergeant Lipari thought how much, when not absorbed by tragedy as it was now, Sally Jackson's own life must resemble her own. Always at the end of a phone. Although she knew Sally had been granted indefinite leave of absence, being a BBC producer was a high-powered job. She guessed Sally was trying to keep in touch with the office. It was admirable, really, a sort of positive affirmation for the future yet unknown . . .

Open common lay to the left and right of the road now. There were plenty of people around, walking, picnicking, or just sunning themselves. It was a beautiful afternoon, Sergeant Lipari mused. How unreal an insane, dangerous situation such as this could seem on such a summer's day. Idyllic. Except, of course, for the smell of petrol and exhaust-gas, the cars and trucks coming at them in a rapid, almost hypnotic stream.

Then came a slight gap in the oncoming traffic. A big tanker of some kind was approaching, backing up vehicles behind it. It was twenty, thirty yards away with nothing in front. *And suddenly she saw Sally Jackson's right foot shoot out and hit the accelerator, pushing it right down to the floor and keeping it there . . .*

Had Sergeant Lipari been expecting something like this all along? *The booby-trap.* Or was it simply that her unconscious will to live took over?

When, an instant later, Sally swung the wheel so that the little Volkswagen was heading – *racing* – straight for a head-on collision with the big container-lorry, Sergeant Lipari's own hand was also on the wheel, wrenching it violently all the way to the right, as far as it would go . . .

This was her – their – only possible chance of survival, and Sergeant Lipari instinctively knew it.

The rest was a blur: the angry roar of a big truck's horn, the shrill snarl of powerful brakes, then the violent jarring of the VW striking the kerb, spinning round and – at least that was the immediate sensation – bouncing into the air.

The car seemed to be suspended there for a small eternity. Sally was still holding on to the wheel, but Sergeant Lipari had already braced herself as best she could, with her hands protecting her face.

Then the car dropped with a sickening crash, bounced again and rolled gently on its side.

There was a hideous silence. Sergeant Lipari thought, *Out of here before the tank goes up.*

And then Sally began to scream . . .

Sergeant Lipari remembered nothing after that until she had an image of standing on grass, staring dazedly out over the common. Sally was crouched on the ground ten feet or so away with her head in her hands, being attended to by a young black man in lycra cycling gear.

The young man kept saying, 'Just keep breathing easy,' and then, 'Do as I say, love, I've done first aid.'

Someone else was standing next to Sergeant Lipari, a woman, asking her if she was all right, and she was mumbling yes, fine, no problem, just a bit shaken.

The car had not gone up in flames. It was just lying there on its side, twenty feet away, with the passenger door open. The rearmost section of the hatchback part looked oddly out of shape. The back wheels were still spinning.

The woman said, 'That was amazing. The way you got her out. Do you want to sit down?'

Sergeant Lipari didn't answer, because she couldn't. Her lips moved, her jaws worked, but no words came out.

Then the phone inside the car rang again. Sally shook off the young man in the lycra, began to stagger to her feet, and Sergeant Lipari found her tongue.

'*Don't let her answer that phone!*' she yelled.

To Sergeant Lipari, her voice sounded like the squawk of an angry mouse, but it must have carried some authority. The man in lycra and another passer-by duly held on to Sally. Half staggering, half running, Sergeant Lipari made her way over to the damaged car. She leaned over, reached down inside, around the slightly twisted gear-leaver, and eased the mobile phone from its cradle.

Sergeant Lipari waited.

'Hello?' said a voice. 'Hello?'

'Yes.' She tried to make her voice unidentifiable, neutral.

'Jesus? Is that you, doll?'

Sergeant Lipari breathed out so hard it was like a long, soft moan.

'Derek,' Sergeant Lipari said. 'Derek, it's great to hear your voice.' She gulped a breath. Her side was sore, and beginning to give her pain. 'We just had a crash. It was deliberate, a set-up. No time to explain. How . . . how did you know where to contact me?'

'You gave me her mobile number before you left, remember?' Vaughan said. 'For emergencies. You OK?'

'Fine.'

No, Sergeant Lipari hadn't remembered that little precaution.

'You sure?'

'Shaken up,' she admitted. 'Sally Jackson's the same, I think. I hope.' Sergeant Lipari saw that Sally was now on her feet, leaning just a little on her rescuers. 'We're lucky to be alive.'

'Yeah.' Vaughan paused. 'Well, someone else isn't.'

'What?'

'Kit Jackson was found dead about half an hour ago, doll. Apparently initial tests make them suspect a massive overdose of insulin. Administered by injection.'

'Oh, shit.'

'Shit is correct. The thing is, the officer on duty saw someone claiming to be a doctor visit Jackson earlier this afternoon and . . . well, it now seems like no one knows who this guy actually was . . .'

'Derek, I think we know who disconnected Kit Jackson's drip a few nights ago while Kevin Harris and the nurse were canoodling in the yard.'

'Yup. Being thorough as well as a sicko, Yardley's now

tidying up those worrisome loose ends. And this time, he's taking no chances.'

'OK,' Sergeant Lipari cut in decisively. 'Here's what you do, Derek. You go round to Yardley's place. If he's there, you pick him up. Be careful. He's even more dangerous than I thought. I think Sally and I just copped one of his little psychological booby-traps, and I wouldn't be surprised if he's got more up his sleeve.' Sergeant Lipari rubbed her aching right ribs, where she must have banged against the steering wheel during the crash. 'So *hurry*, OK?'

'Right.'

'See you back at the station?'

'Yeah. 'Bye.'

Then something truly, truly terrifying occurred to Sergeant Lipari and she felt herself go into overdrive. *Loose ends*, Vaughan had said. *Yardley's tidying up loose ends.*

'Derek! Wait!' she barked. 'Emma Quinn, oh my God! Get me the number of the secure unit! I'll hold on . . .'

It had been a hell of a day for Tony Hutchinson. First thing, one of the kids on remand for TDA had announced he was going on hunger strike. He had held out until an hour ago. The burly, bearded social worker had just got down to writing a report on the incident when the office phone rang. He hissed a curse under his breath, snatched it up.

'Underwood House. Tony Hutchinson speaking. How can I help you?'

'Sergeant Lipari here. Richmond CID.' It was a woman's voice. Lots of traffic noise in the background. She sounded shaky, very fraught, but authoritative. 'I believe you have an Emma Quinn in residence.'

'That's right.'

'Is she all right?'

'No problem,' Hutchinson said. 'She's fine – at least she was a few minutes ago. When I put her phone call through.'

'*Phone call?*'

'Yes, sergeant. The inmates are allowed phone calls. What on earth's the problem?'

When she answered, she sounded calm, icy cold.

'Find her, Mr Hutchinson,' she hissed. 'Now. Quick. And if she's really OK, don't let her take any more phone calls until further notice. Got that?'

'Excuse me, but how do I know you're really a policewoman? Where are you calling from?'

'Mr Hutchinson, where I'm calling from is no bloody concern to you. If any harm comes to Emma, I'll have your arse!'

The caller's voice was sharp, desperate. Not like the usual policewoman's voice at all. Hutchinson considered the possibility that not all policewomen necessarily sounded like policewomen, especially when they weren't calling from a cosy office.

'Fair enough, I suppose,' he conceded. Hutchinson emitted a nervous laugh. Just at that moment, he heard a loud, splintering crash somewhere in the building. Broken glass.

'Fuck. Just a minute . . .'

He dropped the phone. With two, three loping steps he was at the door. He heard a series of long, terrible moans. They guided him through the kitchen and out into the lounge. At first glance it looked empty. Then the slim, pale figure standing by the shattered window turned unsteadily to face him.

It was Emma Quinn. At her feet lay a jagged, blade-shaped shard of glass. She held her hands out helplessly in front of her, almost in a gesture of supplication.

Tony Hutchinson had served with the army in the Falklands. He had seen what fatal bayonet-wounds looked like, had witnessed men blown apart by shrapnel, but for a moment even he went faint. Dark-red arterial blood was pouring from the girl's slender wrists in a vivid, seemingly inexorable stream, splattering on to the plain grey institutional carpet.

TWENTY-EIGHT

Two panda cars from traffic control had arrived at the scene of
the crash. Sergeant Lipari, still absorbing the news of Emma
Quinn's would-be suicide, was talking to a sergeant from one of
them, whom she knew quite well, telling him she was going to
need a lift back to Richmond, when she heard raised voices over
by where she had left Sally Jackson.

'Mrs Jackson,' one of the paramedics was telling her patiently,
'we have to check for whiplash injuries, and also for possible
harm to the foetus. Please. It will probably be just for one
night.'

'No!'

Sally was on her feet now, a little unsteady but with arms
folded and her elfin features set in an expression of stubborn
refusal. She saw Sergeant Lipari glance in her direction, called
out urgently.

'Sergeant! Please come and talk to these people!'

Sergeant Lipari began to walk towards her. She hadn't
spoken to Sally since Vaughan's original phone call.

The senior paramedic, a tall, bespectacled Welshman, gestured
helplessly. His female assistant just stood with one plump arm
around Sally's shoulders.

'Please, Sergeant,' he said. 'Mrs Jackson needs to be in

309

hospital for observation. Please tell her that, will you?'

Sergeant Lipari took him firmly by the arm.

'Could I have a word with you, please?'

'Right you are.'

'Just a moment, Sally.'

Sergeant Lipari took the paramedic aside, whispered an account of what had happened to Sally's husband and daughter, asked him if he had sedatives available. He nodded. She told him to get a shot ready, and he retreated to his ambulance to make preparations.

Sergeant Lipari took a deep breath, walked back over to where Sally and the female paramedic were standing.

Now or never.

Sally greeted her with a tight, exhausted smile.

'Sorry, Sergeant,' she said. 'I nearly killed you.'

'You nearly killed yourself.'

'I . . . I just couldn't help it.'

'No. I know that.'

'It was Yardley. He planted that impulse in me . . .'

'Yes. What did he say?'

Sally's smile was like a wound. 'I can't remember.'

'There must have been a word or phrase. Something he used to put you into a state where he could control you. It's called post-hypnotic suggestion.'

'I'm sorry. I don't know.'

Sergeant Lipari read defeat in the other woman's body. 'Don't worry yourself now,' she said quickly, realising it would be counter-productive to press too hard. 'But he told you to swerve, right? You know that much?'

Sally nodded. '*How did he get me to do that?*' She shook her head in bewilderment. 'Why couldn't I defend myself? I

should never have gone to see him again once I realised he was
. . . evil . . .'

'Don't blame yourself. I'm no expert on mind-control, but I
just had a crash-course from someone who is,' Sergeant Lipari
said. 'No pun intended.' She laughed grimly. 'I think Yardley
got inside your mind while you still trusted him and needed
him. He programmed you then, so no matter how vigilant you
thought you could be later on, there was no way you could
keep him out. So long as he could reach you and give you that
word . . .'

The senior paramedic had arrived with a small bag, which
Sergeant Lipari knew contained the sedatives. She had to tell
Sally now. More delay was simple cruelty.

'Mrs Jackson,' Sergeant Lipari began, 'your husband—'

'Yes! Kit is innocent!' the woman continued, oblivious. 'I'm
so relieved. Just to know that one day we'll all be together
again.'

Sergeant Lipari exchanged a glance with the paramedic, who
looked away. She was on her own here. She took Sally's hand in
hers.

'I'm afraid I've got some very bad news,' she said as gently
as she could. 'Your husband died this afternoon. I'm so sorry.
There are suspicious circumstances.' Sergeant Lipari kept
talking. She had decided to deal with it all now. 'And Emma . . .
Well, I'm afraid Yardley also reached Emma, as he did you, by
phone. She tried to hurt herself, but the staff at the home got to
her quickly and they think she'll be all right . . .'

Sally stared at her with a masklike intensity. At first Sergeant
Lipari thought it was blank incomprehension, but after just a
few moments she recognised the look; it was the same look she
had seen on her own mother's face when her father had died,

leaving her with four children under the age of fourteen. Grief, yes, but combined with a kind of animal survival-energy, a higher anger.

'Mr Hughes here,' Sergeant Lipari indicated the paramedic, 'has something he can give you for shock . . .'

'No.' Sally frowned. 'Did Yardley . . .?'

'It seems so.'

'But Emma's all right, you said?'

'Yes. They got to her in time.' The paramedic was still hovering. 'Please, Mrs Jackson. Just something to help you through the worst of this . . .'

Sally shook her head.

'I haven't taken any drugs so far. Unless you count ginger tea . . . Remember? And I don't plan to start now. I want to be completely conscious. I'll have plenty of time for sleep later. First I want to know they've found him. Yardley, I mean.'

And she stared straight at Sergeant Lipari, facing her down. 'I hope I'm free of him now. Surely Emma will be soon as well?'

Sergeant Lipari was saved from replying by a call from one of the panda cars.

'DC Vaughan, Sergeant!'

Sergeant Lipari told the paramedics to stay with Sally. And no sedative yet. Then she hurried over to the panda and grabbed the radio handset.

'Hi, Del. Got him?'

'Nah. He's done a bunk, hasn't he? A neighbour saw him leave the house and get into his car. He was wearing a yellow bum-freezer jacket, lugging a suitcase and a carry-on bag.'

'When was this?'

'Couple of hours ago.'

'That fits. It would have been straight after Sally Jackson

312

rang him up to cancel her appointment.'

'He's been busy since then,' Vaughan said. 'Across the river to the hospital . . .'

'He must be using a mobile phone. That's how he rang Sally in her car and Emma at the secure accommodation.'

'I've put out a general alert to the ferries and airports. Plus the Chunnel terminal.'

'Nice one. He's not going to be hanging around.' Sergeant Lipari's humourless little laugh held an edge of hysteria. 'I knew there was some use to you, Derek. God knows, sometimes I've wondered. Tell the airports to concentrate on flights to Holland, will you?'

'Bit obvious, isn't it?'

'Sure. Yardley's devious, but he's had to organise all this in a hurry. He's almost certainly got paedophile friends in Amsterdam who'll help him. He'll head for them by the route he trusts and knows. And don't forget, Derek,' Sergeant Lipari added grimly, 'Yardley doesn't know we're so close on his tail. He planned to wipe out everyone who could finger him. In particular, he thinks the emergency services are still shovelling bits of me and Sally Jackson off the South Circular.'

Sergeant Lipari handed the radio mouthpiece back to the patrol car's driver, turned on her heel, and was surprised to see Sally Jackson standing just a couple of feet away, flanked by the two hapless paramedics. Sally's body language told Sergeant Lipari she had been listening in on her conversation with Vaughan. There was no point in official pretence. This had to be woman to woman.

'I've got to get back to the station,' Sergeant Lipari said firmly. 'And you need skilled medical help.'

'I'm coming with you, wherever you're going,' Sally

answered. 'Emma's fine, you said. Well, I'm fine.'

'You belong in hospital.'

'I belong wherever there's people trying to catch that bastard Yardley.'

They looked at each other long and intensely. Sally was pale, there were bruises on her forehead, and she was breathing hard, but she looked totally, dangerously alive, like a female predator tracking a scent.

'All right,' Sergeant Lipari said. 'You can come back to the station with me. We'll give you a cup of tea and try to make you comfortable. Promise to behave yourself?'

'Whatever that means. You're stuck with me, anyway.' Sally tossed her dishevelled blonde hair.

Sergeant Lipari took her by the arm and guided her away from the paramedics.

'Just take it really easy,' she murmured as she eased Sally into the back seat of the patrol car. 'For the baby's sake. And don't you dare get in our way. And . . . don't answer any mobile phones . . .'

They had reached Sheen Road, heading back towards Richmond, when Vaughan came back on the patrol car's radio. Sergeant Lipari craned painfully forward from her perch in the back seat with Sally and took the call.

'You were right,' Vaughan told her. 'Heathrow's the place. A Mr N. Yardley bought a ticket to Amsterdam. For cash. Half an hour ago.'

'What did I tell you, Derek? Just trust your Auntie Cheryl. They're holding the flight?'

'Natch. The bastard hasn't boarded yet, apparently.'

Sergeant Lipari told the driver to head for Heathrow Airport.

'See you at Terminal Four, Del,' she said. 'And thanks.'

'You're very welcome,' Vaughan said. 'Oh,' he added as if it was an afterthought, 'and by the way. His wife that died. She drove her car off a bridge.'

Sally and Sergeant Lipari exchanged a glance that conveyed everything they felt at that moment: horror, anger, mourning and thanksgiving all in one.

Of course, Sally refused to be taken to the first-aid post at Terminal Four, or to be sidelined in any way. She was still in tow, limping slightly but stonily resolute, when Sergeant Lipari rendezvoused with Vaughan and two other constables at the KLM desk, where Yardley had bought his ticket on the Amsterdam flight.

'Hi, doll,' Vaughan said. He looked gloomy, wrung out. He glanced warily at Sally. 'She all right?'

Sergeant Lipari answered with a wry shrug, as if to say, *There's nothing I can do about this, it's a force of nature.*

'Is Yardley on board?' she asked.

'Ah, yeah. The bad news.' Vaughan looked for support to the KLM official behind the desk. 'He still hasn't boarded. And the plane's due to take off in five minutes.'

'*Shit!*'

'He must have realised something was going on.'

Sergeant Lipari nodded. 'Christ, he's clever,' she conceded through gritted teeth. 'And he'll do *anything*.'

'We've got a problem,' Vaughan said. 'This is a big airport.'

Sergeant Lipari looked up at the departures board.

'Listen, get the airport management to do a sweep on the passenger list of every other plane leaving in the next couple of hours, starting with other flights to Holland, then broadening it out to Germany and Belgium.'

They moved their base of operations to the complex upstairs where airport security and the transport police had their headquarters.

Minutes went by. Someone set up a cot for Sally. She was given soup, a blanket.

And still they waited.

No luck with any continental flights. Checks on other major cities dribbled in: Paris, Düsseldorf, Berlin; they even started on the computerised manifests for intercontinental destinations such as New York, Rio, Bangkok . . . yes, Bangkok: that was a sex destination, wasn't it?

Sergeant Lipari, meanwhile, paced up and down, aching with frustration, aware that every minute lost was a gain for Yardley. He was clever, so clever, the kind who would do just what they had no cause to suspect.

Perhaps this was what gave Sergeant Lipari a final, desperate inspiration.

'Wait,' she said to the airport official who was organising the passenger list searches, 'ease off on the overseas destinations. Check the domestic flights, will you? And Ireland. OK? Especially Ireland!'

She timed the search, tapping her foot with each second that passed. Two and a half minutes later, the word came. They had turned up a passenger by the name of Yardley on an Aer Lingus flight to Dublin. Ticket bought within minutes of the Amsterdam one, also with cash.

Anticipating trouble, Yardley had bought this ticket at the same time as the one to Amsterdam. Very devious. He had never intended to fly direct to Holland. They could still have been waiting for him to appear on the KLM flight, if it hadn't been for Sergeant Lipari.

Not, she realised, that she had much cause for self-congratulation.

According to the Departures board in the middle of the concourse, the Aer Lingus flight had already left the gate.

TWENTY-NINE

On a far-flung corner of the tarmac, the Aer Lingus 737 was finally ready for departure. Almost imperceptibly at first, the aircraft started to move, and soon its engines began to build towards the churning, releasing crescendo of take-off. Then, quite suddenly, there was a rumbling jolt of brakes. The plane slowed and stopped.

'This is Captain Morrison speaking,' the pilot's voice came over the p.a. 'We've been asked by flight control to delay our take-off just a little longer. I know we're already running late, so please accept my most sincere apologies.'

Sister Bridget O'Donnell caught the eye of the pleasant-looking man in the window-seat beside her.

'Surely a technical problem,' said the elderly nun with a sigh. 'Well, if they're not completely certain the coast is clear, I'd rather they didn't take off at all.'

'I couldn't agree more,' her neighbour said. He had an attractive baritone that matched his looks. 'Better late than never.'

'I suppose I shouldn't be bothered about such things at my age,' Sister Bridget continued. 'God will be taking me soon enough, anyway. But then, perhaps he still has work for me. I'll tell you, I never thought I'd spend the twilight of my days jetting

319

round Europe as a trouble-shooter for our order!'

Noel Yardley nodded politely. He had long since perfected the trick of appearing to pay close attention while at the same time running his own thoughts like a parallel computer programme.

'. . . You see, there's this debate about whether we should go more out into the world, maybe even abandon the habit altogether . . .' Sister Bridget chattered on.

Meanwhile Yardley was alertly surveying the concrete tundra of the apron, waiting.

As the nun fell temporarily silent, Yardley saw what he had been expecting. Still half, even three-quarters of a mile away, but clear to his watchful eye. A police car and a Land-Rover, approaching fast.

Yardley turned back to Sister Bridget. 'That's very interesting,' he murmured.

'You're a good listener,' she said. 'I know I talk too much. Lucky ours isn't a silent order. I couldn't have borne it, not even for God!'

He smiled politely, said, 'Excuse me,' and reached down into the black leather bag at his feet.

Sister Bridget, meanwhile, peered curiously up the long aisle to the galley. All the flight attendants were gathered there in a bored, gossiping flock. When she happened to glance back at her neighbour, she started at the sight of a hypodermic in his hand, and him testing the needle, expertly and calmly.

'Do excuse me,' Yardley said with a disarming sheepishness. He undid a button on his shirt, then another. 'I'm a diabetic. I hope you don't mind. Perhaps you'd be more comfortable looking away . . .'

Sister Bridget immediately obeyed, more to save this nice

man's embarrassment than anything else. She transferred her attention back to a flight attendant who had moved over by the emergency hatch, where she was exchanging desultory chat with a passenger. Sister Bridget marvelled at how a girl like that, who reminded her of herself when young, could make such a daring choice for a career. She wondered whether, had she been born forty years later, she herself might have chosen to get closer to heaven in a 737.

The tiny stinging sensation in Sister Bridget's left arm took her by surprise. It took her a moment to react. She made to turn, but before she could move she was paralysed by a searing pain in her chest, a sudden, stifling shortage of breath.

When Sister Bridget did manage a big, slow-motion gulp, it made things not better but worse – as if she had swallowed a huge black hole and she was somehow being sucked down into it, down, down, down . . .

Yardley moved quickly, discarding the hypodermic, then pulling the nun towards him as she collapsed. Her head lolled, bobbed round until she was facing him. Their gazes locked for an instant. The remnants of her consciousness seemed to confront him in appalled, uncomprehending entreaty. It was as if in that moment Sister Bridget glimpsed the evil that for almost seventy years she had sought refuge from, and which had now surprised her so quickly that there was no time for prayer or protection or forgiveness. Then the whites of her eyes rolled up and she went limp.

Grateful that the nun was old and slight, Yardley took her in his arms.

He half rose, and called out to the flight attendant: 'Miss! The sister here has had some kind of seizure! I'm a doctor, so just do as I say!'

Easing Sister Bridget out into the waiting arms of the cabin crew, Yardley noticed that she had lodged her boarding-card in the documents net in front of her seat.

'Careful now,' he warned gravely. 'Lay her down on the floor for the moment. Make room. *Please* – do as I say . . .'

It was like a magician's sleight of hand. Yardley moved out into the aisle in Sister Bridget's wake, plucking her boarding-card from the net and slipping it into his own jacket pocket in one easy, swift motion that everyone was far too horrified and preoccupied to notice.

The Land-Rover pulled in below the hatchway. The emergency steps were quickly unloaded and set up. Two officers of the airport's police unit got out of the accompanying squad car and watched the procedure with a kind of languid impatience.

Above, the hatch door opened.

'Right,' said Sergeant Owen to Constable Quigley, 'let's get him.'

'It'll be a pleasure.'

As they moved towards the foot of the steps, an Aer Lingus stewardess appeared at the top, signalling frantically. Owen hesitated, exchanged glances with Quigley. Jesus, maybe the nonce on board had a weapon . . .

'We've got an old lady here who's unconscious!' the stewardess called down. 'There's a doctor aboard and he thinks it's a coronary! He's bringing her down now!'

The stewardess moved aside to make way for two male cabin crew carrying a stretcher. They started gingerly down the steps. Behind them came a distinguished-looking man in a mustard-yellow blouson jacket, carrying a very medical-looking black grip-bag.

Automatically the two airport policemen moved aside to make way for the urgent little procession. When it reached tarmac level they glanced at the patient. She was elderly, dressed all in black, with some kind of headdress arrangement half unbuttoned to allow her to breathe more easily.

Within moments the rear doors of the Land-Rover had been flung open and its driver was revving his engine. The doctor, absolutely concentrated on his patient, supervised the loading of the stretcher into the vehicle. Only then did he turn to Owen.

'I'm a doctor. I'm escorting the sister here back to the terminal building for proper care. Thank you, gentlemen . . .'

He fished a boarding-card from his pocket and flashed it at the police officers. Sergeant Owen caught the name O'Donnell. Fair enough. He waved him on. The doctor jumped in alongside the driver. Within moments the police Land-Rover was roaring off back in the direction of the terminal building.

Owen checked his notes.

'OK, Mr Bastard Yardley,' he muttered. 'We're coming to get you . . .'

He started up the steps, followed by Quigley. At the top he turned briefly, spotted the Land-Rover already closing on the terminal.

In the midst of life, Owen thought, being of a melancholy turn of mind. Talk about drama.

As he advanced into the aircraft, the cabin was in chaos – people wandering around, grouped around the bulkhead windows, complaining to the crew.

'Jesus!' Quigley hissed.

'OK!' Owen said loudly, taking charge. He clapped his hands. 'Now, I want everyone to return to their seats immediately!' He turned to Quigley. 'Just mind the bloody door, will you? We don't want him exploiting this confusion to do a runner.'

'What d'you mean, you can't find him?' the airport police inspector barked over his mobile. 'Get them all back to their seats and search systematically.'

He put his hand over the mouthpiece, turned to where Sergeant Lipari and Vaughan were standing.

'Double trouble, I'm afraid. Apparently an elderly lady passenger has had a heart-attack. She's being brought back to the terminal now, accompanied by a doctor who fortunately happened to be on the flight.'

'A *doctor*?' Sergeant Lipari saw Sally Jackson, who had been hunched in the corner, get to her feet and begin to wander over with a kind of dreamy expectancy. Sergeant Lipari lowered her voice to an urgent whisper: 'What's his name, sir? Quick.'

'I'll ask,' the inspector said. He returned to the mobile, rasped the question, waited. 'O'Donnell.' He frowned. 'Hang on a minute. That can't be right. O'Donnell's the *patient*'s name . . .'

'Where would the patient be taken to?' Sergeant Lipari demanded.

'The first-aid station, a couple of minutes from here.'

'You stay here, Mrs Jackson!' Sergeant Lipari ordered Sally.

Then she was out of the door, with Vaughan at her heels.

They arrived at the medical centre in a lot less than two minutes. Bursting in through the double-doors, Sergeant Lipari saw a female paramedic bent over a stretcher, assisted by a male helper. The patient from the plane was being hooked up to an oxygen cylinder.

The woman looked up, annoyed by the interruption.

'Where's the doctor who brought her in?' Sergeant Lipari panted, flashing her warrant card.

The woman looked around irritably.

'The one from the plane? He was here a minute ago. Now, if you'll excuse me, I don't think this lady's got much of a chance, but it's my job to do my best.'

'I'd start by treating her for a massive insulin reaction,' Sergeant Lipari said, backing towards the door.

The paramedic glared at her. 'You *what*?'

'Insulin. Overdose. Now, if you'll just excuse me . . .'

Sally Jackson approached the balcony rail of the mezzanine. She knew instinctively that Sergeant Lipari and her companion would be too late to catch Yardley at the medical centre. Sally felt close to despair. It would be so easy just to jump into the emptiness, end everything. But she wouldn't do that, for the same reason she couldn't join the hunt, because she was carrying a baby. Kit's child. The baby was everything, now that he was gone. The baby and Emma. They would be her life from now on.

Down below her, business travellers with their briefcases and files scurried self-importantly towards their departures. Families browsed in gift shops. Corralled herds of holidaymakers milled mournfully around the announcement boards, praying that for once their flights would leave on time.

Nice, ordinary people. And none of them knew. None of them knew Kit was dead, or that a loving child could be turned into a murderer, or that a man like Yardley could so cunningly cheat justice. None of them knew how a secure world could be turned upside down. That truly terrible things could happen overnight to nice, ordinary people . . .

Sally checked the faces, happy and sad, bored and lively, all unknown. Except for one: a mustard-yellow blouson, a black bag, a face bobbing among the crowd, making for the door that said EXIT: TAXIS.

Yardley. It was Noel Yardley down there.

Footsteps to Sally's left. Sergeant Lipari and DC Vaughan were hurrying towards her. Sergeant Lipari was talking into a mobile phone, obviously detailing police to cover possible escape routes. Sally turned her attention back to the seething ground floor, once more fixed on the bobbing head and the mustard coat, now approaching the automatic exit doors. She knew what she had to do.

'STOP THAT MAN!' Sally yelled at the top of her voice.

She amazed herself with the power she generated, a force that brought hundreds of people to a halt, to silence. Now they were all frozen, staring up at the diminutive but absolutely magnetic blonde figure above them on the mezzanine balcony. Sally's arm was extended, her finger pointing like fate itself.

Only one human being down there was still moving, with his black bag, not looking back or to either side. The automatic doors had started to open for him . . . and Sally's voice seared the air-conditioned chill of the concourse with its grim clarity and perfect projection:

'THE MAN IN THE YELLOW JACKET! WITH THE BLACK BAG! STOP HIM!'

Heads began to turn. There was nervous laughter among the travellers.

Sally felt a pressure in her stomach and rib cage, an ominous dizziness, but she summoned up the last of her strength and yelled: 'HE RAPED MY LITTLE GIRL!'

And at last Yardley broke into a run.

He moved fast and smoothly, almost seemed to glide towards

the electronically operated doors that led to the outside. For a moment everyone else seemed petrified: it was like a fantasy world, in which time has stopped for all except one errant human being.

Sally, already breathing hard and starting to grip the mezzanine rail, let out a last wail of frustration. Then Sergeant Lipari was at her side, gripping her arm, and Constable Vaughan, her companion, was racing down the steps towards the concourse.

But the door marked EXIT: TAXIS was already sliding open for Yardley, and Vaughan was still a good hundred yards behind him.

And then suddenly a baggage trolley appeared to shoot out of the hands of a woman standing by the door. It caught Yardley in mid-stride. He tipped, seemed to steady himself, then slid right over on the smooth floor of the concourse. His bag went flying.

Yardley quickly checked his fall and began to struggle to his feet. Vaughan was still quite far away, just at the bottom of the mezzanine steps. Yardley must have felt there was still time . . .

In fact, he was already lost. The flight of the baggage trolley had acted as a signal. From nowhere appeared a dozen or more female figures – they were all women, without exception – deserting trolleys, baggage, families without a qualm.

Sally and Sergeant Lipari glimpsed Yardley going down on the floor once more. They caught sight of his face, in that momentary snapshot, just as amazement was turning to terror. An instant later, the group of women had literally enclosed him, silent and all the more dangerous for that, like a parliament of crows settling on a carcass.

Vaughan got to the scrimmage first, closely followed by a couple of airport police. It took them some time to pull off enough of the women to get in and rescue Yardley. When the women finally retreated, they left a man curled in a foetal tuck, groaning with pain. There were bruises plainly apparent on his face, but he was clutching himself down below, desperately shielding his groin.

At first it seemed as if Yardley was too badly mauled to be moved, but as Vaughan leaned over him he straighten out, still sprawled on the ground, and looked up at the policeman. One eye was closing under the pressure of a swelling bruise, but the other shone with anger and defiance. A balled fist reached out, but Vaughan avoided it easily.

Vaughan decided that if Yardley was fit enough to try to put one on him, he could also be moved.

'All right, my son,' Vaughan muttered, 'you asked for it.'

He snapped handcuffs on Yardley's wrists, brutally hauled him into a sitting position.

Yardley let out a yelp. A low hiss of satisfaction went through the watching crowd. Then Vaughan pulled him fully to his feet. Yardley stood there, swaying slightly, Vaughan holding him by the handcuffs like a steer waiting to be poleaxed, staring numbly around him with what appeared an unseeing gaze.

But those eyes could see. They saw Sally Jackson approach, leaning on Cheryl Lipari's arm. The crowd parted in front of them, acknowledging her primitive right to precedence.

The two women stopped just short of Yardley. Beyond the bruising and the blood, it was possible to discern a subtle but total change in the set of this man's features. The mask of kindly concern had been dropped. He now radiated a kind of cold, almost other-worldly arrogance.

Sally said nothing, just looked at him with a distilled hatred. Their eyes met. They remained locked in this silent combat even as Sergeant Lipari stepped forward to do her job.

'Bastard,' Sergeant Lipari murmured. 'You put Emma Quinn and her family through hell. Now it's your turn. I am arresting you on suspicion of the rape of a minor and on suspicion of the murder of Christopher Jackson . . .'

When Sergeant Lipari had finished reminding him of his rights, Yardley was still staring straight at Sally.

'You took my husband,' she said, meeting his gaze. 'You tried to take all our lives, even the baby's inside me. But now it's over. You don't control me any more.'

And then Yardley did the strangest, most chilling thing: he smiled.

'You don't understand. It's not you I want,' he said in a thick, slightly lisping voice that might have been ridiculous but instead made his words sound more deliberate, more wounding. 'What I really want, I'll have for ever. Emma's my little girl. She'll always be mine.'

His gaze was hate-filled, defiant . . . almost triumphant.

Vaughan tugged on the handcuffs.

'Always,' Yardley repeated the word like a mantra as he stumbled away. '*Always*.'

THIRTY

It was early evening but still light when the dark-blue Sierra saloon eased itself into a free space in the hospital car park. The engine stopped, but no one got out.

In the driver's seat, DC Vaughan sat silently, drumming lightly on the wheel, obviously waiting for Sergeant Lipari to speak. After a while, he let out a long sigh.

'I could hang around here, you know,' he suggested. 'Run you home afterwards, doll. No problem.'

'No thanks. I'll get a cab.'

Vaughan kept looking straight ahead, as if at some imaginary film being projected at the far end of the car park.

'You wouldn't have said that a week ago, doll.'

'Sorry,' Sergeant Lipari answered softly. 'All good things come to an end, don't they?'

He glanced at her sharply, then went back to staring through the windscreen.

'I thought you'd been going off me lately,' he said.

'You were right, Derek.'

Vaughan shrugged. 'Not much of a hero's reward,' he said with an edge of bitterness. 'And there was me sort of thinking what a great team we made.'

'I'm grateful for everything you did,' Sergeant Lipari said

331

slowly. 'You were a major help in catching Yardley. Right down to slapping the cuffs on him at Heathrow. I'd never deny you any of that. But it's not the point, is it?'

Vaughan grunted.

'Listen, Derek,' Sergeant Lipari said, suddenly animated, 'it's *over* between you and me. If you're looking for recognition as the big, brave cop, try your wife!'

'It's what *you* think that matters to me, doll,' Vaughan said. He was chewing his words like bitter medicine. For a man like him, this was impossibly humiliating. 'I want my reward from you.'

'Is that so?' Sergeant Lipari murmured. 'Fair enough. Well, your reward from me is, you don't get kicked out of CID, OK?'

Vaughan turned violently to face her. 'You *what*?'

'You heard!' Sergeant Lipari said. 'Listen, how much did Mulligan, the reporter, pay you for the information?'

Vaughan's jaw clenched in anger, but it was faked, and she knew it.

'Come on!' Vaughan blustered. 'If you think—'

Sergeant Lipari didn't even wait for him to finish his sentence.

'I *know*, Derek!' she said. 'I talked to Mulligan just a couple of days ago!'

There was silence once again. It got heavier and heavier, like the quiet before a storm, except that none followed. When Vaughan broke, he was quiet, ashamed, like a small boy found out by his mother.

'A monkey altogether,' he whispered. 'What did he tell you?'

'That you didn't give him the photo, but you did sell him the information that enabled him to go and get it,' Sergeant Lipari said. 'Oh, and you helped him get the address of the friends' place where Sally Jackson was staying.'

Vaughan nodded. He swallowed hard. 'I'm well fucked then, aren't I?' he said. 'Well and bloody truly.'

Sergeant Lipari let that one hang for a while. Then she laughed.

'Not necessarily. I said to Mulligan that I'd have him blackballed by everyone I knew – and then some – if he named you in his campaign against dismissal.'

'And what did he say to that?'

'He said he'd think about it.'

Vaughan frowned. 'Well, what did he decide? Don't stuff me around, doll.'

'Would I do that? Anyway, I heard the next morning he'd been offered a job on another crime desk.' Sergeant Lipari ruffled Vaughan's hair in a way that she hoped was sisterly. 'Mulligan immediately decided to drop the complaint. Nobody likes a whiner, do they?'

Vaughan transferred his attention to the view through the window. It gave out on to a pale-coloured Volvo of no particular interest.

'Thanks,' he said eventually.

'You're welcome. And I'll thank you for the five hundred quid, Del. I want a cheque made out to the National Society for the Prevention of Cruelty to Children. In my hand. Now. For the full amount.'

Wordlessly Vaughan wrote the cheque, handed it to Sergeant Lipari. She granted him a distinctly feline smile as she took it.

'Good boy. And don't do that again.'

Vaughan smiled back, ruefully for his part. Then he put an arm around her.

'How about a kiss, doll? We can still have a good time, can't we?'

Sergeant Lipari wriggled expertly out of his grip, popped the cheque into her bag.

'You give me five hundred quid and then make a request for sexual favours? You're a policeman, Derek. Don't you know there's a law against that sort of thing? Bye . . .'

In a moment Sergeant Lipari had clicked the door open. She slid out swiftly, shot him the briefest of smiles as she closed the door behind her. Then she strode briskly off towards the hospital's main entrance.

Sergeant Lipari didn't once glance back, an act that was a lot harder than it looked. Because at that moment, despite everything – despite, she supposed, her better self – she had wanted a kiss from Derek Vaughan more than anything else in the world.

Sally Jackson was in a private room, propped up on pillows and looking a little dazed but otherwise undamaged. And by her bedside stood her ex-husband, Jonathan.

Sergeant Lipari hesitated in the doorway.

'Hello, Mrs Jackson.'

'Hello, Sergeant.'

'Hello, Mr Quinn.'

'Hi.' Jonathan made a small, indefinite gesture of greeting. 'Well,' he murmured, getting to his feet. 'I'd better be off. I promised I'd drop back and see Emma again before I go home.'

'How is she?' Sergeant Lipari asked.

'Pretty shaken. Not talking. They've told me to say nothing yet about Yardley or Kit. Not until the specialists have had a chance to check out her state of mind.'

Sergeant Lipari nodded. 'This is just the beginning for

Emma, Mr Quinn. She's going to need all your support.'

'I've acknowledged my mistake. I feel a complete idiot.'

This was possibly the nearest either his ex-wife or Sergeant Lipari was going to get to an apology: Jonathan Quinn expressing his personal sense of humiliation.

'We all feel pretty silly,' Sergeant Lipari said. 'Only Sally kept the faith. Without her persistence Yardley would probably still be free to prey on kids like Emma.'

'Right.' Jonathan leaned over and brushed Sally's right cheek with his lips, then walked out with a mumbled goodbye to Sergeant Lipari.

'Thanks for coming.' Sally indicated a chair by the bed. 'Sit down.'

Sergeant Lipari obeyed. 'You look pretty good, considering.'

'Just stressed out, apparently,' Sally said. 'The best thing is, Kit's baby's going to be all right. Emma will be able to look at her little stepbrother, or stepsister, and it will bring back happy memories, not cruel ones.' She bit her lip. 'Excuse me . . .'

Sergeant Lipari handed Sally the Kleenex box, then took her hand. They sat there for some time like that, not moving or speaking, Sally just sobbing quietly.

'Your husband . . . Kit . . . was a good man, Mrs Jackson,' Sergeant Lipari said finally, breaking the silence.

'I know. It's hard to forgive myself for . . . you know . . . doubting him, even for a second. If only he'd discussed his suspicions about Emma with me before setting up that awful charade with Dr Macintyre. Or taken me into his confidence before he went to see Yardley . . .'

'Men don't talk about things, Mrs Jackson. That's part of the trouble with them.'

'There's so much I'd like to ask him. So much we'd have had

to talk about. And so much I'll never really know.'

'If it's any help, my guess is that Emma said something to your husband after you'd gone away to Manchester,' Sergeant Lipari said tentatively. 'Something that made him suspicious of Yardley, I mean. I don't think Kit was looking in that direction until then.'

'Yes. That fits.'

'And so Kit went around to Yardley's consulting-rooms and asked some awkward questions, which was when Yardley decided he wanted him out of the way.'

'Perhaps one day Emma will be able to tell us.' Sally leaned forward painfully. 'Diminished responsibility. That's what Diane Worcester says the plea will be. They'll set my Emma free, won't they?' she asked plaintively.

'I hope so. It's out of my hands now, Mrs Jackson.'

Sally lowered herself back into her pillows. She suddenly looked tired, Sergeant Lipari thought. This woman needed to rest, not to waste energy in speculation. God knows, there would be plenty more time for that. After his cruel taunt to Sally at the airport, Yardley had clammed up completely. If things carried on like this, they would get no insights from his side.

'You'll go and see Emma, won't you?' Sally asked then. 'I mean, you'll give her some support?'

'Of course. She'll get plenty of good vibes from the women involved. Me, you, your friend Mrs Paine . . .' Sergeant Lipari made a face. 'Even that politically correct, gum-chewing solicitor of yours,' she conceded. 'I'm afraid it's Emma's relationship with the male sex that may be a problem from now on.'

'But she'll have her wonderful memories of Kit,' Sally said thoughtfully.

'And she'll have Mr Quinn.'

'Yes. In his way Jonathan's utterly devoted to her.'

Sergeant Lipari gave Sally's hand a final pat, got to her feet.

'Oh, I expect Emma will still suffer with men, Mrs Jackson,' she said. 'Especially the ones she finds herself able to love. But then, don't we all?'

'I hope Yardley hasn't ruined her for love, Sergeant.'

'So do I.'

Sally looked at Sergeant Lipari. Her eyes were unfathomably sad.

'Yardley's got inside her mind. He got into mine. Perhaps he even got into yours.'

'Yes.'

'He raped our minds,' Sally said with a voice like well-tempered steel. 'How do you get over that? Day by day, how do you really survive it?'

Sergeant Lipari had come here to the hospital buoyed up by a sense of professional victory, of a job well done. At this moment, though, she was just a woman wanting to console another woman.

And in that capacity Sergeant Lipari knew only a terrible emptiness, a sense that for Sally Jackson there wasn't – perhaps never would be – a truly comforting reply.

POSTSCRIPT

It had become summer once again. The following summer.

Exactly a year had passed since Noel Yardley had been arrested at Heathrow Airport – and Kit Jackson had died helpless in intensive care. A terrible double anniversary.

The terraced house in Islington was smaller than the Jacksons' old one, but again airy and light. And thankfully a long way from Barnes. Above all, for Sally Jackson, its walls held no memories.

Sally looked through to the living room, where Emma was engrossed in a glossy magazine. She was relieved to see her daughter acting like a normal teenager – hooked on clothes and make-up. It was just over eight months since Emma had been freed, by the same court that had sent Yardley to Broadmoor At Her Majesty's Pleasure for abusing her and killing her stepfather. After his chilling outburst at the airport, Yardley had never admitted another thing. It was still a mystery exactly how Kit had been stabbed, and the court, in a historic decision, had decided this to be an irrelevancy.

Emma had been heavily counselled during her period on remand and after her acquittal. Now she was seeing Carl Thompson, the hypnosis expert who had provided the breakthrough information to Sergeant Lipari which had enabled them to catch Yardley. Once a week, under careful supervision, he gently explored the recesses of the young girl's mind, probing for evidence of Yardley's programming. 'Clearing the last mines from the children's playground,' Thompson called it. The war was over, its chief criminal punished, all foreseeable danger a thing of the past. But the complete soul-cleansing process could take months still, even years.

For the past few minutes Sally had been gently rocking the Moses basket where baby Christopher was sleeping, full of milk and at peace. Little Kit – they called him that, Sally and Emma – was fair like his mother, broad-featured like his father, and at six months he was already going almost through the night. A gift. Something close to a recompense for all the terrible things that had happened before he was born.

After a while, Sally got to her feet. She tiptoed through from the small study to the living room.

'Darling?'

Emma looked up sharply for an instant. Even now, she never seemed truly relaxed.

'Oh. Hi, Mum.'

Sally's daughter had almost stopped growing in height, and was slowly filling out, becoming truly a young woman. A very beautiful one. But sometimes, at such moments when someone broke into Emma's thoughts or entered a room without announcing themselves, Sally thought she caught a fleeting glint of remembered torment, of viscerally imprinted horror, in her daughter's violet-blue eyes.

'Remember that Liz and Harry are bringing Zak over for supper tonight,' Sally said. 'If you want to take a shower and change, do it soon. I'm just going to clear the decks in the kitchen, sweetheart, OK?'

Emma nodded absently, her eyes already back on her magazine.

'Little Kit's gone off to sleep, so don't make too much noise.'

'I'm reading, Mum. It's not a noisy occupation.'

'Well, just in case.'

'All right, all right.'

And then Emma caught her mother's eye and laughed. Sally laughed too and went through to the kitchen. Life was starting to seem good again. Tonight, with their friends, they would be toasting the memory of Kit, but also their own survival, the survival of a loving unit that the world called a family.

Sally was literally up to her elbows in grease, decked out in rubber gloves and wielding an abrasive pad on the big paella dish she planned to use for this evening's fish pie, when the phone rang.

She clucked in annoyance, glared balefully at the wall-phone by the kitchen door. At least phones no longer terrified her. Or Emma. Then the ringing stopped.

'Got it!' Emma sang out gently from the living room.

'Oh. Thanks, darling.' Fortunately it hadn't woken little Kit.

Sally heard her daughter talking on the phone in a low, soft voice. Perhaps some friend from school. Or a boy, perhaps, she thought with a silent little giggle. About time. Anyway, it wasn't Liz and Harry cancelling, which was all she cared about at the moment. Sally returned to her pot, rubbed hard at the last encrusted blemishes, placed it on the draining board.

It was then, as she was struggling to remove her rubber gloves, that a warning shiver ran up Sally's spine.

Perhaps it was something about the quality of the silence in the next room. Emma had gone very silent, but she hadn't hung up the phone. The receiver always made a tiny, crystal-clear *ping* when replaced.

'Darling?' Sally said, trying to sound calm.

No answer.

'*Emma . . .*'

Sally moved quickly to the door, looked through.

Emma's magazine lay discarded on the chair. The phone handset was dangling off the table, still swinging gently.

The silence was thick, suddenly, and horrible, literally horrible.

Sally ran across the living room and into the study where she had left Little Kit in his Moses basket.

It brought back everything from that time a year ago. The way she had felt, like a tigress, protective – except then she had been fighting for Emma . . .

Emma was bent over the Moses basket. She might have been playing with her little step-brother, except Sally knew instinctively that she wasn't. Emma didn't look round when Sally entered. Her smooth, pale young face was stiff with concentration, as if she were completing one of the difficult, intricate craft assignments she was fond of undertaking at school.

But this was no innocent craft assignment. Emma was holding the plump centre-cushion from the living-room sofa over Little Kit's face, pressing down remorselessly, easing her weight on to it.

'What . . . what are you doing, Emma?' Sally said in a firm voice, advancing across the room. 'Stop it! *Stop!*'

Her daughter looked round at her. Emma's eyes seemed dead, devoid of feeling or independent will. As she stared at her mother, she continued to press down on the baby boy's face . . .

Another two steps and Sally was at the basket. She pushed Emma very hard, and the girl staggered back, pillow and all.

Exploiting the moment's advantage, Sally dived in and seized her baby. She held him up, massaging his tiny chest, willing him to be alive, but for a moment Little Kit was terrifyingly still. Then he let out a tiny, desperate breath which exploded into a rasping cry.

Sally turned, the bawling, living child in her arms. Emma had stood up, the fat pillow still in her hands like some other deadly offspring. She was motionless, expressionless, saying nothing.

Sally stared for an eternity of a moment at her daughter. Then she began to back out of the room, holding Little Kit close. Instead of the Emma she loved, she saw a stranger. *Someone else. Or someone else's creation* . . .

She knew she had to get help. For Emma. For herself and her baby. And then she had to find somewhere Yardley couldn't reach them. If such a place existed.

Emma's mine, he had promised. How she remembered that look of triumph, of primitive, nihilistic hatred in Yardley's eyes. *She's my little girl and she'll always be mine.*

Always.

More Enthralling Fiction from Headline Feature

══ Joy Fielding ══

SEE JANE RUN

THE TERRIFYING PSYCHOLOGICAL THRILLER

'One afternoon in late spring, Jane Whittaker went to the shops and forgot who she was. She couldn't remember her own name. She couldn't remember whether she was married or single, widowed or divorced, childless or the mother of twins . . . What in God's name was happening?'

Jane's nightmare is only just beginning. When a handsome, distinguished man, calling himself her husband, comes to claim her, she is taken to a beautiful home she doesn't recognise, kept away from the family and friends she can't remember. And despite Michael's tender concern, she feels a growing sense of unease.

Jane is in a race against time to recapture her identity before it is too late. To do that she must first remember whatever terrible thing made her lose her memory in the first place.

'Finely tuned and convincing . . . suspense is maintained at a high level . . . sharply drawn, articulate characters' *Publishers Weekly*

'Compulsive reading' *Company*

FICTION / GENERAL 0 7472 3753 0

A selection of bestsellers from Headline

BODY OF A CRIME	Michael C. Eberhardt	£5.99	☐
TESTIMONY	Craig A. Lewis	£5.99	☐
LIFE PENALTY	Joy Fielding	£5.99	☐
SLAYGROUND	Philip Caveney	£5.99	☐
BURN OUT	Alan Scholefield	£4.99	☐
SPECIAL VICTIMS	Nick Gaitano	£4.99	☐
DESPERATE MEASURES	David Morrell	£5.99	☐
JUDGMENT HOUR	Stephen Smoke	£5.99	☐
DEEP PURSUIT	Geoffrey Norman	£4.99	☐
THE CHIMNEY SWEEPER	John Peyton Cooke	£4.99	☐
TRAP DOOR	Deanie Francis Mills	£5.99	☐
VANISHING ACT	Thomas Perry	£4.99	☐

All Headline books are available at your local bookshop or newsagent, or can be ordered direct from the publisher. Just tick the titles you want and fill in the form below. Prices and availability subject to change without notice.

Headline Book Publishing, Cash Sales Department, Bookpoint, 39 Milton Park, Abingdon, OXON, OX14 4TD, UK. If you have a credit card you may order by telephone – 01235 400400.

Please enclose a cheque or postal order made payable to Bookpoint Ltd to the value of the cover price and allow the following for postage and packing:

UK & BFPO: £1.00 for the first book, 50p for the second book and 30p for each additional book ordered up to a maximum charge of £3.00.

OVERSEAS & EIRE: £2.00 for the first book, £1.00 for the second book and 50p for each additional book.

Name ....

Address ....

....

....

If you would prefer to pay by credit card, please complete:
Please debit my Visa/Access/Diner's Card/American Express (delete as applicable) card no:

Signature .... Expiry Date..............